THE DOORWAY TO THE OTHER WORLD WILL OPEN

ENDOSYM
BOOK TWO

THE PLANTATION
By J. Henry Thomson

WHEN DOCTOR GEORGE NAH SARDAY, THE LEADER OF THE NEW AGE CULT Dacari Mucomba, purchased the old Johnson Plantation in Johnsonville, Virginia as the site for the *School for West African Spiritual Studies*, Chief of Police Brian Bishop had little reason to be concerned.

Little did he realize that it was far more than just another fake religion bilking money from its followers; the School was hiding the creature whose existence would threaten not only the City of Johnsonville but also the very existence of the human race. With time running out and marked for death, Chief Bishop finds an unlikely ally in Tim Martin, a senior at the University of Virginia who knows to well what they must face when they meet the Endosym.

Learn how it all began.

Read books one and two in the Endosym series.

Available from Amazaon.com

THEY HAVE HIDDEN AMONG US FOR CENTURIES

ENDOSYM

BOOK ONE

THE DARK FACE OF EVIL

By J. Henry Thomson

HANK MARTIN, HIS WIFE LINDSEY AND THEIR TEENAGE SON TIM ARRIVE IN Liberia, West Africa where Hank will be the Defense Attaché' to the American Embassy. What began as the ideal tour for the Martins escalates into sheer terror when an incident from Hank's past haunts his dreams and becomes reality.

Hank is forced to choose between the interests of the United States as it negotiates for the vast oil reserves hidden beneath the Saint Paul River Delta and the destruction of an evil that permeates the Government of Liberia to the very doors of the President's Office.

This is a battle that, if Hank does not win, will cost him far more than his career; it will cost him the sacrifice of his son to the Endosym. A creature that has hidden in the jungles of Liberia for centuries.

ENDOSYM

BOOK THREE
THE ACADEMY

By J Henry Thomson

The events and adventures in this novel are fiction. The names, characters, places and incidents are either a product of the author's imagination or are used fictitiously. Any similarity to persons, living or dead, business establishments, events or locales is entirely coincidental.

The story and the glimpses of the lives and beliefs of the people of West Africa are based on the author's experiences. The ancient statues are real, as is the leopard tooth. Their origins are fiction.

ENDOSYM-THE ACADEMY
Copyright © February 6, 2013 J Henry Thomson
All rights reserved.
ISBN: 0985742623
ISBN 13: 9780985742621

ACKNOWLEDGMENTS

WHEN WRITING A NOVEL, THERE ARE ALWAYS THOSE INDIVIDUALS WHOSE contributions make the novel come to life.

First is to thank you the readers. Whether you are a first reader or a follower of the Endosym series thank you for your support.

The United States Military Academy holds many found memories. For the men and women of the Long Grey Line yours is truly a proud vocation.

To Kim Holmes and Bill Rohrer thank you for you insight.

For this novel Dianna Main, John Main and Larry Hicks who read the draft and told it like it is.

As always, my editor, Irene Hicks, continues to provide the energy, unflagging support and encouragement that get me through the difficult periods. Without her constant efforts none of this would be possible.

ENDOSYM: *Two entities living in one humanoid body whose goal is to become the "Apex Predator" of the Planet.*

March 28, 1779

"THOMAS, IT'S TIME TO WAKE UP."

Captain Thomas Marsh abruptly opened his eyes. In the flickering candlelight, he made out the blurred shape of James standing over him.

"Is it already time?" he asked as he shook off his deep sleep and forced himself to regain a soldier's composure.

"Yes, it's your turn to check the sentries," replied James.

Thomas pushed back the heavy woolen blanket and quickly swung his legs over the side of the bunk, unwilling to waste a single moment between the warmth of his bed and the security of his uniform. In these high, rolling hills, it was cold, very cold, this late at night.

Shivering, he stood, clutched his britches and pulled them to his waist. He tugged his cotton blouse into position squarely on his shoulders before tucking it into his waistband. The shirt served him well both day and night. In another deft maneuver, he forced his arms into the sleeves of his dark blue officer's coat. Finally, he sat down heavily on the bunk and yanked on each of his leather boots. He stood up and reached out to the table where his wig rested on a stand. He carefully positioned it on his head before standing and staring at James.

"Does my wig look all right?"

"It's straight," said James.

Satisfied, Thomas strapped on his pistol and saber. Finally, he placed his four-cornered cocked hat atop his head. It was similar to the head coverings worn by enlisted men, but for officers, the hat formed a rect-angle rather than a triangle. He was now fully dressed as a captain in General Washington's Continental Army.

Once out the door of the officers' quarters, he stepped into the court-yard. It was only minutes before midnight and unusually light. The cloudless sky allowed the moonlight to illuminate the compound. Two large fires burned fiercely at opposite ends of the yard, cutting out the shadows and revealing details seldom seen at this late hour.

Thomas wasted no time. He hastened to the railing where his horse had been tied, saddled and ready for its rider. As he approached his mount, he caught sight of a lone figure hobbling toward him. Thomas could tell by the man's gait that it was General Arnold.

To the young officers, Benedict Arnold was one of the most respected leaders in the colonial forces. Arnold had led an expedition of eleven hundred men into Quebec by way of the Kennebec and Chaudière riv-ers. After frightful hardships en route, his army climbed the heights of Abraham. Yet it wasn't enough. Arnold's forces were insufficient to storm the city. He was compelled to await the arrival of General Montgomery.

In the ensuing battle, Montgomery was slain, and Arnold was wound-ed in the leg. For his gallantry, Arnold was promoted to brigadier general and took command of the siege of Quebec until General Wooster's forces came to their aid. Then Arnold assumed command of the revolutionary armies in the battle for Montreal.

When the British, soon heavily reinforced, drove the Americans out of Canada, Arnold and his surviving troops retreated to Fort Ticonderoga. Arnold's strong resistance during the battle for Montreal discouraged the British. Their commander, General Carleton, was forced to retire to Montreal for the winter. The relief of Fort Ticonderoga made it possible to divert three thousand men from the northern army and to come to Washington's aid.

Thomas had heard the rumors of the sleepless Arnold who patrolled the fort late at night, but this was Thomas's first encounter with the general.

"Who's there?" demanded Arnold.

"Sir, it's Captain Marsh," answered Thomas. "I'm getting ready to inspect the listening posts."

The general approached the young officer, taking note of his appearance. Each of Arnold's men was required to be in full uniform at all times, except when asleep. Arnold himself wore the immaculate uniform of a brigadier general. Thomas was struck by his meticulous attention to detail. Yet it was Arnold's stature that surprised him the most. Arnold was short, standing only a little taller than five and a half feet. Yet, somehow he achieved a commanding presence. Thomas, who was a good three inches taller, felt short compared to the renowned general.

"Hell of a deal," grumbled Arnold. "Here we are sitting in two indefensible forts on the Hudson waiting for the damn British to come from New York City. When that happens, we'll be defeated. Those idiots in Congress have no idea how to win a war. I can't believe how ignorant they are. They wouldn't even listen to me when I told them what to do. Margaret was right. There is no way we can take on King George. He will squash us like a bug on the hearth."

Margaret, his new wife, was half his age. It was no secret that she was a Tory.

Captain Marsh was dumbfounded by the rambling words coming from the mouth of this famous military man. Marsh stood stock-still and forced himself to maintain his serious demeanor.

"Oh, carry on, captain," Arnold barked. Thomas snapped to attention with a sharp salute, turned and mounted his horse.

Thomas now had a story to tell his grandchildren. He had met the great General Benedict Arnold. But now, Thomas was anxious about Arnold's dire prediction of defeat. Perhaps the brilliant man was disappointed that – although ready for battle – there was still no action. Here was Arnold, requiring readiness, yet everyone knew that it would take many days for the British to move up the Hudson.

The men at the gate pushed their shoulders against the heavy wooden gates. Their groans mingled with the creak of timber as the opening widened. Soon Thomas and his dappled mount plodded along on the muddy road. He had a job to do, and he didn't intend to linger.

Thomas shook his head. He didn't have time to concern himself with General Arnold's ramblings. In the moonlight he could see the ramparts of Fort Putnam on the hill above. He turned his horse toward the Hudson. From this elevation he could see the reflection of the moon on the calm water. During winter, the river became a frozen highway. One could walk across the ice between Garrison and West Point. Now in March some large sections of ice still floated lazily in the river. Thomas halted his mount and peered into the distance. He could make out the fires from camps at Garrison.

Thomas knew the area well. His home was in Newburgh, just twenty miles north by boat. Once, he and his brother had started across the ice when it had begun to crack, forming dangerous puddles of frozen water. They barely made it to shore. When they got home and told their story, Mother had forbidden them from walking on the ice again. They didn't – at least that year – but her warning failed to stop them from testing the ice the following winter.

Had that been eight years ago? It seemed like forever. Now here he was fighting in a war that his father cursed as wrongheaded. His family had emigrated from England to the colonies in 1751. When they arrived they had only three children, one boy and two girls. Thomas and his brother Samuel were born in America. They were only two years apart in age, Thomas being the younger.

When the call came for soldiers to serve in the new continental army, Thomas enlisted, refusing to heed his father's admonitions. Because of his father's good reputation, Thomas was given a commission as a captain, even though he was just twenty-two years old. In private, his father had voiced his disapproval, protesting that it was wrong to go against king and country. Yet, with the open hostility toward Loyalists, his father said nothing in public. He had wished that Thomas had followed Samuel into the clergy. Already, Samuel served as the associate minister in Newburg's Methodist Church.

Thomas cantered slowly along the moonlit trail. The horse had no problem negotiating the rough roadway. When he approached the first lookout, he dismounted and prepared to check the three soldiers who manned the post. The idea of the late night inspection was ludicrous. Obviously, there was no problem. No enemy soldier had been reported anywhere in the area.

He saluted the men and continued his ride toward the next lookout.

Once out of sight of the first lookout, Thomas veered to the left. He took a trail that led him closer to the riverbank. He cautiously glanced behind him to see if he had been followed. He passed through a grove of oaks. Still leafless, the branches formed skeletal lines against the pre-dawn sky. They seemed to be reaching up to the vanishing moon. He topped a small rise.

In the clearing below, he saw two horses hitched to a wagon. Five men stood nearby as if waiting for someone. Thomas jerked the reins, gently prodding the horse's flanks with his boots. He rode down the hill and stopped. He dismounted and approached a man who held his arms out to him. They fell into a hearty embrace.

"Sam, you look well."

"It is good to see you, Tom," said his brother, Samuel. "Tom, you know Brother Michael, Brother James and Brother John."

"Yes, it's good to see you all again," said Thomas.

Samuel turned to the last man.

"This is Andrew Wyatt, the silversmith." Thomas nodded and shook the man's hand.

"It's time to get this deed done," said Samuel. "Are you sure that no military fortifications are planned for this area?"

"Yes," replied Thomas. "I went over the plans yesterday. Nothing will be built here."

"Where do you want to put it?" asked Brother Michael.

"Over by that large oak tree," answered Samuel. "It will take all six of us to move the casket."

Samuel moved to the back of the wagon and reached out to lift a heavy tarp, revealing the corner of a wooden casket. It was not the typical burial box built of half-inch pine. Instead, it was constructed of one-inch thick tongue and groove oak planks that had been soaked in a copper sulfate solution to preserve the wood. Two three-inch wide iron straps encircled the casket, each approximately twelve inches from the opposing ends.

"Let's give it a go," said Samuel.

The men lined up at the back of the wagon, three on each side. Even pulling the box to the open edge of the wagon was a struggle, but they put their backs into the task and slowly carried it to the base of the tree. They returned for the tools – two rakes, two shovels and a two-pronged pick.

The silversmith returned to the wagon and cradled a bulky object wrapped in heavy cotton. Alone, he struggled to hoist it on his shoulder and carry it to the casket. He set it down and removed the cloth, revealing an exquisitely formed silver cross.

Thomas guessed that it was nearly two and a half feet in length, one and a half feet wide, and probably three-quarters of an inch thick. He slipped both hands under the cross and tried to lift it. He was amazed at the weight – likely in excess of thirty pounds. He noted that small holes had been bored in each of the four points of the cross.

The smith stepped forward, lifted the familiar object and centered it on the casket. Using four iron screws, he attached the cross to the casket. When the smith finished, each man came forward and touched the sacred symbol as if compelled to do its bidding. Even Thomas paused. It was strange, he thought. Perhaps it was just the effect of the reflected moonlight, but to him, the cross seemed to shine of its own accord.

Without speaking, the men began their work. They raked the dead foliage from a wide area near the tree. They cleared a square about eight feet long and eight feet wide.

Although Thomas had been too cold when the task began, the strenuous toil soon warmed his body. He removed his military coat and rolled up his sleeves. They worked silently. No one spoke. They took turns with the digging. It was hard work, and there was only room for two in the hole. They were careful to dig as quietly as possible.

When the rectangular hole was approximately five feet deep, they stopped and rested their tools against the tree. Three thick hemp ropes were retrieved from the wagon and threaded under the casket. Two men were assigned at each rope. Working together, their muscles straining, they lifted the casket and positioned it over the hole. They lowered the casket, trying to keep their burden level to prevent the shifting of its contents. Once the casket was placed in the musky soil, they let loose of the ropes and stepped back.

Samuel again walked to the wagon and retrieved a large leather-bound book. He returned to the gravesite.

"Please kneel," he said calmly to the five men before him.

He began to read from Saint Luke, Chapter 8, verses 27 to 33.

And when he went forth to land, there met him out of the city a certain man, which had devils long time, and ware no clothes, neither abode in any house, but in the tombs.

When he saw Jesus, he cried out, and fell down before him, and with a loud voice said, What have I to do with thee, Jesus, thou Son of God most high? I beseech thee, torment me not.

(For he had commanded the unclean spirit to come out of the man. For oftentimes it had caught him: and he was kept bound with chains and in fetters; and he brake the bands, and was driven of the devil into the wilderness.)

And Jesus asked him, saying, What is thy name? And he said, Legion: because many devils were entered into him.

And they besought him that he would not command them to go out into the deep.

And there was there an herd of many swine feeding on the mountain: and they besought him that he would suffer them to enter into them. And he suffered them.

Then went the devils out of the man, and entered into the swine; and the herd ran violently down a steep place into the lake, and were choked.

"Only Jesus can drive the devil from a man," said Samuel as he closed the book. "But, we – with the power of the cross – can bind the devil in the box. We will never divulge the location of the cursed tomb. Should any one of us ever speak of tonight, may that person rot in hell for eternity."

They all stood, and Samuel walked to the wagon, placed the Bible carefully under the seat and returned to the grave. The men retrieved their tools and began to cover the box with shovelfuls of earth. They took turns stomping heavily on the soil. When the grave had been filled and leveled, the excess dirt was loaded into the back of the wagon. Then dried leaves and branches were scattered over the site. When finished, they stood back to assure themselves that they had left no evidence of their work.

The men shook hands with Thomas and loaded the tools on the wagon. The last man to climb aboard was his brother.

"Thank you for your help, Tom. I look forward to seeing you again when this horrible war is over."

"And I, too, Sam," said Thomas. The two held their final embrace. Finally, Sam climbed on the wagon. Thomas watched them move into the shadows and disappear from view. He rolled down his sleeves and pulled on his coat. He mounted his horse and rode off to complete his inspection of the lookout posts.

Thomas would never see his brother again. In early 1780, a British attack against an American outpost in Westchester County, New York resulted in fifty American casualties and seventy-five captured in the Battle of Young's House.

One of those casualties was Captain Thomas Marsh.

1

SOME OF THE MILITARY'S GREATEST HEROES REST FOREVER IN THE WEST POINT Cemetery.

The hallowed grounds overlook the Hudson River at the United States Military Academy in New York. The cemetery once served as the burial grounds for American Revolutionary War soldiers and early West Point inhabitants. In 1817 it was officially designated as a military cemetery. The caretaker's cottage was erected in 1872. Still standing, it now houses the offices for the cemetery management. Academy visitors regularly come to the cemetery to acknowledge those heroes who fought for their country. It is one of the major attractions on the academy tour.

Visitors who come to the graveyard walk through history. Each section is a testament to those who served their nation.

They may visit the oldest grave that holds the remains of Ensign Dominick Trant, a native of Cork, Ireland. He was a soldier in the Ninth Massachusetts Infantry. Trant died at West Point in 1782.

Other men who made history include Major General John Buford, Union cavalry commander who set the stage for the Battle of Gettysburg; General William Westmoreland, Army Chief of Staff, Superintendent of the United States Military Academy and the commanding general of all forces who fought in Vietnam; and Major General George Armstrong Custer, commander at the Battle of the Little Bighorn.

Visitors who tour the grounds will also notice many monuments, enough to keep a history buff fascinated for a week or more.

The monuments include the Dade Monument, honoring Major Francis L. Dade and the one hundred ten men who died with him in a battle with Seminole warriors in 1835.

Another is the Cadet Monument. It originally was erected to honor Cadet Vincent M. Lowe who was killed in a premature cannon discharge in 1817. The monument now includes the names of cadets and professors who died in the early days of the academy.

Wood's Monument was erected in 1818 to commemorate the life of Eleazer D. Wood, one of the early graduates, for his notable work as an engineer and his service in the artillery.

The Margaret Corbin Monument honors a heroine of the Revolutionary War. When her husband was killed while manning a cannon, Margaret immediately took his place until she was hit by enemy fire. The injury left her disabled for the rest of her life. She was the first woman to receive a military pension.

2

VICTOR SANCHEZ WAS DEVOTED TO THE SACRED GROUNDS, BUT EVEN MORE, he loved his job. He had worked for the Grounds Division of the Directorate of Engineering and Housing for twenty years. During the previous ten years he had served as the foreman.

He took particular pride in the digging of the graves. When he prepared a gravesite, it was done perfectly. His graves were always precisely cornered and dug accurately to the requested depth. He believed that a meticulously prepared site was important to the kin of the deceased.

Victor's skill with a backhoe couldn't be matched. Even though he was the foreman, he would prepare a new gravesite anytime he got the chance. For that reason, he was currently operating the bright orange Kubota backhoe.

Today he would be digging the first grave in the newly expanded area of the cemetery next to the old Post Exchange. West Point had been the site for burial of graduates and retired instructors as well as their spouses for more than one hundred and sixty years. Because of the high demand, there was a constant urgency to expand the cemetery. It had been a five-year process to reclaim the land where Victor worked. The area had been carefully leveled. New grass had been planted. Finally, it was ready to accommodate the new gravesites.

Victor took another look at the finalized map of the area. Each plot had been located using the latest mapping technology. The first grave would be the final resting place for a retired colonel from the class of 1960. There would be no excuse for any error when use of the land was so critical.

The honor of digging the first grave went to the man selected by the foreman. Victor had told his crew that he, himself, would do the honors. He pulled himself onto the seat of the backhoe and drove it to the predetermined spot. He had spread out a large tarp that was fitted with an opening for the grave. Earth and grass would be placed on one side of the tarp adjacent to the three-and-a-half foot by seven-and-a-half foot opening.

Using a sod-cutting machine, Victor carefully sliced into the thick grass, creating green blocks of turf. Each chunk was laid gently in place on the tarp. He began to remove the dirt from the hole using the backhoe. He carefully dug the soil to a depth of six inches over the entire area of the grave. This allowed him to keep the hole totally even as he dug. He hummed along to random selections from his iPod playlist. He claimed that the music helped mask the noise from the tractor, but, in truth, the songs added to his joy at doing his job as expertly as he could.

He wiped his brow and concentrated on enlarging the hole. It was hot, very hot on this August afternoon. If ever a man could choose a place to be buried, it would be here, he reasoned. It took about forty minutes to reach a depth of three feet. He needed to go to seven feet before he would be satisfied. Then he would use special shoring material to hold up the sides so that the concrete vault could be lowered into the grave without doing any damage or collapsing the soil. He pulled back so he could remove the next six inches of soil. He marveled at how easy it had been to dig at this site.

Suddenly, he heard a crunch as the mouth of the backhoe's shovel hit something unusual. He felt the shovel drop by about a foot.

"What in the world was that?" he said aloud. No one was there to answer his question. He climbed off the backhoe, stood as close as possible to the edge of the hole, and peered into the dark soil.

"Son of a bitch!" he exclaimed, amazed at what he thought he saw. Pieces of the thick, partially decaying plank were visible, likely broken from the top of what looked like a casket. He was virtually certain that he had broken into an old grave. Never, in all his time working in the grounds department, had he ever experienced anything like this. This should not happen at the military academy. Historical records never indicated that this area was used for graves.

No matter now, Victor told himself as he reached into his pocket and pulled out his cell phone.

"Buildings and grounds division, how may I help you?" asked a woman in the office.

"Eloise, it's Victor Sanchez. Is Bob in?"

"He's busy right now, Victor," she answered.

"I need to talk to him right now. It's important."

Victor stood next to the backhoe holding his cell phone to his ear. Soon, Bob Cushman, the director, came on the line.

"What is it, Victor?" asked Bob.

"I just dug up an old grave," said Victor.

"An old grave? Where the hell is it?" growled Bob.

"Right smack dab in the middle of the new area," answered Victor, a slight tremble in his voice.

"There's no record of any graves in that area," said Bob. "Are you sure it's a grave?"

"Bob, I know a casket when I see one. It's an old gravesite." "Shit!" said Bob. "I'll be right there. Sit tight."

Only ten minutes later, the colonel's sedan pulled up. Two men got out and walked up to the backhoe.

Bob, short and stocky, wrung his hands. Victor could see beads of sweat on the man's balding head. His tan suit was wrinkled. The man looked anxious and concerned.

On the other hand, Col. Hal Stevens, the director of engineering and housing, was quite a contrast. Tall and broad-shouldered, Stevens wore a tailored military uniform, complete with medals representative of his many years of service.

Victor explained to his two bosses that while he was digging the new grave at a depth of four feet, the backhoe broke through the top of an old casket.

"Could you see a body?" asked Bob.

"No," said Victor.

Bob turned and headed back to the car. He pulled a flashlight from the glove box. Meanwhile, Victor had returned to the Kubota and brought back a short ladder that had been tied to the backhoe. Back at the gravesite, Bob signaled to Victor that he was the one to climb into the hole.

Cautiously, Victor moved step-by-step down the ladder being careful not to disturb the loose dirt any more than necessary. When he had gone as far as he dared, he bent his knees and pointed the beam between the decaying boards of the casket.

"See anything?" Bob asked in a whisper.

"No, it's empty," Victor, replied.

"Have Stanley Chris come over," said Stevens. "Maybe he can give us some idea where it came from." Stanley, the museum curator, was the go-to guy when it came to historical questions.

Bob pulled out his cell. Fifteen minutes later Stanley showed up. Victor explained what had happened.

"I don't have any record of anything being buried in this area," said Stanley as he peered into the hole. "Let me take a closer look."

Just as Victor had done, Stanley clutched the ladder, bent down in the soft soil, and aimed the beam of light into the decaying casket.

"You're right, Victor. There is absolutely nothing in this casket," he said, shaking his head. Then he poked his finger into the wood. "Strange, it's a lot heavier than a normal pre-twentieth century casket. I've never seen one constructed like this. Look at the steel straps around the casket and the thickness of the planks. Looks like the wood has been treated. That's why it hasn't totally rotted."

Stanley began to brush the dirt away from the top of the casket.

"Wow, look at this!" he exclaimed. He had uncovered a large black cross. He pulled out his pocketknife and scraped the tarnished object.

"Holy shit, it's silver. It must weigh twenty or thirty pounds. It is worth thousands of dollars."

"Hal, can I have your guys dig up this casket and haul it over to the museum? Since there is no body, we don't have to worry about legal problems with possible next of kin. In the lab, I can examine it more carefully. There is no way that we can leave that cross sitting out here. It's priceless."

"Not a problem, Stanley," responded Hal. "I'll have it delivered to the museum right away."

3

THE BLACK DODGE CHARGER PULLED ONTO THE MAIN AVENUE IN HIGHLAND Falls, New York. It approached the main gate at West Point Military Academy.

Approximately three blocks from the gate was a McDonald's. An older McDonald's, it was the first fast-food restaurant in Highland Falls. Almost forty years earlier the first owners had realized the financial advantage of locating their restaurant so close to the main gate.

Nowadays, the town was overrun with newer, more modern fast-food restaurants. Subsequent owners had made half-hearted attempts to remodel the old building, but inside, not much had changed. Eating inside was like stepping into a time machine – it still had the flavor and décor of the first McDonald's from four decades earlier.

The most striking change was in the menu. No longer could a customer count on placing an order for a greasy burger and salty fries. Instead, the choices included turkey, soy and veggie burgers. The famous fries had disappeared, replaced by apple slices and carrot sticks. However, if a customer wanted an old-fashioned hamburger and fries, the vintage fare was listed at the bottom of the menu board in small letters. The cost for each of the "old" items was a good three times that of the new, healthier foods.

The Charger pulled into a parking space near the side door. A young man, still in his early twenties, stepped out of the vehicle. Butch Langston stood well over six and a half feet tall and weighed nearly two hundred fifty pounds. Inside, he found that he was the lone customer at this late hour.

Predictably, he placed his order for three cheeseburgers, a large Coke and a super-size order of fries. As he waited for his meal, he thought about the changes the coming school year would bring. When he had first arrived at the academy three years earlier, he had no idea what to expect.

During those years he had virtually no freedom. Now he was a senior or a "firstie," the nickname for a first-year cadet. He had his own car and could come and go whenever he wanted. Now, at 2330 hours, or 11:30 p.m., he marveled at his liberty to order late-night burgers at McDonald's.

This summer he had only gone home for two weeks. He returned early to take a make-up math course. Then he would be helping the incoming freshmen, called plebes, to prepare for the coming year and their new lives at the Point. He had arrived on campus two weeks ago and had been working with the staff getting ready for what was known as "beast barracks." The incoming plebes would learn all they needed to know to be successful cadets.

Butch was a proud member of the varsity football team. Unfortunately, the football program had a rather lackluster record. Last season the team had squeezed out only four wins. Two of the losses were against archrivals Navy and Air Force. Even so, being a member of the varsity football team made him a semi-celebrity. At least, he thought he was.

Back home, just being accepted at West Point brought him the status of a hometown hero. He had graduated from a small rural high school in Wisconsin. His senior class was small, numbering only one hundred five graduates. All through school he had won honors for his athletic achievements and was considered a star football player. His grades and SAT scores weren't great, but they were enough to get him into most colleges. His dad's friendship with the governor had made the difference. He made the cut and was accepted at the prestigious West Point Military Academy. To his dismay, he was only good enough to play back-up halfback with the Black Knights. Every year he had struggled to keep his grades high enough to be academically eligible to play football. Being on the football team had its perks. Players ate at their own team table and were served far more food than the other cadets. Plus, they were given more time to consume their meals. He liked the camaraderie on the team. His teammates were special to each other. He had made friendships that would last a lifetime. Butch cherished the time he had played football.

It seemed like it was taking forever to get his burgers. He peered over the counter to check on the cook's progress. Finally, the order came up. He took his tray to a table near the window and unwrapped the first burger while nibbling at a handful of fries.

He paused only to look up when he heard the side door swing open. He was a bit surprised to see that a young woman had come in alone. At first, he assumed she was just a pre-teen girl. She was very, very short, maybe no taller than four feet eight inches. Even her hair was short. He tried to remember what they called that type of a cut. A pixie cut? He glanced down and saw that she had on black patent leather high heels. What was most striking was that her skin was white as snow.

Even though he knew it was impolite to stare, he couldn't take his eyes off her. She looked like a China doll. She wore a Goth-style outfit. Her face stood out in contrast with the pale skin because she wore black lipstick and had a silver nose ring. Butch noticed that she had also painted her fingernails black to match her outfit.

He watched as she chatted with the cashier. She paid for a large Coke, and then turned and looked directly at him. Oops, he thought, I've been caught staring.

To his surprise, she walked directly to his table, pulled out a chair, and sat down across from him.

"Hi," she said. "My name is Kelly. I know what you're thinking. You're thinking that I should be home and that I'm too young to be out here without my parents. Let me tell you this, I'm nineteen years old, I graduated from Highland Falls High School last year, and I guarantee you that I am old enough to be here tonight."

Butch smiled at her abrupt introduction.

"Well, I guess I could ask you to sit down, but you're already sitting down."

She certainly wasn't shy.

"You go to the Point, don't you?" she asked.

Butch laughed. "How can you tell?"

"It's simple – your haircut and how straight you're sitting. I've lived all my life in Highland Falls, and I know a West Point cadet when I see one. How come they let you out tonight?"

"It's summer. I'm a senior, and we can get off post anytime. I'm here to prepare for beast week."

Her eyes focused on his short-sleeved shirt and the bulging muscles.

"I'll bet you play football."

"How'd you guess?"

"By your strong arms," she said with a grin. "Listen, when you get done eating, you want to go some place with me?"

She caught him off guard. He certainly wasn't expecting such an up-front offer.

"Sure. Where you want to go?"

"I don't know. Maybe we can just go out and park somewhere."

This can't be happening, he thought. At West Point his social life was somewhat restricted, to say the least. Cadets at West Point don't have time for dates. They have unbelievably long working hours, and they're lucky if they get four hours sleep a night. Dating during their time at West Point is almost unthinkable.

Even during the summer break when the cadets go home to family, they're usually so tired they spend the two weeks sleeping or staring vacantly at TV. Butch had led a celibate life during the last three years – not his choice, just the bitter truth.

About five or six percent of the cadets are women, but the academy discourages fraternization between the men and women. Of course, that didn't stop it from happening, but there were very few male cadets lucky enough to have any encounter with the females. The academy brass seemed to have forgotten what it's like to be young. They prohibited adult magazines and videos. Cadets joked that being at the academy was like being a novice priest at a seminary – except for the luxury of having a laptop computer. Cadets were issued their own laptops when they first enrolled. They all had free access to the academy's wireless network. It didn't take long for the cadets to figure out how to surf for porn. They were careful not to give their email addresses or offer to pay for what they saw. Instead, they tended to surf the free net and did everything possible to prevent anyone from discovering their identities.

Of course, the academy's leaders weren't fools. Obviously, with four thousand horny cadets, porn websites were hit more at West Point than just about anywhere else in the world. Butch had a pretty good idea what might happen tonight. So easy, he thought. Here he had only dreamed about sex during his time at the academy.

Yet, here was this bold young woman inviting him out for a drive and offering to "park somewhere." He wolfed down his last burger, picked up his Coke, stood up, and pushed back his chair.

"Let's go!" he said without hesitation.

As Butch and Kelly approached the door, he caught a glimpse of their reflection in the glass. Butch towered over the petite girl. They definitely made a strange pair.

Just how did he measure up? He knew he was far from handsome. He hated his large nose. His ears stuck out. Despite his nervous habit of pressing them back at odd times during the day, they stubbornly remained in place. Another thing that annoyed him was his tendency to blush easily. It was difficult to hide his emotions as his face turned red quickly when he was angry or embarrassed. His pale complexion kept him out of the sunlight as his skin burned easily. His hair was a reddish brown, likely a trait passed down from his Norse ancestors. He hated the color. More than anything, his hair disturbed him the most – he was just too hairy. Even his forearms and the backs of his fingers sprouted that ugly amber fur.

As for his body, he had issues with his huge hands and super sized feet. His big-boned body would likely turn to fat as he got older. But for now, with all the physical training at West Point and the daily workouts with weights, his shoulders were broad, his biceps huge, and his waist narrow.

Clothes didn't matter to him. He pulled on whatever was semi-clean. He had to look down to remember what he had on. Tonight his outfit was a black short-sleeved polo shirt, Levis and run-down sneakers.

All in all, if you didn't look at his face, he looked great. Nevertheless, he had no idea why this Kelly was so interested in going for a drive.

Standing beside him at the door, she almost looked like a pixie, maybe a fairy child from a children's story. At age thirteen, he had taken his younger brother to see "Peter Pan." That little Tinkerbell was jealous of Wendy, and she had a thing going for Peter. His mind wandered, imagining Peter and Tinkerbell having sex. He wondered if having sex with Kelly would be like Peter having sex with Tinker. Could someone so big have sex with such a tiny woman?

As they crossed the parking lot, he pulled out his car keys and pushed the unlock button. The lights flashed on the ten-year-old Charger.

"That's a cool car."

"Yup," said Butch. "I just bought it. It's ten years old, but it only has twenty thousand miles on it. The guy that owned it bought it new and always kept it in the garage. It has customized exhaust, special performance options for the engine, cool mag wheels and new high-performance tires.

"On the inside it looks like no one's sat in it, and I was very lucky. Most of my fellow cadets will be making car payments for the next six years. I've saved enough money that I could pay cash, and I won't be stuck with all those payments."

Remembering to act like a gentleman, he opened the door for Kelly. Butch walked around to the driver's side. As he got in, he noticed Kelly caressing the soft black leather.

"This even smells like a new car," she said.

"Where do you want to go?" Butch asked, realizing that since she was just nineteen, they couldn't go to a bar; the drinking age in New York was twenty-one.

"I don't know," said Kelly. "Let's just drive around for a while."

Neither of them had much to say, but soon Kelly was making small talk.

"So, is your name really Butch?"

"No," he said, "My first name is Jerald. I was named after my father. Instead of being called junior, somewhere along the line they called me

Butch, and as long as I can remember, everyone has called me Butch. Is your name really Kelly?" he asked.

"Of course, my name is Kelly Anderson. It always has been," she laughed at her own joke.

As they drove out of town heading south toward Bear Mountain, they talked about his life as a cadet, growing up in Wisconsin, and about how boring it was to have to live nineteen years in Highland Falls.

Butch noticed her rifling through her purse as if looking for something. She withdrew a compact and a small white plastic packet.

"Do you want to snort some coke?" she asked.

"Hell, no," said Butch. "They piss us every month. If we come up positive, we're kicked out of the academy. I'm certainly not going to do anything that could ruin my whole career."

"Do you care if I take a little coke?" asked Kelly.

"It's your body. Do what you want," he snapped.

Kelly opened the compact and set it in her lap. She placed two small strips of white powder on the mirror, rolled a twenty-dollar bill and snorted coke into her nose.

"Why the hell do you do that?" asked Butch.

"I can get along fine without the stuff, but when you're a little high, you can really perform sex."

Now there was no doubt. No doubt it was about her wanting to have sex.

"What are you? A prostitute or something?"

"No," she said. "Nothing like that, I just really like having sex. I can't explain it, but I just love to be screwed."

Butch glanced at her, checking out her cleavage and the swelling breasts spilling out of the top of her black low-cut blouse. He felt a thickness in his groin.

He should have heeded his father's warning words. A colonel in the Wisconsin National Guard, his dad often said, "If something feels wrong, you can pretty well bet that it is wrong." That message flashed in the back of Butch's brain.

His father's words and his common sense told him one thing, but his body didn't agree. His other brain in his pants was already geared to go. Butch pulled off onto a dirt road, drove up into the hills and stopped in a grassy clearing.

He leaned over and kissed her gently on the lips, expecting to proceed slowly and carefully so as not to scare her off.

That wasn't Kelly's plan. Her tongue quickly meshed with his. Before he knew it, she was trying to unzip his fly. She was breathing heavily.

"I want you inside of me." Her words weren't a request, but a demand.

"There's no way we can do it in this car. I'm too big," Butch gasped. "I've got a blanket in the trunk. Let's get out of the car," he continued, reaching down to open the driver's door.

Soon, he had the red plaid woolen blanket spread out on the grass behind the car. A full moon provided just enough light to see, and the night sky was dark enough to keep the act semi-private.

Kelly kicked off her high heels, yanked her blouse over her head, released her breasts from her bra, slithered out of her skirt, and pulled down her black panty hose. She wore no panties. She stood about two feet in front of him, boldly facing him. Even though she was short, she had a well-proportioned body. Her breasts jutted out, just ready to be sucked. Butch looked downward at the dark triangle between her legs.

It was just too much.

Butch tore off his clothes, wadding up his jeans, and tossing underwear aside. The rest happened so fast that he couldn't remember anything other than his penis driving into her moist body. He held himself up by his arms, holding his frenzied body in a push-up pose, and plunged in and out. He climaxed in what seemed like seconds. He rolled off of the girl, breathing as if he had just run a hundred-yard dash.

He leaned over and touched her cheek. She didn't respond.

"ARE YOU OK?" he asked.

Still no response. He shook her shoulder. She remained motionless; eyes open, staring blankly at nothing.

"Are you OK?" he asked again, almost screaming. Still no response.

Oh, my God, had he injured her? Maybe he was just too big. But it had been so easy, and she was enjoying it. He was sure of that.

Then he remembered the cocaine.

"Oh shit, she's stoned!" he realized.

Now what should he do? He needed to get her to a hospital. He got up, pulled on his shorts and pushed his legs into his crumpled Levi's while hopping barefoot toward the car. He picked up her purse that was gaping open on the passenger seat. He opened it and took out her wallet. He fumbled through her cards until he found her driver's license. Yes, that was her picture with the name Kelly Jane Anderson. Her address was in Highland Falls.

His eyes focused on her birth date. He looked again. She wasn't nineteen – she was just sixteen! This was bad news, really bad news. He was twenty-two; she was sixteen. That's statuary rape. He would go to jail if the police found out. He collapsed in the driver's seat, holding the girl's driver's license in his quivering hand.

He could take her into Newburg, drop her off near the hospital. Someone would find her. That was the solution. But first, he had to get her dressed.

Her body remained immobile, still on the blanket, her legs spread apart, her tiny form motionless.

"Kelly, you need to get dressed," he whispered.

No response. No movement.

He touched her cheek again. He leaned closer, hoping to detect some breaths coming in and out. He touched her throat, feeling for a pulse. None. He started CPR, pressing on her chest a hundred times a minute. After a few minutes, he again checked for a pulse. Still nothing. He stood up, bracing one hand on the trunk of the car. He took a deep gasp of air, shook his head from side to side, and tried to gather his senses.

Oh, God, he finally realized, she really is dead.

$$4$$

Out! Out! He needed to get the hell out of there right now.

He pulled his shirt over his head and struggled to push his arms into the sleeves. He crammed his feet into his sneakers without tying the shoestrings. He felt into the wrong pocket for his keys. He fumbled his right hand into the other front pocket, stopped, and clasped the keys tightly in his shaking hand. He couldn't just leave her lying on the ground.

"You stupid shit," he shrieked at her lifeless form. "You snort that damn coke. Now you're dead," he screamed.

He would have to get rid of the body. Someone would have seen them leave the McDonald's together. Cops would question him. He pounded his head with his fist. He had a condom in his wallet, but he had been in such a hurry, he didn't think to use it. His semen was inside her, and it even had dribbled over her lower body. Investigators would run the DNA and match it to him. The army kept DNA records on every service member. It identified people better than old-fashioned dog tags.

"Shit. Shit. Shit," he mumbled unconsciously.

The longer he waited, the greater the chance of someone driving by and finding him. He had to do something and do it soon. Where could he take the body to hide it?

Obviously, this wasn't the first time this friggin' chick had picked up some guy. If she didn't come home, her family would probably just assume she had run away. No one would look for her for days, maybe weeks. He could get away with all this as long as no one knew where she had gone. As long as no one found the body, he was free. But where could he hide a corpse where it would never be found?

"The tunnels!" His lips moved, but no sound came out. It was as though a light bulb had turned on in his head. Of course! He could hide the body in the tunnels. Sometimes, he reminded himself, he was downright brilliant.

5

WEST POINT, NEW YORK, HAS BEEN A MILITARY INSTALLATION SINCE BEFORE the Revolutionary War. Forts Putnam and Clinton were built in the 1700s to defend the Hudson River from the British. Numerous redoubts connected the forts by a series of underground tunnels.

When West Point became the United States Military Academy, the buildings were heated via these tunnels by high-pressure steam from a power plant near the Hudson. Over the years, the old tunnels were gradually abandoned and new ones built. Still, history won out. Some of the tunnels intersected with the Revolutionary era redoubt tunnels, dug more than two hundred years earlier. As far as anyone knew, the underground passages had never been accurately and completely mapped.

Everyone heard the stories about cadets sneaking through the tunnels and entering the superintendent's office. Likely, it was just one of the academy's urban legends. Although that part was probably inaccurate, one element of the story lived on in a secret club known as the "Tunnel Rats." No one knew when the club first began, but it was general knowledge that only twenty-five cadets were admitted each year.

New members had to meet certain standards. First, prospective members had to have survived their beginning two years at the academy. Second, they had to meet academic criteria – being in the bottom twenty percent of the class. Finally, they had to be willing to take a secret blood oath.

The Tunnel Rats were the opposite of an academic honor society. The Rats provided a sense of community for cadets who struggled to survive in the highly competitive West Point environment. It gave them emotional support and served as a resource of information on tests, papers and projects. Membership had recently been opened to qualifying female cadets. Ceremonies mimicked those of a secret fraternal organization, but were punctuated by lively beer-drinking sessions. Members had access keys to the mechanical rooms that led to the tunnels. Last year, Butch had become a Rat, and he took pride in his status.

So the solution of what to do with Kelly's body was simple: Take the body underground and hide it far down in one of the redoubt tunnels. The tunnels were dry, and no one would ever find a buried body.

He was confident his plan would work. The hard part was getting the body back to the Point. He glanced at the naked girl on the blanket. He couldn't just drop the body on the back seat of his car. He had to pass through the military police checkpoint at Stony Lonesome Gate. The gate guards always checked the back seat.

Then it came to him – he would use the duffel bag where he kept his field gear. It was in the trunk. He fingered his keys until he found the trunk key. Once the trunk was open, he pulled out his duffel bag, opened it, and dumped his gear on the ground. He took the empty bag over to the blanket and laid it parallel to Kelly's body. She was very small. He figured he could stuff her body into the drawstring bag.

Rolling the body to its back, he positioned the arms tightly at the sides.

Then the dilemma: Feet first or headfirst? Did it really matter?

He didn't want to argue with himself. He began at the head. He worked quickly. It was just like slipping a pillow into a pillowcase, but despite his best efforts, the body didn't fit. The legs were too long.

"Damn! Damn!" he muttered angrily. "I'll go the other way."

He gripped the closed end of the bag and pulled the bag off the corpse. Then he dropped to the ground next to the knees, folded them tightly and pressed them close to the body, making the body parts more compact.

He again threaded the duffel bag over the corpse, beginning at the legs. He bent the elbows, folded them tightly into the chest, and tucked the hands by the face. He turned, picked up the scattered clothing and stuffed it into the bag's open spaces. He took a step backward to assess his work. He stared at the lumps in the canvas – all that remained of the once-living Kelly.

None of this should have happened.

"It's your fault," he said to the body in the bag. "You lied to me, and then you did drugs and died. It's not my fault."

He retrieved the wallet and purse from the car and crammed them into the bag. He tightened the drawstring and picked up the duffel by its handle. It was easy to lift. Kelly only weighed about eighty pounds. He could dead lift two hundred twenty pounds. He settled the duffel inside the wide trunk, stuffing loose gear around it. After slamming the trunk, he climbed into the Charger and punched the start button with his index finger. He slowly drove down the dirt road and onto the highway, heading back toward Highland Falls.

It seemed unreal, so like a nightmare. He couldn't believe what had occurred. His mind kept replaying all that had happened this evening – the movie, the cheeseburgers, and meeting Kelly. Then his world and all of his dreams had turned upside down.

"Oh, shit! Holy mother of God – shit!" he stammered.

His blood froze. He could see red and blue lights flashing in the rearview mirror. A patrol car pulled up behind him. Its front bumper was only a few feet from the girl's lifeless body.

"I'm dead meat," he said slowly and softly. "They must have found out what happened."

As soon as the cop pulled him over, he would be going to jail for the rest of his life. He was tempted to floorboard the gas pedal and outrun the patrol car. The Charger had a special high-performance engine. It had power. No way, he reasoned. He'd seen enough cop movies to know that it wouldn't work.

"No," he whispered. "I've got to keep a clear head. How could they possibly know what happened?"

He turned the steering wheel to the right and pulled onto the edge of the road. He watched in the mirror as the cop car stopped. The officer got out and slowly walked to the driver's window. He tapped on the glass and indicated that the window should be opened. Butch smiled nervously and pushed the window button. The electric window rolled down.

"Yes, officer?" asked Butch.

"Sir, may I see your driver's license, proof of registration and insurance card?" Butch slowly gathered the documents and handed them to the officer.

"You're a cadet at West Point?"

"Yes, sir," said Butch.

"You're out a little late tonight," said the officer.

"Yes, sir. I went to a movie, and I'm on my way back now."

"I thought you guys had some kind of curfew."

"Not during the summer," said Butch. The officer looked in the back seat.

"You're by yourself?"

"Yes, sir," said Butch.

"Well, we're checking all vehicles. We've had a number of overdoses on bad cocaine tonight. We've got four kids in the hospital and one dead on arrival."

The officer looked more closely at Butch's face, particularly his eyes.

"You haven't taken any drugs, have you?"

"No, sir, they test us almost every week. If we come up positive, we're through," responded Butch.

"All right, you take it easy."

"Yes, sir, officer."

Butch exhaled slowly as he watched the cop go back to his car. Then he inhaled and exhaled once again — more of a sigh of relief than anything else. He waited until the officer pulled around him. Then he slowly got back on the road, keeping his attention focused on oncoming vehicles.

He was becoming absolutely paranoid. The next stop would be the MPs at Stony Lonesome Gate. Somehow, he imagined that his car was transparent, and everybody could see Kelly's body bundled in the trunk.

At the gate the MP saluted, checked his ID card, glanced at the window sticker, and waved him through. Butch drove to the cadet parking lot and pulled into an empty space.

He braced his arms against the steering wheel, as if he was preparing to crash into a concrete wall. Yet nothing happened, nothing at all. He continued to look straight ahead, totally immobile. He couldn't focus on what was right ahead.

How could he – Jerald "Butch" Langston – sink into this horror?

6

HE HAD TO GET THE BODY OUT OF THE TRUNK.

The temperature in the car's trunk would likely reach one hundred twenty degrees during the day. The smell alone would overpower anyone who came within a short distance of the car. Some people would retch in dry heaves or spill the contents of their stomachs right there in the parking lot. Some would recognize the smell of death. Someone would call the police to investigate the origin of the odor.

Rigor mortis would set in, stiffening the corpse. Butch remembered the dead body of the family cat. She had died overnight. He was the one who had found her curled in her bed as if she were still asleep. But when he touched the body, he found it as stiff as a rock. A human body, even though it was as small as Kelly's, would make the duffel bag unbendable and difficult to move. He had to get rid of the corpse that very night.

He got out of the Charger, walked around to the trunk, and opened it. He lifted the duffel bag and threw it over his shoulder. He felt the body hanging limply against his back. It was still flexible. He tried to carry it as if it contained only his gear – not a dead girl. He headed down the pathway towards Grant barracks. He prayed that he would not cross paths with anyone, but he assumed that this early in the morning, meeting someone was unlikely. When he got to the barracks, he took the side entrance that led downstairs into the basement where the washers and dryers were located. At the far wall was a locked steel door. A sign on it read:

DANGER
HIGH VOLTAGE
AUTHORIZED PERSONNEL ONLY

He pulled out his keys, fingering them one-by-one until he found the master key. That was one of the perks of being a Tunnel Rat. Each of them had a key to the tunnels.

He set the duffel bag on the floor, inserted the key in the lock, opened the door, and dragged the bag into the room. He flipped the switch to turn on the low-level lighting and quietly closed the door. He double-checked to be sure it locked securely behind him.

He stood in a concrete vault-like room. Rows of tall gray metal cabinets lined the walls. Gauges indicated voltage and amperage. The panels had circuit breakers that served to turn on or shut off power to different sections of the building. He could hear the steady hum of electrical power from the transformers along the west wall.

At the far end of the room was yet another secure door. He used the same key, opened the door, and stepped into the steam distribution room. Here, high-pressure steam entered the huge heat exchangers that took the cool water from the building, reheated it, and sent it back through the radiators. Twenty-five horsepower motors drove the pumps. It was hot inside the room – likely more than one hundred degrees.

He lifted the duffel bag and headed to yet a third door. This one also posted a warning sign:

DANGER
ASBESTOS
DO NOT ENTER WITHOUT
PROTECTIVE GEAR

Again, he ignored the warning. He turned off the light switch and waited until his eyes adjusted to the low light inside. He locked the door behind him.

He stood at the entrance to a concrete tunnel. He'd been there before. The tunnel was twelve feet wide and a good ten feet tall. Compact fluorescent lights spaced every thirty feet ran along the ceiling. A person could drive a car down the wide tunnel. Now, the temperature was even higher than it had been in the heat exchange room. Sweat poured in rivulets down Butch's face. He slung the duffle bag over his shoulder and made his way down the tunnel. He could hear the steady drip-drip of water.

Drains were spaced at even intervals along the floor. Large steam pipes hung from the ceiling, suspended by anchors. Newer pipes were wrapped with ceramic insulation; some of the older pipes were still coated with asbestos. Hundreds of miles of pipe ran under the academy grounds. The asbestos would remain in place. It would be impossible to take out the tons of asbestos. The logical solution was to keep the insulation encapsulated. It was dangerous to be here without a protective mask. Butch stifled a chuckle. This was all part of the mystique of being a Tunnel Rat.

Butch began his trek deeper into the tunnel. The asbestos made this a dangerous place, but the high-pressure pipes and high temperatures made it even more perilous. A break in one of the steam pipes could open up a high-pressure leak. If a person stepped on a crack from a broken pipe, its rupture could cut off an arm or even sever a head from a body.

But that was not an issue tonight. All Butch wanted to do was get rid the damn duffel bag that contained Kelly's body. When he had gone about two hundred feet, he turned into a side tunnel where the lights were spaced even farther apart. He walked down another one hundred and fifty feet to where the tunnel ended at a metal fire door. He rotated the handle on the door and pushed it open, revealing the blackness behind it. He reached into his left pants pocket and pulled out an LED flashlight. It illuminated the space ahead of him. He could see an old steam tunnel. Likely it had been closed for decades. The air was much cooler in this section of the tunnel. He stopped briefly to wipe the sweat from his face and neck.

Here, chunks of concrete, wood from shattered furniture, discarded pipes, and piles of old books littered the floor. Now the tunnel had shrunk. It was only about eight feet wide and eight feet high. He resumed his walk, figuring he was now under the parade field. He came to another side tunnel, even smaller yet. It was only about four feet wide and six feet high. He had to stoop and carry the duffle by its handle.

When he had gone only fifty feet, it came to an end. Here, a makeshift door built of heavy timbers blocked the way. Butch dropped the duffel, walked to the barrier and reached between the heavy boards until his fingers felt a latch. He released it. The boarded wall swung open on hinges. It was a door – not a wall – designed to deceive and discourage anyone snooping around in the tunnels. He retrieved the bag and passed though the opening.

Butch continued another sixty feet until he came to hundreds of bricks scattered randomly on the floor. Beyond the bricks stood an opening on the right. He stooped and dragged the bag through the opening. Once inside, he pointed his light into the brick interior. The steam tunnels were finally behind him. Apparently, he had reached deep enough that he entered the original tunnel construction. The tunnel descended even more deeply into the ground.

After another hundred feet, the tunnel turned sharply to the right. He entered a chamber. It had three small rooms on one side. Could these be the old cells used to hold prisoners during the Revolutionary War? In modern times, the dead were buried under the north side of the plain, near Execution Hollow. If he had his bearings right, he was actually under the tennis courts. He stepped into the first room. He struck a match and ignited a Coleman lantern. He was now in the Tunnel Rats' sanctuary. The three rooms were clean and orderly; in sharp contrast to the littered mess he had passed minutes earlier.

Now he sighed with a sense of relief as he gazed at the neatly arranged furniture. Forbidden reading material was scattered on the low tables. A battery-operated DVD player and an LCD screen had been set up to play sports events and X-rated videos. This is the place where he and his fellow rats liked to hang out and escape the stress of academy life.

It was cooler now. The underground sanctuary stayed at sixty degrees year-round. He sighed as he looked at the bar along one wall. It was well stocked with bottles of beer, a variety of sodas and even some hard liquor. After Butch's stressful night and heavy work, he was thirsty, really thirsty. He grabbed a beer, wiped off the top on his shirt, and twisted the cap. The cool liquid ran freely down his open throat. He tossed the empty bottle on the floor and opened another beer. Then he opened a third.

With the alcoholic euphoria boosting his courage, his thoughts returned to Kelly's body. He needed to take it even more deeply into the old tunnels. The low temperature and humidity meant that as long as he covered the duffel bag with tightly packed dirt, no telltale odor would escape. Besides, he had to make sure that anything that could identify him would never be found. His name and serial number were stenciled on the bag. He told himself that the body must stay hidden for the next one hundred years.

An opening at the back of the third cell led to an older part of the tunnels. It was partially collapsed. As far as he knew, no one had bothered to crawl over the rubble. It looked too dangerous, and there was always the possibility that the ceiling might collapse. It had happened before. In 1984, a sinkhole opened up next to the canoe house. Apparently part of the old tunnel system had given way, opening up a substantial depression. The grounds crew filled the hole with several truckloads of crushed rock.

He dragged the duffel through the opening and carefully picked his way over the rubble. About one hundred feet in, he figured he had gone far enough. It was time to reassess his position. He set the bag down on the rough surface and aimed the beam of light along the walls. On the right, the bricks had fallen away. It looked like there may be an opening behind the wall. With a sigh of relief, he reassured himself that this was the perfect place to get rid of his horrible burden. He placed the light on a brick and aimed its beam at the opening.

Instantly, he stopped. He thought had heard something. Impossible. Where had the sound come from? He froze in place and listened closely once again. He definitely heard a sound – something akin to a moan. His heart rate accelerated. Was it simply the rhythm of his own heart beating out of control?

Then he heard the pitiful sound again. He grabbed his light and began to search the rubble, foot-by-foot and inch-by-inch. A chill ran down his spine. Out of the corner of his eye, he thought he saw movement inside the duffel bag. At first, he was elated. Maybe she wasn't dead after all.

Then his thoughts turned to the awful truth – only Kelly was inside his duffel bag. She was the only thing that could explain the moaning and the movement. If she lived, she would tell the police where he had taken her and what she thought he planned to do with her body.

Then he heard the moan again, only it was louder than before. The duffel began to thrash about as if it had a life unto itself. He imagined knees and elbows poking from side to side in the girl's futile effort to escape. Without thinking, Butch picked up a brick and held it in both hands over his head.

He might have slammed the brick onto the bag had he not seen the hole at the drawstring begin to widen. Two black-painted fingernails emerged. The hole opened even more. Now, one tiny hand emerged. Then another hand joined the first. Soon her head would be free, and she would stare into his eyes, blaming him for his deadly plan.

With all the strength he could muster, he brought the brick down heavily against the bag, roughly near where her left ear might have been. Once wasn't enough. She still cried out, and her shrieks intensified. He struck again – once, twice, three and four times. He pounded at the same spot until he heard the crack of bone. The bag darkened as blood soaked through the canvas. He let the brick fall from his hands. He bent over, almost falling to his knees, and began to sob.

Now, there was no movement. No sound. Nothing at all.

His stomach churned. He grasped his belly, hoping to control the urge to expel the contents of his stomach. But it was too late. Now he knew that he was going to be sick. Vomit swelled in his throat. He turned to his left and spewed forth a lumpy mixture of warm beer and chunks of burger. Stomach acid burned the inside of his nose and dripped over his lips and down his chin. He braced his midsection with tightly folded forearms and retched violently.

God, what had he done? How could he have been so stupid?

He fell to his knees, continuing to cry, moan and beat his fists on the ground. He had no idea how long he had been on the tunnel floor, stretched out alongside the bloody body bag.

Finally, he struggled to his feet and wiped his dripping nose on his shirtsleeve. His mind cleared. He had to finish what he had started. He crawled to the wall and began tearing at the loose bricks. Gradually, he had made an opening large enough to cram the bag inside. He pressed against the duffel, forcing it inside as far as it would go. Then he began to replace the bricks.

"What the fuck?" he said aloud, unable to believe his own eyes.

He picked up his flashlight and aimed its beam directly into the remaining hole. Inside the opening, he could make out a second body. Someone had beaten him to this spot.

He could see that it was the body of an old man, dressed in tattered rags. A long white beard came from the chin and curled itself in a circular shape. The thick yellow fingernails were at least two inches in length. A thin layer of dust covered the entire body. The corpse must have occupied the hole for decades. Yet, thought Butch, it didn't look shriveled like the bodies of mummies he'd seen in magazines. There was almost no decay on this withered form. He willed himself to draw nearer for a closer look.

Suddenly, the eyes popped open and the twisted fingers reached out and encircled his upper arm.

The cadet struggled to loosen the viselike grip. As if caught in machinery, his body fell helplessly to the rough surface. From somewhere close by, he heard his chilling screams echo throughout the tunnels.

Butch Langston had just come face to face with a terror that would change his life forever.

7

ONE OF THE LARGEST COLLECTIONS OF MILITARY MEMORABILIA IN THE WESTERN hemisphere is housed in the west point museum.

The museum and West Point Visitors Center are located next to each other just off of West Point Highway next to the Academy's Thayer Gate. As a department of the United States Military Academy, the museum supports cadet academic, military and cultural instruction. Its collections encompass the history of West Point and the academy, the evolution of warfare, and the development of the American armed forces. While only a portion of the collection is on public display, all artifacts are available for cadet academic instruction, special exhibition and research.

At five o'clock in the afternoon, Stanley Chris, the museum's director, took the elevator to the sub-basement. Chris was proud of his seven-year tenure as the museum's director. This was considered the most coveted position in the entire country's military museums. When the elevator door opened, he stepped out into the large open display area. He walked past several large artillery pieces and a tank from the First World War and glanced at the two floor-to-ceiling murals depicting the D-day Allied invasion of Europe.

To his left, Chris paused briefly to look at the familiar facsimile of the atomic bomb that had been dropped on Nagasaki. He reached for the coded keypad above the door handle, punched in his numbers, and heard the lock click. Hundreds of items of historical significance were stored in the museum's warehouse. In a small room to the right sat the old decaying casket that had been discovered only two months earlier.

Everyone at West Point had been amazed when the news of the casket became public. The grounds staff always took the utmost caution when they dug. No one wanted to desecrate the gravesite of someone's long-dead relative, no matter the date of death. Yet the casket had been empty. It showed no indication that a body had ever rested inside. Since there was no rush, the men had carefully removed what was left of the box and took the pieces to the museum. It had been in this room since its arrival.

With the start of a new year, Chris had been too busy to address the mystery of the empty casket. Even though it was after hours, he had decided to begin the investigation. Earlier, his assistant had brushed off most of the dirt, taken off the silver cross and placed it on the workbench. From the metalwork of the straps and the type of nails used, the museum crew concluded that the casket had been built around the time of the Revolutionary War.

It had been constructed of rough oak planks, each one approximately one-inch thick. They were chemically treated to reduce wood rot. The cross itself weighed twenty-six pounds, eight ounces. Chris had never seen such a large religious item made during Revolutionary times. His assistant had painstakingly applied a cleaning solution formulated to re-move the silver oxide. They didn't want all of it removed – only enough to reveal any lettering or engraving.

Chris used a strong magnifying glass to examine the item more close-ly. The cross pieces had been embellished with Biblical scenes. One scene showed Christ being tempted by the devil. Chris was astounded at the quality of the art. He had examined hundreds of artifacts in his career, but this was one of the finest.

He found the symbol of the cross's maker. He took close-up photos of the symbol and printed several before checking historical records for sil-versmith marks from that era. A little after eight o'clock, he found what he was looking for. The maker was none other than Andrew Wyatt who had been a silversmith for the town of Newburgh, New York, only about twenty miles from the academy. His research showed several of Wyatt's pieces, but none of them depicted religious themes. The current market still offered some of Wyatt's pieces.

Chris decided to return to the museum before calling it a day. Back in the room with the casket, he pulled on his gloves and turned over the cross. Again he examined it with the magnifying glass. He could see something written on the back. It was difficult to read. Using onionskin and a soft lead pencil, he made a rubbing of the letters. He could make out a few letters. Then he looked again and pieced together a few words. Finally, he put together the sentence:

"Whoever removes the cross that binds the demon to the tomb will be damned to eternal hell."

Although he was alone in his familiar workplace, Stanley Chris paused, overcome by the mystery he had just revealed.

Then he felt a chill run down his back.

8

Manhattan's J.P. Morgan Chase building is one of the taller structures in the city.

It might impress those who are unfamiliar with New York City, but to this young man, it was just the building where he worked. He took the express elevator from the forty-ninth floor down to the lobby. It was now ten o'clock. The early meeting had started at seven o'clock. After three hours of staring at the computer screen, searching through accounts, looking for errors, and asking questions, he needed to escape. Talk about boring. This was one aspect of the job he could do without. When the elevator doors opened in the lobby, the man moved ahead and fell into step with the others. Everyone wore a power suit. Everyone was in a hurry to go somewhere.

He walked through the lobby and turned right through the double doors into the bank on the lobby level. Even though the bank was on the first floor of one of the largest financial corporations in the world, under it all, this was just an ordinary bank. It had been disguised to look like a bank built in the last century. It had tall marble columns, shiny tile floors and tiny teller windows.

He reached in his pocket and pulled out the check he had written before leaving home. It was a personal check for six hundred dollars. He wanted it in cash. He approached one of the tellers.

Fortunately, the meeting had concluded two hours before it was scheduled to end. Now he had time to kill. He had considered walking the three and a half miles back to Federal Plaza. He surmised that he could get back to the office more quickly walking than taking a taxi through the thick traffic. It looked like it was going to be a good day. The forecast was for temperatures in the low seventies. Besides that, the brisk exercise would feel good.

Although he was just about to hand his check to the teller, he paused and turned to look behind him. He sensed a certain tension in the air. It often happened like that, although he couldn't explain why he had this feeling. Only a dozen or so people were in the bank lobby. Just three teller windows were open. It should seem like a normal day at any normal bank. But it wasn't.

Four of them – all men – entered the bank through the Park Avenue doors. All wore long black coats over what seemed like Goth costumes. Each one had pink spiked hair. But these weren't teenagers who wanted to set themselves apart from their peers. Instead, they all appeared to be in their mid-thirties – grown, seasoned and fearless. One marched directly to the double doors to the lobby of the main building.

Another approached the manager's desk, bypassed it, and veered to the first teller's cage. He came to a stop ten feet behind a tall, well-built young man wearing a dark tailored suit, highly polished shoes, a crisp light blue shirt and a white tie with thin red stripes. The teller had seen young men like him before. He was one of the successful young executives who frequented Chase's corporate headquarters.

A young woman, the teller smiled at the young executive and glanced momentarily at the Goth impersonator behind him. Her training included courtesy to customers, no matter their age, race or costume. Yet this man gave her second thoughts. She turned her attention to the young executive.

"Good morning, sir," she said. "How may I help you?"

"I need to cash a check."

"Yes, sir, do you have an account with us?"

"Of course," he said as he handed her the check.

"How would you like the money?"

"Fifties," he said.

She counted out the twelve fifty dollar bills. He took the cash and tucked it into his wallet, then calmly returned the wallet to his hip pocket.

"Oh, yes," he said. "There is one more thing."

"Yes, Mr. Martin," she said.

Martin was impressed. Obviously, this was a smart teller, reading the check and remembering his name.

"Under the counter, you have a button for a silent alarm. Please press it," said Tim Martin.

The young woman paled.

"I don't understand," she said.

He smiled calmly at her.

"There's an armed robbery in progress and in twenty seconds you will be ordered to raise your hands and won't be able to push it."

"I can't ...," she started to say.

"Do it now," he whispered. His smile was gone and a serious look came over his face. He meant business.

She reached down and slid her hand toward the alarm button. She hesitated for a second and once again looked into his eyes. She pushed the button.

"If this is some kind of joke, you're in big trouble," she whispered.

Two quick blasts from a semi-automatic 12-gauge shotgun brought their conversation to an abrupt end. The roar from the explosions ripped through the lobby.

"EVERYONE, HANDS IN THE AIR!"

The order came from one man who had positioned himself in the center of the lobby. The other men were wrapping chains around the handles on the doors that led to the street and into the lobby of the main building.

"All right, everyone out from behind the counter and come over here by me. Keep your hands up!" he shouted.

People slowly began moving toward the middle of the lobby. An older man, a bank customer, had the courage to speak out.

"This is an outrage. You can't do this!"

One of the punks moved directly in front of the man, reversed his shotgun, and struck the side of the man's face soundly with the stock of his weapon. The man fell backwards, the back of his head striking against a marble column. He slid limply to the floor and remained motionless. Blood poured from an open gash on his cheek.

A woman screamed in terror. Now it was her turn. The punker pointed the barrel of the shotgun directly in her face.

"If you don't shut up, bitch, I'll blow your fucking head off!"

His threats reduced her screams to sobs. She pressed her fist to her mouth to silence her outburst.

"Now, everyone on the floor. Face down, hands and legs spread out. If you move a finger, we'll blow your head off!"

Not far from the bank building, Eleanor Blatto poked her head in Director Vance's corner office.

"Sir, we have an agent-in-distress alarm."

"Shit!" grumbled Howard Vance. "Who is it?"

"Tim Martin," she answered.

"Double shit," said Vance. "What's the GPS location?"

"JP Morgan Chase World Headquarters building."

"What was he doing this morning?"

"Meeting with the auditors at Chase."

"So, what happened? Did one of them come at him with a paperclip?"

"Ah, come on now. Martin's not that bad," she replied.

"I know," said Vance, "but, my God, Martin sometimes reacts without thinking. I know that his busts are good and internal affairs has always cleared him, but why couldn't it be another agent?"

Vance shook his head.

"OK, let's get a couple of agents down there and see what's going down."

When an agent activates the duress button on his or her pager, no overt contact can be made with the agent. The purpose of the duress button is to indicate that the agent is in a position that he or she needs help, but no acknowledgement can be made that help is on the way. The pager's GPS allows the agency to pinpoint the agent's location.

"Keep me informed on what's happening," said Vance.

Vance took a quick look at his watch. It was only ten minutes after ten o'clock in the morning. He suspected that this was going to be one very long day.

9

AN EERIE SILENCE DESCENDED ON THE TERRIFIED PEOPLE IN THE LOBBY. ASIDE from a few muffled sobs, no noise — other than that of general street sounds — could be heard. Martin lay face down on the cool floor along with the bank's staff and customers. The silence was broken now and then by the clank and rattle of cash drawers being forced open. The robbers moved quickly. Obviously, they had rehearsed their plan and had memorized their roles.

"Dwaine! Dwaine! There are a bunch of cops outside!" shouted the man at the Park Avenue entrance.

Martin sighed cautiously. Christ, he thought. Instead of keeping out of sight, New York's finest pull right up to the front doors.

The robbers' careful plan seemed to be falling apart. No one had figured that the cops would come that fast.

"There ain't no way I'm going down," shrieked one of the robbers. "This will be my third rap. I'll get life!"

"I'd rather die," cried out another man.

"We ain't goin' down!" shouted another. "If they don't drop back, we'll start shooting bullets into all these nice people here. Those pigs won't risk the lives of all these suckers!"

The phone at the first teller's window rang three times.

"Pick it up! Pick up the damn phone," said the one who seemed to be in charge.

"Hello?" said the guy named Dwaine.

"Mark, it's a cop. What do I say?"

"Tell the motherfucker that unless he pulls back those pigs, we'll start popping hostages. Get me someone. I'm going to give them an example so that they know we're serious."

10

HOWARD VANCE LISTENED TO JORDAN DRISTAN'S BRIEFING ON THE BANK situation. Dristan had been relaying the information from a police lieutenant at the scene. Police were already in cell phone contact with one suspect who threatened to shoot the hostages.

"I'm on my way," Vance yelled loud enough so that the man on the phone could hear him.

Racing out of the office, he shouted orders to Eleanor.

"Call D.C. Tell them we have a hostage crisis at Chase. Let them know that we believe one of our agents is in the bank. And, Eleanor, have my car and driver at the front door when I get there!"

11

MY GOD, THOUGHT MARTIN. THESE GUYS ARE SERIOUS, REALLY SERIOUS. They will kill one of us.

"Who do I pick?" Dwaine asked, his voice quivering with anxiety.

"I don't give a fuck who you pick! Just pick one," said the guy named Mark. "Oh, and Dave, you come with me!"

Martin could hear the click-click of footsteps on the marble floor. He had to do something, and he had to do it fast.

"Take a bank employee!" he pleaded, curling his body into in a fetal position. "We're just customers!"

"What did you say, asshole?" screamed Dave.

"Oh, God," Martin cried out pitifully. "Please leave me alone. Take her, she's a teller."

"What?" asked the young woman teller. "You rotten coward, you can go to hell," she screamed.

Mark came up beside Martin and kicked him in the ribs. It hurt like hell. Then Martin began to sob.

"Please, I have three kids! Don't do this!" he cried.

12

Sweat dripped down Lieutenant Angelo Goddard's cheeks and onto his neck. Christ, this could turn out really bad. From what they now knew, this was likely the work of a group of thugs that had been dubbed "The Punk Robbers" by the news media. They had been hitting banks all over borough. Now the police had them trapped, but the place had been full of customers and some guy on the phone said they would start picking them off one by one.

"Where the hell is the SWAT team and hostage negotiator?" yelled Angelo at the sergeant on the radio.

"Stuck in traffic," answered the sergeant.

"Christ, we need help," Goddard said, mopping his brow with his wrinkled handkerchief.

13

"COME HERE, YOU BIG TOUGH MAN, YOU JUST GOT YOURSELF ELECTED."

Two of the men grabbed Martin by the elbows and lifted him to his feet. Then his knees went limp. If they hadn't been holding him by his arms, he would have crumpled to the floor. Totally distraught, Martin sobbed uncontrollably.

"Come on, you chicken shit, act like a man," growled Mark.

The two hauled Martin toward the front door. The toes of his shiny shoes scraped across the floor.

"I'm going to enjoy putting a round in this wimp's puny head," laughed Mark.

Martin's cries intensified.

"Oh, God, I don't want to die. Please, please, no!"

"Shut up and act like a man," yelled Dave as he grabbed Martin by the lapels of his suit coat. He drew back his fist and swung a right hook at Martin's face.

But the fist didn't connect. Instead, Dave found himself flying through the air and crashing onto the floor.

"What the fuck?" growled Mark.

But before he could react, a second blow struck him above the jaw so fiercely that his cheekbone shattered. He fell to the floor unconscious. Martin pulled a .40 caliber pistol from a hidden holster under his jacket. The man who had been stationed by the lobby door turned and brought his shotgun up, taking aim at Martin.

But Martin was faster. He fired, striking the robber in his left shoulder. The shotgun flew through the air. Martin threw himself on the floor and rolled to his right. Two shotgun blasts exploded inches from him, and the buckshot peppered the wall behind him.

Martin, still on his side, swung his pistol around and fired two shots in the direction of his would-be assassin. Two rounds struck Dwaine in the chest knocking him backwards. A blast from the shotgun discharged into the ceiling.

Then there was silence.

14

When they heard the shots, every cop froze.

"Jesus," said one. "What are they doing, killing everyone?"

Lieutenant Goddard stared blankly ahead. He didn't see the man in the dark suit come up to him. All he saw was a shiny badge thrust before his eyes.

"Howard Vance, Director FBI, New York office. What do we have here?"

Goddard blinked and recovered his professional demeanor.

"Shots fired in the bank, a number of shots. It sounded like a massacre. Then nothing."

"Shit," said Vance.

15

Martin rose from the floor, holding his pistol firmly in both hands. He looked around to assess the situation. Dave and Mark were on the floor, unconscious. The man by the door now sat on the floor, leaning his back against the wall, clutching his right shoulder in an attempt to stop the flow of blood from his wound. Dwaine was on his back, his vacant eyes staring at the ceiling.

"All right, everyone. I'm Special Agent Martin, FBI. I want you to slowly and carefully get to your feet. Move over to the front door. Move very slowly and carefully."

The people, shell-shocked and confused, followed his orders. They moved toward the door. In fewer than two minutes, the group huddled together by the door.

"Please turn and face me," Martin said.

He took a moment to make eye contact with the twenty men and women in front of him. He saw terror and shock in their eyes. He approached the young teller who had pushed the button on the silent alarm.

"Sorry about the chicken thing, but I had to get clear so I could take them out," he told her.

Martin didn't really expect a response. The woman just nodded, then she looked down.

Then Martin grabbed the arm of a young woman who had been standing next to the teller. He pulled her out of the group while holding her arms to her sides. He grabbed her other hand and yanked a small .32-caliber pistol out of her grasp.

"You're under arrest as an accomplice for an armed robbery," he told her as he turned her around and snapped handcuffs on her wrists.

"How did you know?" she asked.

"Your eyes," he said. "I could see it in your eyes."

"Folks, I want you all to place your hands on the top of your heads," Martin continued.

"Why?" asked a man.

"So a police sniper doesn't shoot you when you step outside," Martin said as he removed the chains from the front door. Then he held the door open for them as they silently filed out, one after another.

16

BOTH VANCE AND GODDARD WERE SPEECHLESS. HERE WERE THE HOSTAGES – a group of strangers who now had a second chance at life. They walked one by one out the door and onto the street with their hands on their heads.

"Get in there and find out exactly what happened!" shouted the lieutenant. Four police officers approached the door while holding bullet-proof Kevlar shields in front of them.

One officer came to a halt in front of Martin. He didn't have a chance to ask a question. Martin did the talking.

"I'm Agent Martin, FBI. I have five perps. One's dead. One victim is unconscious."

Within minutes, the bank lobby was transformed into a beehive of police activity. The older man who had suffered a head injury and the three suspects who had been hurt were receiving medical treatment.

One of the policemen came up. He shook his head while he spoke to Martin.

"You took all five out by yourself?" he asked.

"I guess so," said Martin.

Just then Director Vance stepped between them and glared at Martin.

"Jesus Christ, Martin. I sent you over here to do an audit, not destroy the Goddamn bank."

17

Tim Martin bounded up the steps, two at a time.

For exercise, he usually opted for the stairs over the elevator. It was an easy workout. He only had to get to the fourth floor.

At number 402, he put his key in the deadbolt lock and soon was inside his six-hundred-square-foot flat. He still couldn't accept the real estate agent's smooth talk describing the place as a view apartment. Sure, it was just one bedroom and only two blocks from Central Park, but to get any kind of a view, a person had to lean out the bedroom window, hold tight and look to the far right. But, the place did have its upside. It was near the park, and within the last five years with the improved economy, its value had almost doubled.

He switched on the lights, tossed his suit jacket on the back of the sofa, and crossed into the kitchen that opened up directly to the living room. He popped a frozen dinner in the microwave. That was his food, but he still needed a beverage.

He took out a beer, screwed off the cap, and tipped his head back, allowing the liquid to pour freely down his throat. While the microwave hummed, he loosened his tie and unbuttoned the top of his shirt. The sound of the bell told him dinner was ready. He gingerly lifted the hot meal and carried it to the coffee table. He opened another beer. Definitely, this was at least a two-beer night.

He had spent nine hours being debriefed. He was put on administrative leave, a short one, most likely only until Monday considering the circumstances of the shooting. His service weapon had been turned in to forensics. Of course, he had been issued a temporary replacement. It was in his shoulder holster sitting right beside the "gourmet" meal on the coffee table.

The world had changed with the fear of terrorism. It wasn't common knowledge, but when someone in law enforcement is put on administrative leave, he or she was still permitted to carry a weapon. Martin just shook his head at the logic of the situation – here he had to be on leave because he killed an armed robber who was about to kill innocent hostages.

Dinner disappeared quickly, washed down with what little beer remained. It was almost ten o'clock. He reached for the remote and turned on Channel 23.

"It's the WNY Ten O'clock News with Bill Bisbee. Substituting tonight for Roxy Anderson is reporter Samantha Dixon-Martin. Jennifer Wells will have the weather.

"We have breaking news," Bisbee continued. "Late this morning an armed robbery was thwarted at Morgan Chase in the World Headquarters Building in Manhattan. Police report that the suspects could be members of a gang known as the 'Punk Robbers.' The group may have been responsible for as many as fifteen recent robberies in New York and New Jersey.

"One suspect died at the scene, and two others were wounded. Authorities have not yet released the names or medical conditions of the suspects. One customer was slightly injured, taken to the hospital and later released. Three additional suspects are currently being held for arraignment.

"Police say that the incident nearly became a serious hostage situation, but was stopped almost as soon as it began due to the swift intervention of an FBI agent who happened to be in the bank when the incident occurred. A silent alarm, triggered by a teller, resulted in a quick police response.

"We have Samara Oscoda who had the opportunity to interview the teller, Regan Tompkins."

"Good evening, Bill. I'm here with Regan Tompkins. Miss Tompkins, could you tell us briefly what happened?"

"Agent Martin – Timothy Martin – came to my window and asked me to help. He told me that he was going to arrest the robbers, and he asked me to set off the silent alarm. Once we were all lying on the floor, Agent Martin pretended to be just one of the frightened customers until he could get the drop on the bad guys.

"I can't begin to tell you how magnificent he was. He saved us all. They might have killed all of us."

"We'll have more details as they become available. This is Samara Oscoda, reporting."

So that's it, thought Tim, shaking his head At least the teller had changed her tune. No longer was he a coward; now he was a hero.

Tim couldn't take his eyes off the stunning woman who was sitting in for the regular anchorwoman. Her skin was a golden brown, her lips full, and her complexion flawless. She was the perfect mix of African-American and Caucasian. It was difficult to tell how tall she was. The three anchors sat behind the news desk. The man appeared to be about two inches taller than the woman. Of course, he knew the producers used adjustable chairs to equalize the heights of whoever was on camera. Wouldn't Bisbee be ticked if the viewers knew that the woman sitting in tonight was six inches taller than he was?

Tim had seen enough of the news. He leaned back and closed his eyes.

18

He was awakened when he heard the lock turn and the door open. There she was. God, she was even more beautiful in person. She stood six feet two inches tall. She had long, slender legs, a narrow waist and a subtle, inner beauty that turned heads wherever she went.

"Hi," he said.

"Hi," she answered. "Did you watch the Ten O'clock News?"

"You were great," he said.

"Yeah, can you believe that the first time I had the anchor position, the lead story is about my hero husband? God, Tim, you could've been killed!"

"Nah, it was a piece of cake," said Tim with a grin.

"I so wanted to tell the world that you were my husband, but the station never wants us to mix our personal lives with the news. At first, I was afraid they would pull me from the anchor chair, but they just told me to be careful not to mention a connection between us."

"Welcome home, Mrs. Dixon-Martin. I would be happy to give you an up-close and personal interview!" said Tim with a coy smile.

Sam smiled right back.

"Wow, I have never interviewed a superhero. Please, sir, let me get into something more comfortable."

She locked the door and took off her coat and jacket. She sat down and kicked off her shoes. She was not wearing stockings. She stood up, unbuttoned her blouse and removed it, and then she took off her skirt. Apparently, she planned to conduct the interview in her bra and panties.

Tim watched, mesmerized.

"What kind of interview are you planning on doing?" he asked hoarsely.

"One very close and very personal," she said with a smile. She unhooked her bra, letting her breasts fall free. Then she removed her panties and stood before him totally naked.

Tim was having difficultly catching his breath. They had been married six years, but every time he saw her incredible body, it was like the first time.

"Oh, my," she teased. "You are way too dressed up for this interview."

She sat on the sofa beside him and began unbuttoning his shirt. Tim wasn't about to stay still and wait for the buttons. He was already getting out of his pants. He was just as aroused as that night so many years ago when they had first made love in her apartment on New Year's Eve.

He pulled his T-shirt over his head, and now he was also totally naked.

"Oh, my God, Tim, look at you!"

"What?" he asked, slightly annoyed by the interruption. He looked down at his groin. He was fully erect and ready to go.

"No," she said. "It's your side."

He glanced at the left side of his chest. It had turned an ugly purple. A huge bruise ran from his armpits to the middle of his thigh.

"Oh," he said. "I must have banged against the desk."

"I doubt that," she said, looking worried. "Did you see a doctor?"

"No," he said. "I didn't even remember hitting it."

Actually, that was a bit of a white lie. After being kicked in the ribs, he had hurt like hell. At the office he had popped a couple of Motrin. He never mentioned the injury in his report.

Sam frowned, "Maybe we better not make love. I could hurt you."

"You'll hurt me far more if we don't," he said with a sorry look into her eyes.

"All right, but we have to improvise. Come with me," she said.

She took Tim's hand and led him to the middle of the living room floor.

"All right, I want you to lie down on your back," she said. He did as she asked. She stood above him looking down.

"Oh-oh," she said. "Shrinkage."

"Not much," he said smiling.

"Well, let's see what we can do about that."

She knelt down and kissed him on the lips. Then she kissed his throat. Then she nuzzled his chest. Then she moved to his belly. Finally, he felt the caress of her lips on his most sensitive spot. Her warm, moist mouth put a definite stop to shrinkage. After a few moments Tim thought he would burst. Then she straddled him and, using her hand, she eased onto him. He felt an almost spiritual connection as their bodies joined. Then she sat up and faced him while slowly moving her body up and down. Tim reached up with his hands and caressed her breasts. Her rhythm increased in speed and intensity. Then, at exactly at the same time, they both came. Tim closed his eyes.

"God, you are so beautiful, so very beautiful," he moaned.

19

At the United States Military Academy, football is much more than just a game.

Army football began in 1890, when Navy challenged the cadets to a game of a promising new sport. The academies still clash every December in what is traditionally the final regular football game of the season. Army football isn't what it used to be when the all-time greats like Army's Doc Blanchard and Glenn Davis captured the hearts of the nation. Known as the Touchdown Twins, the two led the Army team to national fame as the powerhouse of college football in the 1940s. Blanchard won the Heisman in 1945, and Davis took it in 1946.

Unfortunately, times have changed. Today star high school players hotly market themselves for post-college contracts worth millions of dollars. The academies' five-year service obligation delays the acceptance of professional football contracts. No matter how great they are as players, they would not be able to set foot on a pro field until they reach at least twenty-seven years old. That is well past prime time for the best players. Army now competes in an independent division made up of Ivy League schools.

As they have for more than a hundred years, the cadet team, known as the Black Knights, gathers on the field to do battle against a rival college. Football, after all, resembles an ancient military battle. An offense faces a defense. Intricately designed plays are guarded more closely than was the planning for the invasion of Normandy. It is a brutal body-contact sport. Athletes play to win.

No other sport played by cadets is more exciting than football. Alumni pay tens of thousands of dollars to reserve a spot in the stadium parking lot for tailgating parties at home games. The entire corps of cadets is seated in a block for every game. A cannon fires every time Army scores.

Michie Stadium located next to Lusk Reservoir, seats thirty-eight thousand fans. At every home game, the stadium fills to capacity, even if the team has had a losing season. Cheerleaders, known as rabble-rousers, stir the four thousand cadets into a frenzy. The crowd roars as the team mascots – three army mules – gallop along the sidelines. Military officers who buy season tickets sit in groups according to their graduation year. Not only are academy grads included, but also the men and women who obtain their commission through ROTC or OCS. As the years pass, new replaces the old, and the people move up to better seats. For the duration of the game up to the moment the final whistle blows, the crowd roars in support of the team. Finally, as the game ends, the Corps of Cadets and all graduates stand and sing West Point's alma mater.

20

TODAY WAS NO EXCEPTION. AT GAME TIME, AT 1400 HOURS, THE TEMPERATURE would be sixty-eight degrees and sunny – perfect conditions for a football game. The game would be the fourth of the season. Unless the team could turn around their losing streak of two defeats, it looked like it was going to be an exceptionally long season.

As they had done every year while at West Point, Jim and Maggie Parkinson would make their appearance with other members of the faculty.

"Ready to go?" called out Jim.

"Just one second," said Maggie from the upstairs hallway.

They had decided to take the bus to the stadium, even though they had a reserved parking space and could have driven. Had it been raining, Maggie would never have agreed to ride the bus. But it was a beautiful fall afternoon, a short walk to the bus stop, and a direct ride to the stadium. As for Jim, he actually enjoyed taking the bus, no matter what the weather was like. It reminded him of the old days when he had been a junior officer.

Maggie was now ready to make her appearance. As always, she was color-coordinated, carefully coifed, and elegantly dressed. She picked up her new tailored coat, the one done in soft brown wool. She didn't need a coat now, but as soon as the sun went down, it would cool off quickly. She folded the coat over her left arm. She layered a turquoise cashmere scarf over the coat, hung a designer handbag on her shoulder and descended the stairs.

"Ready now?" Jim asked.

"Ready as I can be," Maggie said, smiling fondly at her husband.

They would walk to the bus stop. On the front porch, Jim paused to lock the front door. He stepped down to the walkway and locked arms with his wife. Once out on the sidewalk in front of their quarters, Jim took a quick glance at the sign outside their home. It read: "Quarters Number 3, Brigadier General Parkinson, Dean of the Academy."

Three General officers were assigned positions at West Point. The superintendent was a three-star general, the commandant of cadets was a two-star general, and the dean was a one-star general. The first two officers came from active duty ranks. The dean was the senior position for permanent, full-time professors who had made the decision early in their military careers to become instructors for future officers.

Jim and Maggie strolled arm in arm down the sidewalk to the bus stop, only one block away. They both were aware that people sometimes stopped to stare at them. Even now, the striking older couple could still turn heads. Maggie, a light-skinned black of average height, and Jim, a dark-skinned black man who stood six feet six inches tall, made an instant impression. Maggie regularly wore four-inch heels that helped diminish the height differential. She had a sense of style as well as an outgoing personality. Jim's ready grin and his confident bearing impressed friends and those who soon would be friends. His work ethic and keen intelligence made him a model for the young officers coming through the academy.

They looked ahead to the bus stop where a group of other faculty couples had gathered. It included several full colonels, a couple of lieutenant colonels and a dozen or so majors and captains along with their spouses. The officers, both men and women, all came to attention and saluted as Jim and Maggie approached.

"Please, carry on," said Jim, returning their salutes. The chatter continued. For some reason, the upcoming game seemed to spark more than the usual interest.

One would think that twenty-seven years as an army officer would have prepared Jim for every aspect of his job, but it hadn't. His life and career still seemed unreal. He still had to pinch himself to remember that he had been named to one of the most prestigious positions at the military academy.

When Jim had graduated from the academy, he had accepted a commission in the Ordinance Corps. His first assignment was at Aberdeen Proving Grounds in Maryland. It was a lucky assignment – there, he had met Maggie, a girl from Baltimore, and it had been love at first sight. They married six months later. They had two boys. One was now married and worked as a truck driver. The other was single and serving as a captain in the Army.

Jim had the routine military assignments for an ordinance officer. Then, as a major, he pulled a tour as an instructor in the engineering department at West Point. Following that assignment, they found themselves assigned to the U.S. Embassy in Liberia, West Africa, where Jim worked as the assistant attaché to the ambassador. During that tour, they became immersed in a bloody coup that toppled the Liberian government. It had been a trying time, but they had survived. It was then back to the U.S. where Jim was selected to command an ordinance battalion headed to Afghanistan. When he gave up his command, the army sent him back to school to earn his doctorate in mechanical engineering. Following graduation he was re-assigned to West Point where he worked his way up to the head of the engineering department.

Last year when Dean Roberts retired, Jim and most of the other department heads competed for the coveted position of dean. To his surprise, Jim became the first African-American Dean of the Academic Board of the United States Military Academy.

The bus pulled up and their group climbed on board for the short trip to the stadium. When they arrived, Jim and Maggie made the rounds of the tailgaters, shaking hands with alumni and former classmates. It was part political and part just plain fun. When the time came to take their seats, they moved into the section reserved for the academy's hierarchy.

"Hello, Marjorie!" beamed Maggie when she spotted the commandant's wife. "How's Taylor doing?"

Maggie was skilled at remembering names. The commandant's son was serving with the 82nd Airborne at Fort Bragg. The two military wives and mothers genuinely shared their pride in their men.

Finally, the pre-game hoopla came to an end. The opposing teams ran onto the field. When Army's black and gold made its appearance, a deafening roar exploded from the block of seats reserved for the Cadet Corps. The crowd at Michie Stadium was geared up once more to host one hell of a game.

The cadets were considered underdogs by two touchdowns, and even within the first few minutes it looked like the predictions would come true. The opposing team had won the coin toss and elected to defend. On the return, the kickoff was fumbled and then recovered by the defense that promptly took the ball and marched in for the first score. The extra point was good. Scarcely two minutes had gone by on the clock, and Army was already behind by seven. The home team crowd sat stunned by the poor start to what they had hoped would be an amazing afternoon.

Once more the opposition kicked off to Army. The cadets managed to hold onto the ball and run it back to the 35-yard line. But the opposition's strong defense held them. The cadets lost three yards in three downs and were forced to kick. The opposition took over once again and easily moved the ball back down the field, scoring its second touchdown and extra point in fewer than nine minutes. The first quarter hadn't even ended, and already the score was 14-zip.

On the kickoff, the cadets squeezed out a first down and moved the ball across the 50-yard line. Then the quarterback handed off to the fullback, and he forced the ball through the center of the defense. He broke clear, and it looked like he had the best gain of the game. When he was tackled, his knee bent backward. He lay on the turf, writhing in pain while grasping his knee. Army fans sat quietly, sharing the agony as the young man was helped off the field.

The game resumed. The next play was a pass. The right end ran all the way into the end zone to await the ball. Once thrown, the ball sailed right toward the Army receiver. Just then a defensive player leaped up and intercepted the ball. The opposition once again moved the ball downfield and easily scored its third touchdown. When the second quarter began, the score was 21-zip.

A new fullback, Number 27, took to the field for the cadets. On the first play, the quarterback handed the ball to the untried fullback. The crowd registered its shock – the coach had the nerve to call the same play as the one that had taken out his starting fullback. To everyone's amazement, Number 27 tore through the defensive line, escaped two tackles, and broke free of the secondary. Only one defensive player stood between the runner and the goal. Number 27 easily out-distanced the defender and ran into the end zone. An enthusiastic round of cheers and shouts came from the cadet section. The extra point was good, and now the "zip" had disappeared. The score was now 21-7.

Finally, the Army fans could hear the cannon fired. The crowd stood up and belted out the fight song: *"On brave old Army team. Onto the fray. Fight on to victory for the Army team is out to win today."*

The touchdown fired up the cadet defense, and they held the opposition to a field goal. As the cadets got the ball, the plays began to rely on Number 27. He was making yardage and moving the ball up the field. Ten plays later Number 27 broke into the end zone for the score. Now, with the score 24-14, Army was only ten points down. There was hope.

"Maggie," Jim said, turning to his wife. "Let me take a look at that players' book." After she had handed him the book, Jim scanned the player list to find Number 27, Jerald (Butch) Langston.

"Know anything about this Cadet Langston?" Jim asked the man on his left.

"Yeah," said Col. Dave McDonald who headed up the engineering department. "He's a firstie, at the bottom of his class. Funny, he maxed his last thermodynamics test. Considering his past performance, some of us were concerned that he had cheated. For a quick check, we had him do some problems in the office. He handled them with ease, like he had all this talent and had been holding back."

"Well," said Jim, "it looks like he has some physical talent, too."

When it was all over, the cadets had managed to pull out a 41-38 win. The enthusiastic crowd had reason to cheer. It would be party time after this game.

"That's the best game I've seen in years," said Maggie.

"No doubt about it," responded Jim, "and it looks like we have a new starting fullback. Too bad we didn't find his talent two years ago."

21

In the tunnels that snaked under the West Point plain, a wrinkled old man stared intently at the coleman lantern.

It had taken what seemed like weeks as he battled the conflicting voices in his mind, but — at last — he knew his true identity. His tale spanned centuries, from the Middle Ages to the 21st century. Clearly, no human being could live that long. Nor would anyone alive ever guess what had saved him from death.

His true name was Duncan McDougal. He remembered what his mother had told him about his birth in the Scottish Highlands on the 21st day of June in the Year of Our Lord 1739. She had told him that he shouldn't have been allowed to live. His death should have immediately followed his birth.

From his mother's story, he imagined the moments immediately following his birth when his very survival was uncertain.

The contents of his mother's womb lay on the cold stone within the ceremonial circle of life. A ghostly moonlight illuminated the fateful scene. Tall stone pillars cast shadows over the small body that was coated with a chalky white substance and streaked with blood.

Sisters of the Coven of Perth had served as midwives to the expulsion. It was by decree of the coven that the newborn's life was to end moments after its appearance in the outside world. The pitiful creature with the male sexual organ was to have been immediately butchered, chopped to pieces, and consumed by the twelve sisters of the coven.

The coven served Icesus, the Earth mother. Only she could balance the power in the battle between darkness and light. If a male were to join the coven, the women believed that the powers of Icesus would wither and die.

These women despised all men. Acts of sexual love were conducted only between sisters of the coven. Yet without birthing new sisters to carry on its will, the coven itself would perish. There was no recourse but to require one of the sisters to lie with a man for the sole purpose of birthing a new sister. The woman's impregnation would result in the joyful arrival of another female, or it could result in the necessary demise of a male child.

The choice had been made. Mary, the youngest and most beautiful female in the coven, was chosen to serve as the mother. She was to participate in sexual congress with a man. Arrangements were made, and the union was consummated. Soon after, it was confirmed that she was with child.

As Mary's time grew near, the sisters cautiously slipped from their homes and gathered in their sacred place deep in the forest. A large stone circle surrounded by tall pillars formed an open stage for their secret ceremonies. None dared risk discovery as a member of the coven. Practicing witchcraft could result in the woman being burned at the stake.

Throughout her pregnancy, Mary felt certain that she carried a special girl child. Her birthing time would be near the summer solstice, and the stars promised a time of great magic.

For the first time in a thousand years, the full moon and the longest day of the Earth's cycle would occur simultaneously at midnight on the 21st of June. Mary had prayed that the child would come on that very day. Although only a novice, Mary knew that the birth of the girl-child would bring them strange powers and enrich their lives.

Mary's labor began in earnest on the appointed day in June. Although other sisters had spoken of the excruciating pains that would tear through her body, Mary never dreamed that the ordeal would be so difficult. She already had lain on the cold stone floor for hours and hours, nearly fainting from agony. Each spasm was greater than the last. She begged for death to end her misery. She cursed the male who had caused her to harbor the tiny creature.

Mary had learned about mankind's evil all throughout her life. The old teachings were engraved in her mind and on her heart. The old witch-women had taught her well. She could recite their words:

"This is the reason that we despise men and love only your sisters. A man wants your body for his pleasure then he leaves you to face the torture of giving birth. After all the agony, the tiny creature will bite your tender nipples with its sharp gums until it feeds on your blood. Women are fated to raise the children and serve as slaves to men's obscene desires. Your only release will come on the day you die, a dry husk of your very being."

Finally, at exactly midnight, a searing pain ripped through Mary's body. Her legs parted and the strong bones in her hips ached from the pressure. Momentarily, her spirit hovered over her body. Never did she expect to experience such agony. Her thin frame felt torn, much like a criminal might feel as the executioner's sword split open his mid-section and spilled the internal organs from chest to groin.

Then – after what seemed like days of pain – it was over. A brief silence was broken by the wail of a newborn child.

"It's a male child, a male child," someone shouted. "Kill it, kill it quickly!" Mary could see Sister Elizabeth step forward, holding a sharp knife in her clenched fist.

"Stop, stop, everyone. Look at the child!" shouted Isabella, the coven leader.

Mary's strength began to return, but she couldn't understand where they were looking. She could see the familiar faces of her sisterhood, their naked bodies shining in the moonlight.

"What are they staring at?" whispered Mary. She raised herself up to her elbows so that she could see where they were looking.

Resting between her bloody legs lay the small child; its head flattened and elongated, its wrinkled face in a grimace, and its mouth open in a squall. The birth cord still linked the mother and babe. Mary's eyes focused on the area between the child's legs – it bulged with an exaggerated male member and a large scrotum.

Now Mary saw what had shocked her sisters. Her eyes focused on the upright stones that encircled them. The thick granite pillars rose to twice the height of one of their town's tallest men. Apparently, the sacred site, built eons ago, had been designed to celebrate the summer solstice. On that exact date, the light of the setting sun bisected the circle, cutting it exactly in half. What was unusual on this particular solstice was that the light from the full moon came from the east – directly opposite of the sunset in the west.

Even more incredible was to see that the enraged boy-child lay directly in the light of the moon.

"It is a sign," said Isabella. "This child will possess great powers."

"But it is a male," one sister argued.

"It must be destroyed," demanded another.

"No," said Isabella, "This is a sign from the dark forces. If we destroy this child, we will be doomed."

"You're wrong!" screamed Elisabeth, raising the knife over her head.

Isabella lunged forward, grabbing Elisabeth's hand and wrenched away the knife. With all the force she could muster, she slashed her sister's throat. Elisabeth sank to her knees, and then she fell face forward. As she fell, her blood splattered on the woman and the child who lay on the stone table. Isabella used the same knife to cut the umbilical cord. She placed the mewling babe in Mary's arms.

"Feed your son," Isabella demanded.

22

AND SO IT WAS. DUNCAN MCDOUGAL HIMSELF WAS THAT BOY CHILD BORN into a coven of women who practiced witchcraft. His birth occurred when the sun and the moon conspired to grant unusual power. Indeed, he would live a unique life.

He lived with his mother in a tiny room above a public house in Edinburgh. Mary worked relentlessly all day and all evening as a serving girl to the rough crowd that frequented the tavern. To those who saw her, Mary was no more than the typical unwed wench and her son a common bastard. Somehow they had sufficient food and adequate shelter. In all earthly matters, they lived under the protection of the unseen coven.

Like most people, Mary could neither read nor write, and she had no reason to learn. The same might have been said for Duncan, were it not for the assistance by sisters of the coven. The women saw to it that the child was schooled in reading and writing. A quick learner, Duncan had mastered Latin, French and English by the time he reached his early teens. On his fifteenth birthday, he was initiated into the coven. No one could remember when – if ever – a male had been accepted into the sisterhood. He had been tested by pain and punishment and had exceeded every expectation. Never before had the sisters shared their sacred secrets with a man.

Not only was the sisterhood a unique society, most people would consider it a deviant one. These women detested males, but they relished sexual contact. Since Duncan was the sole male in the coven, he was allowed to copulate freely with the women at his request or at theirs. He learned a variety of sexual techniques, particularly in those rituals performed by the Earth Goddess. By his eighteenth birthday, Duncan had matured into a handsome young man. He was not only a scholar, but also well experienced in the art of sexual pleasure.

His skills with weaponry also advanced well beyond his years. He listened carefully to the soldiers who came into the tavern. They told stories of skill and bravery. They talked of swords, knives and how to kill their enemies.

He put his lessons to use when he was just sixteen when he killed his first man. A burly drunkard had broken into his mother's room, demanding sex. The thick Scotsman who had fought many a battle scoffed at the young whelp when he tried to put a stop to his lust. He threw young Duncan against the wall.

But Duncan was on him in an instant. His dirk drawn, he drew his blade and slit the intruder's throat, nearly decapitating him. After the tavern closed for the night, Mary and Duncan disposed of the body by wrapping and tying it tightly in a tattered blanket. When night had reached its darkest hour, the two dragged the body to the moat surrounding the castle. They tied stones to the gory bundle and dropped it where the water was at its deepest.

For Duncan, that moment was a revelation – he discovered that he enjoyed killing. While his mother worked, he wandered the city streets, searching for anyone who dared test his fighting skills. Incredibly, Duncan always won easily. Once he took on three men at the same time and managed to kill all three.

Duncan learned the magic potions and elixirs, the curses and special ceremonies of the sisterhood. But he found this study boring and without meaning. The so-called mother Earth Goddess had never appeared to him, and he doubted that any members of the sisterhood had actually seen her either. Instead, he began a study of the black arts, which he believed was his true calling. Satan – not Icesus – would be his God.

23

THE FIRST EVENT TO SHAPE DUNCAN'S FUTURE WOULD BE THE DISCOVERY OF his natural father.

One night while Duncan sat at a corner table in the tavern where he could observe those who entered and those who left, he saw an unbelievable image of himself come into the tavern. His inquiries confirmed that the man's name was Duncan McDougal, son of Angus McDougal, lord of the great castle in the Pentland Hills.

For all his life, his name had been only Duncan. He had no last name. He never thought it possible to learn his father's true identity. After all, bastards never could be sure who their fathers were. When he asked his mother, she confirmed that Duncan McDougal was indeed his father.

"Mother, if what you say is true, then I will claim my right as heir to McDougal Castle," he told her.

"My son, that will never happen," she said. "A bastard has no rights of ownership."

But Duncan had no doubt that eventually it would all be his.

24

SADLY, THE SECOND EVENT WOULD CHANGE DUNCAN FOREVER, DRIVING HIM to the madness that would transform his life.

Even though witchcraft was no longer a punishable offense, there were still those who feared the legends of witchcraft and magic. Angus McDougal, the powerful lord of Castle McDougal was one such person. He believed that witches should be burned at the stake. He had personally executed at least a dozen women. If Edinburgh's government knew of his deeds, they never chose to acknowledge them.

Unfortunately, one of the sisters of the coven was caught stealing a sheep on Angus's property. During the horrific torture by old Angus and his son, Duncan, she confessed not only to being a witch, but also revealed the names of her sister witches.

McDougal's men seized five of the sisters and tried them in the castle's great room. The women – including Duncan's mother – were found guilty of practicing witchcraft. They were to be burned at the stake in the castle courtyard.

No one had considered Duncan a witch. Witches were women. Also, he had not been home the night Mary and the others were arrested. There was nothing he could do to save his mother and her sisters. He even went to the ceremonial site and prayed to Icesus for their salvation. No one answered his prayers.

On the appointed morning of the death fires, Duncan stood in the crowd that cheered as firewood was readied for the burning. His anger surged. He vowed to kill all those who supported the horrible atrocity.

Deep holes had been dug into the ground in the courtyard. Poles were firmly set in the holes and one woman was firmly bound to each pole. Dry wood was stacked around each base. The agitated villagers gleefully dripped whale oil and lard from butchered animals over the firewood.

Once ignited, the flames burned vigorously. First, the fires blackened the criminals' feet and then the flames reached the women's legs. The upper bodies initially remained untouched by the fire. The hundreds of commoners who had gathered to watch the grisly spectacle could hear the screams of agony over the crackle of burning timber and the crowd's gleeful roar.

Duncan was among the spectators, yet he failed to share their joy. He stood, fists clenched. He wanted to scream. He wanted to cry. He remained immobile as he watched the women he had loved thrashing about in the flames. Their bodies collapsed into the dying embers and black smoke whirled around their charred remains.

It was soon after that he heard one woman's final scream. It sounded like his mother's voice. At first, the words were unclear, and he strained to make sense of the final plea.

"Kill them! Kill them all!"

It was done. His own grandfather and his own father had destroyed his mother.

He worked his way out of the crowd and away from the castle. He bloodied his knuckles when he pounded his fists against the rough bark of a tree. He slumped to his knees, raised his hands to his face and allowed his tears to flow uncontrollably.

When his sobbing subsided, he rose to his full height and looked up to the night sky.

"I swear on all the powers of heaven and Earth that I will avenge the death of my mother and her sisters. I will strike out against mankind with all the power I possess!"

He turned and walked out of the woods. That was the last time that Duncan would allow himself to be consumed with sorrow. He would conquer his weakness and avenge the horrible crimes that had destroyed those he loved.

25

It took Duncan five difficult years to assume lordship of Castle McDougal.

Constant bickering and unrelenting conflict had consumed the lives of the pitiful people who struggled to survive in the Scottish Highlands. No one could recall times of peace – it had always been an unsettled, warlike land. Clan battled clan. The warrior combatants had forgotten the motives for the conflict, but they fought on out of habit. They refused to acknowledge defeat.

Duncan made use of this ongoing struggle, and he sought out alliances with other clans who also despised Clan McDougal. His desire for revenge was unmatched. In only a few years, the alliance brought the McDougal clan to its knees.

Duncan used his own sword to slay his father and grandfather, showing them no mercy. After all, what mercy had they shown his mother or the sisters?

"Kill them! Kill them all!" his mother had demanded in her dying breath as the flames consumed her body.

"I will avenge the death of my mother and sisters," he had vowed. "I will strike out against mankind."

With the deaths of his father and grandfather, McDougal Castle now belonged to him. No one could dispute his claim. How could they? Duncan's face clearly resembled those of the McDougal Clan. Standing beside the portrait of his grandfather, painted when the man was Duncan's age, anyone might even assume they were twin brothers.

He consolidated his belongings and called his remaining sisters to his side. With wealth and power, he again turned to the mystic ways of the sisterhood. He researched secret books, consulted magicians and listened to stories passed down through the ages, but he still could not find a true source of spiritual power.

26

ONE POSSIBLE RECORD REMAINED. PERHAPS IT WOULD LEAD HIM TO THE truth of magic and power.

The Codex Gigas, known as the Devil's Bible, was steeped in mystery. According to legend, a monk was walled into a room for having committed a sinful deed. To absolve his guilt, he promised to write the world's largest book in a single day. Since this was impossible, he called on the Devil for help. To prove the existence of the Devil, the monk sketched the Devil's image in the book.

Hand written and illustrated, the six hundred twenty-four page volume weighed more than one hundred fifty pounds. Each page was nearly three feet tall. One hundred sixty donkeys had been slaughtered so their hides could serve as its pages.

Written in 1229 AD, the book is considered to be one of the seven wonders of the Middle Ages.

The book was Duncan's last hope to uncover the mysteries of spirituality. For six months he journeyed over land and sea to reach the crumbling monastery that housed the book. Duncan sought permission to read the book. The monks agreed to his request. A scholar as well as a warrior, Duncan dedicated himself to the book. He would spend months in deciphering its message.

The following excerpts tell the monk's story:

"I was brought to this monastery when I was but 11 years. The monastery is built on a high cliff overlooking the river. The side of the monastery facing the

river is built into the rock bluff and the lowest level connects to a large cave where the monks who die rest until the resurrection.

I was taught to be a scribe and spent each day writing the word.

A year ago I was given the additional duty of going to the village twice a week to obtain eggs and cheese for the brothers. It was there that I fell into sin with a young wench. No one knew of my secret until brother Bartholomew discovered us fornicating. As was his duty, he notified the monsignor who judged me guilty of a grievous sin against not only the Brotherhood but also our Savior Jesus.

Duncan was fascinated by the text. Could this volume provide written proof of the existence of spiritual power?

My punishment was to be sealed in the Catacombs until the Lord Jesus called the monsignor to his kingdom. I was told that every three days bread cheese and water would be brought to me. I was also given writing materials and sheets of beaten animal skin. I would write about God. I had no idea how long I would be imprisoned, but I knew that the monsignor had lived for uncountable years.

The catacombs were located in large rooms with high stone walls. At the top of the wall facing the river were openings that allowed light to enter. To the back was the tunnel that led into the bowels of the Earth.

Duncan nodded silently. Only total isolation would allow a man to search the depths of his soul.

Thirty days after I was placed in the catacombs I began to hear whispering. Perhaps it came from the dead monks whose bones rested in the cave.

I felt that someone was looking over my shoulder. I turned quickly, but there was nothing to see. Later I sensed movement in the corner of the room. "Who's there?" I asked, but there was no answer. Days later I saw the figure again.

Now, Duncan sensed, he will learn the truth.

I approached slowly, but this time the figure did not disappear. I screamed, even though no one could hear. The Devil himself stood next to the wall. His skin was gray as in death. His genitals were like those of a man. Behind him dragged a tail. Horns came out of the top of his head.

Duncan sighed, feeling faint. This man actually saw the Devil!

"Why do you torture me, Satan?" I pleaded.

"I do not torture you. You torture yourself. I can grant you great power." He said he would help me write. He explained that he was not the Devil, but a being that lives hidden through magic. He and those like him gain power from men but only when they die by decapitation or burned at the stake.

To enhance their power, his kind must capture more souls. Those who agree to serve them are given great gifts. His kind becomes so powerful that they can live forever. They can only be destroyed by one of their own.

On Earth, their bodies are not solid, but they are more like clouds. Once they enter the human host, they will co-exist, becoming two beings in one body.

I could leave this place if I allowed him to enter my body. I had no choice; I would go mad if I remained in the tomb. So I agreed.

He stepped forward. I felt fear in my heart. Then I knew myself, but also knew the creature that lived within me.

Duncan was overcome with relief. The old story had much truth in it.

I sat down at the table. My fingers flew across the page creating perfect letters; the words flowed from our joint minds. I required no sleep. The dark of night was like day. The monsignor had told me that if I completed the great book, I would be set free, my sins absolved. In one half year, I completed the book.

When I was released, the creature that now lived within me promised me great riches. I would leave the monastery and persecute those who failed to follow the true religion. They would die by decapitation or be burned by fire. With each death, our kind grows stronger, richer and more powerful.

Duncan gently closed the great book and laid his head in his weary arms. There was much to ponder. He concluded that it was not the book itself that he sought, but it was this creature that had entered the monk's body. Since the book – now five hundred years old – promised eternal life, the monk could still exist.

27

It would take Duncan another year to trace the trail of the monk whose name had become Carlos Medina.

Duncan McDougal combed the known world to study the documents that could reveal what had happened to Medina. He poured through leather-bound volumes, their pages so fragile that even the slightest touch might turn them to dust. He scoured church documents to uncover historical records – those approved by the clergy as well as those that blasphemed accepted beliefs. He studied civil records that listed names of those who were born and those who died. He accessed names of criminals who were hanged or burned at the stake.

Duncan also studied the oral legends, passed by word of mouth through the centuries. The stories told of mythic heroes who defeated terrible beasts. More than anything, he paid heed to the whispers of his own soul that spoke only to him during the nights' darkest hours.

It appeared that – with the aid of the creature – the monk had lived five times longer than a mortal man.

From his studies, Duncan learned that through his lifetime, Medina had acquired five ancient statues. Each was a replica of the creature that lived within him. These identical statues dated back to the time of ancient Egypt. Through sacred rites, they would allow a curtain to open. The statues would come to life.

Most would question such a story. Yet with the information Duncan had found in the Codex Gigas, the creature did exist. Duncan vowed to search the world over to find one of the statues.

Although it took another two years, Duncan followed the clues to a curio shop in the British West Indies. At first, the savvy proprietor denied that such a relic existed. Duncan added another pouch of gold to his offer, and the man recalled that indeed such a statue did exist. He pried open the lid of an old wooden box. The thick boards splintered in his hands. When he had completed his task, he pushed aside the splinters of wood and pulled out a dark figure. Duncan saw immediately that this figure was the key to the power he sought.

Only ten inches tall, the statue was exquisitely carved. It was a man, and yet it was something else. Two horns sprouted from the large hairless head. The ears were long and pointed. Its face looked Egyptian, judging from the thin artificial beard worn by the Pharaohs. It had the sunken chest of an old man. Below was a potbelly. Its arms were thin and its legs appeared to be strong and muscular. One hand held an axe; the other carried a spear. A loincloth covered its genitals. On the back, one could see a long tail that rested on the ground. Around its neck was a beaded necklace.

He purchased the statue. For the first time in his life, he could feel the power emitting from the image. Duncan returned to Scotland. During the pilgrimage, he realized it would be far more beneficial to leave Scotland. He placed the sisters in charge of the castle and immigrated to the New World settling in Newburgh, New York.

He carried the statue with him, hoping to find the secret that would allow him to evoke the statue's power and bring the creature into the world.

Duncan maintained a low profile as a gentleman farmer. Very carefully, he began to recruit women into a new coven. Soon he served as the warlock in a sisterhood of twelve. Several of the sisters had practiced witchcraft before. Others were novices. One was the wife of Reverend Samuel Marsh, the minister of the Methodist Church.

When the colonies declared their independence, many men left their homes to enlist in the Continental Army. Soon the coven began to grow as lonely women sought to be serviced by this handsome warlock.

It was time for Duncan to invoke the creature's power from the statue. From the ancient writings of the Codex Gigas, the small statue could only reveal the creature through human sacrifice. At the release of the soul, the window to the creature's world would open.

Duncan enlarged the cellar beneath his home. He built a stone sacrificial altar. Now, after twenty years – half of his life, he was ready to test the power of the statue. All he needed was a victim.

He soon found one. A boy, perhaps ten or eleven years of age, was fishing in a nearby stream. A simple spell easily charmed the child. He rested the limp body on the saddle of his horse and rode quickly to his home. He had not noticed the boy's young brother who saw his evil deed. The brother ran home to tell their mother what he had seen.

Duncan carried the boy down into the cellar, stripped him naked and laid the body face down on the altar. He lifted the ceremonial sword and whispered the ancient words to invoke the creature. The polished metal of the blade gleamed in the candlelight. He lifted the sword high over his head and brought it down quickly on the boy's outstretched neck.

It easily sliced through the spinal column and continued through muscles and soft flesh, severing the head from the boy's body. The head landed with a thump on the dirt floor. A red mist was expelled from the headless corpse as the lungs released the dying breath, and the body contracted from massive shock. The arteries continued to allow blood to pour from a heart that was unaware of the fatal trauma.

When the lifeless head rolled on the floor, the entire area seemed to take on a reddish glow. When the head finally stopped its rolling, a dark circular opening appeared in the wall behind where it lay.

Duncan pressed his hand to his lips and stood frozen in amazement. He saw the cloudy apparition – the same creature he had read about in the ancient book. The creature appeared confused and turned to retreat into the opening. Duncan rushed forward and tightly wrapped his arms around the creature to prevent its escape. As he embraced it, Duncan could feel the essence of the creature enter his own body. He fell to his knees, weakened and unable to move. Confused, he struggled with the creature that had become a part of him. Through force of will, he fought against the creature's presence in his mind. He opened a hidden door in the wall that led to a secret cavity in the cellar. He laid the statue and the sword inside. Yet, still his thinking remained unclear.

"The body, the body," he said. "I have to dispose of the body."

He wrapped the thin body and its severed head in a blanket and carried the bundle up the rickety ladder. He closed the entrance to the hidden passageway to the cellar. At the barn, he hitched the horse to the wagon and laid the bundle in the back.

Although he was in his familiar world, flashes of a strange world inhabited his thinking. He could see other creatures like the one that now shared his own body. Unsure of where to go, he allowed the horse to find its own way to the river. Although the current would carry away the corpse, it was foolish to dispose of the body in daylight and so near the town of Newburgh.

Again, fate handed him a deadly blow. The boy's brother saw the man in the wagon, the man who had stolen his brother. Directed by the boy, two men on horseback chased after the wagon. But Duncan wasn't thinking clearly. He should have been able to escape.

When he was stopped along the road, the men questioned him. But Duncan couldn't speak. He only babbled like a madman. When the men searched the wagon, they discovered the boy's head and body. Soon joined by angry townspeople, the men bound and gagged the hapless Duncan. No matter, he knew his words made no sense. He had no control of his body or of his speech.

A noose made of coarse rope encircled his neck. The men threw the rope over a thick limb of an oak tree at the base of a hill. Suddenly, he lost his footing. His body was jerked off the ground. The rough rope tightened on his throat. No longer could he utter a sound or even breathe. An unbearable pain filled his very being. The demon spirit began to withdraw from his body.

"No! No!' he tried to scream, but no sound came out.

His body swung and twisted. It was now late afternoon. The undulation ceased. He now faced the setting sun.

The light dimmed and daylight turned to darkness.

28

It had been two months since his awakening.

Duncan stared at the glass on the magic box. The soldier named Butch had called the box a laptop. He now knew it was a computer. Yet for a man who last lived more than two hundred years ago, this was only one of the mysterious magical devices that he had encountered. Even the great magician Merlin would have been driven to the edge of madness by the confusing experiences Duncan had endured in the past sixty days.

In his younger days, Duncan had dabbled in the black arts, never imagining where his quest might lead. Now, he and the demon shared one body and co-existed in a suspended sleep. He had learned much about the creature that had become a part of his being.

The demon was young for its kind but well versed in the ways of this world. Without its mortal host, the demon was like the wind – an unseen force without substance. In order to share the human's body, the demon had granted him great powers. Yet the demon continued to demand that it be fed. Its source of energy came from the essence of a human spirit as its life force ebbs from its mortal body. To maintain its power, the human host hunts and kills fellow humans. Thus, the demon and its host are bound together for eternity. Jointly, they become an *endosym* – two beings in one body.

Duncan's immersion in the black arts had brought him great power. His master – Satan – had initially led him to the demon. When Duncan's body twisted in the hangman's noose, he had only existed in a void. But when his eyes adjusted to the bright light, he saw the face and form of the soldier called Butch. Because Butch had taken the life of the young woman, her spirit had been released. Duncan and the demon each fed on the woman's essence, allowing them both to return to the material world.

How the world had changed during the centuries while he slept! So much magic now surrounded him!

He saw horseless carriages as well as great dragon-like beasts that rolled on steel lines carrying boxes of fuel and food as well as human passengers. He saw gigantic metal birds that roared through the skies over land and sea. He saw the wonders revealed by the magic box right before him. The strange new world overwhelmed him. Had not the demon lived within him, sharpening his mind and body, Duncan would have surely gone mad.

At first, he had been weak, yet his co-existence with the demon brought him strength. The deaths of humans fed their mutual essence. Now he could feel the powers coursing through his body. He could go on for days without sleep. His mind absorbed information at a rate impossible for a mere mortal.

When Butch showed Duncan the laptop and instructed him in its operation, it made the other marvels of this strange new world pale in comparison. The laptop was truly Merlin's crystal ball. He could ask a question, and it would provide the answer. Butch used the term "surfing the web" to describe this process. He also showed him how to use Google Earth to magically carry him to anywhere in the world. It took Duncan only a few weeks to take in more information than any one human being had ever learned.

As the days passed, Duncan found that the demon was not just a spiritual entity. Indeed, it was something far more unusual. In the 1700s, no one could conceive of alternate universes or that billions of other worlds even existed. He suspected that the demon co-existing in his body was a creature from an alternate universe. Even more surprising was the fact that the demon that he once hoped to serve was just a stupid creature whose singular goal had been to destroy humans so that it could feed on their essence. As his learning advanced, he realized that the demon was unable to read his thoughts.

Without the demon dwelling in his body, he would be a mere human existing within a normal life span and wielding little power. Just like the armor worn by the Knights of the Round Table, the demon was a heavy and uncomfortable burden. Like the armor, it was hot in summer and cold in winter. Yet without its protection, the knight stood no chance of survival.

So Duncan resigned himself to the reality that he and the demon would forever live in one body. But, unlike in the past where the demons controlled their hosts and killed recklessly, their roles would be reversed. This new world was a far different place. Now, men and women would become masters over the demons that shared their bodies.

He learned that human sacrifice increased his power. Those humans who served him were also granted enhanced power. He could pass on his gift to them. But, at the same time, he could take it away. He indeed was evolving into a being similar to those of the ancient gods. Satan had given him an amazing gift. For his power to grow, he would need more sacrifices. He wasn't concerned. He knew that his human recruits would provide all the human essence he wanted. Even now he knew that two of his cadet followers and a recruit were hunting for their next victim.

29

IN NEW YORK CITY THE NUMBER OF HOMELESS PEOPLE BEDDING DOWN nightly in municipal shelters may exceed forty thousand.

Countless others sleep in cardboard boxes, crawl into dumpsters, curl together under bushes or hide in doorways of abandoned buildings. They come in all ages, colors and genders. Some wander in families, real or imagined. Packs of children roam like feral animals, picking through garbage in search of nourishment. The homeless come from all walks of life. Some are well educated; others suffer mental illness. Some simply have fallen on hard times and have slipped through the cracks in the social network. For all the homeless, it is a precarious existence. Abuse and even death are real – any day and any time.

Urban legends tell of the "Mole People" – perhaps the most unique among the homeless. They dwell in abandoned subway and railroad tunnels that wind beneath city streets. Some experts claim the stories are exaggerations, yet the cops and church people would disagree.

Despite efforts by the transit authority and the persistent do-gooders to save those beings that hide out in the multilevel labyrinths, hundreds still struggle to survive in these dark places, seeking to eat, to sleep and to simply exist.

The city periodically sends down teams of cops to round up the moles, but the patrols cannot navigate the vast underground neighborhood with any degree of efficiency. Of all the homeless in New York, those living in the underground tunnels are the least visible. Little is known about these underground people and the disappearance of one or more of these poor souls fail to register with those in power. It is commonplace to discover the decaying remains of what was once a human being in some dark, twisted turn in the tunnels.

This was the perfect place for Duncan McDougal's followers to hunt for the next victim for sacrifice. Here was a human life that could easily be subdued and brought back to the tunnels under West Point.

30

THE HOMELESS MAN WAS RESOURCEFUL, TO SAY THE LEAST. HE HAD UNCOVERED a partially eaten hamburger and a handful of stiff fries in the trash. He'd purchased a bottle of cheap wine. It had given him enough of a buzz to silence the nightmares that haunted him when he fell into a restless sleep. He had worked his way down to the third level – much warmer here than up higher where the cold weather had first begun to settle.

In summertime, he preferred a doorway or a cluttered alleyway for a few hours' rest. But the previous night was too cold to stay up on the streets. He had slipped into an abandoned subway tunnel and curled up between two sheets of cardboard.

All his meager belongings were stuffed in an old rucksack that also served as his pillow. He curled tightly in his makeshift bed and closed his eyes. Hopefully, the sounds of warfare would not haunt his dreams. He drifted off into an alcohol-induced sleep.

The sixth sense from his other life cause him to abruptly awaken. He sat up and looked around. Only the dim glow from the few service lights that could be found interspersed along the tunnel offered a clue as to what he sensed.

He saw them moving stealthily among the shadows. There were three of them. They carried a fourth person. As they passed a light, he could barely make out a few details. All three wore black. They had on black combat boots. They wore black ski masks. Two were men. The third was a woman. The first could have been a special ops guy. Draped over the shoulder of one was the limp form of the old man he had noticed earlier.

He'd been asleep on the street-level platform. The old man was trussed up like a steer. Wide duct tape was stuck firmly over his closed mouth.

These three weren't cops, he was sure of that. He had seen the old man several times within the last month. The man was not a friend, for he had no friends, but another of the lost ones who, like himself, avoided others. When they passed each other, there was always that slight nod, an acknowledgment that this was another being lost to humanity but still willing to accept the other's existence.

He got up and staggered after the group.

"Hey!" he yelled. "What are you doing?"

The group came to a halt.

"Beat it, buddy. Your time is not tonight," growled one of them. He got close. The ski mask hid their faces, but he could tell that one of the men was white and the other, black. The woman who was small, just a little over five feet tall, was also white.

"Put him down!" he yelled. "He ain't hurting anyone."

"Get rid of him," said the white man. The woman approached him.

What was this little thing going to do, he wondered.

It all happened so fast that he had no time to react. Her hands shot out and grabbed him by both arms. She lifted him like he was a small child, and he found himself flying through the air. Only the years of training saved him from a broken neck. He tucked his chin in and kept his body in tight ball. He hit the concrete and rolled several feet. At that point, he was on autopilot. As he came up, his right hand was in his pocket, pulling out and flipping open the buck knife with its four-inch blade.

He held the knife in a back grip, as he had been trained. The woman came at him again; she was ready to strike. This time he was better prepared. But again, he had been astonished at her strength. She walked up casually, in no big hurry like he wasn't going anywhere. She swung her right fist toward his face. He threw his left arm up to block the punch. Her fist struck his forearm. He had heard a bone snap on impact.

Her left hand reached out and her fingers grabbed his throat. It felt as if a vise had been tightened on his larynx. He had been trained to live with pain, accept it, and still function. Without a second thought, his right hand snaked up, and the blade of the knife sunk into the woman just below the ribs. He felt the knife penetrate flesh. She wasn't wearing a flack jacket. The blade went all the way to its hilt. He felt the warm blood flow freely over his hand as he twisted the knife in place.

She let go of his throat and staggered backward. He knew from experience that the wound would be fatal. He was gasping for breath, expecting to see her drop to her knees. Instead, she looked down at the blood on her sweater, then looked up at him and smiled. He could see her eyes; they seem to glow from an inner force. It wasn't possible that she could still stand. She took a step forward. He couldn't survive another blow. He stood waiting for the inevitable.

"Police!" came a load voice echoing through the tunnels.

"Cops!" yelled the white guy who apparently was in charge.

"Come on, we can't cause a scene. Leave the old guy, and let's get out of here!" yelled the man.

They released the old man at the same moment, allowing his body to fall carelessly on the damp cement. They turned and ran, disappearing into the darkness.

The alcohol must be affecting his mind. The woman was running as if she had not been touched. Strange, he thought, recalling vividly the twist of his knife under her ribs.

"Drop the knife, buddy. Otherwise, you're dead!" yelled one of the cops. At first he didn't move.

They all held flashlights in one hand, guns in the other. The strong beam blinded him temporarily. He began to make out the images of four uniformed transit cops. They stood in a line in front of him with their weapons drawn.

One hand held a flashlight; the other, a gun. For an instant, he considered charging their line. Maybe deliberate suicide by police gunfire was better than continuing to live this miserable life.

Not this time, not now, he thought. His fingers released the knife. It fell, useless, on the ground in front of him.

31

THE GRANDFATHER CLOCK IN THE LIVING ROOM STRUCK TWICE.

Jim Parkinson hadn't been asleep. He stood, stretched, and ambled to the refrigerator to get a bottle of cold water. He twisted the cap, took a swig and returned to his easy chair.

Maggie was down in Baltimore, caring for her dying mother. The house was far too quiet. Maybe they needed to get a cat. Staying alone in the creaky old home without another human or even a pet seemed too lonely. It was like living in a tomb.

When they moved into the Dean's Cottage, Maggie had insisted that the house retain the 19th century furnishings that came with the quarters. Unfortunately, people who lived in that era were much smaller than folks today. At six and a half feet in height and two hundred sixty pounds, Jim feared that if he dared sit in one of the vintage chairs, his weight would demolish the pricey antique.

At least Maggie let him have his stuff in the rear sitting room or den, as he called it, and, of course, in their bedroom upstairs. The two of them had always been night owls, seldom going to bed before midnight. As the dean, Jim kept bankers' hours and usually wasn't in his office before nine o'clock. Now he did his running in the evenings. He was no longer required to participate in morning physical training. Those late hours had shifted their bedtime to as late as two o'clock in the morning. With Maggie out of town and a good mystery novel under way, he had decided to stay up even later and finish the book.

When the doorbell rang, he was momentarily startled. He looked at his watch. It was 0245, way too late for visitors. West Point is a closed installation. If Maggie's mother had passed away, Maggie would have called on the phone. Even an emergency at the academy would normally be called into the house. Who in the world would be ringing the doorbell at this late hour?

Jim got up and walked through the living room to the front hallway. He snapped on the front porch light and peered out the cut glass window in the front door. He recognized the anxious face peering back at him. He opened the door.

"Cadet Wiggins, what on earth are you doing here at this late hour?"

"I'm sorry, Dean Parkinson, sir. I didn't know what else to do," responded Wiggins. The young man seemed unusually anxious.

"Well, come in. Tell me what the problem is."

Cadet Wiggins looked around behind him as if he expected someone to be lurking in the bushes alongside the porch. He entered the hallway. His hands trembled. It seemed like the cadet was scared to death.

"Go on back to the den and take off your coat," Parkinson said as he waved the cadet inside. When Wiggins pulled his arms out of his long gray coat, Jim was surprised to see him wearing a black sweater, black jeans and black boots — not the prescribed uniform. But Wiggins was a firstie, and it was after hours, way after hours.

"Would you like something to drink?" Parkinson asked.

"Could I have some water?"

"Sure," said Parkinson. "You want a glass or is the bottle OK?"

"Bottle's fine," replied Wiggins.

Parkinson brought the bottle of water and settled into his easy chair. Water bottle in hand, Parkinson waited. He'd let Wiggins take his time.

At the military academy, the staff and faculty sponsor cadets during their final years. Together, Jim and Maggie sponsored eight cadets. Ambrose Wiggins, a black cadet from Biloxi, Mississippi, was one of them. He was a firstie and on the football team. He played right guard and weighed nearly three hundred pounds. He would be one of the players who would have to go on a crash diet as soon as the season ended. The academy allowed the ballplayers to bulk up during the years they played, but if they kept the weight on, they would not meet the weight standards for commissioning as second lieutenants.

It seemed strange seeing this huge man acting so frightened. Whatever was going on must be something bad. Parkinson was almost reluctant to hear Wiggins' concerns. As the dean, it would be his duty to take action if Wiggins had violated the honor code or committed some crime. Yet at the same time, the sponsorship was designed to give these young men and women someone to talk to. Wiggins still was on his feet, pacing back and forth like a caged lion.

"Calm down, cadet," said Parkinson. "Sit down, and take a drink of water."

Wiggins perched on the edge of his chair and took a long drink of water before he began to speak.

"Dean, I did something bad, something really bad. You know that academics have always been hard for me. I've made it through three and a half years, but math has always been my most difficult subject. I've been in bonehead math since I was a plebe. Calculus is the really long pole in my tent. I just do not understand it, and I had no prayer of passing the final exam. That's when another cadet told me about Duncan."

Parkinson started to ask who Duncan was, but he decided he would just let Wiggins do the talking. It looked like he was about to hear what could be a cheating issue that could cost Wiggins and this cadet Duncan – whoever he was – his career at West Point. The academy had a no-tolerance policy on cheating. Those found guilty would be dismissed from the academy.

"This cadet was a tunnel rat, and he said that several cadets had discovered a secret in the tunnels that gave them great power and enhanced knowledge. Now, I didn't believe any of this, but Butch and I were teammates, and I went along for the ride. So after lights out, five of use went down into the tunnels," Wiggins said.

When Parkinson had been a cadet, he had heard stories about the tunnels. Some cadets claimed that they could travel underground from one building to another. They even claimed that in addition to the stream and utility tunnels, that other, older tunnels and rooms were buried under the parade field. Some said that they dated back to Revolutionary times when Fort Putnam had been built to guard the Hudson from British warships.

To Parkinson, the stories had no merit. They were just stories. But he did remember back in the early '80s a big hole had opened up next to the boathouse below the plain. Part of the old tunnel system had collapsed. Before the engineers got around to filling the hole with rock and concrete, he had walked by and stared into the hole. He could see the old clay bricks and part of the wall of an old tunnel.

"The guys had a key that let us into the maintenance room in the basement of Pershing Barracks," Wiggins continued. "They also had keys that got them into the electrical vaults and steam tunnels. The tunnels are huge, and they have lights running through them.

"We came to a locked door that led into to the abandoned part of the underground complex. Once in the old section, we all carried our own lights. We traveled deeper, and I think we were under the plain. Then we came to a side tunnel, built of bricks. At the end of the old brick tunnel was a wooden door. We unlocked the door and entered an area that had some of those old kerosene lanterns.

"Man, this was weird. Like I never knew anything like this could exist here at West Point," Wiggins said, pausing momentarily to gather his thoughts. "Dean, there are rooms under the plain, I mean like jail cells and all kinds of stuff. One room was really big, like a church or something. It had a brick table in the middle. When I first saw it, I actually felt afraid.

"Dean, there ain't much that scares me, but that sure did," Wiggins said. He closed his eyes as if he were seeing it all again for the first time.

"Then stepping out of a side room was an old man. His hair was cut short, and he looked like an old soldier. Butch called him Duncan, and he told Duncan that I wanted to be a follower.

"This old Duncan guy walked right up to me. He had something like a Scottish accent and his words were kind of funny. He reminded me of those pirates you see in old movies. He said that he could grant me great power and wisdom, but I would then have to serve him," Wiggins said.

He paused to run his tongue over his dry lips. He took another gulp of water before he began to speak again.

"Then he reached his hand towards my head. When it came within a few inches of my head, a spark snapped from his finger striking the side of my head. I couldn't believe what happened then. I could hear his voice talking inside in my head.

"He said, 'You will see now what my power will grant.'

"I mean like that was weird. Then he turned, walked back into the darkness and was gone."

Wiggins stopped talking. He hung his head, once again collecting his thoughts before he continued.

"We left and worked our way back to the barracks. The next morning when I took my calculus test, I couldn't believe what was happening. As I looked at the problems, for the first time in my life I understood the theory and concept. Each problem was so easy to solve that I had to slow down. As a matter of fact, I deliberately made a few errors. If I aced the test, my prof would have thought I had cheated. I got a B- on that test, the highest grade I ever had.

"Major Eckert was even suspicious of the B-. He called me into his office and gave me a couple of problems to solve. I could have solved them in seconds, but instead I took about thirty minutes. I got both problems right. Eckert was impressed. I told him that I had been tutored and for the first time in my life was beginning to understand calculus."

Parkinson recalled hearing a similar story recently. Nevertheless, he made no comment.

"But there was even more," continued Wiggins. "At football practice, I found myself for the first time being able to keep up with the team during laps. I wasn't even winded. Then in the weight room I found myself pushing sixty more pounds on the bench press. I was sure that I could have pressed even more.

"Butch had warned me not to show too much of what I could do. Like the math test, I faked being pushed during runs and pressed less than I could. I was hooked; I had joined "Duncan's Coven," as he called our group of five cadets. One, April, was a female cadet.

"Then the truth of Duncan's source of power was made evident. The others knew what was coming, but it caught me blind-sided. We started one of them witchcraft ceremonies. We all got naked. That was kind of cool. April has a neat body, and you don't get to see many naked women here.

"Then Duncan led this old bum into the chamber. It was like this guy was drugged or something. He just pointed and the guy climbed up on the platform made of old bricks. It was like an old brick lab table about three feet high, three feet wide and maybe six feet long. It was made of old yellow bricks.

"Anyway, the old bum, who is naked like us, lies down on this brick table with his head hanging over the end. Then the other cadets begin chanting some weird language. Me? I just stood there not sure what to do. Then Duncan picks up this sword and whacks off this bum's head with a single swipe of the blade. Holy shit! I couldn't believe it. There was blood all over the ground. I screamed like a girl. But no one seemed to notice. Then there were sparks snapping in the air. I knew that I should have run, but I was suddenly charged like I had just swallowed a super energy drink.

"I never took drugs. Hell, my parents are Baptists. I never drank alcohol before last year. But if this is what a drug high is all about, I was hooked. I wanted more."

Parkinson had been mesmerized by the cadet's story. Initially, he had thought that Wiggins would require lots of questioning to confess to his indiscretions, but the opposite had been true. It almost seemed like the venerable dean was watching it all unfold before his eyes.

"God, forgive me, but I looked forward to the next sacrifice," Wiggins continued. "Duncan told us that he was the next step in the evolution of the human race, and that he had the power to make us all like him. I know this sounds like bullshit, but you would have to feel the power surging through your body to know what it was like. The only problem was that I could not get the sight of those headless corpses out of my dreams. I wanted the power, but I knew it was somehow wrong. My folks didn't raise me that way. Yet, at the same time, I found myself going back.

"Duncan said that for us to retain the power, we had to continue sacrificing human beings. He said the power came from the electrical energy released when people die. His power came from that energy, and it charged his followers. But how do you kill people without the authorities finding out? The answer was surprisingly simple: We became hunters.

"New York City has hundreds of homeless people. If they disappear, who knows or even cares? We kind of considered it a public service. As firsties, we have the freedom to leave the academy. One old redoubt tunnel can be accessed from outside of the academy. We would go down to the city, bag us a bum, and then bring him back through the tunnels. There are old cells down there where we kept our victims alive until Duncan needed a sacrifice.

"Tonight Butch, April and I went on a hunting trip under the subways in Grand Central. We found an old bum sleeping in a doorway. After we had him all bound up, things started to go wrong. Another one of those street guys came out of nowhere and tried to stop us. April started beating the crap out of him. But this new one stabbed April under the ribs and fought like a son of a bitch.

Then transit cops showed up, and we got the hell out of there. I thought April was going to die. She should have died – there was so much blood. But by the time we got back, her wound was already healing. Besides acquiring strength and wisdom, we can even heal ourselves physically.

"But tonight scared me big time. What we're doing just isn't right. No, it's downright evil. I can't go on, but I don't know what to do. Dean, can you help me?"

Parkinson's chin rested on his chest. His eyes were half closed. His pleasant smile had become a grimace. How should he deal with this bizarre story? My God, he thought, this would be the worst scandal to ever hit the academy, but only if Wiggins was telling the truth. How could it be – cadets killing people in tunnels?

Then Parkinson's finely honed military mind kicked into gear. OK, what has to be done? First, he needed the names of the other cadets. Then he had to find this horrific place in the tunnels. He needed to get to this

Duncan and find out how he could ever have convinced cadets to kill people.

It was now early Sunday morning. He had to take the investigation slowly and carefully.

"Cadet Wiggins, I want you to go back to the barracks. Do nothing and say nothing. Monday morning at 0700 hours I want you in my office. Bring a list of the names of all the cadets involved in this. Can you do that?"

"Yes, sir," Wiggins said as he rose to his feet.

"All right, you get back to your room."

After Wiggins left, Jim sat down, pulled out his iPad and keyed in everything he could remember about Wiggins' story. He then recorded the sequence of events to ensure that justice would be served. He would have his secretary and Colonel Anderson with him when Wiggins reported on Monday.

Parkinson was torn between calling the MPs immediately and going directly into the tunnels to find out the truth. If this had been just a simple crime, he might have continued the investigation on his own. But the story was so bizarre that Parkinson was still having difficulty believing what he had just heard.

This was so unreal that it might only be a delusional story told by a cadet high on meth. Yet, if his story was true, and they were actually killing people, they didn't belong in the army, they belonged in jail.

Hopefully, Wiggins wouldn't change his story by Monday.

32

Parkinson couldn't fall asleep after Wiggins left.

He had gone to bed, but just tossed and turned. He finally got up and cooked himself breakfast. He cut four slices of bacon into small chunks, diced a quarter of an onion, chopped up half a green pepper, threw in some shredded cheddar, and then beat it all together with three eggs. He poured it into a buttery skillet. This recipe was his own invention. He called it his famous "egg delight." He fixed two slices of whole-wheat toast, telling himself that the whole-wheat bread would absorb all the fat and cholesterol. After all, Maggie had insisted that he adhere to his diet. He drank two cups of coffee, hot and black.

He tried to finish the mystery novel, but it no longer held his interest. Within two hours he had a bad case of heartburn so he munched on three Tums. He thumbed through the Sunday paper, and then found himself in the den surfing channels on TV. He flipped back and forth between two football games.

He must have dozed off for a few minutes. The insistent ringing of the phone brought him brought him back to awareness.

"Were you out?" asked Maggie.

"No," said Jim groggily. He glanced at his watch. It was seven o'clock, and it had been dark for several hours.

"Are you OK?" asked Maggie.

"Yeah, I just dozed off. I think I might be coming down with a cold."

"OK," she said. "You take care of yourself."

"How's your mom doing?" asked Jim.

"She had a good day," Maggie answered. "I know that her days are numbered. The oncologist gave her maybe a month. Hospice sure helps."

He could hear Maggie choke back a sob. He knew how difficult it was for her to deal with her mother's failing health. He wanted his wife back home, yet he also could not begrudge the few days Maggie would have left with her mother.

"So what's new with you?" she asked, changing the subject.

"Same old story," said Jim. "I spent the day reading and watching football."

He wasn't about to tell Maggie what Cadet Wiggins had told him. If it were true, she would know soon enough. Besides that, the fewer people that knew about this, the better it would be.

If cadets had really committed murder, then the staff would be circling the wagons. Damage control would become the word of the day. It would all come out eventually, but there would be a lot of discussion before their spin was released to the media.

Jim and Maggie continued to chat for about half an hour. They talked about minor things. Jim certainly did not bring up what was haunting his mind.

"I miss you," said Jim, feeling the distance between them.

"I miss you, too," answered Maggie. "Love you," she said as she said goodbye.

Jim switched off the phone. He had missed the news. He decided he didn't feel like watching any more TV and pushed the off button on the remote. He felt sluggish and bloated. The eggs tasted great this morning, but now he regretted having eaten them. Maybe a run in the cold, fresh air would help. He went up to the bedroom and put on a gray sweatsuit and his running shoes. He pulled a black watch cap over his head and headed down the stairs and out the back door.

It was below freezing, and the car was coated with frost. The night sky was clear. The days were still mild but the temperature dropped below freezing at night in the Hudson Valley. He headed out to the street in front of the house, crossed Washington Road and headed towards the cemetery. The main roads were well lit. He jogged along at a slow pace.

On Sunday night at eight o'clock, there were no cars on the road. He saw only one other runner on the opposite side of the road. He saluted the famous West Point graduates who were buried in the cemetery.

He took his regular route that followed Bowman Loop and ran past the quarters where he and Maggie first lived when they returned from Liberia. He still loved those quarters better than the last two places. He knew Maggie liked the prestige of the single-family quarters where they now lived. The Dean's Cottage was as high as they would go. He chuckled. All those years ago as a young cadet, he ran this same course. He never dreamed at that time that some day he would be the dean. He turned right on Lee Road and started down the hill towards the housing area.

There was a stretch about six hundred feet long where there were no streetlights. He slowed his pace, making sure he didn't stub a toe on a raised piece of sidewalk.

"Good evening, sir!"

Parkinson's heart skipped a beat as he heard a young woman's voice. He looked to his right. A female cadet in sweats and a hoody had fallen in step with him. She looked just like a kid. She was short; he was tall. He looked too tall, but this gal was short, really short.

"How are you this evening, cadet?" Parkinson asked.

"Just fine, sir. It's a great night for a run, isn't it?"

Parkinson expected her to run on ahead. After all, he was poking along at an old man's pace. But she stayed right beside him as they headed towards the bridge across the creek.

"Sir, do you believe in predestination?"

The question caught him by surprise.

"What?" he asked.

"You know, like it was predestined that we would meet on this spot at this time?"

"I hadn't thought about it," Parkinson said. A little alarm bell went off in his head.

"We had planned to go to your quarters later tonight. Now, we won't have to."

Parkinson felt his heart rate quicken. He stopped running. He didn't need this attitude, not tonight.

"Cadet, I want your full name. Tell me what exactly you're talking about."

He glared down at the short woman, but he could not make out any details of her face. It was dark on this stretch of pavement. The hood on her sweatshirt made it appear that he was staring in a black hole, rather than at a human face. He wasn't afraid; he could pick her up with one hand. But he was angry. He couldn't believe that a cadet would have the nerve to be so insolent.

Without warning and so quickly that Parkinson didn't see it coming, the woman stretched out both arms, palms out on both hands and struck him firmly on the chest. She hit with such force that he was thrown backward off the sidewalk. He fell backward down the bank and came to rest next to the stream. He landed so hard that he was momentarily dazed.

He wasn't certain what had happened. He had caught a glimpse of the female cadet leaping through the air toward him. She landed on her feet in front of him. She bent over and grabbed him by his arms. Her grip was as tight as a vise. She lifted him off the ground, swiveled and slammed him against a tree. His feet didn't touch the ground.

"My strength is still off," she said. "Took a knife below the ribs last night. I think it nicked my heart. Now, I want you to listen very carefully. Forget everything that Wiggins told you. There is nothing going on in the tunnels. If you go down there, you will find nothing. However, you will become a widower. It will be a shame if Maggie has an accident down in Baltimore. Who will be there for her dying mother?"

She released her grip and Parkinson crumpled in a heap at the base of the tree. Then she was gone, like she had never even been there.

33

PARKINSON KNEW HE HAD TO GET ON HIS FEET AND GET BACK HOME.

Although the drop was only about eight feet, his body felt as if it fallen out of a second-story window. Rolling to his side, he took several deep breaths before running his hands over his arms, down his sides and along his legs. Apparently, there were no broken bones and no obvious blood.

Finally on his knees, he grasped a tree branch and pulled himself onto his feet. Even though it hurt to walk, he was able to reach the sidewalk. He slowly made his way to Washington Road and cut across to the opposite side. The headlights of an oncoming car startled him at first, and he moved into the shadows.

What would people say if they heard he was found staggering along the highway at this time of night? Parkinson was embarrassed, frightened and even a little ashamed. All he would need now was for the MPs to come by. They would haul him off to the emergency room. What would he tell them? He couldn't tell the truth: a one hundred ten-pound female cadet had beaten up the dean.

Slowly, he limped back to his quarters, choosing to enter through the back door. Finally in the sitting room, he went directly to the closet opened the door and pulled down the metal strong box that had been stored on the top shelf. He twisted the combination lock and took out the 9mm pistol. His hands shook as he shoved shells into a magazine, slammed the magazine into the pistol, pulled back the slide, and chambered a round.

Then he searched the entire house from attic to basement. Satisfied that he was alone and that all doors and windows were locked, he went into the bathroom, stripped out of his sweats and studied his body in the mirror. His chest felt like a baseball bat had hit it. There was no obvious bruising, but his ribs hurt like hell.

The worst damage was on his arms. He had deep scratches and bruises where the woman had grasped his arms and lifted him off his feet. Now he could see where blood had soaked through his sweatshirt. The wounds were probably dirty. Maybe he should have seen a doctor, but he wasn't going to let that happen. He popped three Aleves. Once in the shower, he winced as the hot water ran over the torn skin on his hip and arms.

After the shower, he blotted the moisture with a towel. He bandaged the cuts and put ointment on the abrasions. Slipping on a pair of shorts and a T-shirt, he staggered to the bed. He tucked the loaded pistol under Maggie's pillow.

What was going on? What was he going to do? He resolved that he would be at the office at 0700. If Wiggins came in, he would get his story. Then he would order police protection for Maggie.

Finally, the Aleve was starting to take effect. He closed his eyes. At five o'clock in the morning the phone rang.

"Dean Parkinson, this is Captain Easley, the duty officer. We've had a cadet die."

"Die? How?"

"We think it might be natural. His roommate found him in his bunk. When the roommate came in yesterday, the cadet was in bed, apparently asleep. The roommate didn't do anything. This morning when the alarm went off, the cadet didn't move. Rigger had already set in. He's been taken to the hospital. They are going to perform an autopsy."

"What's the cadet's name?" asked Parkinson.

"Wiggins, Cadet Ambrose Peterson Wiggins. He's a firstie."

"Thank you, captain," said Parkinson. He turned off the phone.

"My God," he said. "Oh, my God!"

34

THE TAXI PULLED UP JUST ONE BLOCK AWAY FROM NEW YORK CITY'S PUBLIC safety building.

Samantha Dixon-Martin paid the fare plus the tip and asked for a receipt. It was easier following up on a story by taking a taxi, but even the reporters needed to keep receipts if they wanted to claim the expense. She slipped the receipt into a side pocket of her purse and skirted the barriers near the well-guarded front doors.

The building housed NYPD headquarters, the prosecutor's office, and other city offices including the mayor's. This was one secure building. It could survive a variety of threats. It had no windows for the first five floors; the windows on the upper floors were heavily reinforced.

She passed through the front doors and went down a long hallway that turned to the right after about thirty feet. Suicide bombers would have a tough time here, she thought. They'd have to thread their way through a maze even before they reached the lobby. After another turn, she stood in line to pass through the metal and bomb detectors. Since there had been no bells, she continued on, passing by the visual scrutiny of the armed guards. Now she stood in line at the bank of elevators, pressed the "up" button and waited. That gave her time to check out her reflection on the polished metal door.

Not bad, she had to admit. She wore tight black slacks, black heels, a white blouse and a black leather jacket. Her thick dark hair fell straight to her shoulders. She wore diamond studded earrings and pale peach lipstick.

She had deliberately tried to dress like one of the policewomen on TV. It was the perfect attire for the show "New York's Most Wanted." It aired the first Sunday of the month at four o'clock in the afternoon. She had been the co-host for the last two years. Tony DeAgastenio was the other half of the team. The show had been a successful clone of the old "America's Most Wanted." The production crew had worked with a station in Washington State to develop the show's format. It was a simple process: They identified a major crime, covered the story, and offered a reward to someone who could provide the information that brought the bad guys to justice.

Tony was a third-generation Italian and had the "look" of law enforcement. Samantha suspected that she had been selected because she was black, but not too black, and tall. They had decided that her looks would bring in the male viewers. Her light mocha complexion appealed not only to the black and Latino communities, but white guys, too.

Sam loved the role she played for the show. If she hadn't chosen television news reporting for a career, she might have enjoyed being a cop. That is, of course, if she could have started out as a detective and skipped the police academy.

No more daydreaming. The elevator bell rang, and the doors slid open. When she got out on the fifth floor, she entered the lobby for NYPD headquarters.

"Good morning, Rita," Sam said, flashing her smile at the receptionist. "I have an appointment with Abe Wilson."

"Good morning, Samantha. Abe is expecting you. Go on in."

Rita pressed a button that released the door lock, and Sam walked into the main headquarters. The large, open bay contained numerous cubicles for lower ranking staff. She walked through the main hallway to the rear offices. She acknowledged a number of people who spoke to her. She was well known because of her work on the show.

She stopped at the last office on the right. On the door was a plaque that read "Lt. Abraham Wilson, Public Affairs." She rapped softly on the door and waited. The door opened. Standing in front of her was a huge man in a blue suit. He was almost as tall as Sam, but his girth filled the entire doorway. He had a round face with almond-shaped eyes. His skin color was similar to Sam's. She had to stifle a chuckle. A Sumo wrestler in a blue suit? But Abe wasn't fat; he was just big. His father was a black retired sergeant major; his mother was Korean. Abe had been on the force for twenty-five years. He had started out on the streets and worked his way up through the ranks. He was one of the most articulate men Sam had ever met. He had a master's degree in public affairs from NYU and had authored two books.

"Come on in," said Abe. "Would you like a Danish and a cup of coffee?" he asked, pointing to the carafe and a tray of pastries on a side table.

"I'd love both," said Sam who had missed breakfast.

"So is that FBI husband treating you OK?" asked Abe.

"Of course," said Sam smiling.

"It's a good thing. Otherwise Uncle Abe would have to pay him a visit."

Sam laughed out loud. Actually she and Tim had been to Abe's house a number of times, and they all had become good friends.

She bit into the Danish. It was delicious.

"These come from that deli on 134th Street?" she asked.

"Only place I would ever buy them," said Abe.

Together, they went over a list detailing several robberies and one murder. Sam took notes. Later, she would meet with Tony, and they would select one or two unsolved cases, then they'd do more follow-up. She appreciated the freedom of story selection allowed by the production people.

"Anything else going on?" she asked.

"We had kind of a weird thing happen last night at Grand Central. I don't know if it would be good for the show or not."

"What happened?" Sam asked.

Abe pulled out a folder and opened it.

"Let's see, four transit cops patrolling the lower tunnels trying to roust homeless people encountered a confrontation involving five people. It looked like some kind of fight. Happens a lot down there. There are a lot more folks going down there when the weather gets cold. The patrols find a body down there almost every week.

"Anyway, the cops shouted at the group, and three of them took off running down toward the lower level. You really don't chase these guys down there unless you have a platoon of cops. The mole people know the tunnels, and they know all the best places to hide.

"So that left the cops standing there with nothing to do. When they approached the two remaining perps, they could see that one was still holding a knife. It was all covered with blood. The other guy was lying on the tunnel floor. His hands and feet were tied with zip ties, and his mouth was taped shut. At first, they thought they would have to shoot at the guy with the knife, but he finally dropped it. When they went to cuff him, they found that his left arm was broken. He had a compound fracture. The bone was sticking out through the skin. He was obviously drunk and was also having problems breathing. They called in backup and did a search, but they could not locate the other three."

"Well," said Sam, "that doesn't seem like much of a story."

"Oh, it gets better."

"How?" asked Sam.

"When they got the two down to the station, the guy that was bound up was one of the local crazies. He had a bump on the head and was claiming that guys in black had been kidnapping people in the tunnels for several months and that he was one of the victims."

"So the other guy was kidnapping him?"

"Doesn't appear to be that way. The other guy was not a regular in the tunnels, and it looked like one of the other three was beating the crap out of him. Once we got him sobered up, he claimed that when he woke up, he saw the three. One was carrying the old bum over his shoulder. When he confronted them, he claimed that one of them was a woman. He said she weighed less than one hundred ten pounds. He swore that she was the one who had attacked him and would have killed him had the transit cops not stopped her."

"What was she, some kind of kung fu expert?" asked Sam.

"Can't say, except when we got him to Bellevue, his arm was broken, he had bruises and scratches like he had been thrown off of a train, and his throat had almost been crushed. Now, here is the weird part – when he was brought in, he was covered in blood, but when they got him cleaned up, it wasn't his blood. He claims he stabbed the woman. From the amount of blood, whoever he stabbed should have been dead."

By now, Sam was definitely interested. Abe, who loved to milk a story, just smiled.

"There is more."

"All right, out with it," said Sam.

"Get this, the guy is retired military. When we went through his rucksack, we found a savings book for Chase. We assumed it was something he had ripped off, but his fingerprints came back as the owner of the account. When we checked the account, it seems that his retirement pay goes into that savings account. Would you believe that the balance in the account was $325,891, and this guy had less than ten bucks in his pocket? Looks like he's been on the streets for years."

"God, I would love to talk to him. It sounds like a real human-interest story."

"Well, if you would like to talk to him, he is in a holding cell downstairs."

"Is he under arrest?"

"No, we're waiting for the VA to pick him up. He obviously needs help."

"Come on, Abe, let me talk to him."

35

THEY HAD TO TAKE THE ELEVATOR TO THE SUB-BASEMENT. THE PUBLIC SAFETY building didn't have its own jail. However, it had four secure rooms just off the parking garage. These were temporary holding cells for special cases until the individual could be booked into the regular jail. Each cell had a bed, desk, several metal chairs, and its own bathroom. There was also a bench anchored to the wall. It was fitted out with leg irons, if needed, for unruly individuals.

Abe approached the desk outside the holding rooms. An armed officer was always stationed there if anyone was being held inside.

"Good morning, lieutenant," said the officer whose nametag said Jenkins.

"Morning, Russ. We're here to talk to Quincy."

"Sure, lieutenant. How are you today, Ms. Dixon-Martin?"

"Call me Sam," said Samantha.

"Sure, Sam," said Jenkins.

He punched in a code that unlocked the outer door. Inside was a short hallway with four doors, two on each side. They walked up to room number one and looked through a window in the door. Actually, it was a one-way mirror with one-inch thick tempered glass. An individual in the room would only see the mirror. From the hallway outside the room, people could look in at whoever was inside the room. Sam peered through the mirror.

What she saw was not what she expected. Sitting on a chair facing the door was an old man with a short gray beard. His hair was long – almost shoulder length. He was very thin and had one of those thousand-yard stares so common in Gulf War veterans who suffered from post-traumatic stress.

"His name is Gary Quincy. He was medically retired from the Navy with the rank of chief petty officer. He's forty-seven years old," said Abe.

"Forty-seven?" whispered Sam. "My God, he looks like he's seventy."

"It's a rough life on the streets," said Abe.

"Is he dangerous?" asked Sam.

"Nah, just sad and confused. Don't worry, I will be right there with you."

There was a box next to the door. Abe took off his Glock and placed it in the box. Russ unlocked the door and Sam and Abe stepped in. The door closed. Sam heard the lock engage.

"Chief Quincy, I'm Lieutenant Wilson, and this is Ms. Dixon-Martin. Would you mind talking to us?"

"No problem," whispered Quincy. "Sorry, I can't speak much louder. That bitch really hurt my throat."

Quincy slowly got to his feet. He wore one of the prison's orange jumpsuits. His left arm was in a cast. Sam noticed the bruises around his throat.

"Go ahead and use the chairs. I'll sit on the bunk," whispered Quincy.

"Mr. Quincy, is it all right if I record this?"

"No, no problem, Miss …?"

"Just call me Sam," she said.

Sam pressed the record button and began asking questions.

"Lieutenant Wilson tells me you were in the Navy?"

"Yes, Ma'am. For seventeen years."

"So why did you get out?"

"I guess they threw me out."

"Why would they do that?"

"Because of the dreams."

"Dreams?"

"Yeah, the dreams. The man kept showing up each night, he wouldn't leave me alone. He just stood there staring at me in his bathrobe."

"What man?"

"You know, the big guy, the one who took down the World Trade Towers."

"I'm afraid I don't understand," said Sam, shaking her head.

"The man, the man! You know, Osama bin Laden."

"Why do you see him in your dreams?"

"Because I killed him," said Quincy.

"Killed him?" asked Sam.

"You know, 'BAM, BAM,' one shot in the chest and one in the head. Then he was dead, and we took his body back to the chopper. But, the bastard, he won't die. He visits me each night. If I don't get drunk, there he is, just standing there."

Whoa, thought Sam, this guy is not playing with a full deck of cards. She tried a different approach.

"Mr. Quincy?"

"It's Chief Quincy, retired US Navy," he said. "Oh, hell, just call me Gary."

"All right, Gary. Can you tell me what happened last night?"

"Sure," he said, his voice croaking.

"I decided to sleep in the tunnels last night. It was getting too cold to sleep up on the streets. Then I sort of felt something. Even though I had drunk a bottle, I guess I was sober enough to still have that sense.

"When I opened my eyes, I saw three dudes carrying another guy. When they got closer I recognized the old guy they were carrying, all trussed up like a pig. Them guys were dressed in black with black combat boots and were wearing black ski masks. It was like we used to dress in the team. Two were men and the third person was a woman.

"Well, hell, I got up and asked them what they thought they were doing. That's when the shit hit the fan. The big white guy – did I tell you that one of the guys was black and the other one was white? I don't remember. Anyway, he tells this little bitty white chick to take care of me. Can you imagine that? I could kick all three of their butts when I was on the team.

"Anyway, this little woman comes walking up to me. Now what could that little girl do, I wondered, hit me with her lipstick?"

He paused long enough to squint at Sam.

"Now, you might be different. How tall are you?"

"Six-two," answered Sam.

"Well, anyway, I wasn't worried about this little girl. Then would you believe it? She grabbed me, and the next thing was I'm flying though the air. Well, that wasn't going to cut it. So I pulled out my buck knife, you know, just to scare her. By the time I was on my feet, she was on me, swinging her fists. I easily blocked the blows, but, my God, she hit me with the force of a sledgehammer. She broke my Goddamn arm. Then she grabbed me by my throat. She was going to kill me. I had no choice. I stuck her with the knife. I felt the blade go in under her ribs. I felt the blood gush out and drip through my fingers. It was a fatal blow; I know it. But the bitch just turned and smiled."

"How did you know it was a fatal wound?" Sam asked.

"Hell, I ain't no cherry boy."

"Cherry boy?" asked Sam.

"You know, one of the team that hasn't made a kill up close and personal. You know, not a hundred-yard shot with a rifle, but a nice and close shot where the blood gets on your hands. When we did the mission to get the man, there were no cherries on that mission. We all had killed up close. That guy was my number five kill.

"Let me tell you, the knife cut an artery. I felt the blood pulsing out from the wound. She should have been dead in sixty seconds. I may have been drunk, but I knew what I was doing. Then the cops showed up and the three ran away. Can you believe that – that little girl ran away? She wasn't human; that's what I believe."

Sam sucked in her breath.

"What else do you remember, Gary?"

"Not much. She hurt me bad. I was about ready to pass out," he said, and then he paused.

"Oh, I guess there was one other thing I remember. Her eyes – they seemed to glow, but not from the lights, like from within."

Sam stared at this derelict of a man. She wanted to collect her thoughts before her next question. Before she spoke, Abe jumped in.

"What team were you on, chief?"

"SEAL Team Six," answered Quincy.

After the interview, Sam and Abe returned to his office.

"Quite a story, huh?" Abe commented.

"Yeah, I wonder how much of it is true," mused Sam.

"Well," said Abe, "I was in the MPs during Desert Storm. SEAL Team Six was the elite force that handled the special assignments for the Navy. As I recall, SEAL Team Six killed bin Laden. They never identified members of the team.

"The guy was in the Navy, and the medical examination papers listed a number of scars from what looked like combat wounds. He also has a tattoo on his right arm. It's the SEAL badge. I suspect his story about Osama bin Laden might just be true, but you could never print it. I mean who would believe Gary Quincy?

"As for what happened in the tunnels, I really don't know what to say. The old guy that was trussed up was babbling about people being kidnapped from the tunnels. The cops did see three other perps down there, and they said there was a lot of blood. None of the blood came from either of the two guys we have in custody."

Sam frowned. Unless she got something more substantial, this would be a great story for the national scandal rags, but not for "New York's Most Wanted."

Sam said her goodbyes, took the elevator to the lobby, flagged a cab, and returned to the station. On her way, Quincy's words kept replaying in her mind.

"She was not human, and her eyes glowed from within," he had said. Those words sent a chill down her spine. God, she thought, now that's in the past, yet for a moment, it all had come rushing back. She'd lived this story six years ago.

The pictures remained too vivid – the cavern in Virginia, the drums, and the people with those eyes that were not really human. No, she thought, all that was over.

It couldn't be happening again.

36

THE BLUE BMW CRUISED AT 80 MPH ALONG THE PALISADES PARKWAY.

The call had come totally out of the blue. He had been sitting at his desk closing out a case when Jaime told him that there was a general on the phone.

"Agent Martin," he said.

"Agent Martin, my name is James Parkinson. Is your father Lt. General Hank Martin?"

"Yes, sir, is there a problem?"

"Not with your father. I served with him in Liberia twelve years ago," said Parkinson.

"Sure, I remember you. You were Dad's deputy."

"Yes," said Parkinson. "Currently I'm at the U.S. Military Academy. I realize that this may sound strange, but I need to talk to you about a problem. I would prefer to talk to you in person. I would be glad to make an appointment and drive down to the city."

"That's, OK, sir. I could come up to the academy. How about next Wednesday?"

"That would be fine. Let's meet at my quarters, say 1000 hours. It's quarters number 102," said Parkinson. "I apologize about being so mysterious, and you may not be able to help, but I have no one else to turn to," added Parkinson.

Tim Martin took a vacation day to drive up to West Point and meet with Parkinson. He couldn't decide whether this was an official call or a personal call, so he drove his BMW. He and Sam only had one car, and it cost them a fortune for insurance. Most people who live and work in Manhattan don't even own a car. But with both sets of parents living in the DC area, they needed a car. The BMW hadn't been driven in six weeks. Martin was grateful that it had even started.

It was a beautiful fall day and trees along the Palisades Parkway were decked out in fall foliage. He had tried to talk Sam into coming with him, but she was following up on a story involving the disappearance of some homeless people. Sam had been trying to land one of the evening anchor spots, and that meant that she had to tackle some of the more bizarre stories. Sometimes he wished she wasn't so gung ho.

"Parkinson," he said aloud. "I remember Parkinson."

He realized that it had been twelve years since he'd seen Parkinson. That was when he and his parents got caught up in that Liberian coup d'état. It almost cost them their lives. Tim had been fifteen then. He remembered that Parkinson was tall, and he was black. He and his wife had two young boys, about nine and eleven years old. They'd be grown and gone by now.

Martin drove through Bear Mountain State Park and took 9W north towards Newburgh. He got caught behind a slow-moving line of cars. The idiot up front was poking along at fifteen mph under the speed limit. Stupid drivers like that made his blood boil. Finally, he saw an open stretch. He pulled into the left lane and mashed the gas pedal to the floor. By the time he passed the four cars, he was doing one hundred ten mph.

"Stupid idiot," he said as he swerved back into the right lane.

He had failed to spot the state cop car idling under the bridge. He slowed as he saw the cop's emergency lights go on as the car took off after him.

"Wonderful," Martin grumbled as he pulled to the side of the road. "Just wonderful."

The trooper stayed in his car doing a license check. Martin fumed as he watched the four cars he had just passed drive by. He saw a woman in her sixties with short white hair turn and stare at him from the passenger seat of the lead car. She grinned and mouthed the words, "Serves you right."

"Fuck you, too," he said back at her.

Finally, the cop approached the driver's window. State law required a driver to notify an officer immediately if he or she was carrying a weapon.

"Good morning, officer. I am carrying," Martin said as he rolled down his window.

The officer's hand moved to his gun. Martin held his badge in his hand.

"Agent Tim Martin, FBI."

The officer took the badge and Martin's ID.

"Are you on official business?' asked the officer.

"Yes, I am on my way to the United States Military Academy to meet with General Parkinson."

"Sir, you passed on a double line back there. I should give you a ticket, but if this is official police work, then try to keep the speed down."

"Yes, sir," said Martin, "I apologize."

"Have a good day," said the cop as he went back to his cruiser.

Tim breathed a sigh of relief. He could have gotten a speeding ticket even though he was a law enforcement officer. He vowed to keep his speed down – as difficult as it was – at least for the rest of the way.

A few miles later he saw the signs for Highland Falls, then a sign for the United States Military Academy Visitors' Gate. The academy restricted vehicle access. There was special parking for visitors and shuttle buses to take them to historic sites. Tim assumed that his FBI credentials would allow him to drive directly to Parkinson's quarters.

Martin pulled up to the gate. He had his credentials ready.

"I'm Special Agent Martin. I have an appointment with General Parkinson."

"Yes, sir," said the guard. "I'll issue you a temporary pass for your vehicle that will allow you access to the main campus. Are you familiar with the academy?"

"Yes," Martin answered. "Both my grandfather and great grandfather are buried in the West Point Cemetery."

He placed the pass on the dash.

"Turn the pass in when you leave, Agent Martin," said the MP.

Martin followed the road past a sign that said "Restricted Access, Authorized Vehicles Only." The road took him past Michie Stadium. When his dad had been stationed in Washington, DC, the family had attended a number of football games there. They would spend the weekend at the Thayer Hotel, always finding time to attend the cadet parades.

Three generations of Martins had graduated from the academy. He would have been the fourth. Unfortunately, he wanted to play soccer at a top-notch school, and the University of Virginia recruited him, much to the disappointment of both his father and grandfather. At least they felt some satisfaction as Tim enrolled in ROTC and would be commissioned as a second lieutenant.

Then a twist of fate changed everything. The nightmare that followed him from Liberia to Johnsonville, Virginia had almost cost Tim and Sam their lives. It also led to a new direction. Now married to Sam, Tim would stay in the U.S. He would no longer train to participate in foreign wars. Instead, he would commit himself to catching the bad guys here at home.

Following the drawdown of the military after the Afghanistan war, ROTC scholarship students were allowed to apply for the FBI academy following their college graduation. Tim applied and was accepted. Special Agent Tim Martin was now a five-year veteran of the FBI.

Martin peered at the house numbers as he drove down Washington Avenue past Professors' Row. The larger homes were designated for the full professors who had moved from being career officers to career instructors. The full professors would spend their remaining service time at the military academy. They were the academic elite – all held doctorates from the nation's finest educational institutions.

Finally, he saw Quarters 102, the Dean's Cottage. A brass plaque on the front steps read, "BG James M. Parkinson, Dean of the Academic Board." Martin was pleased to know that this fine man had become the Dean, the highest and most prestigious academic position at the United States Military Academy.

Martin turned into the driveway. He took a moment to look around, an ingrained habit of any successful agent. He could see men and women dressed in cadet gray uniforms. They moved freely along the streets and between buildings. This looked like any college campus, except for the wearing of uniforms.

Martin walked up the steps onto the covered porch and knocked lightly. When the door opened, a tall black man with closely cropped gray hair greeted him. Parkinson wore a sweater with the stars of a brigadier general on his shoulders.

"Sir, I'm Tim Martin."

"Tim, my how you have changed. I remember you as a skinny teenager. My gosh, you're taller than your father. Please come in."

$$\frac{37}{}$$

QUARTERS 102 HAD CHANGED LITTLE SINCE IT WAS BUILT IN 1856. MANY people thought it looked more like an English cottage than government-built quarters for a general officer.

Once a visitor entered the front door, Quarters 102 could have passed for an elegant antique shop. Many of the furnishings had been in the house more than one hundred fifty years. Usually, most of the space downstairs honored the rich military tradition of West Point. Upstairs, the residents used their own personal furniture to reflect their personal style.

Parkinson must have been used to the "shock and awe" on visitors' faces when they first walked into the living area.

"Have you ever been in the Dean's Cottage before?" asked Parkinson.

"No, sir, I have toured the Superintendent's Cottage once, and Dad and I attended a few football games at Michie Stadium. We stayed at the hotel and watched a couple of parades. My great-grandfather and grandfather are both buried in the cemetery," answered Martin.

"Did you serve in the army?"

"No, sir, I joined the FBI right out of college."

"I thought you might have followed your father into the military. Especially after what your family went through in Liberia," said Parkinson.

"But let's not hang out here," he continued, leading Martin back into the den. "I feel more comfortable there. It's the only place my wife, Maggie, lets me have my own things."

Martin understood what Parkinson meant when the two went into a large room that they used as a den. It featured several large leather chairs, designed for tall men like the two of them. An over-sized couch and several seating areas with tables and side chairs finished off the main furnishings. Then there were the necessary evils – a portable bar, a refrigerator and huge flat screen TV that sat directly across from the couch. A half dozen pairs of 3-D glasses were stacked in a large bowl on the coffee table.

The far wall featured a series of pictures and plaques, illustrating the life of the man who lived here. Martin noticed a miniature battalion flag, a shadowbox filled with military awards, and photos of Parkinson as a young officer. There were diplomas from a variety of colleges and universities, as well as dozens of certificates of achievement in math and science.

"Whew!" said Martin, impressed by Parkinson's amazing career. "I always knew you were a cool guy," he said with a smile. "But I didn't know how cool!"

Martin was a bit taken aback – all he had was a degree in political science. He had no head for math or science.

"Oh, that's all Maggie's work," Parkinson said. "She's the designer here."

Parkinson changed the subject quickly.

"May I offer you coffee or a drink?" he asked.

"Diet Coke would be great," Martin answered.

"Glass or can?" asked Parkinson as he opened the refrigerator.

"Can's fine."

Parkinson pulled out two cans of Diet Coke. He saw Martin looking at a photo of a young black officer in his battle dress uniform.

"My oldest son," said Parkinson. "He's in the 82nd Airborne Division. He graduated last year from the academy."

"Don't you have two sons?"

"The youngest lives in Newburgh. Drives a beer truck," said Parkinson frowning. Martin sensed disappointment in Parkinson's tone of voice.

"Is he happy driving a truck?"

"Yes, he seems to actually enjoy what he is doing. But he had so much potential. It seems like such a waste."

"Be happy for him," said Martin. "There is no greater joy in one's life than doing what makes you happy."

"You're right, of course," mused Parkinson.

The two men settled into facing easy chairs and sipped their Cokes.

"I know that you must be wondering why I contacted you," said Parkinson.

"Yes, sir," said Martin.

"Call me Jim. I get tired of being the dean all the time."

"All right, Jim," Martin said, recalling the first time his family had met Parkinson back in Liberia. He'd asked them all to call him Jim then, too.

Jim leaned forward, his fingertips touching lightly together as he began talking.

"Tim, do you believe in witchcraft?"

The question blindsided Tim. He had to think for a moment.

"Let's just say that I have seen things that cannot be rationally explained in the everyday real world. Why do you ask?"

"I was there during the coup in Liberia when you were kidnapped. There were things that your dad said that made me believe that there was something going on that defied reality.

"Let me get right to the point," Jim said. Clearly, Jim knew how to get down to business.

"Last week, one of our cadets died in his bed of a brain hemorrhage. The coroner ruled it a natural death. The office concluded that the cadet may have accidentally hit his head and was unaware of the severity of the injury."

"Doesn't that happen?" asked Tim.

"Yes, but the cadet was one that I sponsored. The staff and faculty sponsor cadets during their stay here. It's kind of like a home-away-from-home. Maggie and I have eight cadets.

"Cadet Ambrose Wiggins came to me the day before he died. He told me that he was being initiated into a coven that conducted ceremonies in the tunnels."

"The tunnels?" asked Tim.

"That's right. You're not a graduate, but your dad would know about the tunnels."

Jim explained the history of the steam tunnels. The legends seemed to have grown over the years.

"Don't know how much of that is or isn't true," Jim said, looking down at the floor. He paused, and then he got back to the story.

"Anyway, Wiggins came to me and said that he was pledging membership in a witches' coven. Apparently, this group of upper classmen, all seniors, we call them firsties, were conducting some kind of ancient ceremonies down there. It was supposed to enhance their physical and mental abilities.

"Of course, I assumed that this was just BS. We try to discourage such nonsense. According to Wiggins, part of their initiation was that he and two other cadets were to go into New York City, kidnap a homeless person, and bring him back to the tunnels."

Tim held up his hand to interrupt Jim's story.

"That's interesting, as well as ironic. You see, my wife is currently investigating a story dealing with the disappearance of homeless people in New York."

"Your wife?" asked Parkinson "Is she an FBI agent, too?"

"No, she's a news reporter for WNY-TV. Her name is Samantha Dixon-Martin."

"You mean the good-looking black woman that sometimes anchors the weekend news?"

"The same one," said Tim with a wide grin.

"Maybe this is somehow connected," said Jim. "Anyway, apparently the three cadets actually tried to kidnap a bum. It turned out that he was tougher than they realized. They found they were lucky only to end up with just a few bruises.

"Cadet Wiggins decided that he wanted out of all that, and he came to me. I was ready to recommend that the commandant initiate an Article 32 investigation. I told Wiggins that I would need names of the cadets involved. He said he would bring me the names on Monday morning. That never happened. They found Wiggins dead in his bunk over the weekend.

"The same night Wiggins died, I was jogging after dark. A female cadet ran up alongside of me. As we neared a wooded area, she shoved me into the brush. As you can see, I am a big man – all right, maybe a little bigger than I used to be and certainly not as tough as I was in the past.

"She likely wasn't much more than a hundred twenty pounds and probably not more than five feet four inches tall, but she had unbelievable strength. She shoved me up against a tree and warned me to stop asking questions about Cadet Wiggins.

"Then she said that she hoped my mother-in-law would get better. It would be unfortunate if my wife Maggie had an accident and was unable to care for her. Maggie is currently in Baltimore staying with her mother who has terminal cancer.

"This cadet let go of me and ran off into the dark. It was then I felt the pain in my arms where she had grabbed me. There was blood on my sweatshirt. I headed back to the house. When I got my shirt off, this is what I found."

Jim pulled up the sleeve on his sweater. The purple marks on his arm looked as if a person with small hands had gripped his arm and squeezed so tightly that the fingers themselves had broken the skin. Tim took a closer look at the marks. He had seen this kind of super strength six years ago back in Johnsonville, Virginia. Could it be possible that somehow these two events were connected?

"Did you ever find out the names of the cadets who were allegedly a part of this coven?" asked Tim.

"Not officially. I think Cadet Langston may be the leader. He's a running back on the football team. Last year he was second string. Now, he's one of the best backs in the league.

"Then there are his grades," Jim continued. "He's always been at the bottom of his class. Then he suddenly aced his last thermodynamics test. Colonel Reilly was convinced that Langston had cheated. He gave him several problems to do and sat down right in front of him to watch him doing the work. Langston solved the problems with complete ease."

"Is there any way I can observe Cadet Langston without him knowing I'm watching?" asked Tim.

"Why don't you join me for lunch at the cadet mess? You can be my guest. Lots of times we take family members or visitors to the mess. We will be eating at one of the cadet tables. I'll point out Langston," said Jim.

"Don't tell me who he is," said Tim. "If he is what I think he is, I will recognize him."

They walked from the Dean's Cottage to the cadet mess in Washington Hall. Tim had eaten there before and was familiar with the family-style dining. The cadets spoke only if spoken to. They sat ramrod straight. The entire corps of cadets could be fed in sixty minutes.

Jim selected an athletes' table. Tim sat down next to him. As they ate, Tim watched the cadets at nearby tables. He studied their faces, their eyes and their gestures. He saw the first one, then another. Soon he had counted four. One was a woman. He hadn't seen an *endosym* in six years, but he was familiar with the impact they could have on supposedly normal human beings. Although these cadets were not *endosyms*, Tim was certain that each of the four was under the power of one of these creatures.

38

THE ENDOSYMS WERE BACK. MORE LIKELY, THEY NEVER HAD LEFT. HE remembered the witch doctor's words.

"*Chea Geebe, is it really you?*" *said Tim smiling.*

"*So now you remember old Chea. I have tried to bring you the warnings of the endosym, but you ignored my warnings.*"

"*It was you who made me see the demons in those men?*" *asked Tim.*

"*No, my son, your eyes saw the true inner spirit of those men, I only helped you to see the inner man.*"

"*I don't understand,*" *Tim said.*

"*Tim, the endosym is back. You must stop him before it is too late,*" *Chea whispered.*

"*I still don't understand,*" *Tim said again.*

"*You are now the Chosen One, the one who walks with the spirit of the leopard,*" *answered the old man.*

After lunch, they walked back to the Dean's Cottage.

"Why didn't you ask me to point out Langston?" asked Jim.

"He was the tall guy with the freckles sitting at the third table over," said Tim.

"How in the world did you know that?" asked Jim.

"There are four of them. One was that small woman. All four of those people are controlled by an *endosym*," replied Tim.

"What the hell is an *endosym?*" asked Jim.

"That's the name the *zos* of Liberia gave them. It's believed that they have existed for thousands of years. In the New Testament, Christ even encountered them. They are men possessed by a demon. The result is a creature that is more than human and preys on humans, somehow feeding off of their deaths," Tim explained.

"You've got to be kidding me! There are no such things as demons or *endosyms* or whatever they are called," said Jim.

"Look at your arms again. As you said, no human could have done that," Tim said. "Jim, do not ask any questions about what happened to Cadet Wiggins, and don't tell anyone what I just told you," said Tim. "I've got to get back to the city. I'll be back. When I return, we are going to stop this thing!"

The two men shook hands, and Jim stood in his doorway and watched as Tim turned onto Mills Road. He quietly closed the door and returned to the den.

"This is impossible," Jim said aloud. "This cannot really be happening!

39

MARTIN TURNED LEFT AFTER PASSING THROUGH THE STONY LONESOME GATE and headed back to New York. The drive would give him time to process what Parkinson had told him. Usually, getting behind the wheel gave him an opportunity to think things through, but, for some reason, the *endosym* business kept returning to his thoughts. The feeling finally passed, but it left him unsettled. He had more questions than answers. One of the biggest questions was what he would tell Sam.

As Tim Martin drove south into the city, another car – a black Dodge Charger – traveled north. The driver was an older man with closely-cropped hair. Neither Martin nor the northbound driver was aware that they had come so near to each other. While Martin had just left West Point, the other driver followed the signs directing him to Newburgh.

40

THE CHARGER'S DRIVER ADHERED PRECISELY TO THE POSTED SPEED LIMIT. HE was careful to stay in the right lane, except to pass a slower vehicle.

The *endosym* Duncan McDougal continued to be amazed at the magic ride of this modern carriage. His enhanced brain had quickly mastered the ability to maneuver the vehicle that Butch called a car. Once he learned the rules of the road, Duncan could maneuver it at will. Butch had warned him that he must maintain the speed limit on the gauge in front of him by matching the number on the gauge to the numbers on the speed limit signs along the road.

On this trip, Duncan was paying another visit to the home where he had lived in 1779.

Six weeks ago he found the house on Google Earth and mapped the directions to the house on the car's GPS. He had typed in "McDougal" and "Newburg, New York." Up popped a web site that told him what he needed to know:

"Only four miles North of Newburgh, New York off Highway 87, The McDougal House offers the believer a unique experience. This is a place where the spiritually enlightened can relax, enjoy a cup of herbal tea, experience a tarot reading, and, of course, shop for books, herbs, candles, organic soap, crystals, tarot decks, incense and much more. Come any time. Guests are always welcome."

Was it possible that after all those years, descendants of his coven still practiced their arts in this modern world? He soon found out.

Duncan followed the GPS directions and pulled up on a rough dirt road. The house was just as he had remembered it. Even the aging oak trees were still alive, only they were much taller than he remembered. He pulled into the gravel parking lot and stopped to assess the place. At first, he was puzzled. Could it be only coincidental that the house was used to sell things used in witchcraft? Perhaps Satan kept his followers there to meet their master.

The saltbox house had small leaded glass windows and a wide front porch. The structure had changed very little from the time when Duncan had lived there. A large brass knocker was centered on the eight-foot front door. A large white pentagram stood out on its red paint. Strings of sparkling crystals hung in the windows. He tested the door handle and found it was unlocked. He pushed the door open and stepped inside.

At the counter stood a young woman, perhaps thirty years old. She had decorated her face to fit in with her occupation. A tattooed pentagram was centered on her forehead, silver rings pierced her nose and each eyebrow, and a black substance added color to her lips. At first, her appearance caused Duncan some consternation. In the past, such a blatant display of sensuality would have resulted in a woman being burned at the stake. Now, such displays were commonplace.

"Hi," she said. "Welcome to McDougal House!"

She paused and stared at the visitor.

"Do I know you?" she asked.

"What's your name?" Duncan replied.

"My name's Constance Marsh. What's yours?" she asked.

"I am the master, the one that you have been waiting for," he answered.

The woman seemed momentarily confused. She looked as if she were trying to speak, but only stared blankly at him.

Duncan reached out his hand.

"Come, my dear, let me show you my home."

Constance took his hand. Duncan pushed aside the useless baubles and charms. He led her to the large, open fireplace. He pressed the palm of his hand against one of the old bricks on the lower right side of the fireplace. With little resistance the bottom part of the wall swung inward to reveal a narrow opening and a dark stairway. Stone steps led into a musty chamber.

"Yes ... yes," murmured Duncan. It all looked familiar. The glow from his phone revealed thick, dusty cobwebs that draped from the rough-hewn beams. He had been here before, and this is where he was destined to return.

He had initially planned to sacrifice the woman to his master, Satan, but as he read her thoughts, he discovered that Constance was a true descendent from the original coven he had established in this very house. This woman had been chosen to await his return.

After Duncan had been hanged, his corpse had been buried in an unmarked grave at what later became West Point. Andrew Wyatt, the silversmith, had created a large silver cross that was placed on Duncan's coffin to hold his soul for eternity.

But the women of the coven had secretly disinterred and hidden his remains. They passed down the tale of that fateful night, assuring their future sisters that Duncan would indeed return. Satan had paved the way. This house, Constance and this coven would the touchstone for the renewed conquest of the human race.

Duncan's mission took a new direction. He ran his fingers along a shelf until he found a stack of books on demonology and satanic worship. His fingertips finally located a wooden box. The lid was easily dislodged. Inside, he found an ancient statue. Working alongside Constance, the two carried the statue and books up the stairway and placed them into the back of the car.

"Come," he said. "Come back down with me," he whispered to the woman.

She had followed him without question. Once again in the chamber, he found a box of beeswax candles. He placed them in a circular pattern around the altar. The dim light cast eerie shadows in the chamber.

"Here," he had demanded. "Lie here."

And so it began. He let his seed flow repeatedly into the female's womb. He knew his essence would produce the beginnings of a renewed coven.

Constance was instructed to gather followers. Two weeks later, he met with them at midnight to deliver his message from the grave. Since then, he regularly returned to his former house to visit, just as he was doing today.

The tunnels provided the passageways for the cadets to locate the human beings he used for sacrifices. Duncan had not revealed the existence of the coven. He kept his groups of followers separate. Yet this plan would soon be insufficient, soon, he realized, more covens would be required.

As his power increased, Duncan bestowed some of his power on his loyal followers. This gave them – at least temporarily – superior strength and knowledge. These powers did not last in the followers, and they gradually wore off.

He soon realized that a single *endosym* was insufficient. What his master Satan wanted now was for the door to the demon world to open.

It was his destiny to create a renewed race of *endosyms*.

41

SAM WAS HAVING ONE OF THOSE 'MORNING AFTER' EPISODES WHEN SHE HAD
partied too hard the night before.

Then, at least, Sam might have alcohol to blame for feeling the room
spin and her stomach churn. No, it wasn't booze. It more likely was the
rigor of her late-night stint as a temporary anchor on the "Ten O'clock
Nightly News." Even if the station had offered her a raise, she wouldn't
take it. Last night was her final show. Shirley Higgins would be back on
Monday. Then Sam would go back to filling in for the anchors on the
"Five O'clock News."

"It doesn't make sense to have to set the alarm to wake me up at nine
o'clock in the morning!" she complained. She slapped the top of the clock
radio, sat upright, and swung her legs over the edge of the bed.

"Some day, some day," she said aloud. "I'm going to wake up when
I'm ready to wake up."

She staggered into the bathroom, stripped off her panties and T-shirt,
and stepped into the shower. The hot water seemed to revive her. At least
for the moment, the dizzy feeling had disappeared.

She stepped out of the shower, toweled off, powdered and walked
absent-mindedly to her wardrobe where she slipped on her bra, panties,
white blouse and matching blue linen jacket and pants. She sucked in her
stomach and zipped up the slacks.

"Damn!" she swore. Eating after the late show hadn't been such a
good idea. Somehow she'd lost track of eating healthy. She resolved to
get back on a better schedule that included a long stint every day on the
treadmill. No way was she going to move up a size. After all, she was

only twenty-six. Marriage had been great. She was happy. But, there was no way she would become one of those dumpy wives. She needed to hit the gym.

She picked up the remote and checked the local weather. It was an unusually warm and humid day in the low-eighties with no chance of rain. Just walking to the subway would make her break out in a sweat.

Back in front of the mirror, Sam put on light makeup. She decided to wear the small turquoise earrings. She switched off the bedroom TV and headed for the kitchen where she clicked on the news. She swung open the refrigerator door and didn't see anything worth eating. Even the thought of breakfast made her nauseous.

Once more she sighed with relief, knowing that she wouldn't be coming home from work at two o'clock the next morning. Finally, she could have dinner with Tim tonight. Lately, they'd been like two ships passing in the night. He was asleep when she got home; he was already gone when she got up.

"A Pop-Tart!" she said, trying to convince herself that she could swallow it. She shoved it into the toaster. She didn't wait for it to come up by itself. She raised the lever, pulled it out, and took a big bite. She swallowed a nearly full glass of water. The combo made her think of how a wooden shingle might taste. At least, she'd have something in her stomach, even if it were indigestible.

"Out! Out!" she told herself. It was already a quarter to ten. She flew out the front door, closed it, snapped the deadbolt and headed for the elevator. Finally outside, she was almost bowled over by a blast of muggy heat. It was already seventy-eight degrees, and the weatherman was predicting another eighty-degree day. It was only a three-block walk to the subway, but it seemed like a mile. It was hard to believe that the temperature in New York City could reach the eighties in mid-October.

She forced herself to go at double her normal speed down the wide stairway to the turnstile. Even at ten o'clock in the morning, a small crowd had gathered, waiting for the next train. Lights flashed and bells rang, warning of the train's approach.

"Train 464 to Manhattan," said a voice on the recorded announcement. A whoosh of air pressed through the tunnel in front of the decelerating train. The cars finally halted, and the crowd surged through the doors. Sam was lucky. There were still several empty seats. At least she wouldn't have to stand for the entire trip downtown.

Where to sit? She looked around. The gangbanger with an empty seat next to him was definitely out. She didn't need some young punk hitting on her. A better choice was two rows farther back. She saw a vacant seat next to a white woman in her early fifties. Sam collapsed in the seat beside her.

"Oh my!" the woman said. "You're that lady on Channel 23 aren't you?"

Sometimes it felt good to be recognized.

"Yes," said Sam. "Yes, I ..."

The subway lurched forward. Sam's stomach did a flip-flop. She sucked in a breath of air.

The woman had already introduced herself as Emma Ferguson, but Sam's deep breathing interrupted her chatter.

"Your first?" she asked.

"My first what?" asked Sam, a little puzzled. Subway ride? TV show? What?

"Baby, dear," Emma said with a knowing smile. "I've had three. I know the signs."

"Oh, no," said Sam, "I'm recovering from the stomach flu. Had it all week."

"Oh, I'm sorry. I could have sworn that you were pregnant," said Emma.

Unlikely, thought Sam. Since she had sat in the anchor seat for the late night news, their sex life was almost non-existent. Besides, she was on the ENGYN patch, one of the most reliable birth control methods around.

The two women kept up a conversation until Samantha got off at Rockefeller Plaza. Once in the outside air again, Sam paused for a gasp of air. She cut across the plaza and entered the lobby of the TV station offices. As she entered, she pulled her press pass from her purse and showed it to the guard. She took the elevator to the nineteenth floor.

"Good morning, Ms. Martin," said the guard.

"Morning, Jerry," she said, not missing a step as she entered the pandemonium of the newsroom.

Tim had teased her about the tight security at the station, telling her it was more restricted than at the FBI. Sam understood the competitive nature of the news business. Getting one up on rival stations was critical to staying on top.

42

As usual, the newsroom was a beehive of activity. Most people worked out of cubicles, although the anchors had private offices near the sound studios. To add to the ongoing chaos, several huge LCD screens flashed real-time, silent images from the rival stations and major international channels. The video remained on mute unless one of the stations had breaking news. The sound then came on and all heads turned toward the screens.

Sam loved the vibrant climate in the newsroom. Close to forty individuals scurried from desk to desk, each fulfilling a vital job. Sam worked her way back to her cubicle, exchanging nods and tidbits with co-workers. She plopped down in her chair, clicked her mouse and entered her password. First, she'd scan her email, and then she would send a memo to her boss with suggestions for priority placement. In many ways, she liked being a reporter better than being an anchor. The past two weeks as anchorwoman had just been too exhausting.

Before she realized it, four hours had flown by. Her stomach gurgled, announcing its need for food. That Pop-Tart simply didn't last long enough. This isn't nausea, she told herself, it was downright hunger.

"I'm going out for a bite to eat," she told Greta who sat in the adjoining cube. "I have my cell phone with me."

She grabbed a Caesar salad, an iced tea and a piece of chocolate cake at the station's snack bar. She had a moment of guilt about the cake. Her suit pants were too tight this morning, and she should have stopped at the salad. But she couldn't pass by the chocolate. Recently, chocolate had been like an essential drug. She had to have it.

"Craving?" she whispered. "Craving … as in pregnant?" She lowered her hand to her waistband, patting her mid-section lightly.

The morning's image of that kindly woman on the subway popped into her mind. What exactly had she said? Was it "Is this your first?"

Impossible, Sam concluded. Nevertheless, when she finished her lunch, Sam headed back to the station. She suddenly came to a stop, turned right, and stepped out onto the sidewalk. Drug Emporium was directly ahead.

"May I help you?" asked a clerk who had been stocking the shelves. Sam realized that she had been staring at the boxes, but not really seeing what she needed.

"Pregnancy tests?" she stammered.

"Of course, aisle six."

"Thank you," she muttered. How could she be so totally embarrassed at her age? Then she laughed out loud. She remembered Tim's story about his senior prom night. His buddies figured they all needed condoms, just in case they got lucky. They had selected Tim to make the purchase, but, at the last minute, he had chickened out. Even brave Tim had been too embarrassed to buy condoms.

Aisle six had too many boxes. Too many choices, she concluded. She randomly picked up two different brands and headed for the cash register. The clerk, a young man, seemed oblivious to her product selection. He was just doing his job; Sam, on the other hand, was possibly on the verge of a life-changing discovery.

She headed back to the station, dropped her bag into the bottom desk drawer next to her purse, and got back to work. The pregnancy test could wait until she got home.

Ten minutes later, she pulled out the drawer. The people around her seemed to be totally engaged in their work. They wouldn't notice that she had taken out the bag and headed for the restroom. In the end stall, she opened the first box and read the directions.

"Simple," she said softly. "Just pee on the strip."

Not so easy, she realized. "Damn it!" she swore. She had wet her fingers. She pulled back her hand and grabbed a handful of toilet paper.

Wiping her hand, she had forgotten about the test strip. She glanced down at the box top and saw the bright blue on the strip. She read the directions once again. Pregnant? That was impossible. It must be an error. She would use the other test.

There was one problem – Sam couldn't just pee on demand. She needed to have a full bladder. Great, she thought, she needed to hydrate. She took the soaked strip and its box and stuffed them into the sanitary napkin container next to the toilet seat. She stood, pulled up her pants, and walked to the sink. She scrubbed her hands for several minutes. Her brother, Eddie, had often called her prissy. Well, she was concerned about cleanliness.

Sam headed back to her desk, picking up a bottle of water from the fridge on her way. She puttered around on her computer and managed to drink the entire bottle. Fifteen minutes later, she still didn't feel the urge. She returned to the fridge and grabbed a second bottle. Finally, she began to feel that she could pee. She headed back to the bathroom. She returned to the end stall to repeat the process. She took care not to get urine on her hand this time. She pulled out the strip. Thankfully, it was clear. She breathed a sigh of relief and got ready to open the door. When she looked down, she saw that the strip was beginning to change color. After a long minute, it, too, turned blue.

Two positive pregnancy tests? Maybe she needed to get another test. No, she would see Shelly. She pulled out her cell phone and punched in Shelly's number.

"Manhattan Gynecology," answered the receptionist.

"Yes, this is Samantha Dixon-Martin, would it be possible for me to see Dr. Badger later this afternoon? It's an emergency."

"Her calendar is filled for the rest of the day. Could another doctor see you?"

"No, Dr. Badger is my personal doctor."

"What is the problem?" asked the receptionist.

"I think I may have an infection," she lied.

"One moment, please," the woman said.

Samantha waited impatiently.

"Dr. Badger can see you at 5:30."

"Wonderful!" Sam said, "I'll be there."

Shelly's office was only four blocks from the station. The Badgers owned a home next to her parents. Shelly's younger sister was one of Sam's sorority sisters. When she and Tim moved to New York, Sam was surprised to find Shelly, practicing medicine just four blocks from the station. Shelly had been her doctor for the last three years. She had been the one who had prescribed the patch.

43

SAM DIDN'T WANT TO WAIT ANY LONGER THAN NECESSARY. SHE CHECKED IN at the doctor's office forty minutes early. The five-doctor clinic catered to the rich and famous. No one else could afford the high prices. The group specialized in women's bodies. Many clients were in their childbearing years.

Sam took a seat and picked up a glossy decorating magazine. She had trouble concentrating. Her mind wandered. She checked out the other women in the waiting room. Two were obviously pregnant. She might soon look like them. Or not. The longer she waited, the more time she had to think.

She couldn't possibly be pregnant. She and Tim hadn't really even discussed having children. Both were deeply committed to their careers. She figured they had more time to think about it before making a decision. There was even the possibility that they wouldn't have children at all.

Even in this day and age, Sam wasn't keen on raising a child from a mixed marriage. She remembered how opposed to her marriage her dad had been when she fell in love with Tim, who was about as white as anyone can get.

"Mrs. Martin? Mrs. Martin, would you please come this way," said the neatly dressed nurse. "How are you today?" the woman asked with a smile, obviously trying to ease Sam's concern.

She took Sam directly to a dressing room that had a locking closet. A crisp light green hospital gown was sitting neatly folded on a chair. Sam was about to say that she only wanted to speak with Dr. Badger when she realized that she would have to be examined.

She removed her clothes and placed them in the closet. A few minutes later, the nurse knocked on the door at the back of the dressing room.

"Yes?" asked Sam.

The nurse opened the door.

"Follow me, please." She led Sam to an examination room complete with an exam table and stirrups. Sam took a seat in the chair next to the table and began waiting again.

Twenty minutes later Shelly walked in.

"Sam, it's good to see you. I hope there is nothing serious going on."

"Me, too," said Sam.

"What's the problem?" asked the doctor.

"I've been very tired, and in the mornings, I have felt sick to my stomach," Sam answered, speaking too quickly. She paused and took a deep breath.

"All right, Shelly, I think I might be pregnant. As a matter of fact, I did one of those tests – actually two – and they both came up positive," she said. Then she continued, "Well, I'm glad I got that out," said Sam with a smile.

"Well, let's take a look," said Shelly. First, she gently pressed in several places against Sam's abdomen. Next, she reached inside to do a pelvic exam.

"I need to do an ultrasound," Shelly explained without revealing any information.

The nurse wheeled in a machine, rubbed a slick substance on Sam's middle below her navel. She rolled the transmitter over Sam's skin, and then she pushed a button to print a report.

Shelly studied at the paper.

"Well?" asked Sam.

"You're pregnant," said Shelly.

"That's not possible! I'm on the patch. I haven't even had a period in three years," Sam exclaimed, holding her face in her hands.

"Well, although the patch has a ninety-nine percent success rate, there is that one percent," the doctor said. She looked directly at Sam. "How do you feel about this?" asked Shelly.

"I really don't know. How far along I am?"

"Well, that's a problem," said Shelly. "Based on the size of the fetus, I would say five months."

"Five months? How? I don't even look pregnant?"

"That's because of the patch," said Sally. "It suppresses the estrogen. I'll give you a shot today that will counter the patch, and you will notice the changes within two weeks. You, of course, must realize that you're past the time when an abortion is possible. As a matter of fact, had the fetus not been curled up, I could have probably told you the baby's gender."

Samantha stared at the ceiling. She didn't know what to say or what to do. She was going to have a baby in four months, and Tim didn't even know. Then she had a horrible thought.

"Is there a chance that the baby will be deformed because of the patch?" she asked.

"I see no reason to be concerned about that," said Shelly. "Usually, when a woman is on the patch, the egg doesn't adhere to the womb and she naturally aborts. But, this guy has his – or her – own ideas, and it's well attached. You should have no problem carrying this pregnancy to term.

"You can go ahead and get dressed. Then I will give you the estrogen shot and a prescription for prenatal vitamins. Oh, and the morning sickness should just about be through. Normally, by the sixth month, it goes away," said Shelly with a wide grin.

"Things are going to start changing pretty fast. Your breasts will get larger, so will your rear. You're going to need new clothes. Get ready to go shopping!"

Suddenly, Sam was on the subway once again, but this time she was going from Rockefeller Plaza back to her home. Everything had happened so quickly that she hadn't stopped to process what her next steps would be.

Tim should already be home. So, what should she do? She figured that she might wait until they crawled in bed together. Usually, a couple has a lot more time to plan. But here she was – five months along.

OK, she decided as she took the elevator to the apartment, she would wait until bed to tell him the news. When she unlocked the door, she saw Tim right away. He was sitting in his recliner watching TV.

"Hi, hon. Did you have a good day?" Tim asked.

"I'm pregnant!" Sam said, surprising even herself.

Tim's jaw had dropped. He stared directly at her, totally speechless.

"Well, that was tactful," she chided herself. It was certainly not how she had planned to make her announcement.

"How?" asked Tim.

"You know, the normal way. Although with our crazy hours the last two months, I can't say we've been working on it on a regular basis."

"No," said Tim. "I meant how did this happen because you're supposed to be on this patch thing, right?"

"Oh, yeah, I guess I'm in the one percent where it doesn't work. God, Tim what are we going to do?" she asked, bursting into tears.

Tim stood and raced to her side to embrace her.

"We're going to have a baby. That's what we're going to do."

"You're not upset?" she asked.

"Hell, no, I've always wanted a son."

"Whoa, there, Daddy, we don't know it's a boy."

"It's a boy," said Tim with unusual certainty. "You don't even need an ultrasound, and it is a boy!" he said smugly.

Speechless no more, the two spent the rest of the evening talking about the changes that would be taking place in their lives. Like Sam, Tim couldn't believe that they were already five months into the pregnancy.

"Dad's in Iraq," Tim said. "He won't be back until just before Thanksgiving." They decided to hold off on telling him and everyone else in the family until Thanksgiving. At six and a half months into the pregnancy, it would be hard to keep it a secret any longer than that.

Then, there was the problem of Sam's job at the station. When should she tell the management?

And then, there was the shopping – by her doctor's orders, she needed to add to her wardrobe.

And what about baby names? They tossed around names, but Tim insisted on suggesting only boy names. He also declared that he didn't want to know the gender before the birth. Sam said that they'd have to buy two different sets of clothes.

"Oh, Tim," Sam said, nearly breaking out in tears once again. "We haven't eaten yet! I'm so starved!"

"Can't let that happen!" Tim declared.

They dashed out to a sandwich shop and picked up two hoagies. Sam needed another piece of chocolate cake.

They got back to the flat at almost two o'clock in the morning. By then, they were both ready to collapse from the excitement.

Tim watched as Sam undressed.

"Hey!" he said. "I kind of like this. Your breasts look bigger!"

"One of the side effects," Sam joked. "I'm glad that makes you happy!"

"Do you suppose junior would be OK if his parents enjoyed a little sex?"

"Tim, we can't do that," she said laughing.

"Of course, we can," said Tim. "Show me where it's written that we can't."

He nuzzled her neck.

"Stop that!" she scolded, but she knew he wouldn't stop. The baby would have company tonight. She laughed as they fell into bed naked.

"I love you," she whispered in his ear.

"I love you, too," he said as he caressed her middle. "I love both of you."

44

Two men sat at a window table in the second floor restaurant at Bear Mountain Inn.

It was one of those historic park lodges that also had a reputation as one of the best restaurants in the area. Built in 1915, the hotel and restaurant business was located on Route 9W, seven miles south of West Point.

On the US National Register of Historic Places, it is on the "must-see" list for visitors. The stones used in the foundations, wall façades and fireplaces were reclaimed from old walls found on the property. Timber for the building was milled on site. A major renovation project between 2005 and 2011 had brought the old place into the modern world.

It wasn't too busy for a Sunday night. Only five other tables were occupied. That was OK with Tim. He had been hungry – that's the way it was for soon-to-be fathers. They needed to keep up their energy.

Tim had knocked off a huge porterhouse steak and was looking at the dessert menu with heightened interest. Jim had been more reasonable. He had ordered chicken Parmesan. In the old days, he, too, would have gone for a steak, but tonight he didn't want to risk the upset stomach that would surely follow. Since this whole thing started, he had been chewing Tums like they were candy.

While Jim held back, Tim ate like a warrior in the olden days. They gorged themselves on huge meals because when the battle began, their next meal would be uncertain. Tim thought of the old saying, "Eat, drink and be merry, for tomorrow we may die."

The waitress had taken their plates, and they waited for their coffee and Tim's chocolate mousse. Jim reached for his briefcase and pulled out the information he had obtained from Hal Stevens, the USMA engineer.

"This place has been an important part of American history since the Revolutionary War," Jim said. "It didn't become the United States Military Academy until 1802.

"It sits on an open plain on a point of land that juts out on the west side of the Hudson. During the Revolution, they built forts here to stop the British advance. Underground tunnels and redoubts set up a good defense," he continued. "But even today, we know that there are numerous tunnels and underground chambers that exist, but are not identified on any official map."

Jim knew his history, and he also loved the academy. Clearly, the recent revelations had bothered him.

"Your coffees, gentlemen," said the waitress. She returned a few minutes later with Tim's large helping of chocolate mousse. Tim had to grin. Sam would have loved this, he thought.

Tim ate his dessert while Jim summarized the physical history of the academy. Tim listened carefully, focusing on the details that might be critical later.

"One thing particularly interesting is the area under the current tennis courts. That whole area used to be known as Execution Hollow. Allegedly, that's where they performed the hangings. Most experts believe that several secure cells were constructed underneath to hold those found guilty of supposed crimes against the American forces.

"We're pretty sure that the ground has its spots of instability. Back in 1983, an old tunnel collapsed and you could see the original stone and brickwork. Quite a historical find, except they didn't treat it as such. They just threw in a bunch of gravel to fill in the hole."

Tim learned about many of the old buildings and how so much of the academy's campus was truly a lesson in American history and a story of American heroes.

"Another thing you might find interesting is the old steam plant and the tunnels that lead to various buildings to provide heat. For two hundred years, this place underwent construction and re-construction. Underground tunnels have provided water, removed waste, connected networks and, of course, provided electricity and heat. Some of those tunnels are wide enough to drive a car through. Others have been closed and forgotten."

Finally satisfied, Tim set his fork on his dessert plate and cradled his coffee cup in his hands.

"So what you're telling me is that you don't know for sure what's really under this place, right?" asked Tim.

"That's right, Tim. Maps of the underground are likely accurate only for the last seventy years. Earlier than that, what lies under the academy is unknown and unexplored," concluded Jim.

"So how do we go about getting into the tunnels?" asked Tim.

"That part is easy. We will go through Mahan Hall. I taught in that building for sixteen years. I taught a class in thermodynamics. We used to tour the steam plant and mechanical room under the building."

"So, you've actually been in the tunnels?"

"Only in the entrance to the system. The engineers don't allow us to go into the tunnels. It's too dangerous."

"Dangerous, how?"

"Well, the power lines running through the tunnels carry fifteen thousand volts. A short in one of the high voltage lines could electrocute someone.

"But far more dangerous is the steam," Jim continued. We run high-pressure steam to the buildings. Heat exchangers provide hot water. The problem with high-pressure steam is a pinhole leak could cause the pipe to rupture. People inside could die instantly.

"Then there is the asbestos, miles and miles of asbestos pipes. If the covering is damaged, a person risks exposure to the asbestos fibers."

"If it's dangerous why in the world would the cadets want to go there?"

Jim laughed.

"It's simple. They go in there because they're not supposed to. It becomes a challenge."

"How easy is it to move around?" asked Tim.

"The new tunnels are well lit. It's easy to walk around. Older tunnels that we still use are also lighted, but they're more dangerous. Then there are the abandoned tunnels with no lighting. They were built with brick. The moisture and heat has caused the mortar to fail. Some have already collapsed.

"Then, of course, there are the unknown areas," Jim said. He thumbed through the documents and pulled out a stack of detailed maps.

"Hal gave me these maps of the complex. It shows all the tunnels in use. The tunnels are marked with numbers and arrows. For example, P is for Pershing Barracks and G for Grant Hall. By looking at the letters and codes we can get a general idea of where we are. One problem is that we can get lost. For that reason, Hal suggests we carry spray cans of orange fluorescent paint. By marking small spots on the wall, we can backtrack."

"That should work better than breadcrumbs," laughed Tim.

Tim glanced at his watch. He'd been with Jim since he arrived at five o'clock. Sam was scheduled to anchor the "Ten O'clock News." She wouldn't expect him to return until the next afternoon.

It had been a pleasant dinner. The two talked as if they were just a couple of friends having dinner together. They had avoided talking about the possibility of witchcraft. Jim still had a hard time believing that something supernatural was involved. As an engineer, he relied on facts. Yet, in his gut, he knew that some things still remained unknown. But for him, acknowledging demon-possessed men called *endosyms* was just one step too far over the edge.

"What are we expecting to find in the tunnels?" Jim asked.

"If I am right, I believe that what Wiggins told you is true, and that those cadets are killing people in the tunnels," Tim said.

"But how in the world will we be able to locate this place? We could wander around for days, maybe years, and never find answers to our questions."

Tim reached under his shirt and pulled out a leopard's tooth attached to a leather strap.

Jim looked at Tim as if he had just lost his mind.

"What's a tooth have to do with all this?" he asked.

"I can't explain it, but I know the tooth will glow green if there is an *endosym* in the tunnels," said Tim.

"Green?"

"Yeah, like a chemical light. It happened to me six years ago in Virginia."

"Look, Tim, I am still having problems with these *endosyms*, but I have to tell you that it is not scientifically possible for an old tooth to glow green."

"I know, Jim, but it happens. An old witch doctor gave it to my mom, said it would protect her. Somehow, it works."

"For anyone?" asked Jim.

"No, I think it only works for me."

Jim stared across the table at this unusual young man.

"Jim, do you believe in God?" asked Tim.

"Sure," said Jim.

"Have you ever seen God?" asked Tim.

"Well, no," said Jim.

"Have you ever had God speak to you?"

"I'm afraid not," said Jim.

"Yet, we believe in God. We accept it on faith. You'll just have to accept on faith that an African witch doctor from Liberia has given this old leopard tooth some kind of power that causes it to glow. Kind of like a forked stick, a water witch, that allows you to find water."

"Tim, I'm going to have to see it to believe it."

Tim smiled.

"I believe you will get the chance. All the signs point to something quite unbelievable," Tim said.

45

THE DEAN AND THE FBI AGENT RETURNED TO THE ACADEMY.

The seven-mile trip in a fourteen-year-old Lexus driven at five miles under the speed limit was almost too much for Tim. He tapped his feet on the floor in front of the passenger seat as he watched Jim crawl up to the gate.

The MP saluted as Jim pulled to a stop. Both men took out their ID cards – Jim's was military; Tim's was FBI. The guard knew Parkinson by sight, but he'd never before seen him with an FBI agent. Trained to be cautious, the guard took a second look at Tim before waving the car through the gate.

Instead of returning to the Dean's Cottage, Jim turned off on a side road and parked in a restricted space across from a tall granite block building.

"Mahan Hall," Jim announced.

After they had gotten out of the car, Jim pressed the key fob to lock the door.

"Damn," Jim said. "I forgot to take out my pistol."

He unlocked car and reached into the glove box for his loaded pistol.

"You know it's illegal to carry a concealed weapon on academy grounds," said Jim.

"I'll bet they would make an exception for the dean," said Tim. "Besides, I'm with you, and FBI trumps MPs."

Jim laughed nervously.

"Right, but I still don't feel good about carrying this."

"Let me assure you if we need weapons, then you'll be glad you have it," Tim said. "Oh, by the way, if you have to use the gun, go for a headshot."

"Headshot!" gasped Jim, "You mean shoot to kill?"

"You never pull the trigger unless you are planning to kill someone. People that are under the influence of an *endosym* possess super-human strength. You saw what that female cadet could do when she grabbed you. We found six years ago that the only way we could shut down that power, was a direct headshot. You scramble their brains, and they stop functioning."

Jim was speechless. He just stood there. There was no way he could shoot one of the cadets in the head. He prayed that this would turn out to be nothing more than just a wild goose chase.

The building alarm sounded immediately after Jim slid his keycard in the box by the double glass doors of Mahan Hall and they stepped into the hallway. Jim disabled the alarm as soon as he punched in his access code.

"When I was a cadet, they didn't have the academic buildings monitored by alarms and video," said Jim. "Times have changed."

Tim scanned the area around the long polished hallway. The building reminded him of the academic buildings at the University of Virginia. Somehow he had expected West Point's academic buildings to look more like a standard military facility.

"Mahan Hall is built into the hill above the Hudson. From this street, it raises four stories and goes down underground for three stories," explained Jim.

They strolled casually down the hallway.

"Before I was dean, I was the department head for engineering. That was my office," said Jim pointing to the door with windows along the wall next to it. Tim noticed the receptionist's desk in front of an office with a plaque reading "Department Head."

They took the flight of stairs leading to the lower floors. Neither man had dressed up for their dinner. They wore jeans, sweatshirts and running shoes. The shoes squeaked as they walked along the polished tile floors.

Three levels down, Jim led Tim to a door marked "Mechanical Room." He unlocked the door and pushed it open.

They walked onto a concrete balcony that overlooked a brightly lit room. Tim could hear the hum of large electric motors that drowned the noise from the gray transformers mounted along the far wall. Alongside the transformers were rows of electrical panels with numerous switches and flashing lights. Larger steam pipes led into heat exchangers. To Tim, the room wasn't too different from a boiler room on a large ocean-going ship.

"The buildings are all heated by high-pressure steam. Steam and electrical power come from the steam and power plant we passed on our way here. In a lot of ways, the academy runs like a huge ship. We burn bunker fuel just like the freighters you see on the ocean. The boilers generate steam for both electric power and heat. The main electrical and steam for all the buildings pass through this room."

Jim pointed to another section.

"Those openings over there carry the power to the other building," said Jim.

"So, how far did you say you've gone into the tunnels?" Tim asked.

"Just to here and to the power plant," Jim answered.

"Is it easy for the cadets to access the mechanical rooms?"

"The rooms are always locked, but cadets are innovative, and everyone knows that cadets get into places they shouldn't be."

"Whew, it's hot in here," said Tim.

"Wait until we get in the steam tunnel. The temperature in some areas is around one hundred ten degrees. We need to wear just T-shirts when we go into the tunnels. Also, we need to bring water."

Jim opened a refrigerator along the wall and pulled out two belts with canteens filled with cold water. On each belt was also a small can of orange fluorescent paint that the crew used to mark directions on the tunnel walls.

His next stop was a table where a number of flashlights sat in battery chargers. Each light held twenty small bulbs.

"These flashlights will show a steam break," Jim said.

"Steam break?" asked Tim. "Why would you need a flashlight? You would be able to see the water vapor.

"This is different," said Jim. "Those huge steam pipes are pressurized at over a thousand PSI. The temperature of steam exceeds a thousand degrees. A pinhole leak is invisible, yet it could cut off your arm like a laser beam."

"You've got to be kidding," Tim scoffed.

"No, these aren't your common radiator steam pipes. Also if the power goes out, you will need the flashlights to find your way back through the tunnels," Jim explained.

Next, he handed Tim a walkie-talkie.

"We use these if we get separated. They have limited range in the tunnels and operate on the same frequency. Clip it on the belt with the canteen.

"Man, they are well prepared," said Tim.

"Remember what I said, the tunnels are dangerous," said Jim.

"More dangerous than the maintenance staff realizes," Tim said, thinking of the potential danger inside.

They walked down the heavy metal stairs to the ground level. Tim followed Jim toward a large opening along one wall. It was at least ten feet tall and twenty feet wide. Along one side, Tim saw the huge, asbestos-wrapped steam pipes attached to the wall. Stenciled on the insulation of the pipes were signs that read:

WARNING: ASBESTOS
DO NOT PUNCTURE OR DAMAGE

On the opposite wall near the ceiling were large metal conduits. They also came with warnings:

DANGER: HIGH VOLTAGE

In the center of the tunnel was a metal grate about four feet wide. Tim looked down. He saw huge return water pipes through the protective grate.

"Wow, this is like we're walking into a different world!" Tim said.

Compact florescent bulbs encased in glass-sealed fixtures were situated along both walls, spaced about every ten feet. The lights operated on several separate circuits so a short would not shut off the entire lighting system. Even though the tunnel was brightly lit, both men turned on their lights, shining them directly ahead.

They continued down the tunnel. Neither man spoke. After about one hundred fifty feet, the tunnel branched off in three directions. Jim stopped and consulted the map. His finger traced the direction of the arrows.

"Let's see," Jim said. "To the left is Pershing Barracks. If you go straight ahead, you're under Washington Hall. If you go to the right, the tunnel services the gymnasium, and then it runs under the road. The main tunnels also have bisecting tunnels, and they are all connected to each other along the way. Kind of like a spider web."

"This could take all night," said Tim.

"Well, according to Cadet Wiggins, they enter through Pershing Barracks. He said they went under the field and eventually reached a door that belonged to an older tunnel complex."

Jim paused as he thought about what they should do. "Let's take the right tunnel," he concluded.

It took them thirty minutes, backtracking twice, before they finally were stopped at a locked metal door.

Stevens, the engineer, had given Jim a key ring with perhaps twenty different keys. The sixth key that Jim tried opened the door.

From the hot, humid air in the live steam tunnels, they were confronted by a blast of cold air. It felt like they had walked into a huge refrigerator. The tunnel construction hadn't changed – it was made of concrete. Abandoned steam pipes ran along the walls. There was no indication of electrical power. Their flashlights revealed chunks of concrete mixed with broken furniture and piles of old books strewn along the tunnel floor.

"This must be part of the old section built back in the early 1900s after the steam and power plant was finished in 1903," whispered Jim.

"That's it for the maps," Jim said. "There are no maps beyond this point. And no lights."

Tim ran his finger along the wall.

"Don't stir the dust," warned Jim. "It's probably mixed with asbestos."

"Look!" said Tim pointing his flashlight at the ground.

They could see footprints in the dust on the floor. It looked like whoever had made the prints had gone back and forth numerous times.

"Let's go on ahead," Tim said. "It should be easy to follow the prints in the dust."

In some places, the tunnel was covered with white efflorescence from water seeping through cracks in the concrete. Both men shivered for several minutes until their bodies adjusted to the sixty-degree temperature.

"I'll bet the temperature down here remains constant year-round," said Tim.

They came to a dead end.

"What's up with that?" Tim asked. He pointed the beam of his light on the floor. The footprints had disappeared.

"Let's backtrack and try to find out where they dropped off," suggested Jim.

"There!" whispered Tim. "Look over there!"

There was a side tunnel. The tracks entered a tunnel that was only about four feet wide and six feet high. They both had to stoop as they entered.

Jim spray-painted an X on the wall before they entered the opening. When they had gone fifty feet they came to an old wooden door. It stood wide open. They entered the tunnel and walked another sixty feet until they came to a pile of broken bricks. There was an opening to their right.

"This is part of Fort Clinton's tunnel complex built during the Revolutionary War," Jim concluded.

"Holy shit! What's happening under your T-shirt?" Jim said.

Tim reached under his shirt and pulled out the leather cord. The leopard tooth was glowing green.

"I'll be darned, you were right," said Jim.

"Yeah," warned Tim. "This means that there is an *endosym* somewhere up ahead."

Tim pulled out his 40 cal H&K, carefully pulled the slide back to ensure a round was chambered. He held the gun in his right hand and the flashlight in his left.

Jim felt for the outline of the 9mm pistol in his front pants pocket. His heart rate quickened. He could feel his heart pound in his chest. This was unreal. Not even in Iraq while he was commanding his battalion did he feel so much stress.

Cautiously, they moved forward through the partially collapsed brick tunnel. Jim picked each step carefully, willing himself to keep on going although the engineer inside him warned him to turn around. Not safe, he knew. Not structurally safe. They continued another one hundred feet.

At the next corner, Jim saw three openings to the right. Tim stepped ahead and clicked off his light, indicating to Jim that he should do the same. The only light came from the emerald glow of the leopard tooth. They both moved ahead. The intensity of the tooth's brightness seemed to increase as they continued ahead.

They both stopped. Tim pointed to his ear and Jim nodded in response. They both heard chanting coming from up ahead.

Tim pushed the tooth back inside his T-shirt, and then he slowly moved down the hallway toward the mysterious sound.

Both men blinked their eyes to make a better assessment of the interior. It seemed like they had entered an underground building. Of course, they were under the ground. They both knew that, but it appeared that they had entered something distinct. A long hallway with evenly spaced doors ran down the right side. Each was open. Ahead, a yellow flickering light streamed downward. They could hear the hiss of gas from Coleman lanterns.

The chanting increased as they stepped forward. At the end of the hallway, they saw even more lantern light.

Jim slowly dipped his hand into his pants pocket and brought out his pistol.

"Damn," he muttered under his breath. His hand had begun to shake so badly that he hooked his flashlight onto his belt and gripped the pistol with both hands to keep it still.

The first room on the right lit by lantern light revealed tables, chairs, books, and partially eaten packages of chips and cookies. The second room contained air mattresses, blankets and four piles of neatly stacked cadet uniforms.

"Shit," he whispered. It looked as if people could live down here undetected for several days in a row.

At the third room, Jim gagged at an unbelievably foul odor. He knew that smell. It was the stink of a rotting corpse. There was no light in that room, and Jim did not want to see what was inside.

At the end of the hallway, the space opened up to reveal a larger, open room. What Jim saw made no sense at all. There were four people in the room. Actually, Jim counted five people, if he included the person bound and gagged and lying on a brick altar in the middle of the room.

Three people – each totally naked – stood at one end of the altar. One was a woman. Jim recognized them as the cadets they'd seen in the mess hall.

The fourth person was none other than Butch Langston. He stood behind the man stretched out on the altar. The guy looked like an old street person – a bum – dressed in ragged clothing. Langston's arm lifted. He held a long sword overhead.

"My God!" Jim realized he was about to witness an execution. This cadet who had been a football hero only weeks earlier was now going to kill a man in cold blood.

Langston stretched, readying the sword for its fatal descent.

"No! No!" screamed Jim. "Stop! Stop right now!"

While Parkinson pleaded for the man's life, Tim fired his .40 caliber handgun. The round struck the hilt of the sword, blasting it out of Langston's hand.

But Langston didn't miss a beat. As the sword fell to the hard earth floor, Langston rushed the two men with incredible speed. Tim was just as fast. He lifted his weapon and drew a bead on Langston's forehead. His finger touched the cool metal trigger.

As quickly as it had begun, it was suddenly over. Neither Langston nor Tim completed their intended moves. Langston had frozen in place, his eyes focused on the two intruders. He seemed like a man who had lost his way. Tim gently lifted his trigger finger, yet held his stance.

A piercing scream echoed through the chamber. Tim fell to his knees, and Jim was only seconds behind him. Both were engulfed in a bright red glow. As quickly as it had come, it faded and then disappeared.

"What in the hell was that?" asked Jim.

Tim didn't answer. There was no answer.

With his right hand still pointing his weapon at Langston, Tim reached inside his shirt with his left hand and pulled out the leopard tooth. It was cold to his touch and no longer glowed green.

"Holy sh ...!" Tim yelled. Before he could spit out the rest of his oath, the ground shook under his feet. A cascade of bricks began to let loose of their mortar and crash to the floor around them.

Langston's trance evaporated and the cadet made a dash towards them. The other three cadets stood frozen in place next to the altar. Then the entire ceiling collapsed, burying the three cadets and their intended victim. Langston paused momentarily to turn and look back. Just then Tim saw a portion of the brick ceiling fall onto Langston. He fell face down, his legs buried in brick and rubble. A fine white dust filled the air, reducing visibility even more. Only the dim light from the lanterns in the adjoining rooms allowed the men to maintain their sense of direction.

Tim thrust his gun into his belt as he rushed forward and began to throw broken brick and mortar off Langston's legs. He freed the cadet's arms and dragged his unconscious body into the hallway.

"Jim, give me a hand. We have to get him out of here!"

"If he comes to, he might try to kill us. He's possessed by that *endosym* thing!" argued Jim.

"Not any more," said Tim. "The *endosym* is gone, and the leopard tooth is no longer glowing."

Tim took another look at Langston. The man was in poor shape.

"Wait here, Jim," he said. He ran into the adjoining room, returning moments later carrying two gray blankets. One was tied in a bundle. Tim spread the other blanket on the ground near Langston.

"Let's move Langston to the blanket. We can carry him that way. We've got to get out of here now," Tim said. Then he paused and stood completely still.

"Listen! Can you hear that?" Tim asked.

Jim tried to focus on a noise, but the gunshot, the scream and the rumble of falling bricks seemed to have caused a momentary loss of hearing. He closed his eyes and concentrated. Then he began to hear a low, steady rumble.

Jim stared at Tim – whatever it was, it couldn't be good.

"I don't know, but I think it's bad news. When the gun discharged, it might have caused the roof to collapse back there," said Jim.

A stream of water gushed through the debris of the collapsed room and began to swirl around their shoes. Tim reacted quickly, spreading the blanket on the floor near Langston.

"Open it up, and grab the edges. We're going to have to carry him with us," Tim yelled.

The water came up fast. It was nearly at their knees.

"Where's all this water coming from?" Tim shouted.

"It must be coming from the twenty-four-inch water line that runs along Washington. The collapse back there must have ruptured the pipe," said Jim.

"Won't they shut it off?"

"Sure, but it will take them some time."

"Won't the water tank run out?"

"I'm afraid not. It comes from Lusk Reservoir. There are millions of gallons of water in that reservoir."

"Then we need to get back to Mahan Hall, and we'd better get there fast!" Tim said.

Both men had turned on their lights and hooked them to their belts so they had hands free to carry Langston. They moved quickly, but they had to pick their steps carefully along the rough passage.

"How much farther?" Tim asked, looking back at Jim over his shoulder.

Before Jim could answer, they saw bricks splashing into the rising water around them.

"Looks like the whole tunnel is going to cave in," screamed Jim. "Move! Move fast!"

In a matter of minutes, they made it out of the brick tunnel and into the old concrete one. Finally, they reached the newer concrete portion. A heavy metal door stood between the old and new tunnels.

"Wait! Let's stop," Tim called out. "Help me close this door. If we can lock it, it may reduce the water flow."

They laid the unconscious Langston down in the two-feet deep water. The concrete was fairly level, and the water had formed a shallow lake. Tim took a second look at the cadet to verify that he was still breathing. They managed to prop his head against the wall and out of the water. It took both men to push the heavy steel door closed. They picked up their ends of the blanket and headed in the direction of Mahan Hall.

Both men were gasping with exhaustion as they plodded along through the main tunnels. Here, the water was only running in the lower grating.

"I need to stop and get a breath!" Jim said. "Tim, I'm not as young as you are."

"We can't," yelled Tim. "We have to keep going. If the old tunnel collapses, it will blast open the steel door and a wall of water will come roaring down this tunnel. If it reaches those power panels along the walls, we could be electrocuted, but that's only if we're not drowned first."

Right on cue, the lights in the tunnel went out.

"The guys in the power plant must be concerned about the same thing," concluded Jim.

Now, the only light came from the flashlights swinging from their belts. They made it to the junction and could see the mechanical room up ahead. It, too, was dark. It appeared that all power in the system had been shut down.

Then they felt the rumble.

"The rest of the tunnel is collapsing!" yelled Jim. He used the last reserves of his strength to keep moving.

Following the rumble, a strong wind rushed through the tunnel.

"The water is pushing the air," yelled Tim. "We have got to get to the steps of the balcony."

A few emergency lights were still on in the mechanical room, giving them just enough light to see the steps. They had almost made it when a wall of water burst into the mechanical room, causing them to lose their footing. They pulled the corners of the blanket close to their chests, all the while struggling to keep Langston's head above water.

As suddenly as the water had come, it quickly began receding. Within minutes, the water had reversed direction and was flowing back into the tunnel. The flood was over.

The two men found a flat spot on the wet concrete and both sat down to catch their breath. Jim leaned over to check on the cadet. He was breathing, but still unconscious.

"We've got to get him to the hospital and call in a rescue team to save those other three cadets and that guy they had tied up," said Jim.

"That's not going to happen," said Tim. "They are all dead. As a matter of fact, I am not sure their bodies will ever be recovered."

Jim considered Tim's words.

"You're right. There must be hundreds of tons of rubble on top of that room," he said. "So this *endosym* thing must be dead, too?"

"Yeah, Jim," murmured Tim.

But Tim was not sure that the *endosym* was dead. True, the tooth had stopped glowing, and Langston had seemed confused before the room began to collapse. Could the *endosym* have caused the room to collapse?

Tim didn't know. He thought that this horror had all ended six years ago. At that time he believed that Sarday was the only *endosym* in existence. Now this Duncan guy might be another one. How can they exist without us being aware that they are out there?

Right now, they needed damage control. He grabbed the bundled blanket and opened it. Inside were Langston's cadet's uniform, shoes and underwear. Tim had gathered the stack of clothing in the room when he retrieved the blankets.

"Come on. We've got to get him dressed," said Tim.

"Dressed?" asked Jim.

"This is weird enough without having him naked," said Tim.

The clothes were wet, and they had to wring them out.

"This doesn't seem right," said Jim. "This delay might cause him to die. We should call the medics."

"If he dies, so be it," said Tim. "How do we tell your bosses and the news media that four cadets were in the tunnels sacrificing victims under the orders of some demon creature? With the collapse of the tunnels, there is no proof. Do you want to spend the rest of your life labeled as a nut? Your career would end for no good reason. What we talked about at dinner is just that – talk. We can't prove that *endosyms* existed six years ago, and because of what just happened here, we still have no proof they exist today.

"Come on. Let's get him dressed then call for help. "By now, the entire academy knows that there has been a catastrophic event down here."

"You can say that again. This will cost millions of dollars to repair," said Jim.

The two of them got Langston dressed. It wasn't easy pulling on the damp clothing. It took them both longer than expected to complete the job. Then they used the emergency phone to report that they had a seriously injured cadet in the mechanical room.

As they waited for help to arrive, Tim turned to Jim.

"All right. We need to come up with a plausible story of what happened."

46

Tim Martin and Jim Parkinson sat with academy brass in the superintendent's office at 1600 hours on monday. The administrative offices were operating on emergency power.

Joining in the briefing were Col. Brad Ross, chief of staff; Major General Don Moring, commandant of cadets; and Lt. General Wallace Scow, the academy superintendent.

"Jesus, I can't believe this whole thing. Washington Road has dropped twenty feet. Part of the plain has sunken ten feet," said Scow.

"We'll have to inspect all the electrical panels in the tunnels. It will cost a fortune to repair damaged insulation. Worst of all, we have three dead firsties and another one in a coma with brain damage. If he gets out of this alive, he'll likely have to be institutionalized for the rest of his life. The engineers say that it would be too dangerous to attempt to recover the bodies. So we'll have to deal with next of kin. We'll have to come up with some memorial to honor their deaths.

"And, damn it, they were all screwing off when it happened. Hell, for all I know, they might have caused this disaster," grumbled Scow.

"Jim, I still am having trouble grasping what you and special agent Martin were doing in the tunnels at 2300 hours."

"Sir, the Parkinsons and my family served in Africa together. We were having dinner at Bear Mountain when a cadet called Dean Parkinson and said that some of his classmates were planning some kind of prank in the tunnels. We decided to check it out.

"When we got down there, some old tunnels collapsed. We found one cadet, Langston, injured. Then the water started coming in, but we still managed to get him out. We didn't see the other cadets," Tim reported confidently.

"Your dad was in the army?" asked the General Moring.

"He still is, sir."

"What's his name?"

"Hank Martin," answered Tim.

"Lt. General Hank Martin, the deputy chief of staff for operations?" asked General Scow.

"Yes, sir," said Tim.

"Damn," said Scow. "Your dad and I were roommates here," he laughed. "Hell, we pulled a few pranks here ourselves. But at least we didn't kill ourselves," he sighed.

"I guess now we start damage control," Scow said as he turned to the chief of staff.

"Brad, I want to review the press release before it goes out."

Tim sat back and listened to the conversation. Whew, he thought, they bought the story. Now, he needed to get some sleep and get back to New York City. He would like to keep the *endosym's* existence from Sam.

But they didn't keep secrets from each other, and she knew better than almost anyone that *endosyms* really do exist.

47

DUNCAN MCDOUGAL CHUCKLED WHILE HE SAT AT A CORNER TABLE IN A manhattan starbucks.

He was beginning to get a taste for espresso, but more than that, he enjoyed watching the customers come and go.

"Stupid mortals," he snickered under his breath. These creatures were so foolish. Little did they realize that the time of their enslavement was coming sooner than they would ever expect. These ignorant beasts would soon give up their essence and give rise to a new legion of *endosyms*, the man-demons who would take over the Earth.

Duncan had learned a great deal in his transition from human to *endosym*. The simple Christians thought that a man possessed by a demon had an unclean spirit abiding in his human body. The Catholics had even ritualized an exorcism to drive out the demons. But Duncan knew that their understanding was far too superficial. The demon changed a human at the cellular level, transforming it into a totally new creature. The DNA sequence would reveal a combination of human and demon.

Even more unique was the *endosym's* brain. No longer were man and demon simply two separate spirits residing in one body. Instead, it was total assimilation – the two brains were fused as one. Their thoughts, memories and desires were intermingled.

The more rational human might control the creature's thought process. If the wild demon was dominant, it determined the *endosym's* thinking. In Duncan's case, his human side had taken total control.

Duncan had used his impressive powers to assume a different identity. He now dressed in Armani, wore silk shirts and strolled confidently in Italian leather shoes. He had become Harold Weinstein. The passport photo was of Weinstein. Any fool could see that the faces didn't match. But that didn't matter. Duncan could convince others to believe whatever he wished, as long as they were nearby. Yet Duncan had no plans to be around others who might know the real Weinstein. Duncan was headed for Edinburgh, Scotland. He'd use Weinstein's passport, ID and credit cards. Weinstein would no longer need the documents – his cold body was rolled in a Persian carpet and left in the bathroom of the dead man's flat.

Recently, Duncan altered his plans.

He had discovered that the woman, Constance, was descended from his mother's original coven. Moreover, she practiced witchcraft, used his former home to sell objects of the occult, and she led workshops to instruct would-be witches in the dark arts.

"And that, my love, proves my point," Duncan had told the young woman while pointing at a cracked oil painting above the mantel. When she turned to study it, Constance gasped.

"That's you," she whispered. "That's really you – the one we've been waiting for."

The likeness was unquestionable. The painting was commissioned in the late 1700s when Duncan lived in the house.

Since his return, other witches, warlocks and willing followers had flocked to Newburgh to listen to his teachings. Once the human sacrifices had begun, his power had multiplied. He now controlled a cadre of cadets as well as the women and men in his coven. Their service and obedience awarded them powers beyond those of normal humans.

He had come to the conclusion that the demon inside him was not a spiritual being, but a living creature from another dimension. For centuries, humans were terrified by the idea that the demons controlled the humans. Duncan believed that the reverse was more likely true. He was determined to open the doorway between the two worlds by selecting the strongest hosts – those who were powerful enough to wrest control from their internal demons. These super man-demons would rule the world.

The key to his plan was to learn how to use the ancient statues to open the portal to the demon world. Already, fate had taken his side.

As the number of believers grew, he was certain to find the hosts who would serve in his new world order.

When he returned to West Point that night, Duncan encountered a force that challenged his power. He discovered that two humans had interrupted a sacrificial ceremony conducted by Langston. Duncan had warned the cadet never to attempt the ritual without him, but Langston had defied him.

Each human sacrifice had enhanced Duncan's powers, but despite the two centuries of ritual executions, he wasn't yet as strong as he desired. Had he been stronger, he would have crushed the two humans. But one of the humans radiated an opposing power. All Duncan could do now was to destroy the site and escape detection. He raced through the tunnels winding his way through haphazard piles of rocks and bricks. He wound his way through the cascading bricks and finally came out into the open by the railroad tracks where he had left Langston's Dodge Charger.

With the interference from the two humans and the destruction of the ceremonial site in the tunnels, he had decided to relocate to his ancestral home in Edinburgh.

He drove to the city the people had named New York. It had grown beyond comprehension in only two centuries. Even Duncan, with his amazing brain, had to marvel at the wonder of the city. Although the metropolis was new to him, he was confident he would find a safe place to sacrifice more humans and continue to build his strength. He would keep a low profile while seeking the appropriate hosts for the man-demons.

He had met the human Harold Weinstein in an all-male bar. He quickly discovered that this was a meeting place for men who sought out other males for sexual pleasure. Duncan agreed to visit Weinstein's apartment where the wealthy man satisfied his lust. He had consented to Weinstein's bold requests, but it would be Duncan who would eventually benefit from the encounter.

When Weinstein finished, Duncan had snapped the man's neck. He took the chance meeting as an opportunity to feed off the man's essence, adding to his own powers. It was easy – very easy. Now, using the man's identity, Duncan was ready to travel to Scotland and continue his quest to conquer the world. In two days he would ride in one of the great shining metal birds called airplanes that carried humans through the air.

Duncan tipped the paper cup to his lips, savoring the last swallow of the strong coffee. He dabbed at the corners of his mouth with a paper napkin. He casually brushed croissant crumbs from the table top, allowing them to fall to the floor. Yet he still wasn't finished. Watching the foolish humans was too entertaining. He enjoyed observing the parade of his future slaves. He wasn't ready to leave just yet.

Then it happened.

For the first time in his life, Duncan felt a deep-seated fear. It emanated from memories stored within the demon side of his brain. Upset and frightened, Duncan sensed the presence of a human who could identify him as an *endosym*. Duncan somehow knew that thousands of years ago a similar human power had diminished the *endosyms'* dominance of Earth. Now that power had reappeared.

"Twice! It's happened two times now!" Duncan said under his breath. He shook his head, astonished at the double setback. First, something had interrupted his work at the academy. Now, this uneasy feeling evoked fear and anxiety.

He stood and walked out onto the street. He turned to the left, stopped, and looked to the right. What human could possibly be the source of his angst?

It was unusually cold, with temperatures in the low thirties. People walked briskly, wearing dark knit caps, thick scarves, heavy wool coats and tall leather boots. They reacted to the weather, yet Duncan ignored the cold. He fell into step with the others who were going somewhere and nowhere. He'd know when he was close to the source of his fear. He'd feel its presence. He'd destroy the human and eliminate the threat.

A tall, light-skinned Negro woman approached, walking confidently toward him. In his past life, a person looking like this would have been the product of a liaison between slave owner and one of his human possessions. That was no longer the case. Now people came in random shades. The darker ones called themselves blacks or African-Americans.

This one towered above the others. From her appearance and stately walk, she proclaimed herself a step above the common people. A member of society's upper class, this woman walked with purpose.

She ignored him; yet he felt the stirring of a presence.

He followed her at a discreet distance. She turned into the lobby of a building and came to a stop before a bank of elevators.

48

WHEN THE DOORS OPENED, HE JOINED THE OTHERS WHO CROWDED INTO THE elevator. He held his breath, fearing that the dark-skinned young woman would acknowledge him. If that happened, he would be forced to kill everyone around him. Yet she completely ignored him. When the elevator came to a halt at the fifth floor, she stepped out. He followed.

She moved down a hallway and entered an office. Interior windows allowed him to observe her approach to a reception desk. A number of women waited in the office area. The dark woman smiled as she spoke to the receptionist and then took a seat.

Duncan was startled at the sound of the elevator doors opening behind him. Another woman waddled toward him and reached out her hand to open the office door. He used his powers to cause the woman to freeze in place.

"What place is this?" he asked.

She told him that this was the place where women visited when they were with child.

"Ah, a midwife," he concluded, releasing her from his powers.

So, he understood, the tall Negro woman was pregnant. Then the revelation struck him – it was not the woman who sent out the signals – it was the child inside her womb. It was no threat now. Until it reached maturity, the new life was no reason for concern. Yet, why wait? The solution was simple – the child must be destroyed now.

He could just walk into the midwife's office and kill the woman. Yet in this modern world, even with Duncan's powers, escape would be difficult. A better course would be to follow the woman, find out where she lived and then destroy her.

Duncan hid in a corner by the elevator. When the woman left the midwife's office, he could follow her to a more convenient location. He waited patiently again. Later that same afternoon, Duncan had learned everything he could about Samantha Dixon Martin.

Even though he'd studied the woman's life, he still did not fully comprehend the child's threat to his kind. Memories passed between the generations of those who had come before him. He knew that thousands of years ago, a human had amassed sufficient power to stop an ancient invasion. The Earth survived because of this one, powerful human. Perhaps this unborn child would become one of those creatures strong enough to thwart Duncan's plans of world domination.

It didn't really matter – the simple solution was to kill this Samantha Dixon Martin. Unfortunately, the armed men, known as the police, had made a simple murder more difficult. Their tools included modern machines that captured an image and allowed these police officers to observe someone's actions.

But Duncan came up with a plan. The inventive humans had also created a vehicle that would serve him well. He would use a horseless carriage to crush her body and steal her spirit. Eventually, she would exit this building. When she did, he would end her life. He continued to wait patiently.

When he saw her leave the building, Duncan called for one of the yellow horseless carriages that carried people around the city in exchange for touching their plastic cards. When one came to the curb, Duncan rapped on the driver's window.

"Can I help you, sir?" asked the man with a wide band of cloth wrapped tightly around his head.

"I want your horseless carriage," said Duncan.

The man said nothing as he slid over to the passenger side and stared straight ahead. Duncan climbed inside and sat behind the steering wheel. He could see the woman walking along the sidewalk. The motor in the carriage continued to rumble. He felt for the lever that would make the carriage move forward. On Cadet Langston's carriage, the lever was located between the two front seats. But he couldn't find the lever in this machine.

He almost panicked. Then he noticed the letters behind the steering wheel. Moving the lever caused the tires to turn. He pulled it from the letter P to the letter D. The carriage obeyed and moved forward. He had already learned how to use the right pedal to hasten the carriage and the left pedal to halt it. He pressed his right foot to the floor, and the carriage shot forward.

He scanned the crowd, searching for his victim.

49

SEEING HER OBSTETRICAN THIS AFTERNOON HAD ACTUALLY BEEN ENJOYABLE.
Sam actually liked the idea of being pregnant. Every time she came to Shelly's office, she learned something new, and she plotted her baby's growth.

The couple had checked the calendar and made some critical decisions. On Monday she would make the announcement to her boss and co-workers. Some were already noticing the subtle changes in Sam's belly and breasts. They talked quietly among themselves after seeing her at lunch and during breaks. Obviously, Sam had something to celebrate.

They had decided to wait another three weeks to make a Thanksgiving announcement to their families. Tim's mom and dad, Lindsey and Hank, would join the Dixon family in Washington for the holiday. Sam had to grin; Lindsey would be ecstatic. The baby would be the first grandchild for the Martins. Sam smiled again. Wow, would this be one spoiled child!

Sam was overjoyed when she imagined the family's response. Everyone would excitedly anticipate the baby's birth. Shelly had projected a mid-January due date. Already the baby was kicking up a storm. When Sam felt movement, she'd call out to Tim, and he would lean his ear to her belly and lightly caress her skin. Sometimes the baby would hold still; other times it threw a knee or an elbow at Tim's hand. He had no choice but to conclude that this child was not only a boy, but would become an accomplished athlete, probably a soccer player like his father.

"Sure you don't want to know the baby's gender?" Tim had asked Sam once again.

"I'm sure," she said with a smile. "I'd rather play this guessing game with you!"

Despite their "baby talk," Sam was fairly certain that Tim was right.

Now she was on her way home. She left the doctor's office and walked quickly along the sidewalk. She grasped the lapels of her heavy coat and held them tightly around her neck. It was getting colder. After all, it was nearly winter. The rare October warm spell had passed.

She'd taken her doctor's advice and had gone shopping. The oversized sweaters helped disguise her changing shape. The stretch slacks with the elastic waistband had been a godsend. At six and a half months along, she was reaching the upper limits of hiding her condition. Fortunately, Sam was tall and lean, allowing plenty of growing space for the baby. It still rode fairly high, but that would change as her pregnancy advanced. Well, it really didn't matter if people guessed the truth. After the Monday announcement everyone in the office would know.

On the way to the subway, she passed the newsstand and noticed the magazines with stories about pregnant actresses. She was one of them now, part of the baby crowd. She stopped to buy a magazine to read on the subway.

Suddenly, the baby gave a jolt. It began to thrash about in her womb. This was an unusual event. It startled her. She dropped her hands from her lapels and held her belly from the bottom, cradling her precious cargo. She worried about miscarrying. She wondered if she should call her doctor or go straight to the hospital. She considered going back to the television station and asking security to call an ambulance. She whirled around to check behind her.

A yellow taxi was heading directly at her. It was going too fast. It looked like it was going to jump the curb and clear the sidewalk.

It wasn't even four o'clock in the afternoon. There was still plenty of light to see the driver. When Sam finally focused on the face, she screamed in terror. The driver resembled the demon she'd seen when they had been inside the cavern in Virginia. Tim called it an *endosym*. She could see the two horns and the pale white eyes. The taxi was being driven by a demon from hell.

She had to get out of the way. She threw herself to the left, but she was too slow. The front fender clipped her right hip and forced her upward. Pain surged through her body as she slammed into the metal shelves of the newsstand. Newspapers, paperback books, candy bars and souvenir trinkets flew through the air.

She landed on the tangled pile and heard the vendor shouting for help. She caught a glimpse of the taxi's taillights as it swung back onto the street, ripping gouges along the side of a parked car. Yes, the demon was still there. She saw it get out of the taxi and glare at her.

Now she was surrounded by dozens of concerned bystanders. Someone knelt beside her.

"An ambulance is on the way," said a man holding his cell phone in one hand while wrapping his strong fingers around her slender hand.

"Don't try to move," the man cautioned.

Move? She couldn't move. She felt as if she had broken every bone in her body.

She closed her eyes and waited for darkness to fall.

50

SAM'S DOCTOR HAD FINALLY ALLOWED HER TO SIT UPRIGHT ON THE EXAM table in Bellevue's Emergency Room.

She was still a little dizzy, but she resisted the urge to fall back on the table. She managed a smile for the three people standing around her – her doctor, Shelly; the intern in the emergency room; and her husband, Tim. Although she was still in pain, at least she was alive.

"Well, Sam, I can find no problem with the baby. It's perfectly healthy, the heartbeat fine, and under no stress whatsoever," Shelly assured her.

"You have a large hematoma on your right hip. We had to stitch up that cut on your arm. Apparently, it happened when you hit a sharp shelf on the newsstand. And, needless to say, you have minor cuts and abrasions in a number of places. I think we should keep you at least overnight."

"No," said Sam firmly. "I want to go home."

Tim held her hand tenderly.

"Honey, maybe it would be a good idea to stay in the hospital to-night. I will stay right here with you."

"No, I want to go home," she sobbed.

"All right," said Shelly. "I don't want you stressing the baby. If you go home, we need to arrange for an ambulance to at least drive you there."

Tim rode in the ambulance with Sam. Tim and the driver used a wheelchair to move her up to the flat. Shelly restricted her to a mild, over-the-counter pain medication. She warned that anything stronger might affect the unborn fetus.

Tim helped her into a nightgown. Sam usually wore a large T-shirt and panties as bedclothes. Now the panties were too tight around her waist, so she had switched to a short nightgown. Tim lifted her legs carefully to ease her into their bed. He was pulling up the covers when he heard his cell phone go off.

"Agent Martin," he said. He listened to the man on the other end, asked several questions, clicked the cover shut, and returned the phone to his pocket.

"Who was that?" asked Sam.

"NYPD," he said. "They've finished interviewing the driver. It's weird. The driver claims he doesn't remember running the taxi up onto the sidewalk, hitting you, or crashing into the parked car."

"Well, I have the bruises to prove that it happened," moaned Sam.

"Funny, the guy is a respected member of the Indian community, and he has no prior accident record."

"A Sikh-like man wearing a turban?" asked Sam.

"Right," said Tim.

"No, no," she said. "The guy with the turban was the passenger; someone else was driving."

"You're sure?" asked Tim.

"I was there, I know what I saw. There was someone else driving. He got out of the taxi and walked away."

She sucked in her breath; she wasn't about to tell Tim that the guy looked like an *endosym*.

"Wait a minute," said Tim. He pulled out his cell phone to call back the police officer.

"Sergeant Morgan? This is Agent Martin again. My wife thought she saw two people in the front seat of the taxi. She thought the Indian Sikh was a passenger, not the driver."

"I see," said Tim, "Twenty witnesses? Sure, I understand. I know that trauma can do that."

He switched off the phone.

"Well?" asked Sam.

"Multiple witnesses say that there was only one person in the taxi. No one got out."

"But, I am certain – absolutely certain – that there were two."

"I know, Hon, but it was broad daylight, and the street was crowded with people. You've suffered a traumatic experience. I want you to close your eyes and try to get some sleep."

"I'll try," she said turning her head into her pillow.

Sam was certain she hadn't been mistaken. She knew an *endosym* when she saw one.

51

It was impossible to sleep in the stifling heat.

Whenever Sam moved, her body hurt. Her hip throbbed where the taxi fender had hit her. She managed to nap on and off, but only when she was lying flat on her back. She tried to push away the covers. Surely, the extra blankets were adding to her discomfort.

She blinked, suddenly aware that there were no covers. And, she wondered, what about the bright light above her? With her eyes closed, she still saw redness through her eyelids. She pressed her hands over her eyes. Gradually, she adjusted to the brightness.

Instead of staring at the ceiling in her New York apartment, she saw only blue sky and golden sunlight. She leaned to her right, and felt Tim's back beside her. He had curled up on his side, facing away from her. She reached out to touch his shoulder.

"Where are we?" Sam asked.

They were lying in soft red dirt in the middle of a primitive village in the jungles of Jamaica or maybe Africa. Strange, she thought. She was wearing the same short nightgown she'd had at home.

"Tim, Tim!" she pleaded. "Wake up! Where are we?"

"Not again," he groaned. "Not again."

"Again? What do you mean 'again'?"

"In Hawaii," he mumbled. "Seven years ago. Like the dream I had seven years ago."

"Whatever are you talking about?" she asked.

"Come on," Tim said, getting to his feet. "Let me help you up." He reached out for Sam's hand and pulled her gently to her feet.

"Can you walk?" he asked.

"I think so, but my hip hurts like hell," she said.

They were in a village. Small huts nestled on a stretch of low-lying land. In the distance, Sam could make out rugged mountains covered by dense trees and shrubs. To the east was a tabletop mountain covered with a triple canopy of lush green trees. Unlike so many other forested lands maimed by clear-cutting, the surrounding area appeared to be a thick blanket of dark green – truly a virgin forest.

She was still too hot. The tropical sun warmed her back. Tiny droplets of perspiration dotted her forehead and began to stream down her face. It was humid – impossibly humid. She recalled her family's villa in Jamaica – it was hot there, too. And she remembered that vacation when she and her twin brother, Eddie, were sixteen. They had gone on an African safari. Wherever they were now was clearly in the tropics – certainly not in New York.

Supported by Tim, the two walked by the thatched huts and passed by gardens. These were well-tended farms, she realized. Orderly rows of vegetable crops were enclosed by loose fences; herds of healthy goats roamed freely.

If this was a dream, it was far too realistic. Sam seldom dreamed, and when she did, she couldn't recall any details of the dream. This didn't seem like a dream – it was like she had truly been transported to a tropical world.

Smoke rose from cooking fires behind huts, creating a strange mingling of smells – burning charcoal, roasting meat and steaming vegetables. She saw animals, crops and primitive cooking fires – but not a single human resident.

"Come on," said Tim, tugging on her arm. "They're waiting for us."

"They?" she asked.

"You'll see," he said looking at her with a tender smile.

They walked across the clearing toward the huts on the far side of the village.

"Ouch!" she exclaimed, reaching down and rubbing the sole of her foot. The hot sun on the dirt path made it hard to walk. The bottoms of her bare feet felt like they burned with each step.

"It will be cooler once we get in the shade," said Tim.

"I thought you couldn't feel pain in dreams," mumbled Sam.

"Not a dream," said Tim.

Sam waited for Tim to explain where they were and what was happening, but he focused on moving ahead out of the sunlight and into the shade.

"Wow!" gasped Sam. "Look at that! Look at that, Tim!"

When they had reached the last hut nearest the forest, they had both stopped suddenly. Twenty-five feet in front of them stood a huge adult leopard. It groomed its paws and seemed oblivious to the presence of the couple. Stranger still was the second animal sitting on its haunches beside the leopard – it was a gray domestic cat, like any other housecat so common back home.

The leopard stopped its licking and turned its head to the right. The cat's attention followed the leopard's lead. Sam did the same. She saw an old man and an old woman sitting on a bench built of rough-sawn planks. Both were shirtless and barefoot. The man wore a short leather loincloth. The smooth top of his bald head poked out from a fringe of white fuzzy hair.

"I knew you would be here," said Tim as he smiled and waved. They returned his greeting.

"I see you married da gal," said the woman. Her wide mouth formed a delighted grin.

"Of course, dey be married, you silly ole woman," scolded the man. "How else could dey be here together?"

"Who are these people?" whispered Sam.

"That's Chea Geebe. He was a *zo* who lived in this village. The woman is Michelle Johnson. Remember the gray cat in the cavern in Virginia? That's it, sitting next to Chea's leopard."

"Why are we here?" Sam dared to ask.

"Because of dem *endosyms*," Chea answered.

"The *endosyms?*" she asked, startled by his use of the word.

"Dey know dat baby be inside you. Dey afeared he be out to stop der planning. If dat baby don't make it, it be de end of all peoples. We all just turn into slaves for dem devils," he said.

Then he interrupted his train of thought. His sad eyes turned toward Sam.

"You know dey try to get you today. Dat baby he done warn you. But you be lucky. You done see it in its true shape."

"You mean the *endosym* that tried to run me down?"

"What *endosym?*" asked Tim. Sam hadn't mentioned any demon.

"I couldn't tell anyone. They would say I was crazy."

"Not me," said Tim. "I've seen them before."

Chea ignored their talk. He had more to tell.

"You be in big danger til de chil be born. Its mind is already put out feelers. De *endosyms* dey know it bein your womb. Once out on its own, de chil know how to hide its thoughts from dem creatures. When chil be grown, it be able to get dem."

"Wait, this makes no sense," said Samantha. "Besides, how can I stop them?"

"You must hide until dat baby be born. To do dat, you gotta travel to dis place and hole up here until de baby be born."

"That's not possible. There is no way that I am going to have my baby in an African village!" Sam shrieked, shaking her head furiously from side to side.

Suddenly, she was in a darkened room. She was in their own bed. What a crazy dream, she thought.

"You're back," said Tim.

"You mean awake, don't you?" asked Sam.

"No, back," he said. "I just arrived also."

Sam reached out to turn on the bedside lamp.

"What the hell are you talking about?" she asked, dropping her arm. She stared at Tim, unable to grasp what he was saying.

"Zigda, he said.

"What?" she asked, "Whatever are you talking about? Do you mean you had the same dream?"

"It wasn't a dream," Tim assured her. "It wasn't a dream."

Sam rose on her elbows, trying to sit up.

"Ouch, it hurts," she said, falling back on the bed. Certainly, the bruises weren't a dream. She reached for the light again and turned the switch. She rolled toward Tim who had pushed back the covers.

"Tim, what's going on? You've got to tell me what's going on."

"Before I say anything, I want you to look at the sheets."

Sam saw a red powder – no, not powder, but red dirt discoloring the white sheets.

"Now, take a look at the bottoms of your feet," Tim said calmly.

"I can't, Tim," Sam cried. "My body hurts so much. There's no way I can sit up high enough to look at my feet."

"Then, look at mine," Tim said. He lifted his right foot so that Sam could see it. "See this? It's covered with red dirt from our trip to the village of Zigda."

"Timothy Martin, that is simply impossible."

"Then tell me what just happened?"

"All right," she said. "I'll analyze it as a reporter. Let me interview you about what just happened."

She asked the questions, and Tim told her the details of his dream. Sam nodded. He was right.

"OK, we dreamed the same dream. But it still has to be a dream."

"What about the dirt?" asked Tim.

"Maybe we got something on our feet before we went to bed."

"Come on, Sam. It happened."

"Wait a minute!" Sam said, holding up her hand to halt his words. "Didn't you say that this had happened before?"

"It wasn't a dream," insisted Tim.

"Hey, let me call it a dream! I am trying not to lose my mind."

"All right, it was a dream," conceded Tim.

"So there!" she said. "I knew I was right."

Tim stared at the floor. He dragged his toes through the red dirt, making parallel lines on the floor. Sam felt she'd been too harsh.

"All right," she said. "When did this happen before?"

"Do you remember our trip to visit my parents in Hawaii? Do you remember our last night there?"

Sam nodded. She would listen to his story, even if it didn't make any sense. She didn't remember him telling her about a dream.

"Chea and Michelle warned me about the *endosym* in Virginia," he began. Even the thought of that terror sent cold chills down his spine.

"Well, why didn't they just call or send you a letter?"

"Because they are both dead."

"Dead!" squealed Sam. "You have got to be kidding me – what is this some sort of supernatural mumbo jumbo?"

"I really don't know, since I was just a teenager when I was first in that village. I have had these visions about *endosyms*. Surely, you haven't forgotten about what happened in Virginia. Then that coven business happened last month at West Point, and now you almost died at the hands of one of them."

"I know, I know," she agreed. "But I just want the world to be normal."

"I know, honey, but you were almost killed yesterday, and you say that you saw an *endosym* at the wheel. Sam, get real here. They're telling us our son is in danger."

"There is no way that I am going to Africa to give birth to our baby. Shelley Badger will deliver our son at Bellevue, and there's no more discussion."

"All right, all right, you need to stay in bed and rest. I'll go out and get us some bagels and cream cheese for breakfast. We'll talk about this later."

He got dressed. He pulled a warm jacket out of the closet, slipped it on, and headed out the front door without looking back.

52

Tim had to grasp the handrail in the elevator as he rode to the lobby of their apartment building. His stomach felt queasy; he had trouble catching his breath.

Now, people had a better understanding of post-traumatic stress, but only those who suffer from it can truly understand what it does to someone. For the past twelve years, Tim had battled his demons. If his colleagues at the FBI were ever to learn what had happened to him in Africa, he would be fired and probably committed to a psychiatric hospital.

Only a handful of people would believe that he was experiencing a supernatural event, dealing with something beyond the scope of the normal senses. Sure, the nut cases would rally around him, but whatever was happening now could destroy his family.

Endosyms defied rational explanation. He had prayed that the past horrors were behind them. He had hoped that they could live a normal, rational life like millions of people enjoyed. It wasn't the bad guys that he feared; it was this thing that had crossed the invisible line between dreams and reality.

53

WHEN TIM REACHED THE LOBBY, HE SAW THE BROAD BACK OF THE DOORMAN standing at the main door.

"Good morning, sir," the man said as he reached to open the door.

"Morning," Tim mumbled as he passed through the doorway and stepped out on the sidewalk. The cool autumn air felt good after the heat of the African jungle.

"Wait a minute," Tim said softly. "Just wait a minute here." Something was wrong. They'd lived in the building for three years. He thought he knew all the doormen, their shifts and even the rare substitute doormen who filled in when the regulars were sick or on vacation. He knew their names. He had delivered the holiday wine, candy or fruit baskets that Sam had put together for them. But, for the life of him, he didn't know who this one was. Tim felt an uncertainty about this strange man.

It was that tattoo, he realized. When the man had reached out to open the door, Tim had noticed the tattoo on the back of the man's hand. Normally, Tim had ignored tattoos, but his FBI training had taught him to pay attention to body markings. Some were gang markings; some had some other special significance.

This man's tattoo was a pentagram, a five-sided star. Was this guy a witch or a warlock, or was the tattoo just the random selection by the man as a teenager who wanted to look tough? He didn't want to think about it now. He pushed these thoughts to the back of his mind.

54

Tim made his way to the corner deli and bought a half dozen bagels, a small container of cream cheese and a couple of red apples. The pentagram tattoo on the back of the doorman's hand continued to haunt his thoughts. He clutched his brown paper bag close to his chest and jogged back to his building. He'd been gone long enough. He wanted to be back on the bed with Sam and their breakfast.

When he reached his building, he pushed on the front door. Usually, it opened immediately, but this time it held fast. He tried the door handle, but it, too, wouldn't give.

"Damn thing must be locked," he growled as he leaned on the door buzzer, pushing it angrily again and again. Sometimes a doorman was on the phone and couldn't open the door right away.

He held up both hands, shielded his eyes, and peered through the glass door. The lobby seemed totally unoccupied. No doorman, no residents. He focused on the elevator light.

"Four," he said. "It's on the fourth floor. My floor."

Now, Tim was more than angry. He felt his heartbeat in his throat. He pounded on the door and rattled the handle. He pulled his pistol. Even when off duty, agents carried their weapon. Using the side of his gun like a hammer, he tried to break the glass. But the tempered glass wouldn't give. The gun just bounced off the window.

Now, he had reached his boiling point.

"Shit!" he shouted. If he was wrong now, he faced dismissal from the FBI. But right now, he didn't care. He held the pistol firmly in his right hand, stepped back and aimed at the door.

His shot echoed off buildings all along the street. Thousands of crystal splinters carpeted the entryway. He stepped gingerly into the lobby, expecting to see the worried doorman looking at him in fear.

But no one was there. Tim was alone in the lobby. He rushed to the elevator and pushed the up button, but the car didn't move. The fourth floor light was still on. That meant that the door was being held open on his floor. He ran to the stairwell. When he tried to open the door, it wouldn't budge. It was locked. But it had never been locked before. He wouldn't be able to knock it down; it was a solid metal fire door.

Tim had his usual reaction to an immoveable force: After he had used his physical strength, he saw only one resort – his weapon once again.

"Oh, hell," he said. Then his granddad's words came back to him in that old saying: "In for a penny, in for a pound." He'd already fired once, why not twice?

He aimed at the lock and pulled the trigger. The round struck above the lock, sending fragments of lead back at him, nicking his cheek.

This wasn't like in the movies. There, when you fire a round, the door flies open. He had no choice – he fired again. Then he fired twice more, each time closing his eyes in hopes that the ricochets wouldn't blind him. He kicked out with his right foot and the door fell backward with no resistance.

He held his weapon in a two-handed hold and rushed up four flights. He pushed open the fourth floor fire door and stepped into the hallway. He paused; he was breathing too fast, too hard.

"Can't stop. Not now," he said, barely able to get the words past his lips. He swung the gun to the left and then quickly to the right.

"Oh, God, no!" he whispered. The door to their apartment stood wide open. He rushed to the doorway and stepped inside the living room.

The strange doorman stood in the middle of the room. He turned and sneered.

Tim fired two shots striking the man directly in the face. Blood and brain matter splattered against the wall behind him and streamed in rivulets to the hardwood floor below. The man's body was thrown backwards by the force of the .40-caliber rounds. He crumpled in a broken heap against the living room sofa.

"Sam! Sam!" screamed Tim. "Where are you, Sam?"

The bedroom door was partially open. He shoved the door all the way open with his left hand, his gun gripped tightly in his right, his finger on the trigger. He would never forget the sight he witnessed – it would haunt his nightmares for the rest of his life.

A large dark-haired woman, perhaps in her fifties, pressed Sam against the wall. One hand was wrapped firmly around Sam's throat; the other held a ten-inch butcher knife. She raised the blade and aimed its sharp tip at his wife's swollen belly.

What could he do? If he fired now, the bullets would pass through the woman. They'd strike Sam and their unborn baby.

Tim dove to the floor and rolled to his right. He lifted his arm and fired a round upward through the woman's side. She should have died right then, but somehow she stayed on her feet. She came at him, holding the knife high over her head.

"The child will die," she shrieked. "We will not stop until we've cut out its heart!"

Tim, still lying on his side, fired four more rounds. She fell to the floor, but still didn't die. Her wide-open eyes seemed to continue to leer at Tim.

He held the weapon steady and fired point-blank at her forehead.

"Die, bitch!" he said. Tim could no longer see her eyes. They were obliterated by chunks of bone and tissue.

"Sam! Sam!" he cried as he gathered his sobbing wife in his arms. "Sam, Sam, it will all be OK," he said softly into her ear.

"I promise that all three of us will be OK," he vowed. "If it's the last thing I ever do ..."

55

"WE ARE BEGINNING OUR DESCENT TO EDINBURGH INTERNATIONAL AIRPORT. Please adjust your seatbacks to the upright position," the pilot announced.

Duncan McDougal pushed the button on the armrest of the first-class seat and felt the seat back move slowly forward. He looked down at the small computer screen in his lap.

He didn't have much time to kill, but he did have a few minutes to re-visit some of his favorite sites. He rejected the standard encyclopedic descriptions and went directly to those dealing with Scotland's mystic and murderous past.

Humans have inhabited the Edinburgh area since the Bronze Age. Traces of primitive settlements are found throughout the Pentland Hills. Celtic cultures from central Europe influenced the area, bringing mystic religions of the Druids. Many historians believe the Druids built the strange rock monoliths found throughout the area.

The Druids maintained strict order within the clan. Both male and female sorcerers were able to communicate with the spirit world.

Survival was based on successful crops and healthy animals. Disease, droughts and storms were all believed to have been the result of contact with unclean spirits. Defeating spirits required powerful magic. Human sacrifice was often necessary to appease the spiritual beings.

Christianity was introduced around four hundred A.D. In an attempt to divert the people from the Druids' powerful nature-based religion, traditional Celtic practices were incorporated into church rituals. The result was a religion of magic and wonder. Celtic Christianity had one foot in the new world, and the other in the land of the faeries.

Despite attempts to meld the differing beliefs, the battle between those holding onto the old beliefs and those committed to Christianity continued to rage. Christians were taught to fear sorcerers and witches in order to prevent demonic forces from influencing mankind. Between 1563 and 1700, thousands of innocent men and women were accused of practicing witchcraft. Many were tortured, and as many as four thousand were executed.

Duncan reluctantly shut down his computer as requested by the pilot. He closed his eyes and allowed visions of the mystic past to fill his thoughts. He loved those words – "sorcerers, witches, demonic forces ... human sacrifice."

Duncan's daydreaming was interrupted by the jolt of the plane's wheels touching down on the tarmac.

He joined the other passengers who were the first to disembark. At the luggage carrousel, he pushed forward to be among the first to retrieve his suitcase. He spotted the large bag. Its nametag indicated that it belonged to Harold Weinstein. Despite weighing more than a hundred pounds, Duncan lifted it easily, as if it were filled with nothing but feathers. He crowded into the line at the customs desk. Some people had their passports closely inspected; others passed through in seconds. Only a few suitcases were opened.

Duncan's bag contained no clothing or personal items. All he had packed were his cherished, leather-bound books from his medieval collection. The volumes were museum pieces, among the oldest books in existence. He found immense pleasure in studying the ancient customs of the first people who had lived in the rugged country.

"So many secrets to unravel ... so much to learn," Duncan whispered as he stood in the customs line. The wait gave him another opportunity chance to plot his next move.

Following the deaths of his two followers at the black woman's apartment, Duncan had made the decision to visit Newburgh once again.

Constance wasn't concerned about the possibility of their identities being traced to the coven. They were recent recruits, not originally from the local area.

Duncan, however, had been more anxious about the black woman's husband. The man was the same human that he had encountered in the tunnel. Twice now, Duncan had attempted to kill the woman's unborn child. The first, "a taxi accident," hadn't done the job. The latest attempt had also been unsuccessful. The husband had burst into the apartment at the last moment and had attacked Duncan's loyal followers.

The child must die, but the new world was a dangerous place to attempt murder. It was filled with unknown technology and an unseen power that hindered Duncan's efforts.

By returning to his home in Scotland, Duncan would have more privacy.

The child's death must be postponed until Duncan had gained even more power.

He instructed Constance to discreetly keep track of Samantha Dixon-Martin. When he was ready, he would finish off mother and child.

Duncan's thoughts were disrupted by a request from the official at the counter.

"Your passport, please?" the man asked.

"What?" asked Duncan.

"Your passport, sir," the agent repeated firmly.

Duncan stared at the man in uniform. He handed over the blue booklet. The agent opened the document, looked at the picture, compared it with Duncan's face, and frowned. Duncan focused his mind on the agent. The man took a second look at Duncan, and then quickly flashed a smile.

"Welcome to Edinburgh," said the agent as he stamped the passport and returned it to Duncan. "By the way, it won't be necessary to inspect your luggage."

From customs, Duncan followed the signs to the car rental desk. He filled out papers and showed his passport and driver's license. The woman at the counter told him that he could have a Range Rover. He was directed to a waiting area. He had been sitting for only a few minutes when a shiny black SUV approached the curb. A young man got out and dangled the keys between his fingers.

"Would you like to see how to operate the Rover?" the young man asked.

"Yes, that would be very helpful," Duncan replied.

"What's this?" asked Duncan. "The controls are on the wrong side."

"Oh," answered the young man. "You must be from the United States."

"Yes," said Duncan, "from New York."

"We drive on the opposite side of the road. The controls work the same, but you must remember to drive on the left side."

The young man struggled to fit the suitcase in the rear of the Rover behind the back seat. Breathing heavily, he closed the back hatch and turned to Duncan.

"Is there anything else?" asked the young man.

"One more thing," said Duncan. "Could you tell me the directions to the village of Innerieithen?"

"Of course," said the man. "Let me program it into your GPS."

He showed Duncan how to work the GPS navigation system. He explained that the system was voice-activated and would give verbal directions, telling the driver when to turn. Duncan thanked the young man and handed him a ten-pound note. In New York, he had learned that people who waited on you expected money. A strange custom, but he did not want to attract attention, so he handed the man a wad of currency.

Duncan started the vehicle and drove away from the airport. A woman's voice gave him directions. He laughed. Merlin would have loved to have a talking voice machine in King Arthur's court.

He drove south out of Edinburgh. So many people populated the modern world. He figured the humans must reproduce like rabbits. Since the *endosyms* would feed on their essence, it was great that the humans liked to procreate, as each new human would potentially add their essence to the powers of the *endosyms*.

After several miles, the landscape began to look more and more like the countryside he remembered. Soon he would be back home.

56

DUNCAN'S ROOTS WERE FIRMLY PLANTED IN THE ROCKY SCOTTISH SOIL. IT was through his great-grandfather that Black Castle first became a McDougal possession.

Robert McDougal had been a loyal government supporter and had served bravely in the Royal Army. When mobs of defiant rebels openly protested government policy, three thousand troops attacked, slaughtering hundreds in the streets of Edinburgh. Fifteen rebels were accused of leading the revolt. They were hanged, drawn and quartered.

To the victor go the spoils – and so it was with Robert McDougal. He was given land and the castle that had belonged to a rebel leader. The dark structure became known as Castle McDougal.

Although the Scottish government ceased persecuting witches in 1736, the McDougals continued to destroy those whom they believed were the devil's spawn. They pursued those who refused to accept the official church. Hundreds of witches were burned at the stake by the order of a McDougal.

Five women died in the righteous flames at Castle McDougal in 1759. Although the gruesome deaths were witnessed by dozens of peasants, no charges were ever brought to bear on the true criminals – the McDougals.

No one knew that one of the supposed witches had given birth to a McDougal. That woman was Duncan's own mother.

In the ensuing years, Duncan sought revenge for his mother's murder. Some McDougal men mysteriously met with accidents, some died of unknown illnesses, and some simply disappeared. After a span of five years, only one McDougal remained to claim title to the property.

The last man was Duncan.

He closed the castle and took on only women to serve as its care-takers. Townspeople whispered tales of strange rituals conducted on the castle grounds.

Located on the edge of Pentland Hills Regional Park, the castle was still owned by Duncan but remained closed to the public. The entire estate of seventy acres was enclosed with an eight-foot chain link fence.

The castle's original name had disappeared. It was no longer called McDougal Castle. Likely due to the fact it was built of black volcanic basalt, the local people call it Dubh Castle. Dubh is the Gaelic word for black.

"So 'black' it is," Duncan said aloud as he drove up the winding road toward his ancestral home. "Fitting, oh so fitting!"

57

MALCOLM CAMPBELL CLIMBED OUT OF THE WORN AND BATTERED LORRY. A wizened shepherd dog slid out of the bed of the truck and tagged slowly behind Malcolm as he moved along the fence line. Malcolm carried a metal toolbox. He inspected the rusty barbed wire, stopping from time to time to put in a nail, bending it over the wire and pounding it solidly to affix it tightly to the soft wooden post. Each time he came to a halt, the dog tucked each of her four legs under her scrawny body and watched her master at work.

The sun hung low in the southwest offering little warmth on this crisp December day. Malcolm stood still for a few moments to assess the force of the north wind. He sensed the smell of a coming snow. By this time tomorrow, the ground would be frozen white. Malcolm's arthritic fingers ached. He had lived a rough sixty-eight years.

He, like his brother and sister, had been born in the old farmhouse. The family homestead was called "Quarry Side," named for the spent rock quarry three miles to the north. He looked behind him toward the house and barn. Both were built of black basalt, same as the stones that had been carried uphill to make the Black Castle, on the high ground to the east.

Malcolm's family had raised sheep on this barren piece of rock, dirt and scrub grass for three hundred years. Lord McDougal himself had passed down the property to Malcolm's ancestors.

Malcolm started down the fence line to the next post. The old dog struggled once again to her feet. Like her master, the cold played havoc with her old bones. She was his best dog, now fourteen years old. Instead of herding sheep, she stayed close to her master and spent her nights in-doors, nestled in a low box near the stove.

"Neither one of us should be doing this today," said Malcolm to the dog. The dog looked him in the eye and showed her agreement by slowly wagging her thin tail.

Sadly, his was the last generation who would raise sheep at Quarry Side. Malcolm, his brother Donald and his sister Chrissie jointly worked the farm. Donald and Chrissie had both lost their spouses years ago, and Malcolm had never married. Most of the family had moved away. Chrissie's daughter worked in Edinburgh; she was their closest kin. All three siblings were in their late sixties. Within three, maybe four years, Quarry Side would go on the block to be sold. If they weren't all dead, they would end up in one of those retirement homes where old people were stored four to a room in a dilapidated building that smelled of urine. Well, right now, the fences needed fixing. Close to a hundred head of sheep depended on their care.

Suddenly, the old dog let out a deep growl.

"What is it, girl?" asked Malcolm. The dog stared toward the next hill. A black SUV crested the hill, heading down, then up again on the narrow road that led to Black Castle.

Probably just another tourist trying to visit the castle, thought Malcolm. Well, they'll find a locked gate. No one had ever gotten inside the Black Castle in all of Malcolm's life. Even the caretakers were rarely seen, and they never spoke to the locals. When the siblings were children they used to talk about sneaking into the castle. But no one ever dared attempt the deed. According to local legend, the castle housed demons. Malcolm shook his head. A confirmed disbeliever, Malcolm scoffed when he thought about the gullible fools who still believed those stories.

As the vehicle approached, the dog became more excited. This was unusual for her, who calmly had accepted life's challenges.

"Quiet, girl," ordered Malcolm. "Down! Stay!"

The dog dropped down, but continued to growl deep in her throat. Malcolm walked over from the fence line, drawing closer to the road and stood on the loose soil of the shoulder. He could see the vehicle come slowly down the road. Despite the cold day, the driver's window was open. At first, Malcolm assumed the driver was going to stop, perhaps to ask a question about Black Castle. The driver looked directly at Malcolm as he passed by, but the car did not stop.

As the sleek vehicle continued up the road past him, Malcolm realized that he had been holding his breath. He gasped; his head was spinning. His knees were so weak that he had to sit down. The dog came over and laid a paw gently on his leg and whined.

What had he just seen? He was still trying to make sense of it. As the driver had looked at him, at first Malcolm thought he was looking at a man with short gray hair. Then for a second, he thought he was looking at the devil or a demon or something else. Whatever it was didn't seem human. It had the features of a man, but had a large round head, sharp horns and pointed ears. The shiny black Rover had continued up the road. No one would believe him if he described what he saw. It didn't matter – no one would ever be told. He looked at Black Castle.

"My God, girl, it is the devil's den. We need to get out of here."

He slowly headed back to the truck. Fence repairs could wait until another day.

58

Sitting on the bed in their hotel room in Bamako, Mali, Sam cradled the phone to her ear.

"Samantha, your daddy is absolutely furious. How could you do this?"

"Mom, we're not talking the end of the world. My God, we'll only be gone three months," argued Sam.

"But why now? All the holidays are just coming up. It's almost Thanksgiving. Why didn't you wait till after Christmas?"

"Mom, I told you that Tim is on official business for the embassy here in Mali."

"What on earth is so important?"

"It's FBI business. You know he can't tell me what they're doing," Sam explained.

"All right. All right, but you could have stayed in New York just a little longer and then come down for Thanksgiving," said Sam's mother, who wasn't about to let her off the hook too easily.

"Mom, the station wants me to do a story on the impact of climate change on the arid regions of Mali. That's great for us. I get to work on the story while Tim does his job. We won't have to be separated during the holidays," said Sam.

"Oh, dear, what will we do at Thanksgiving? You know we've invited the Martins. Now you and Tim will not even be here. What will we talk about?"

Now it was out – Sam's mom wasn't just upset because she and Tim were in Africa. It also had to do with the fact they would be entertaining

Tim's parents. Besides their children, the two couples had nothing in common.

"Oh, Mom! Hank Martin is a three-star general, and he's due to be stationed at the Pentagon. It's not like you'll be having Thanksgiving with the janitor. Besides, Hank is a Redskins fan, just like Daddy. They can watch the games together.

"Lindsey is a college graduate, just like you. You'll have Eddie, his wife and kids there, too. Usually you plan something with some of Daddy's law partners and their wives. They'll be good company.

"Come on, you'll get through it. We plan to be back the last week in January. We can do a late Christmas. I'll find some gifts over here."

Like maybe a new grandson, Sam smiled at the thought.

"Mom, I'll call again, but if you don't hear from me for a few weeks don't panic. I'm not supposed to use the satellite phone except to talk to the producers at the station.

"I love you, Mom, but I've got to go."

"I love you, too, Samantha. You need to be careful. From what I hear, you're going to a very dangerous place. Remember, drink only bottled water. A person can pick up those terrible tropical diseases."

"I know, Mom, I'll drink only bottled water, and we've put together a medicine kit. We've included all the pills recommended by the FBI. I'll have medicine if I get the trots."

Sam clicked off the phone.

"Did she buy your story?" asked Tim.

"Yes," replied Sam.

Of course, Sam thought, there was some truth to what she'd said. The FBI had ordered Tim to leave the country, but only because of what had happened in their apartment just ten days ago.

She put her hands over her eyes and took a few deep breaths. She still found it difficult to think about the horror of that day when the crazed woman had held the sharp knife just inches above her swollen belly. That was the closest she had ever come to death. The woman had super-human strength and intended to commit murder. She was so strong that Sam knew it would have been impossible for her to stop the woman.

Thank God, Tim had arrived there in the nick of time. His quick thinking and fast actions had saved her and their unborn son.

The police had arrived within minutes. Sam had no idea that the cops could move that quickly. Tim had bundled her in a blanket and taken her into the bathroom so she wouldn't have to view the bloody scene any more than necessary.

When Tim held out his ID, the FBI agents had moved in and sealed off the site. At first, Sam was convinced that Tim would be in big trouble. After all, the man had been shot twice in the face. Maybe that could be justified as self-defense. Although the medics had worked frantically on the woman, Sam was almost certain that she, too, was either dead or dying. The woman had fallen to the floor after the first shot. How could they justify a separate shot to the head when she obviously wasn't a threat?

Right now, Tim could be incarcerated, but too much evidence pointed in other directions. First, the police had discovered the real doorman. They found his beheaded body in a storeroom. Then, when they searched nearby apartments, the cops had found the lifeless bodies of the members of the Lewis family, their next-door neighbors. Jim Lewis had innocently opened his door to pick up his Sunday newspaper. Unfortunately, his timing couldn't have been worse. At the same moment, the two intruders had broken in the door on their apartment. The two had reacted immediately, shooting Jim, his wife and their two children.

Internal Affairs had come up with a plausible story. Tim signed a statement claiming that the older woman vowed to avenge the death of her son – the same man whom Tim had killed in the Punk Robbers attempted bank robbery several months ago. They had found out where the Martins lived. If other suspected gang members chose to continue to escalate their quest for revenge, Tim Martin's life would be in jeopardy. Clearly, Martin's wife would also be subject to their wrath.

The director decided Martin would be better off out of the country for a few months until the FBI could look into the possibility of more plots.

"Hey, Sam?" Tim had asked her. "How would you like a three-month vacation in Timbuktu?"

Sam couldn't laugh at Tim's attempted humor. They'd have to come up with a better story than that to tell their families. The truth was that the *endosyms* intended to destroy her, Tim, and their unborn child.

Sam's eyes filled with tears.

"Families?" she sighed, wrapping her arms around her belly. "Mom, Dad, Tim's parents ... they don't even know about their grandbaby."

59

Once they arrived in Africa, Tim had made a call to Liberia.

Two days later a black Mercedes 500 SL pulled up to their hotel. Three men dressed in dark suits stepped out of the car and entered the lobby. A tall, well-built African with closely cropped hair, graying at the temples, approached the desk and asked the concierge to ring the Martins' room. When Tim answered the phone, the familiar voice of Joe Weah greeted him.

Minutes later, all five of them sat at a table in the bar. Sam had heard a lot about Joe Weah, the former minister of defense. Joe and Charles Moray, who became the President of Liberia, had saved Tim's life after his kidnapping by thugs sent by the former regime. Sam took an instant liking to this friendly, confident man who treated Tim like a member of his own family. The other two men were from Joe's tribe. They now served in Liberia's special forces.

"So, Tim, what is this all about?"

"Joe, do you remember Sarday?"

"How can I forget that bastard?"

"You knew he was an *endosym*?"

"Of course. I was with your dad when we found those ancient ruins. Although Charles Morray accompanied your dad into the ruins, years later the council of *zos* showed me the original entrance. They showed me the ancient hieroglyphics illustrating the Egyptian *endosyms* trying to enslave my people," said Joe.

"But I'm confused. Your dad, Hank, had told me that the *endosym*, Sarday, had been killed in Virginia."

"Well," said Tim, "I'm afraid that there was more than one *endosym*. Last month I discovered an *endosym* at West Point, New York. Now that *endosym* and its cult are trying to kill Sam."

Sam covered her face with one hand and gently stroked her belly with the other. Tim reached out and touched Sam's shoulder.

"Why would an *endosym* want to kill your wife?" Joe asked, astonished by Tim's words.

"That's the strange thing. There was an attempt on her life by two *endosym*-possessed individuals. One claimed that they would not rest until our unborn son is dead."

"I thought you looked kind of pregnant," laughed Joe, trying to ease Sam's concern.

Sam looked in Joe's eyes and smiled at Tim's old friend.

"I'm afraid that there is no such thing as 'kind of' pregnant. I'm due in mid-January."

"So why in the world are you in Africa? I mean like couldn't you have security provided in the U.S.? And, where is your security right now, if bad guys are really after you?"

"Sitting right beside me," answered Sam, looking directly at Tim.

Tim cleared his throat. "Ah – there's more," he said quietly.

"More?" asked Joe.

"Yeah," Tim answered. "Sam and I had an identical dream. Well, not really a dream, more an out-of-body experience."

"Whoa, Tim Martin, that's far out even for us primitive Africans," said Joe.

"Tell me about it. Sam and I found ourselves in Zigda. We both talked to Chea Geebe and an old woman. They told us that our child is a special being. He will be able to see *endosyms*. Even before he's born, the *endosyms* can sense his presence. Chea told us that the only safe place until the baby is born is in Zigda.

"I know how crazy this sounds, but back in New York, Sam was almost killed by a hit-and-run driver. She swears that behind the wheel was an *endosym* with horns. And, then later, two intruders broke into our apartment and tried to kill Sam and our baby. It's just too dangerous there. So what we are hoping is that you can take us to Zigda."

Joe frowned and didn't respond to Tim's request.

"I realize, General Weah, that we must sound crazy," Sam said. "Perhaps this was a mistake."

"No, no" said Joe. "There are stories in our culture of such a person, one that could see the *endosyms* as they truly are, not as men.

"Chea Geebe was the greatest *zo* in Zigda. Many of the old people believe that his ghost still walks on moonless nights. Zigda, hidden deep in the Nimba Mountains, is one of the oldest places in Liberia. My people believe that it is a magic place. To this day, it has neither electricity nor modern conveniences. No guns are allowed. The power of the Poro guardians secures the entrances to Zigda. Even during the bloodiest years of the civil war, no forces have ever entered the village.

"My father is the chief," Joe continued. "When he dies, as his eldest son, I will give up all I have and become chief."

Joe laughed. "I will even have to take young wives to ensure the lineage continues."

Joe paused for a moment, then looked up at his two friends. His voice took on a serious tone.

"So, what you have just told me is something that I believe. What I do not understand is how you became the one to bear this child. Perhaps it is the strange relationship that existed between Tim and the old *zo*, Chea. But another possibility is the fact that your ancestors came from this continent. Perhaps it is because of who you are, Samantha Martin," Joe concluded.

"I don't know," said Sam. "Dad's grandparents came from Jamaica. Mom's mother was French, and her father was an African American from Chicago."

"Ah," said Joe, "but don't you see? Black slaves came from the shores of this great continent. Many of these slaves came from what is now Liberia. In the 1700s many of the men, women and children came from Zigda. They were captured and sold as slaves to the Southern states and even to the British colonies in Jamaica. From what you are telling me, I believe that one of your ancestors once walked the paths of my home. This is the true reason why you must accompany us to my home, the village of Zigda."

60

Joe Weah came to pick up Sam and Tim in the black Mercedes the next morning.

Sam settled into the back seat. She was glad that she was now over her morning sickness. They drove out of downtown and headed for the international airport. When they arrived, instead of going to the main terminal, they drove around back of the warehouses to the commercial terminal. At the gate, they stopped for the guard. Sam reached for her passport.

"No need," said Joe. "It will be better if there is no record of you and Tim leaving Mali and entering Liberia."

Joe stepped out of the car and walked up to the guard. He handed the man an envelope, shook hands with him, and got back into the car. The car's tinted windows prohibited anyone from seeing inside, yet allowed the occupants to look out.

The car was waved through the gate. They drove to a parking apron where a Liberian military transport awaited takeoff. The Mercedes was driven up the ramp into the cargo hold. They all got out and walked to the front of the plane. While the crew anchored the Mercedes to the floor, the pilot saluted as he directed Joe to the front row. The others spread out among the dozen seats that accommodated passengers.

"Please have a seat, folks, and fasten your seat belts. We will be departing in a few minutes," said the Liberian pilot as he smiled at Joe Weah, his famous passenger. "Our flying time to Voinjama is three hours."

Joe explained that Voinjama was the capital of Lofa County. It had an airport large enough to accommodate the jet transport.

Soon, they lifted off and were on their way. Sam closed her eyes and tried to stifle her fears about their uncertain future. As the plane leveled off at 29,000 feet, the drone of the engines lulled her into a half sleep.

Sometime later, she felt the change in the pitch of the jets, and she opened her eyes. Even the baby seemed to know that something was happening. He kicked hard enough so that Sam could see a bump go up and down on left side of her belly. Finally the plane began its descent. As the wheels touched down on the runway, Sam peered through the small porthole window. The countryside around Voinjama reminded her of the land around Nairobi when her family went on safari.

The Mercedes was backed down the plane's ramp, and they all got back in. One of their men started the car and headed down the red laterite road. Dust clouds billowed around them each time they encountered another vehicle going in the opposite direction. When they caught up to a slow car ahead of them, their driver rode its back bumper and raced around the vehicle despite the poor visibility.

Sam checked her ill-fitting seat belt that wrapped around her lower belly. She grasped the strap that hung from the car's ceiling, hoping that she could anticipate the car's gyrations and provide more support for the baby. If they were in a head-on collision at these speeds, she feared that they would all be toast. Ahead, they spotted a roadblock manned by a rag-tag band of men. Tim reached for his gun.

"Not a problem," said Joe.

He stepped out of the car. The men at the roadblock leveled their guns directly at him. Joe didn't even seem to move his lips. After a few hand gestures, each of the men lowered his weapon. Joe climbed back in the vehicle, and they drove around the primitive roadblock.

"Bandits," said Joe. "They shake down wealthy travelers."

"Why didn't they demand money from us?" Sam asked.

"They honor the Poro. It crosses all boundaries and is honored by local tribes."

"I guess I don't understand this Poro," said Sam.

Joe laughed. "That's right. You are not familiar with our ways."

"When Kapel boys and girls reach puberty, they go to bush school to learn how to become adults. The Poro spirits run the bush school. The Poro governs our lives. It is a secret society that guides and protects us from the evil spirits that live in the bush," he explained.

"The Kapel believe that a supreme force created the world. The missionaries must have been surprised to learn that the native people already believed in God. But it's a little different. We believe that God is far too busy to have time for the Kapel. Instead, good and evil spirits affect our lives. Even after a person dies, his spirit continues to dwell in the bush and influence our world. The Poro fight the evil spirits. It also acts as a judge and jury for crimes."

Sam nodded her head. This was certainly a different take on the African history she had studied in college.

"When we become teenagers," Joe continued, "a masked Poro spirit called the *Ga Me* takes us from our homes during the night. We go into the bush where we must live for six months. There, we learn the history of our people, how to hunt, how to build weapons and how to make magic potions. The boys become Kapel men and warriors. We learn many secrets that we share with no one, unless they are Poro, too. Those bandits at the roadblock, like myself, were members of the Poro. I saw the scars on their chests."

"How do they get the scars?" asked Sam.

"On the night the *Ga Me* comes for us, our fathers whisper in our ears that our time has come. We are both happy and afraid – happy that at last we would be a Kapel warrior, but afraid of the unknown. That night we all lie awake, waiting to be taken.

"At midnight, the drums begin to beat. We can hear them move through the village. They stop outside each of our doors. Our mothers' sob, but our fathers ignore them. Our fathers take our hands and lead us to the door. We step into the darkness."

Joe looked down and avoided Sam's eyes. He seemed to drift off from the general re-telling of the ancient rite and become engrossed in his own personal story.

"Outside, the *Ga Me* warned us not to speak. If we did, we would be punished. It led us out of the village, along the old bush trail, and into the mountains. Several hours later, we came to a raffia wall, blocking the entrance to the sacred Poro bush. Without a Poro escort, no one could enter. Those who tried would die.

"The days became weeks. Our physical limits were tested each day. We learned to hunt, to make weapons and to kill with our bare hands. We learned to speak using only hand gestures. This language crossed tribal boundaries and dialects. One Poro may speak to another across a distance without moving his lips as I did today to the bandits.

"When eight weeks passed, our boyhood flesh became firm. The soles of our feet hardened, like rocks.

"One night a masked figure woke us at midnight. It had the face of a young woman with light brown skin. We followed her into a deep valley. We approached a large compound surrounded by a tall fence. Stacks of burning wood illuminated the open areas, but we did not know what might be hiding in the dark shadows.

"We were told to line up. One by one, we were called forward. Each of us was required to lie on his back in the damp grass. One man grasped our shoulders; another gripped our ankles.

"Drawing out a finely honed knife, the masked figure pulled at each of our penises and stretched it to its full length. The blade sliced through the foreskin. Some shrieked with pain; some fainted.

"After we were circumcised, we were taken back to the hut. Several of the young men required support on the strong shoulders of others. They could barely walk – such was the their agony. Yet inside the hut, it was less painful to stand upright than to sit. Men came in, washed us, and applied a healing salve to our wounds. Soon, our misery eased. Then we were fed a broth made from the flesh of our severed foreskins. By consuming the broth, we became one with the Poro spirit.

"Now our lives in the bush school were transformed. We all gained weight. We felt vital and alive. We were proud Kapel men, not mere children. Our teachers no longer hovered over us, alert to a violation of the rules. Now we all obeyed out of our own will, not out of fear. We hunted together in teams. We ate what we killed.

"The day of our final test came. We would battle the great *Nangma*. We gathered together at dusk and filed into the bush. We reached the sacred home where the *Nangma* dwells. Each of us carried a spear and a knife. Men gave us cupfuls of a dark liquid. It would give us the power to fight the *Nangma*. They warned us that not all would survive the battle. Those who died would become the beast's servants for eternity.

"Each of us faced our greatest fears during the ordeal. Then once again we found ourselves back in the hut. We could hear the moaning of our brothers. We were told that the *Nangma* had chewed us up and spit us out. We would live. In two weeks, we would be welcomed into the Poro. A sense of well being came over us, and we all fell into a deep slumber.

"It took ten days to heal the wounds from the bite of the *Nangma*. Finally, we were released from the hut. Our teachers stood in the clearing. The *Ga Me* who had come for us so long ago, pronounced that we were all brothers of the Poro. Once again, we were permitted to speak. Our voices croaked. We all laughed and embraced one another. Out of the bush came our older brothers, our fathers and our uncles to join in the celebration. To the beat of the drums, we all marched back to the village.

"All the people lined the trail. They called to us, using our old names, but we ignored their words. Now we had new Poro names, the names we will carry for the rest of our lives. My new name was Nah Weah. The child had been lost in the jaws of the *Nangma*, and a man had been born. We did not acknowledge our mothers who wept at the loss of their children. As Poro warriors, women served us. We no longer followed women's orders. We were now men.

"Of course, after the ceremony, we went back to our families, and even hugged our mothers and told them that we still loved them. However, from that day on, in the streets of our village, our mothers were submissive," Joe said, ending his story.

Sam stared at the man who had gone through the Poro experience and come out stronger. She couldn't help but admire his courage. Joe remained silent while the car continued down the rough road. Despite the bumps and jolts, they were able to sleep for brief periods of time.

Shortly after leaving Voinjama the landscape changed from savanna to jungle. Over the remaining hours that they journeyed, Joe entertained Sam with more stories of life in Zigda. She felt that he was infatuated with her. No, he wasn't putting the make on her, but a woman can tell when a man likes her for herself. Joe was sending those vibes. She guessed that Joe was about the same age as Hank, Tim's father. Without a doubt, he was a good-looking man. He probably had no problem linking up with women. At mid-afternoon, they reached the town of Zorzor.

"I'm hungry," said Joe. "How about some country chop? Everyone game?"

"Sure," said Tim, "I haven't had country chop in twelve years."

"What's country chop?" asked Sam.

"It's the main food dish of Liberia. It's steamed rice and mystery meat, palm butter and hot peppers."

"Just what a pregnant woman needs," laughed Sam.

Zorzor was a town of perhaps three thousand people. The main road passed through the center of town. There were a number of stores built out of scrap wood and chunks of rusty metal. Sam saw a couple of gas stations. Most of the homes had clay walls and tin roofs. Others had rounded walls and thatched roofs. The streets were crowded with people rushing in all directions. Women balanced baskets of fruit and vegetables on their heads. The people looked much like the Kenyans she had seen on the family safari trips, except that they were shorter in stature than the east Africans. All in all, Zorzor seemed like a typical African village.

The driver stopped the Mercedes along the side of the road and turned off the ignition. At her first step out of the air-conditioned car, Sam felt as if she had entered a blast furnace. The muggy afternoon heat almost caused her to sink to her knees as her body began to cope with the insufferable humidity. Her blouse was soaked from the sweat draining the fluids from her body.

Joe led them to what appeared to be a restaurant with a large covered porch. The rough wood deck was randomly furnished with crudely built tables covered with brightly colored oilcloth. Worn chairs with chipped paint and cracked seats surrounded each table. Joe walked to a table large enough to seat the group. He pulled out a chair for Sam after rocking it back and forth to check its stability. Sam nodded her appreciation for Joe's concern.

The proprietor, a short dark man with a bulging stomach, approached them. Joe greeted him in Pidgin English. Sam thought she recognized a language similar to that spoken by the poorer people in Jamaica. When they had ordered, Sam asked the man for a Coke, using the same language she and her brother Eddie had learned when they played with the local children in Jamaica.

Joe looked at her in surprise.

"You speak Liberian country English?" he asked. "I thought you had never been in Liberia."

Sam laughed.

"Just a fast learner," she said with a grin.

The meal came. At first, Sam was concerned that the food might upset her stomach, but she was hungry. She spooned up a big bite of the chopped vegetables and chunks of spicy meat.

"Oh, this is good," she said. "Really, really good."

As she cleaned out her bowl, she rested her palms on her belly. Apparently, the baby didn't object to the flavorful food. She leaned back in her chair and finished off her Coke.

Soon, it was time to go. She waved goodbye to the proprietor as they headed toward the car. They continued down the main road arriving in Gbarnga just as the sun set.

"We will stay in Gbarnga," said Joe. "Tomorrow we will go to Zigda."

They stayed in a government house. It was primitive by U.S. standards, but did have queen-sized beds, electricity and air conditioning. Sam suspected that this would be the Ritz compared to what they would likely find in Zigda. Despite all the good things that had happened, she was still worried about giving birth to their son here in Africa.

She settled into the double bed and curled up next to Tim. She knew that their lives had been in danger and this escape to Zigda was in their best interests, but the whole adventure still seemed like a dream – or maybe a nightmare. She reached out her hand and caressed Tim's strong arm. She nuzzled close to his neck and closed her eyes.

"Dear God," she prayed. "Will we get out of here alive?"

61

SAMANTHA OPENED HER EYES AND LOOKED AROUND.

At first, she didn't realize where she was. The hum of the air conditioner in the window reminded her of the drone of the engines of the military jet that had flown them to Liberia. She wasn't as hot as she had been. It was cool enough in the room to require a blanket during the night. As a matter of fact, she felt quite comfortable.

The room smelled of fresh paint. Room-darkening shades fit tightly in the windows. Even the furniture was better than she could have thought possible. They had two queen-sized beds, a desk, and two overstuffed chairs. A small refrigerator sat next to the desk. It was packed with plastic bottles of cold water. The bathroom had new, highly polished fixtures and a double shower with two sprinkler heads. Fresh, soft towels were neatly folded on the counter. This luxury wasn't at all what she had expected in the middle of Liberia, West Africa.

Joe Weah had explained that many years ago when Tubman was in control, a number of presidential houses were built in all the major cities. Even in those days, the facilities had electricity, powered by small generators. After Master Sergeant Doe overthrew the government, the presidential houses fell into disrepair. Much of the furniture and fixtures had been stolen and the rooms vandalized.

After the discovery of oil, the government used some of its increased revenue to restore the facilities. Guests were restricted to government officials and visiting businessmen. Gbarnga now had its own power plant, providing full-time electricity. The paved road from Monrovia had been extended to Gbarnga. Most of the main streets in Gbarnga were now paved.

Samantha rolled to her side to touch Tim's pillow. She found a note scrawled on a half sheet of paper.

"In the dining room having coffee. I'll wake you in an hour."

She laughed out loud. What was he thinking? Obviously she couldn't read the note if she had been asleep. And when did Tim's hour start?

She could just wait for Tim to come back, but she couldn't go back to sleep now. She got up, picked up her clothes and went into the bathroom. She found Irish Spring soap next to the towels. She turned on the shower; the water came out clear. To her surprise, she didn't have to wait for it to get hot.

Maybe this Africa thing wouldn't be so bad. But she knew that the Zigda in her dream wouldn't have this level of comfort. There wouldn't be running water or electricity. This might be her last shower for several months. She washed like it was the last thing she did in life, taking her time and basking in the flow of warm water on her hair, her face and over the taut skin of her swollen belly.

Everything she had – her clothes, cosmetics and toiletries – was in one suitcase. She and Tim had limited themselves to only two suitcases between them. She kept clothes to a minimum, but brought the essential items for two months, including aspirin, sunscreen, a small first aid kit and four tubes of Vaseline with vitamin E. She planned to rub the Vaseline on her expanding belly and breasts to reduce stretch marks.

Before dressing she looked at her naked body in the large mirror on the wall. Sam had always been proud of her figure. Now she had large breasts – her nipples had doubled in size – and her belly was huge, its skin stretched tight. She spoke to her unborn child.

"You know that you have destroyed my girlish figure."

All right, she realized that even this far along, she was no larger than some of the women she worked with who were not even pregnant yet their stomachs were as large as hers was right now. With an extra-large T-shirt over her stretch pants, she looked not much different than many mothers whose abdominal muscles had stretched so much after childbirth that they looked somewhat pregnant for the rest of their lives.

Sam felt like a fat water buffalo. She put on her clothes and applied some make-up, and then she packed everything tightly back into her suitcase. She stifled a sob. She should be back home, getting a nursery ready, attending baby showers and anticipating the joy of motherhood.

God, she didn't have any baby clothes; she had nothing. Yet they didn't dare let the fact that she was pregnant be known back home. When their son was born, what would they do for baby clothes or diapers? This was sheer madness. She bit her lip. She had no choice. They had to do this. She blew her nose, turned and walked out of the room.

She wandered down a short hallway. The presidential villa was small – just six guest rooms like the one where she and Tim had slept. The larger, presidential suite was reserved for the exclusive use of the Liberian president. The hallway opened on a large reception room. Behind it she could see through to the dining area that held several small tables.

Sitting around a low coffee table in the larger room, Sam saw Tim and Joe, as well as the two assistants. Sam learned that their names were Amos, who would be their driver, and Fuji. After spending so many hours together on their journey, they were all at ease with each other. The men had been drinking coffee together.

"Good morning, Samantha," said Joe as he stood and greeted her. "We waited until you were up to have breakfast. We're glad you're here. We are all very hungry."

The others got up, and they walked together into the dining room. Near the open window, one table was set for five. It had white linen, fine china, and polished flatware. A low arrangement of pink and yellow orchids sat in the center of the table.

Joe held Sam's chair for her as she took her place. After she was comfortably seated, the others sat down. A teenage serving boy filled their china cups with steaming coffee and stood back, anxious to keep the cups filled. Within minutes, two Liberian women dressed in bright tropical caftans carried out large bowls of steaming rice along with chunks of meat covered in a savory sauce. Then came dishes of cassava and a platter of roasted chicken.

"My God," thought Sam. "They eat like this at every meal?"

She thought that the women were done serving, but, to her surprise, they came in again with scrambled eggs, fried ham, and toasted bread. The final items had been placed on two small serving plates. One held a small bowl of bright yellow butter; the second, a jar of Smucker's raspberry jam with a teaspoon poking out its top.

She smiled, realizing the American food was brought out just for them. Normally, she would have preferred to try Liberian food, but last night's country chop had kept the baby kicking most of the night. Since they faced another long drive before reaching Zigda, she gratefully accepted the ham and eggs.

After breakfast, the luggage was loaded into the SUV that had replaced the Mercedes, and they headed toward the morning sun. Still early, the temperature was cool. They continued along the main street that was filled with vendors, shoppers and workers heading to the fields. Dogs and chickens scampered about; barely clad children ran along beside the car and called out greetings. Old men sat cross-legged on low benches and watched others go by. They drove on. Gradually, the huts became spaced farther apart. Fields of rice, cassava and green vegetables grew in the rich, dark soil on both sides of the road. Soon, the pavement vanished, and the car continued down the road.

Small villages consisting of no more than a half dozen huts appeared every few miles. Then, the distance between them became even greater. Nearly two hours later, the driver slowed the vehicle and turned left onto a narrow road that consisted of no more than parallel ruts in the grass. Amos shifted into four-wheel drive, slowed to a crawl, and constantly jockeyed the steering wheel to avoid the deeper holes.

The road narrowed even more, scarcely accommodating the SUV. Branches and brush scraped against the car's sides as it moved deeper and deeper into the dense forest. Overhead, tall trees formed a dark green tunnel. The vegetation was so thick that it nearly cut off the sunlight.

They hadn't seen a living creature since they'd gotten off the main road. Perhaps nothing lived in this part of the forest, Sam thought. Yet she couldn't shake the feeling that they were being watched. She scanned the forest for movement, but saw nothing. If there was something out there, it was hiding.

62

Amos guided the vehicle around a corner. The road widened. The forest opened up. Ahead, Sam could see that a narrow bridge had once spanned the chasm. Only the left side of the bridge remained; the right side had fallen and disappeared into the thick brush below. The vehicle could go no farther. When they came to a stop, everyone got out.

"We have to cross to the other side," said Joe.

Samantha assessed the span. All that was left was a steel girder, maybe ten inches wide. She shivered at the thought of stepping across, like a tightrope walker in a circus stunt. Although she had relished sports while she was growing up, she wasn't sure how her bulky body could balance on the narrow beam. Along the left side of the span was a rope attached to stakes on each side of the chasm. At least they would have the rope to hold onto as they made their way across.

"I'll be right in front of you," said Tim.

"Don't look down," said Joe. "I'll be right behind you."

Sure, thought Sam, tell a reporter not to look down. She took a tentative step, followed by another. Grasping the rope tightly in her hand, she began to slowly work her way across the sixty-foot gap. She couldn't help it. She took a quick peek at the dark chasm below. She sucked in her breath. It was at least a hundred feet down, so deep that the bottom looked like a tiny crack in the ground. She froze in place, unable to move ahead. Tim reached back and touched her hand.

"You'll be OK," he said.

She took a deep breath and picked up her right foot and moved a tiny step forward. Then she moved her left foot ahead. Gradually, the group started moving again. What had seemed like more than an hour had actually taken a matter of minutes.

"You made it, Sam!" shouted Tim when Sam finally reached the firm soil on the opposite bank.

She turned around to check on the others. Joe followed close behind her, then came Amos and Fuji. She couldn't believe what she was seeing. The two men balanced the heavy suitcases on their heads, walking across the beam as if it were only a sidewalk.

"From here, we walk," said Joe.

At one time, there had been a road on this side of the bridge. Now only a narrow trail cut through the jungle.

"Do you think you can walk?" asked Joe.

"Of course," said Sam. She had no idea how she could conjure so much courage, but she did.

They followed the road. It was hotter than she had expected; the humidity was insufferable. Within minutes, her shirt was soaked. After about an hour and a half, they came upon a clearing, about half the size of a soccer field. She scanned the perimeter, checking the edges that bordered the deep forest. She saw a battered vehicle. It looked like an old army Hummer with a wide stance and a low cab. The tires were gone as was its canvas top. She had no idea how long it had been there and couldn't begin to hazard a guess.

Tim, however, walked directly to the vehicle. He put his hand on the front right fender. He recognized the vehicle – it was the one his mother had driven across the bridge just before it collapsed twelve years ago. Their friend, Joe, had lain unconscious in the rear seat, near death from a bullet wound. Tim hung his head, recalling the danger they had faced the last time he'd been to Joe's village.

"How close are we to Zigda?" asked Sam, totally exhausted. Tim looked at his wife with pride. She had summoned the courage to save herself and their child.

Sam didn't notice Tim's look of admiration. She had more physical challenges ahead. She had been a runner. She had run 10K races, but not in the tropics and not carrying an extra thirty pounds of baby weight.

"Seven miles," replied Joe.

"Seven miles?" groaned Samantha.

"Don't worry," he said smiling. "It will be easier from here."

"Down hill?" she asked.

"No, we will go up more than fifteen hundred feet in elevation before we reach Zigda."

"I don't understand. How will it be easier?"

"You'll see," said Joe with a wide grin. He pointed towards the jungle across the clearing. Between twenty-five and thirty men had emerged from the undergrowth. They wore only loincloths. Each carried a spear.

To Sam, this looked like a scene from an old Hollywood movie. Even in Liberia, men no longer dressed like savages. Yet here they were, walking straight toward them. Leading the group was a man about Tim's age. He walked up to Joe.

"I see you, Nah Weah."

"I see you, Salah Saye."

The man then turned to Tim.

"I see you, Tim Martin."

Tim answered, "I see you, Salah."

Tim and the man hugged like old friends. Two of the other men came forward and also greeted Tim with smiles and hugs. Clearly these three men not only knew Tim, but held him in high regard. In all the years she had known Tim, she had never seen Tim exhibit such emotion except toward her brother, Eddie, and his dad, Hank.

Salah came up to Sam.

"Are you Tim's woman?" he asked.

At first, Sam's reaction was to snap back, "No, I am his wife." But she understood that the man was asking sincerely.

"Yes," she answered.

"He has made a good choice for his mate. He was wise not to select one of the virgins when we danced on the night after the games," said Salah.

One of the virgins? What was all that about?

She turned to speak to Tim, but quickly averted her gaze. Joe had removed his Western clothes and shoes and was slipping into one of the loincloths. His loincloth was made from the hide of a leopard. Although he faced away from her, she could not help but admire his strong body. He had to be in his late forties, but he had the build of a twenty-year-old. When he turned back to the group, Sam noticed the tribal scaring on his chest.

"It's time for us to go to Zigda," he said.

Sam saw that Joe now carried a long spear.

"You'll have to give Amos your weapon. You know that no modern weapons are allowed in Zigda," said Joe.

To her surprise, her husband, the FBI agent, removed his service weapon and shoulder holster and handed them to Amos. She would never have believed that Tim would give up his weapon so easily.

Amos and Fuji passed the suitcases to two of the warriors who hoisted them to their heads. Another two men came forward, each one pulling the pole of a wooden, two-wheeled cart. To Sam, it appeared to be an African version of a rickshaw.

Joe and Tim both looked at Sam.

She shook her head and planted her feet – making it clear that she wanted nothing of their plan.

"No way!" whispered Sam to Tim. "I can't ride in that."

"You have to," he said. "If you refuse, they will be offended. Besides, look at yourself. You look beat, and we still have seven miles of rugged terrain to cover."

"I'll walk some of the way," she insisted. "I feel like a white slave owner carried by servants."

"Hey, you're a modern black Goddess carried by her admirers," teased Tim.

"Whatever. But I tell you, I don't like the idea at all."

Reluctantly, she stepped up onto the seat. The two men each grasped a pole, and Sam's African chariot moved ahead into the bush.

They followed the wide path that had been hacked out of the under-growth. As Sam's rickety cart fell into a steady rhythm behind the others, she had the opportunity to observe the beauty of the lush forest around her.

Wide, leafy trees towered above. Coming from their upper branches, she could hear the chirp of birds and the chatter of monkeys. On the stretches of trail where the sun filtered through the trees, multi-colored butterflies settled briefly on the broad leaves, and then flitted away. In some areas, the jungle growth formed a green arch overhead. Sam had the impression that they had entered a massive green cathedral, home to a sacred culture. She leaned back and took in its beauty, feeling strangely in tune with the forest and its inhabitants.

Their trek took them over small streams, some spanned by rough-hewn log bridges. At one point, they crossed a fast moving river via a suspension bridge built entirely of tightly woven vines. It stretched more than a hundred feet across a ravine. It was held only by the knotted vines tied to thick trees on either side of the river. An engineering marvel, she thought, made without modern tools.

Sam dismounted and walked across the bridge. Again, she argued that she could walk, but the men insisted on carrying her along the trail. At one spot along the path, she glanced to her right. On a log near the edge of the trail, she saw a short-bodied snake basking in the sun. Its head was as wide as a man's hand. The snake turned toward her, and its eyes locked on hers. Then it slithered away and disappeared. No one else had noticed the snake. She knew that snakes were common creatures in the jungle – she had no reason to worry. But the brazen stare from its bright green eyes sent a chill down her spine.

Occasionally, the trail would lead to the top of a hill. In the distance, she could look out at rolling hills blanketed in African green. Farther off, she made out higher peaks partially hidden in misty clouds.

63

YET ANOTHER HOUR PASSED, AND SAM THOUGHT SHE COULD HEAR THE BEAT of distant drums. At first, the sound was only a faint rumble, but soon the drumbeat became unmistakable. They finally reached an open spot on the crest of the hill. In the valley below, she made out a pattern of dwellings and garden patches. It was Zigda – and it was exactly as she had seen it in her dream.

The village nestled on a stretch of low-lying land. Rugged mountains stood to the east. Closer to the village a tabletop mountain rose several thousand feet out of the thickly forested jungle.

"I've never seen anything like that," said Sam to Tim.

"They call it the Mountain of Darkness," explained Tim. "It shades the village until about nine o'clock each morning. The people of Zigda believe that it is a sacred place. Only the *zos* can approach the Mountain of Darkness."

It seemed as if the dense forests and steep cliffs kept the village almost totally isolated. There appeared to be no other way to enter – or escape – except on this one trail that skirted the rock cliffs and snaked through the thick vegetation.

Finally, Sam could see the actual village up close. The huts were roofed in natural thatch. Here, no rusty tin roofs like the shacks in Jamaica marred the landscape. She saw well-tended farms, herds of healthy goats and orderly rows of crops.

"Stop!" cried Sam.

"What's wrong?" asked Tim, as he ran up to her cart.

"Nothing," she said, "but I want down. There is no way I'm being carried into Zigda riding in this thing."

Following Tim's instructions, the two men came to a complete halt and helped her get down. She smiled gratefully at the two men who seemed unfazed, even after having pulled her for seven miles. "Thank you for the ride. I'll walk the rest of the way."

"You're welcome, missy," they said in unison. Then their escorts nodded, smiled and headed off down the trail.

They rounded a bend. Sam stopped abruptly. She couldn't believe what she saw. Ahead, lining both sides of the trail stood the ebony-skinned villagers – every man, every woman and every child had come out to greet the visitors. A country band consisting of a variety of crude instruments made from elephant tusks, gourds and native drums played a tune from the dawn of history.

A murmur rose from the crowd as Joe Weah led the group through the chattering gauntlet with Tim and Samantha right behind him. The other men followed a few paces back. A boy, perhaps five years old, reached out and touched Sam's arm. She laughed and bent down to return his touch. He grasped her fingers, grinned and held them in his small hand. Soon, more children surrounded her. More giggles and laughter accompanied the group as the guests and the welcoming party moved ahead into the village and stopped at the center square.

The crowd opened up and stepped back. Sam saw an old man and woman walk slowly toward them. It was impossible to know their exact ages, but Sam guessed that they could be in their mid-seventies. The man used a cane made of black ebony. The woman wore the traditional lappa, a colorful band of cloth wrapped around her bent form. The old man's loincloth was made from the same type of hide as Joe's garment.

"It's Joe's father, Togba, and his mother, Salamatu, Togba's first wife," whispered Tim.

"First wife?" asked Sam.

"He has five wives. He's the chief."

Joe moved toward his father.

"I see you, my father."

"I see you, my son."

The two men reached out and clasped each other's forearms. Joe said nothing to his mother. Sam remembered Joe's words about how the Poro do not speak to their mothers in public. She realized that in this village, women were second-class citizens. She probably shouldn't even have spoken to their escorts.

"I see you, Tim Martin," said Joe's father.

"I see you, Chief Togba," said Tim.

Then the old man's words were replaced by a burst of laughter.

"Tim, you have grown into a man, a strong man and warrior. How are your mother and father?"

"They are well."

"That is good," said Togba.

"So you are the one," he said as he turned to Sam.

"The one?" asked Sam, unsure of his meaning.

"Yes, in my dream, the old *zo* Chea Geebe told me of a young woman, Tim's woman, who would come to this village. In her womb, she would be carrying the greatest of all the *zos*. The one who will destroy the *endosyms* that have haunted mankind since the beginning of time."

Sam's mouth opened in disbelief.

"I, I don't know why I am here," she said. A tear ran freely down her cheek.

"It is OK, my dear," said Togba. "All the people of Zigda are at your service. Come, let us take you to your hut."

64

IT HAD NOW BEEN FIVE WEEKS SINCE TIM AND SAM HAD ARRIVED IN ZIGDA. She had grown accustomed to the daily rhythm of the village and the friendly welcome of its people.

Never left unaccompanied, Sam moved clumsily down the trail to the women's bathing area. This morning Lanai and Ananau joined her; Mamamu had stayed in the hut. Even when she visited the area in the bush just outside of the village where women went to relieve themselves, one of the three women would accompany her.

At first, Sam felt that her presence imposed upon these kind people who went out of their way to help her. Strange, she thought, that she could have felt so alone in New York, one of the world's largest cities. Yet here in this tiny village, she was never alone. Warm, smiling and generous people always surrounded her.

At first, she wasn't sure she could handle this primitive way of life. How could she live without all the modern conveniences? That first day, they had been taken to their new home, a simple mud hut with a dirt floor and a thatched roof. One side had a window that could be shuttered. The only door could be closed and locked by a narrow wooden bolt.

Compared to the people here, the American visitors would live in luxury. First, only the two of them occupied their hut. Sometimes as many as a dozen villagers lived together in a single hut. Second, they were fortunate to have furniture. They had two cots and a hand-built table with four chairs. Other conveniences included kerosene lanterns and a small kerosene refrigerator. Next, they had real dishes – cups, bowls, and a mishmash of other plates and silverware. Sam particularly appreciated the clay water filter. Finally, they had four old woolen army blankets. In Sam's previous life, the Hilton had been a step below her family's standards.

Sam would never again take running water and flush toilets for granted. Here in Zigda, the women's toilet area was simply an open area encircled by a rough-woven raffia fence. To relieve themselves, women had to squat over a trench while teetering on rough boards. They cleaned themselves with a soft dry grass. The first visits were a bit of adventure, but as the days turned into weeks, every day, day-by-day, it became a grim task. Sam had more difficulty than most as she was now eight months pregnant. Just maintaining her balance while squatting was quite an achievement. Recently, the women had changed the procedure to include one woman to hold Sam's arm and keep her steady. Without their help, Sam may well have fallen into the trench.

Individual families were responsible for preparing their own meals. This was a problem as Sam could barely boil water. Mamamu, one of Togba's wives, was in her mid-forties, and she took charge of the household food.

The other two women were young teenagers, not yet married. Each had learned to speak some English in a local school run by the Peace Corps. Mamamu had picked up a little English, but she mostly relied on the young women to translate. Sam could ask simple questions in Kapel. They communicated using simple words and hand gestures.

Today, Tim was out hunting with the village men. When they had first arrived, Tim had completely discarded his Western clothes and wore the britches like those worn by the native men. They were similar to what the Native American men wore in the late nineteenth century. She had teased him, calling him "George of the Jungle." But by the end of the first week, she, too, had rejected her shorts and blouse and had begun to wear the lappa. The women had helped wrap the long band of cloth around her body. Initially, Sam had insisted on wearing a bra and panties, fearing that the lappa would unravel at an inappropriate moment. Soon, however, she gave in and was totally naked under her garment.

Sam learned the layout of the town and the daily routine. Zigda was laid out in a wide, circular pattern. A broad, common area sat at its center. Nearly one hundred huts of varying sizes fanned out from there. Behind each of the huts, women hovered over wooden mortars, grinding grain. Small charcoal fires burned in their cooking areas.

The people were a happy and active group. Children played in the streets. Workers went out each morning to tend the farmland. Men hunted for game. Whatever they killed was divided among the families. Most nights, once the sun set, people withdrew to their huts. But, on some nights, fires were lit in the center of the village, the country band would play, and people would dance. Other times men only gathered by the fires, and women retreated to one of the huts to engage in women talk.

During the five weeks in Zigda, Samantha had come to love these genuine and outgoing people. They didn't waste their time listening to radios or watching TV. They knew little and cared little about the outside world. What did it matter? Life went on here much as it had for the last ten thousand years.

Since they were still trying to convince their friends and families that they were in Mali – not Liberia – they used the satellite phone to touch base with the station and their parents. They sent and answered in text messages explaining that talking used up the batteries too quickly. That part was true. They also had three back-up batteries. When Joe visited, he brought charged batteries. The satellite phone didn't work in the valley where Zigda was located. Tim had to hike up the trail to the jungle to get reception. It was too difficult for Sam to walk that far now, so Tim sent the texts. Since no one could hear their voices, Tim just pretended to be Sam when he sent a text supposedly from her.

One day Sam and her teenage escorts approached the bathing area. Several other women were already in the water. They exchanged greetings.

Sam removed her lappa and stepped into the water. Never in her life would she have believed she would feel comfortable taking off her clothes in front of other women. But here it didn't matter. Two of the women already bathing were also pregnant. No one paid any attention. Pregnancy was part of nature. Bathing was a natural act, and never once did she feel that she was treated differently.

Her skin was lighter that the Liberians, whose race was pure, but they didn't seem to care about the shade of her skin. It was so very different than at home. Many things were different here.

She laughed inside when she thought about how her attitudes had changed. Here, women either covered their upper bodies with their lappas, or just tied the cloth at their waists, letting their breasts fall free.

One particularly hot afternoon, she had tied her lappa around her waist. It was cooler to leave her breasts uncovered. Now that her pregnancy was so advanced, her breasts were larger than ever. No longer was she small. Instead, she was as large as most of the native women of her age.

When Tim returned from a hunting trip, he stopped in shock when he saw his wife sitting on a bench outside their hut. He freaked out – here was his half-naked wife sitting with her full breasts right out in public.

"Sam, what are you thinking?" he shouted. "Why aren't you covered up?" He rushed to her and stood between her and the people who were passing by.

"What do you mean?" she angrily replied. "It's not like we're in downtown Manhattan on a sunny afternoon! It's different here – this is Africa. I'm not doing anything wrong."

"Yeah, but you're my wife!"

"So? Look at yourself, tromping around in a skimpy loincloth, letting it all hang out!"

They settled the dispute in the usual way later on that night. Now, if she felt like wearing her lappa tied at the waist, she did it. Tim had to admit that her bare breasts aroused him. He wasn't any different from any other normal male raised in Western culture.

Once they finished bathing, the women strolled back to the village. Mamamu had prepared lunch for the four of them. It included streamed rice, boiled chicken, fresh coconut milk and fruit – melons, oranges and grapefruit. When they had first arrived in Zigda, Sam worried about getting proper nutrition, but Mamamu seemed to know the right foods for a pregnant woman. Admittedly, Sam felt better than she had ever felt before. She was probably consuming a better diet than she had eaten in New York. No longer was she eating modern foods packed with preservatives or supposedly enriched by additives.

Just one more month, Sam sighed, and it would all be over. She prayed that everything would continue to go well as it had gone already.

Yesterday, Sam had been awakened during her afternoon nap.

"Hey, Trevor, what's going on in there?" she asked her swollen belly. She caressed her taut skin with both hands and continued to speak in soothing tones.

They were using the name "Trevor" more often now. Tim had been so convinced of his baby's gender that he had even suggested the strong name. Neither of them had known a Trevor, but the name seemed to fit.

Normally, Sam had become accustomed to his gyrations and didn't give them a second thought. But now, he was so active that he had awoken her from a sound sleep. She was lying on her side on her cot. Side sleeping was her only option. In the past Sam had always slept on her back. But the weight of the baby pressing on her spine, she found it difficult to breathe if she tried to sleep on her back.

She definitely was ready for Trevor's birth. The baby thrashed around again, kicking out with both feet. Do they do that just before birth? Is this a sign that she was beginning labor? This pregnancy thing was totally new to her. She had friends who had children, but she really hadn't paid attention to what they experienced during their pregnancies.

When she left for Africa, she had told her doctor, her old friend, Shelley, that they were going to be out of the city when the baby was born. Her story was that Tim had been assigned to the American Embassy in Mali. Shelly didn't think it was a good idea for her to have the baby in that primitive country.

Sam had told Shelly that the embassy would fly her to Germany in time for the baby's birth. She had hand-carried her medical records and a prescription for pre-natal vitamins. The only other medication she had was her weekly malaria pill. Of course, before they left, she and Tim had gotten the usual immunizations for anyone traveling to Africa. Those shots wouldn't hurt the fetus, but actually would help the baby, giving it an initial immunity from diseases that killed so many people who lived in undeveloped areas of the world.

Unfortunately, without a doctor, Sam was on her own when it came to dealing with late-stage pregnancy, labor and delivery. Somehow, she had to keep in tune with her changing body. The only resources she had were a couple of paperback pregnancy books she'd bought before they left for Africa.

Somehow, her tattered copy of "My First Baby" seemed woefully inadequate.

65

THE HEIR TO BLACK CASTLE HAD ONLY BEEN IN SCOTLAND A SHORT TIME, BUT he was already leaving his mark.

Black Castle had been considered a mysterious place for more than two hundred years, but it now took on a more sinister appearance. No longer would the eight foot high chain link fence serve to intimidate trespassers. Now sharp razor wire stretched along the top of the chain link fence surrounding the infamous landmark. Electrical sensors affixed to posts along the perimeter picked up any border activity. Video cameras focused on the main gate. The castle was dressed to deter – not welcome – potential visitors.

The number of employees had increased from only a few women to more than thirty staff members. A noted Edinburgh architect had been engaged to plan for the renovation and expansion of the castle itself, as well as to improve the scattered outbuildings. Already heavy equipment had been brought in to scrape the dark soil, readying the earth for its new foundations. It was obvious that this Duncan McDougal was a man of means.

He had slept for more than two hundred years, and he could never get enough of the modern wonders. He had walked the streets of the city as if he were just another tourist, but taking in everything new to him. No one could have imagined that he had strolled there as a child so long ago. He could recall some of the buildings that had existed two centuries earlier, although the magical changes had transformed nearly everything else.

Duncan had developed a taste for spending hours at a time in coffee houses. He had entered a Starbucks just below Edinburgh Castle and had passed the afternoon drinking coffee, reading newspapers and watching people. Now it was past three o'clock on the brisk winter day. Only a handful of customers were inside the small café.

He was lost in thought when a voice spoke to him.

"You must be careful with your thoughts. There are humans who can see what you are if you let your guard down. Then they will follow you and destroy you. They have hunted us down in the past. They possess powers that far surpass those of normal humans. They call themselves zoutari."

There was little that could surprise Duncan, and nothing he feared, but this voice inside his head startled and unsettled him.

He cast furtive glances around the establishment, seeking the source of the words. Then he saw her – a Negro woman, young and quite sensual. Her presence reminded him of the light-skinned Negro woman in New York who carried the child in her womb. He had tried – but failed – to kill her and her unborn child. Unlike that tall woman, this smaller one was exceptionally dark skinned and much shorter, maybe five and a half feet tall.

She came directly toward his table. He studied her intently, his quick mind analyzing her thoughts. When she was an arm's length from him, he realized that two beings existed in her one body. One was the woman herself; the other, a demon. Finally, he had met another *endosym*. That revelation alone would have measured high on Duncan's scale of astonishing events, but the fact that this was a female creature simply astounded him. He would never have imagined that a female *endosym* could even exist.

Duncan couldn't move. He stood mesmerized by the fascinating creature. Then, as suddenly as he realized her hidden truth, the demon disappeared, and she became a singular human.

She slid onto a chair opposite Duncan and smiled.

"I had no idea that there was another one of us here in Edinburgh," she said.

"Who are you?" asked Duncan.

"My name is Florence Kroma."

Duncan guessed she might be thirty years old. She wore a tight-fitting pale green cashmere sweater and a full-length blue and green tartan skirt. She spoke with a lilting British accent.

"And you are?" she asked.

"Duncan McDougal," he answered.

"Why don't we go to my flat where we can talk without being observed by the ones who hunt us?" said Florence with a sly smile.

In a matter of hours, the two knew everything possible about each other – mentally and physically. He was particularly enlightened by her ability to successfully navigate in the human world.

66

Her story began in Liberia, West Africa.

Her real name was Yenplu, in the Kapel language of Liberia, it means, "white woman," not because of the color of her skin, but because she was considered a beautiful girl child. When she was only twelve, she had been sent to bush school, where she was initiated into the Mende women's secret society.

Yenplu did not want to attend bush school. The first night while the other girls trembled in fear in the initiates' hut, she crawled through an opening at the rear of the hut and disappeared into the dark.

The bush school was conducted along the Saint Paul River. This was a time when the interior of Liberia was unexplored. There were no roads, only animal paths snaking through the forests. The initiates had been told that on the other side of the river was a place of dark spirits. No one was ever allowed to cross to that other side.

It was the dry season, and the river was low. The old *zos* who ran the bush school would be afraid to search for her on the opposite side. She easily waded across, stepping effortlessly in the shallow water.

As she moved stealthily along the river's edge, she came to a place strewn with large stone blocks. The jungle had overtaken an ancient village built of stone. She wandered aimlessly through the ruins. Without warning, she felt a cold wind come directly at her. A round opening, tall enough to swallow a man, appeared before her. Curious, she approached slowly until she reached a vantage point where she could peer into the aperture.

Something moved inside. A man? A beast? She couldn't tell. She was frightened to the depths of her soul. Her legs wouldn't move – not forward, not backward. She stood, almost hypnotically drawn to the peculiar creature.

It stood on two feet. Its body was gray in color. Its eyes were black orbs. The naked body was formed in the shape of a young female. Atop its head sprouted two horns. Its ears were long and pointed. It turned, and Yenplu could see a long tail coming from the base of its spine.

"A demon of the bush," Yenplu whispered.

Yenplu crouched behind the pile of stones. Her eyes remained open, wide with surprise as she watched the opening behind it disappear, leaving the female demon standing alone on Yenplu's side. It turned as if in search of a means of escape. It panicked and danced around in a frenzy of fear. Finally, it dropped to the Earth and stared at the point where the opening had first appeared.

Yenplu felt pity for the forsaken creature. She stepped out tentatively from her hiding place.

"My name is Yenplu," she said confidently. "What is your name?"

The demon snapped to attention, jumped to its feet and started to run.

"Wait! Don't leave," shouted Yenplu. She reached out toward the creature's shoulder. As her hand touched the ashen flesh, she felt a sharp crack of static electricity. Then the demon vanished.

Yenplu realized that the demon had entered her being. She was seized with uncontrollable panic – she ran, turning, twisting and tearing through the tangled forest.

"So this is why we were told to never cross the river," she said aloud. The ancient warnings were not just tales passed down by old crones. They were not baseless – they were true.

Eventually, Yenplu found her way back to the other side of the river. She wandered aimlessly through the bush. When the *zos* found her, she was chastised for having left the school. Her punishment would mark her for life as a senseless female who violated their rules.

She was sentenced to a branding on her right cheek. A cutlass was heated by immersing it deep in the fire's coals. Two strong women held her motionless on the ground while a third drew the glowing metal from the fire.

Yenplu fought valiantly. The demon had endowed her with exceptional strength. She writhed, twisted, and pulled away from her two captors. She pried the cutlass from her attacker's hands. She lifted it high above her head. With the full force of both her arms, she brought the weapon down swiftly at an angle. It tore into her attacker's throat, separating the woman's head from her body.

Then Yenplu faced the other two who staggered to their feet in an attempt to escape. She held out her right foot and tripped one; she threw her left elbow into the other's midsection. Both women lay on the rocky ground, shivering in fear, looking up at Yenplu. They begged for mercy. But Yenplu ignored their pitiful cries. She lifted the cutlass once again and brought it down on the closer of the two women. She raised it high once again and let it fall forcefully on her companion. In two swift strokes, their heads rolled on the hard earth, their bodies writhing senselessly. Finally, all their movement ceased. As their spirits left their bodies, Yenplu felt a surge of power come into her body. The essence of the dying women was sucked up and internalized by the demon inside her.

Yenplu left the bush school once again, this time never to return. For a number of years, she hid in the bush, surviving by killing the hapless humans who made the mistake of traversing the thick bush unprotected. Slowly, she gained more knowledge and became aware that she must keep the secret demon hidden inside her.

Eventually, Yenplu found her way to the capital city of Monrovia. Men followed her, relentlessly seeking sexual favors. Her life changed forever when an Americo Liberian, who had ascended to a high position in the Liberian government, found her and fell in love with her. He arranged for her formal education at an English finishing school. He visited her frequently until they could finally spend all the rest of their days together.

That was more than a century ago. Throughout the past one hundred twenty-five years, she had amassed great wealth. More importantly, she had learned how to successfully live among the humans as an *endosym*.

67

HER NAME CHANGED MANY TIMES. NOW KNOWN AS FLORENCE, SHE GAINED control of several highly profitable corporations, but her true identity remained shrouded in mystery.

Duncan listened carefully to the woman's words. She was indeed a brilliant creature. She gave him some of her most valuable secrets as to how to live as an *endosym* in the human world.

"Hide in the shadows," she warned him. "Don't make yourself well known."

She told him of another Liberian *endosym*. She had never met him, but she had heard that he had been foolish enough to develop a follow-ing, claiming that he channeled an ancient sprit. His name was George Sarday. Six years earlier he had opened a school in Johnsonville, Virginia. It served as a cover for his teachings and ritual sacrifices. A cataclysmic event occurred that destroyed the school. Sarday was foolish, Florence contended. His own pride and stupidity destroyed him when the humans learned that he was an *endosym*.

For three days, Duncan stayed in Edinburg in Florence's flat. He told her about his transformation, his death in 1779, and waking up in this new century. He told her about the light-skinned Negro woman in New York and the child in her womb. He feared that the unborn child had frightened his own demon.

As Duncan and Florence shared their life stories, Duncan became even more certain of the potential power of the *endosyms*. He and his kind were indeed the rightful rulers the planet.

Of all the revelations offered by Florence, none was greater than her open sexuality. As a warlock, Duncan participated in frequent sex with the women of his coven. After he and the demon had forged themselves into one being, everything changed for the worse. Copulation with a female had never been a problem, but the act itself now gave him little satisfaction. He enjoyed killing a woman far more than sleeping with her.

But with Florence it was different. They become four beings simultaneously copulating. The male and female *endosyms* enjoyed a union like two passionate lovers joining together for the first time. Sexual pleasure was, unfortunately, the only benefit. Had the demons of both sexes been able to unite with humans producing *endosyms* as offspring, then the possibility to expand their kind would have doubled. But an *endosym* could only be created by a living human and a living demon uniting to become one creature. Yet the joy Duncan experienced with Florence was the closest he had ever come to loving another person.

Duncan was also pleased to learn that Florence knew of the existence of two more *endosyms*. Furthermore, she knew how to contact them.

For so many years, Duncan had devoted his life to his quest to find the demons. He had studied the ancient stories of the small statues of demons, made from metal, not of earth. They had represented the demon world. Under precise rituals he had learned that the statues would lead to the entrance between the two worlds. But now, it satisfied him to know that other *endosyms* walked the Earth. He wanted to meet the two creatures. He asked Florence to arrange a meeting with the other *endosyms*.

68

Duncan's guests had arrived late in the night.

Nearby farmers later reported that they had heard the whirr of helicopter rotors. Some were temporarily blinded by the aircrafts' running lights. Two loud contraptions touched down quickly and then immediately took off in the moonless night.

Now in the great room of Black Castle, two men and one woman sat face-to-face with Duncan. Not since the days of ancient Egypt had *endosyms* gathered with a common cause. These four, for better or worse, had managed to control the demons inside them.

Their demons were not destroyed; they were just under control. Instead, the human side had taken charge. The demons simply resided within human bodies. The new man-demons had become *endosyms*.

Duncan had acknowledged that there might be other *endosyms* in the world, but he had doubted it. However, he had learned a great deal since his awakening from the grave. He had reached another level of understanding – he realized that *endosyms* controlled by the human mind would evolve into something far more powerful.

Yet Duncan had exceptional self-confidence in his ability to deal with the future. Due to his two hundred year sleep, he was the youngest individual in this group of four. He believed that he was destined to become the apex predator of the planet.

He studied the others. Wealthy and powerful, they managed their own empires with iron hands. They had kept their secret from the humans who surrounded them.

On Duncan's right was Krill Morozov, a leader in the Russian mafia. He had lived three hundred years, changing his name many times. He had amassed billions of dollars. It was fitting that he took the name Krill, meaning "the lord."

The second was the oldest in the group. Now called Roberto Mendoza, he was born in 1211. Then he became known as Carlos Medina. As a young monk, he wrote the greatest book in the occult world, the Codex Gigas.

Next to him sat Florence Kroma.

Had there been someone listening to their conservation, they would have been astonished that the four could easily communicate in Russian, Spanish and English. As they spoke in their native tongues, they also shared their thoughts through mental telepathy.

Morozov opened the discussion.

"You are a fool, Duncan McDougal. We live wonderful lives, have great wealth, and all the worldly possessions one would ever want."

"True," chimed in Mendoza. "I have my own jet, ten villas and billions of dollars."

Duncan grinned knowingly.

"That's wonderful," agreed Duncan. "But you have tapped but a hundredth of your full potential. You must feed secretly on human essence. To gain your full power you must sacrifice at least ten humans within just one hour. To obtain full power, the human's head must be separated from the body."

"This world isn't as it was when you became one with your inner demon, Duncan," protested Morozov. "Modern weapons can dispatch us with ease. It is better to remain hidden and live well. How can just the four of us expect to conquer the entire world?"

"We can't," answered Duncan. "It will take thousands of demons, each with thousands of willing men and women in key positions, all willing to become *endosyms*."

The two men stubbornly refused to accept Duncan's argument.

"Don't you understand? The doorway to the demon world does not open on demand. It may take years or centuries before the portal opens once again. This is just wasted time," concluded Mendoza. "No one controls the doorway. No one."

"I will open the doorway using the ancient magic that I learned from my mother and her sisters. I will use the power given me by my lord, Satan," vowed Duncan.

"There is no magic. There is no God. And there is no Satan," scoffed Morozov.

"But you are wrong," said Duncan. "All these modern miracles change nothing. The dark forces of our ancestors still can control the destiny of the planet. We can become the rulers of the world and humans will become our slaves. There are billions of them. Once we've done this, we can reach our full potential."

Florence nodded. Duncan had great respect for her grasp of the potential power of the *endosym*. He welcomed her support.

But Florence had more to say. She added a chilling new element to the discussion.

"Very good, Duncan, but there is a threat to your plan. I have heard from our sources in Liberia that Samantha Dixon who is with child hides in the sacred village of Zigda. The *zos* believe that the child within her has even greater power and is capable of destroying all of us," warned Florence.

"The old legends told in Liberia speak of her," she said. "About ten thousand years ago, the door to the demon world opened in the ruins close to the Saint Paul River in Liberia. That is near where I became an *endosym*. The Egyptian rulers had begun to form an army of *endosyms*. But they failed in their quest. An army of humans, led by a woman, defeated the *endosyms* and forced the portal to close."

"Then we must prevent this child from being born!" declared Duncan.

"That is not as easy as it seems," explained Florence. "Zigda is a place of powerful magic. No *endosym* has ever been able to enter there."

"We'll take care of that problem. What I need now is your help," he said appealing to his guests.

Despite Duncan's convincing arguments and Florence's knowledge of Zigda, Morozov and Mendoza refused to acquiesce to his request. The final dissent came, not from the Russian, but from Mendoza.

During his six hundred year lifespan, Mendoza had been a deeply religious man, and he had written the greatest book on the occult. Now, he cared about nothing but himself.

"I have no desire to conquer the Earth," he said calmly. He stood and glared at Duncan and Florence in disgust.

"If you want to destroy humanity, you're on your own."

69

AS THE ROAR OF THE SECOND CHOPPER FADED INTO THE DISTANCE, DUNCAN stared into the fire's dying embers. Florence approached him and gently touched his hand. Blue sparks arced as her slender fingers caressed his cheek.

"We will not give up your plan. I will work with you to discover not only how to destroy this unborn threat to our kind, but also to learn how to open the doorway to the demon world."

Duncan's lips formed a satisfied smile. He looked deeply into her eyes.

"I know that Satan would never have let me live had he not had a greater plan," Duncan said. "I know in the ancient writing there is an answer to our questions."

Florence nodded in agreement. She was not sure there was Satan or a God, but she did know that she relished the idea of mastering of the human race.

"Tonight, let our bodies connect as one. Tomorrow, we will concern ourselves with the plan for the conquest of Earth," whispered Florence.

Duncan stood and followed her to his chamber.

70

The unique bond between Duncan and Florence flourished.

They were two *endosyms* whose powers had multiplied as they joined physically and mentally. It was their good fortune to have found each other and to have acknowledged their common history. They were two beings, truly joined as one. Between them, their superior union stood on the brink of accomplishing their mutual goal of conquering the Earth.

Duncan and Florence lay together in Duncan's chamber, their bodies still entwined and their passion temporarily satisfied. Florence had fallen asleep, and Duncan rested at her side, quietly admiring his treasured partner. He ran his fingertips lightly over her pale cheek, down her slender neck and brought them to a stop at her full breast.

Unlike the human male, Duncan's active mind could concentrate on his physical needs while simultaneously focusing on the myriad of questions that came into his conscious mind. He marveled at the brain's ability to control the body's physical functioning while forming complex thoughts at still another level.

"Only twenty percent?" he whispered. He had read that scientists had concluded that the human brain uses only twenty percent of the brain's potential. "How could that be? What happens in the other eighty percent of the brain? What powers we would have if we could only harness that power!"

He had committed himself to the study of the brain. He reasoned that if he and Florence used their combined powers, they could unlock the secrets of mental acuity and use their knowledge to extend their powers over mankind.

Duncan rolled onto his back and focused his vision on the rough boards on the ceiling. His mind raced – too many questions remained unanswered. Too many so-called miracles had been dismissed as fantasy rather than fact.

A series of physical and mental examples flashed through his mind: What about the one hundred ten pound woman who lifts a passenger car off of her husband's body? What about the child who had been under water in the family pool for more than an hour, yet still survives? What about twins who can read each other's minds or feel the same pain, or the mystics and shamans, who pierce their bodies, show no pain and heal instantly?

Duncan's own past provided a unique perspective on the brain's untapped powers. He wondered if the ancient druid sect had access to powers that modern mankind had forgotten. Was it through them that he had gained his powers?

The existence of the *endosym* itself presented many questions about the potential of the man-demon brain. First, its brain is nourished by the release of electrical energy from a dying brain that is in close proximity to the receiving *endosym*. If the victim is mentally advanced, even more power enters the host *endosym*. Second, the combined cellular structure of the man-demon brain far exceeds the capacity of the brain of a normal human. Even more amazing is the fact that the *endosym* has supreme self-healing power. Only the destruction of the brain or heart can kill an *endosym*.

Duncan was now fully alert. He sat up on the edge of the bed, stood and walked to the open window. Already he could see that the dark of night was diminishing and the sun would soon brighten the eastern horizon.

"Why …?" Duncan murmured. "But why do so many *endosyms* fail to thrive?"

Could it be because of the internal conflict between the demon and its host? Could it be that the ensuing mental battle between human and demon never cools? If so, the weakened *endosym* would always fail to reach its full potential.

"That's it!" he said aloud. If the *endosym* could overcome its internal struggle as Duncan and Florence had, their potential power would be without limit.

Duncan formulated a plan of discovery and conquest. The two *endosyms* would embark on a journey that would lead to the creation of the most superior being ever known. They would find out how to open the portal to the demon world. They would draw selected demons through the portal, link them with the chosen humans, and develop a super race of *endosyms*.

Achieving this supremacy would be impossible had it not been for his partner, Florence. The two had become like a single entity. From the first time that they had slept together, they both knew that they had a superior connection. They would set out to find the answers to their questions.

When Florence awoke, she already knew his thoughts. That very day they began their research. Together they began to study the ancient texts that Duncan had brought with him, and they surfed the web for additional information.

Over a period of weeks, they studied the physical material that had been used to create the ancient statues. This metal could be formed into the tools that might open the portal to the demon world.

They employed their enhanced brainpower to decipher ancient writings. From ancient inscriptions, it appeared that the energy from one statue was insufficient to keep the door open. It would take several statues to make that happen. But where had the other statues gone, and how could they find them? They still didn't have the answers to those questions.

They also learned more about their own powers. They traveled to the Middle East and Africa where the bloody civil wars allowed them to indiscriminately take human life and drain the essence from their victims.

Physical battle did not deter their quest. Both Florence and Duncan could be riddled with bullets, yet they could survive. Their bodies healed instantly.

Their strength increased tenfold, and they discovered that they could control a number of humans by using only their mental powers. They could enter any business establishment and empty the cash drawers. They could walk out unchallenged. No one would remember that they had even been there.

All was perfect between them. The only point of disagreement was their dispute about the origin of the universe.

Florence believed that creation was just an astronomical event, with no divine intervention. Duncan believed that two mighty entities had battled for control. One was the God of the Christians who had killed his own mother. The other was Satan, the God he worshiped. What troubled him most was his belief that the child in the womb of Samantha Martin was somehow linked to the sword of the God that murdered his mother. For the *endosyms* to rule the world, the child must be destroyed.

Florence's spies in Liberia had found out that the woman was staying in the village of Zigda. According to Florence, *endosyms* could not enter the village. If they did, their strength would dissolve. This, more than anything, convinced Duncan that the humans' God truly protected the woman.

Florence, on the other hand, believed that with her enhanced power, she could easily enter Zigda and destroy the child. Both agreed they needed to find out more about Tim and Samantha Martin.

71

Duncan called Constance who had assumed leadership of his newburgh coven in his absence.

Since his departure, his followers seemed to have lost their powers. They were no longer the enhanced humans he required. He concluded that he needed to be in close proximity to his followers for their power to thrive.

After he discussed the issues with Constance, she told him that she also had news. She announced that she was carrying a child from the result of their coupling. Duncan knew that the child would be born human, but he promised Constance that both she and their child would one day become *endosyms*.

Now he had to learn everything possible about Samantha Dixon-Martin and her husband, Timothy Martin. He wanted to investigate their relationship to Zigda and find out if the Martins had ever faced an *endosym* before. He told Constance to do whatever was necessary to learn more about this couple. Certainly, Duncan's superior intellect and research would lead to their destruction. Not only the parents – but that unborn child, too – must die.

He and Florence were confident that they had taken the first steps that would eventually lead to the enslavement of the entire human race.

72

NEARLY 350 PEOPLE FOUND DEAD IN THE REMOTE
NIGER VILLAGE OF ZINDU, MASSACURED BY UNKNOWN
ASSAILANTS

The London Times: Niamey, Niger — *Shockwaves continue to ripple throughout the world today as leaders of civilized nations react to the bloody execution of every man, woman and child in this formerly tranquil village. The apparent genocide occurred about four days ago, according to authorities at the scene.*

Dr. Juan Ramirez, representing Doctors Without Borders, was among the members of a medical team who made the grisly discovery while on a routine visit.

"The scene was unbelievably gruesome," Ramirez told reporters. "Not only were the people brutally assassinated, the attackers also killed every living creature in the village."

Sources claim that the villagers had been decapitated, possibly while still living, based on the pattern of the blood spatter. A number of goats and dogs were also beheaded.

No group has claimed responsibility for the brutal attack. Warring factions from neighboring Chad have been recently involved in border skirmishes, but evidence has not been found to link them to the murders. The villagers had maintained neutrality in the conflict.

Investigators say that there appeared to have been no firefight. Many victims were found with loaded guns near their bodies. Most villagers had been inside their huts and were found murdered in their beds.

Investigators suspect that a number of individuals carrying machetes entered the village after midnight. Attacking simultaneously, they caught the villagers by surprise.

"Those responsible for this heinous crime must be brought to justice," said U.S. Secretary of State Hillary Kenton. *"We call on the peaceful African community to join with United Nations forces to stop such atrocities. This cannot be allowed to happen again."*

73

FLORENCE KROMA FOLDED THE LONDON TIMES AND DROPPED IT ON THE empty first class seat beside her. She adjusted her seatback.

"More champagne, Miss Tubman?"

"Yes, thank you," said Florence. The flight attendant poured champagne into her glass and returned to the galley.

Adeline Rousseau and her partner, Marie Duval, prepared to stow away the beverage items. The flight attendants on Swiss Air Flight 687 from Zurich to Monrovia both marveled at the distinguished woman who had ordered the most expensive champagne.

"She's so mysterious," said Adeline. "I don't believe that I have ever met anyone so fascinating. My skin just tingles every time I'm near her."

"I know what you mean," said Marie. "She must be someone very special. She also must have lots of money. She paid for both first class seats. That's one passenger I'll never forget."

The pilot announced that the plane would land at Roberts International Airport in one hour. Florence had finished reading the newspaper and had decided to take a brief nap before their arrival in Liberia. She was content; Duncan's plan had been unfolding to her satisfaction.

The biggest threat to their success was the woman with the unborn child. She and her husband had fled to Zigda where they believed that they would be safe from harm. Legend had it that no *endosym* could enter the ancient village. It was believed that an unknown force there sapped their power. Normally, Florence was far too practical to believe in magic, yet history suggested that Zigda might be the exception. The old village was rife with stories of mystical happenings.

Duncan's plan was to create a super *endosym* with such exceptional powers that Zigda's magic would be unable to stop it. Only in sudden death does a living creature release sufficient energy to reinforce the powers of an *endosym*. The more intelligent the creature, the more energy is released and internalized by the *endosym*.

Quickly killing large numbers of humans within a relatively short period of time would charge the super *endosym*. As mankind had become more sophisticated, randomly murdering and decapitating large numbers of humans was becoming more of a challenge. Florence couldn't be sure of the number of deaths that would be necessary to give the *endosym* sufficient power to enter Zigda and achieve its goal. She had committed multiple murders throughout her long lifespan, but she had only taken one life at a time. She only could come up with a "best guess."

Florence had been born in Liberia and knew its landscape and its people. She readily volunteered to destroy the pregnant woman who hid in Zigda. She had flown in her private jet to Cairo, Egypt, where she wandered through the city's slums, stabbing and slashing a number beggars and thieves. She knew her powers were increasing; she felt far stronger than she had ever been before. Still, she was uncertain if she possessed sufficient power to succeed. It was her idea to go deep into the sierra, enter a remote village, and murder every living creature she came across. She'd gain tremendous power to use in Zigda.

She had flown in her private jet to the airport in Illzi, Algeria. There she acquired a useable four-wheel drive vehicle and headed for the sparsely inhabited mountains in Niger's north. Only by chance did she enter Zindu. The gullible people were unfazed by the well-dressed, educated Liberian woman who came to their village in a Land Rover. Florence spent the night in a hut, the lodging offered by a friendly woman who spoke some English.

Her murdering spree began at three o'clock in the morning. The first to die was the woman who had unknowingly shared her hut with the visitor. Florence had stripped naked, reached for the woman's machete, and separated the victim's head from her body.

Immediately, Florence felt the familiar charge of energy enter her being. She arched her back and stretched out her arms, enthralled with a renewed strength.

Then she stepped out of the hut and stood silently amidst the scattered huts surrounded by the open desert. She prepared for her next move.

Fortunately for Florence, she could make use of one of the *endosym's* most unique powers – the ability to pass undetected among others. She could move from hut to hut without alerting the villagers. It took a great deal of mental energy to achieve this state of being. The power lasted only briefly, but that was all it took. She randomly stabbed, bludgeoned and beheaded her victims in her urgency to finish her task.

In one hut, she found ten family members lying on their mats on the dirt floor. She held them all in a stupor by the sheer force of her willpower, then she killed each one as the others slept, blissfully unaware of their impending demise.

By first light, she had finished her bloody binge – every living creature had been killed.

Again she raised her arms in exultation, but this time she screamed with intense joy. She felt her body had been re-born. She stepped up to the well in the center the village and rinsed the caked blood from her body. She returned to the Land Rover and tilted the side mirror so that she could observe her face. Outwardly, she saw no change, but she felt the charge of electrical energy course through her veins. No humans or even other *endosym*s could stand up to her now.

She returned to the hut where she had left her Western clothing. She couldn't help but to glance around at the carnage she had created. It had been a good night, a most successful night.

Back in the vehicle, Florence drove for twenty hours straight without rest to return to Illzi. She needed no sleep. She only consumed one meal within a twenty-four hour period. That was enough to sustain the human part of her being. She drove directly to the airport, boarded her plane and flew directly to Europe. She would fly to Liberia by commercial air. She was "Florence Tubman" on her passport. She gloried in her brilliance of having selected the surname of the nation's former president. Once back in Monrovia, her contacts would drive her to Sanniquellie. Then, in the dark of night, she planned to take the hidden road through the forest to the village of Zigda. No power on Earth could stop her now.

She felt the jet begin its descent. Duncan had it right all along, she conceded. They had stayed in the shadows too long. They should claim their destiny to rule the planet. Once the human race was under their control, they would plan great festivities.

The Earth was home to more than seven billion humans – plenty to quench the *endosyms'* thirst for power.

74

With a traditional lappa tied at her waist, Florence Kroma ran barefoot along the trail that led to Zigda.

The moon was full, and the path before her was easy to follow. Even if it had been totally dark, Florence's enhanced vision would have made the trail appear as clearly as if it were daylight. She could run for days at this pace and run faster than any human who ever ran a marathon. After all, she was an *endosym*.

All of a sudden, she stopped. She'd hit a wall.

Any racer knows what it is like to confront a blocking, physical force field. She slowed, struggling even to put one foot ahead of the other. Duncan had been right once again. Without the essence she had gained from the murder and decapitation of dozens of human beings, she would have had to turn around and return to safety.

She started again. Although her pace had slowed, she pushed onward. Uphill was nearly impossible, but she pressed ahead. She finally reached a high point and was rewarded by the sight of the village below her.

"Zigda, finally, Zigda," she said, her breathing labored. She came to a full stop, bent over and rested her palms on her kneecaps.

Soon she'd made her way down the hill and stood near a dirt pathway that circled the village. She strolled triumphantly into the center of the village, focusing her mental powers on the task ahead.

There was little activity at this early hour. It appeared that the inhabitants still slept. Only the scuffle of goats' feet and the occasional cluck-cluck of chickens interrupted the morning's quiet. She chose to kill the entire village right then. Even the dogs that should have been guarding the villagers didn't sense her approach. This was an opportune time to begin her search for the woman and her unborn child.

It didn't matter if she found them or not. Like in the village of Zindu, every creature in the valley would die a bloody death before dawn. She let the Lappa fall to her feet and stood naked beside a thatched roof hut. Its door appeared to be bolted shut. She noticed wide gaps between the boards in the hut's shutters. Nothing here was safe from her.

She was pleased.

75

Thin stripes of moonlight ran in horizontal lines along the back wall. The boards on the shutters fit loosely, but that was good. Besides letting in moonlight, the random vents allowed a little air to pass through.

Tim sprawled on his cot beside his wife. He snored, as usual, when he slept on his back. Tim had flopped from back to side and back again all throughout the night. Now, he rolled to his side, and the snoring ceased.

During the first year of their marriage, his snoring had been a nuisance. Now, Sam rarely heard him. She tried to ignore his tossing and turning. She threw off her lappa. It was all that had covered her nakedness. She was too hot, way too hot. Her hormones continued their relentless rampage.

She'd try it again. She rolled to her side and began to breathe deeply. Maybe sleep would finally come. She found herself wishing that the shutters were wide open, but she had heard stories of leopards entering the huts and stealing children or small animals during the night.

Her restless mind and the insufferable heat wouldn't allow her to sleep. At this altitude the air temperature would usually drop by twenty degrees at night, allowing comfortable sleep. But not tonight. To Sam, the interior of the hut felt like a sauna.

Now, the baby took up his turn in the war against sleep. He thrashed about, stretched and shoved his elbow into the soft flesh under Sam's rib cage.

"Cut that out, Trevor," she whispered. She put her fingers on the skin above his elbow and pushed gently.

But the baby chose not to hear. He continued to do his belly dance for several more minutes. Finally, he settled down.

She closed her eyes. It was then she noticed the unusual silence. Here, miles from civilization and roads and people, she had found the nights to be surprisingly filled with noises. Every creature that could make a sound played its part in the night symphony. Frogs croaked, crickets chirped, dogs barked – strange, unknown noises came from the forest around them. In the village, a cough could be heard from inside a nearby hut or a child might whimper in a dream.

But tonight was different. Sam felt like she had been secluded in a soundproof room. Even Tim had quieted. His snoring had been reduced to just a steady breathing. She lay perfectly still and strained to pick up even one sound from outside. It was so quiet that when the baby thrashed about again, she could hear the gurgle of the amniotic fluid in her womb. She suddenly was overcome by concern for her baby. Never before had he been so active except for that horrible day back in New York when the *endosym* had attempted to kill them.

The *endosym* – she had not even thought about the horrible creature since they arrived in peaceful Zigda. It was then that she felt a chill come over her. She felt goose bumps on her arms. Moments ago, she had been sweating; now, she shivered.

In their mutual dream, both Tim and Sam had agreed that the old man Chea Geebe had told them that they would be safe in Zigda. Togba had announced that the Poro had sealed the village. No one could enter. She had no reason to feel threatened. Was she simply being paranoid? She listened intently once again. Still nothing. Now she was certain that sleep was impossible.

She swung her legs over the edge of the cot and stood up. She bent over Tim and studied his sleeping form. He had a wool blanket tangled around his legs. He rolled back onto his back, and the blanket slid to the side of the cot. She was touched by the love she felt for this man. She suddenly felt foolish that she had wanted to wake him. Was this another of the strange things that happen when a woman is pregnant?

She was about to return to her cot when she noticed the leopard tooth necklace that Tim always wore around his neck. It was the same amulet given to his mother when the family left Zigda twelve years ago. It had served her mother-in-law well, keeping her safe from the government's goons. It had also protected Tim's dad, Hank, when he battled the *endosym*-possessed minister of defense. It had already saved Sam once when Tim rescued her from deep inside the cavern at the plantation in Johnsonville.

Sam knew how precious the leopard tooth necklace was to the Martin family. Now it also protected her as it would the newest Martin child – little Trevor in her womb.

To the people of Zigda there was no person more honored than the person who wore the leopard tooth. It was the equivalent to America's Medal of Honor. Whoever wore the sacred relic won instant respect from every warrior. They all knew that Tim had earned the right to wear the necklace.

She leaned closer to Tim. It was difficult to see in the dim moonlight that entered their hut from the gaps in the shutters and the cracks between the roof and the walls. Something drew her closer to the tooth. Then she thought she saw it glow with a light green hue. It became brighter, and then the tooth appeared to pulsate.

The baby inside her seemed to take his cue from Sam's anxiety. He again began thrashing about in her womb, this time more violently than before.

"Tim? Tim?" she whispered, shaking his arm.

"What? What's going on?" Tim said groggily.

"Tim, the *endosym* is here," she said quietly.

Tim was immediately alert. He sat upright and looked around the hut.

"Where?" he asked. "Where is it?"

"Not in here," Sam answered. "It's outside."

Tim shook his head. Sam was just overreacting.

"Honey, you must be having a dream. Let's just go back to sleep."

"No," she said firmly. "Trevor woke me. He's kicking up a storm, just like he did in New York."

"Sam, listen to me," Tim said, gripping her shoulders tightly with both hands. "The *endosym* can't get past the Poro."

"Tim, look at the tooth!" she said, her voice shaking in fear.

He held the cord out from his chest so he could get a good look at it.

"Oh, shit!" he said. The tooth was pulsating in his fingers.

He stood and swore to himself. Here he was without his gun just when he needed it most.

The only weapon around was the machete that leaned against the wall near the door. Every person in the village knew how to use a machete. It could be a formidable weapon, but he'd have to be close to his opponent to strike effectively.

"Stay here!" he said as he picked up his weapon and lifted the latch on the door. "Lock the door after me when I'm out."

They both knew that the flimsy latch on the door wouldn't stop an *endosym*-possessed man, but Sam did as she was told.

76

T<small>IM SILENTLY STEPPED OUT OF THE HUT AND ONTO THE EDGE OF THE CENTRAL</small> square. The brilliant moonlight had transformed night into day. He looked right, and then left. He kept to the sides of the square, weaving his movements by each hut as he hunted for the *endosym*.

Nothing moved. The villagers and every living creature seemed to have disappeared. He stopped every few seconds and listened carefully. Certainly, he would hear some movement. But he didn't hear anything but the rhythm of his own respiration – the air coming in, and his breath going out.

Still nothing moved. He was beginning to think that they'd been mistaken. Perhaps it was only a fluke.

Off to his left, he detected movement. He was relieved to see a young woman step out of the shadows. Most likely, she was a member of the tribe that inhabited Zigda. She appeared to be in her late teens or maybe early twenties. She would be a friend, not an enemy.

She was small, likely weighing a hundred pounds, and she was short, slightly more than five feet tall. Tim was startled by her smooth skin and curvaceous form. She conveyed outright sensuality. Any male would stop to admire this stunning woman.

Although her lips didn't move, Tim heard a voice speaking to him within his head.

"If you think that power of the leopard will protect you, you are a fool," said a female voice. *"I have come for the child. You will not stop me."*

The woman held her arms out toward Tim and took a tentative step forward. Never in his life had Tim even considered the possibility of striking a teenage girl with a sharp machete. But now, all his inhibitions vanished.

He charged at her, swinging the machete with all the force he could muster. The girl blocked his swing with her left forearm, knocking the machete to the ground and far from Tim's reach. She lashed out with her right arm, her fist striking Tim's chest with enough force to send him flying backward. He fell heavily to the hard ground. Now, he had trouble regaining his breath. He felt as if a semi truck had hit him. He rose to his knees and struggled to stand.

He realized that he had been mistaken about the young woman. She was strong, too strong for a simple village girl. She was a true *endosym*.

Tim assumed a defensive karate stance. He was no amateur. He held a second-degree black belt. Immediately, he threw a vicious kick to the girl's mid-section. The force knocked her backward, but just by a few feet. It should have sent any hundred-pound female flying farther than that. As for Tim, he felt as if he had kicked an NFL tackle, not a slight teenager. His kicks weren't going to be enough.

"*You cannot stop me,*" said the voice in Tim's head. "*We are growing in strength. Soon, you will all be our slaves. Now, where is the child? I can feel its presence. I will grant you a merciful death if you will just tell me now.*"

But the woman didn't intend to bargain. She just was preparing for her next move. She rushed at Tim with a speed impossible for any mere human. Without his training, Tim would have been dead by now. He managed to elude the woman's attack. He danced around her, avoiding her attempt to strike him down.

"Whew," breathed Tim. He took a half second to take in more air. He was tiring quickly. It was only a matter of time until she'd overpower him.

He had to come up with another plan. He remembered that in Johnsonville, Virginia the only way to stop one of followers was to shoot them in the head. To kill this *endosym* with only a machete he would have to behead the damn thing.

During the fight, he realized that no one had come to help him. Somehow the *endosym* had placed everyone in the area under its control.

Apparently only he and Sam hadn't been susceptible to the creature's powers. He danced to his right, near to where the machete had landed. He snatched it up quickly, held it firmly with both hands, and turned toward the woman. He raised it overhead. She reacted by placing her forearms in front of her face in a defensive posture.

At the very last moment, Tim stepped to the side. He swung the sharp blade as forcefully as he could and connected with the *endosym's* back. She howled as blood gushed from the gaping wound.

Tim stopped to assess his next move. He was astonished to see that the blood ceased to flow. Instead, the gash appeared to have begun to heal itself. He was learning more and more about the powers of these powerful creatures. None of it was good news.

He needed a different approach. He lowered the blade and rushed the creature, attempting to stab her in the gut. But she laughed out loud; she had read his mind.

"You foolish human. You cannot stop me. I will easily defeat you."

Tim tried to think. What could he do? If he could get the thing on the ground, he would have a chance.

He rushed the *endosym* again, but this time, he threw himself to the ground and slid feet forward at her like a runner sliding to home plate. Both his feet connected with the *endosym's* legs, and she toppled over. As she started to get up, Tim was already on his feet, bringing the machete down on the *endosym's* neck. He let it slam into her thin neck with all the strength he could muster. Yet it wasn't enough. The thick blade sunk less than an inch into the flesh. Just a little more, and her head would have totally separated from her body.

Quickly, he swung at her again and again, hacking until the head fell loose from the body and rolled into the middle of the road.

At that moment there was a red flash – Tim saw a translucent demon come out of the corpse. It faded and disappeared into the dark. Whatever magic the *endosym* once had was now gone.

Villagers began to come out of their huts to gather around Tim and the remains of a young woman. They spoke in low tones, occasionally pausing to stare at the corpse, and to look at Tim in wonder.

As for Tim, he leaned against a hut, tilted up his chin and gasped for air. He looked straight ahead when he heard that Chief Togba had come to see for himself what had happened. At first, Tim thought that he might have violated some sacred code in this peaceful village. To the casual observer, it might appear that the white man had taken the life of an innocent young woman.

"This woman is not from this village," Togba said calmly. "I felt her in my mind, but I could do nothing. She was here to kill your child."

Togba stood in silence. Tim could see that the man was deep in thought.

"We must increase the power of the Poro, to stop the *endosyms* like this one from doing more harm."

Tim nodded his approval to the wise man. He couldn't agree more.

Two of the *zos* carried the remains – her head and body – into the bush. They started a fire. When the wood had burned down to red-hot coals, they threw the two pieces of the corpse onto the inferno. They waited until there was nothing left of the evil woman. Unless the body was totally incinerated, they feared that the demon spirit might return to her mortal remains.

Word of the *endosym* spread among the mountain villages. Joe Weah learned what had happened, and he returned to Zigda.

How had the *endosym* been able to bypass the protection of the Poro and enter the village? Perhaps other evil beings would try to repeat her deed or make an attempt to seek revenge for her death.

The people would increase their vigilance. From this moment until the birth of the child, the *zos* would guard Tim's woman, Samantha.

77

Waiting for Florence to return had been an ordeal for Duncan.

Like a cloistered monk, he had set up a harsh routine. He seldom left the castle's great room. He sat cross-legged on the polished marble floor. Head bowed, he had maintained the same position for days.

The pounding inside his head had softened to no more than a dull throb. He now knew that Florence was dead. Somehow, she had been defeated by the powers in Zigda.

Both Duncan and Florence had been certain they would succeed. They had constructed a foolproof plan.

Somehow, some way, something had gone wrong.

"Damn. Damn. Damn. Damn," he mumbled, his words coming like the rhythm of drumbeats. For Duncan, the curses became a prayer-like mantra.

"*If only*...." he thought.

"*If only* he had insisted on joining Florence when she flew to Africa. *If only* he had been with her when she murdered the villagers in Zindu. *If only* he had gone with her to Zigda..."

Duncan teetered from self-assurance to self-recrimination. They both had been certain that it would be a simple task to destroy the woman and the child within her. She had laughed when Duncan offered to go with her.

"You? With me?" she said in disbelief. "If the two of us were there it would be like using a bomb to kill a housefly."

He had stayed behind. He slept and read – all by himself in the castle's great room. He rarely ate. Sometimes the cook would bring him hard bread and thin soup. He read constantly. He poured through dozens of ancient texts, and he had just closed the thick leather cover of the last volume. He would read them all over again.

Without warning, Florence's screams had echoed throughout Black Castle. Duncan felt a searing pain at the back of his neck. He dropped to his knees and screamed her name, but it was late – far too late.

"Why?" he pleaded. He lifted his eyes to the high ceiling above him and cried out once again.

"Why? I have served you well. You saved me from death. You gave me Florence in gratitude for my services. Now she is gone. You gave me Florence, and now you've taken her away!"

There was no answer. He didn't expect an answer.

He closed his eyes again. He saw himself as a small speck on the surface of the planet. Above him shined the brilliant light of the God of the Christians. Below him opened the portal to the black depths of Satan, the God of darkness. Duncan was no more than a single pawn in their chess game. He spat out his venom for each of them – the two super beings took turns playing the game of life, pitting one wretched soul against another.

Did the God of the Christians protect the child?

Duncan seethed with anger. He vowed he would amass a great army and storm that African village, destroying everyone and everything in his path.

"You will not defeat me, God," he screamed. "I will overcome your powers and destroy the child."

He slowly rose to his feet. His head spun. He felt momentary vertigo. Then, clenching his fists, he walked to his desk and picked up the satellite phone. He punched in a series of numbers.

He waited for the familiar voice in Newburgh, New York.

"Duncan, I was waiting for your call," Constance said.

"What have you found out about the Martins?"

"His wife comes from a wealthy family in Washington, D.C. Tim Martin's family also lives there. His father serves as a general in the U.S.

Army," Constance said as she read from a long list of details about the Martin family.

"They were stationed in Africa twelve years ago. Tim Martin and his mother lived in Zigda for a time. While there, the family was involved in the overthrow of the Liberian government.

"Six years ago Tim Martin met his wife, Samantha Dixon, in Virginia. They participated in the total destruction of an *endosym* named George Sarday. It is rumored that a witch doctor from Zigda has endowed Tim Martin with the power to defeat an *endosym*."

So, thought Duncan, this is why Tim Martin had been able to destroy Florence. An outside power was protecting the Martins.

"Constance, I want you to monitor both families," he said, his voice seething with anger. "If there is any contact from Martin or his wife, let me know immediately."

He turned off his phone. He needed to keep a clear mind. As he paced around the room, his resolve strengthened. He realized that there was little he could do at this point. But, he reassured himself; the Martins could not stay in Zigda forever. His spies in Liberia would be watching their movements. When they left the protection of Zigda, Duncan would be ready.

He would avenge Florence's death.

78

Tim watched the road as Joe drove.

Tim breathed in deeply, still recovering from the previous days frightening and near fatal clash with the *endosym*.

His nerves were frayed. His muscles ached. He had nearly died in the evil creature's attempt to murder the woman he loved and the precious son who would soon be born.

"Don't go," pleaded Sam when Tim told her that Joe Weah had asked him to go somewhere with him.

"Don't worry, Sam. You'll be safe here," he assured her.

"It's not me I'm worried about, it's you," she said, tears welling in her eyes.

"You needn't be concerned about me," he reassured her. "Twelve years ago, Joe saved my life. If he tells me now that I have to go with him, I know it's important, and I'll go."

Joe had learned of the events at Zigda and had rushed to the village. He pulled Tim aside and told him that the two of them had to make a journey together. They'd left the previous afternoon and spent their first night in Gbarnga. The two men hadn't slept much. They spent the night drinking beer while Joe told Tim about Zigda.

"Tim, what I am about to tell you has never been disclosed to an outsider. Even the people of Zigda have never heard some of it. You need to know why Zigda is so important to our people."

"Joe, don't tell me then," Tim said shaking his head. He didn't want Joe to put himself in jeopardy by revealing secrets about the sacred village.

"No, Tim, you don't get it. I believe that you, Samantha and your child are part of the mystery of Zigda. What you will see tomorrow will explain everything.

"Tim," Joe continued, "Do you remember the valley where you and Sabo were held by the *endosym,* Sarday?"

"That's something I could never forget."

"Did your dad tell you what he and Charles had found in the underground tunnels?"

"Not that much. I knew he found that statue of the *endosym* down there, but Dad didn't say much other than it appeared that an ancient civilization had once occupied the area."

"Well, there is more to the story. It goes back more than ten thousand years. At that time, a group of Egyptians came up the Saint Paul River to a site near the valley where you were held. They were led by an *endosym* who masqueraded as a priest. He was a short creature, only as tall as a dwarf. He was also an inconsequential individual – but that was before he and the demon became one being.

"The Egyptians enslaved my ancestors and forced them to build a great city. The *endosym* priest found a way to open a doorway to the demon world. He began to create an army of *endosyms.* They fed off the essence of my people – beheading them and stealing their life force. As their strength grew, they spread out from the great city. Had they been able to continue their evil ways, today we would all be slaves to the *endosyms.*

"The village of Zigda was small back then, composed of just a dozen or so huts. Even then the *endosyms* could not enter this valley. We believe it is because of The Night the Sun Came to Earth.

"One night, the people were awakened. The sky had turned as light as day. The people left their sleeping places, ran out of their huts, and stared upward, but they were blinded by the brightness in the sky. They shook with fear and dropped to their knees.

"The bright light began to fade, and the night gave way to a second twilight. When the people were able to regain their clear vision, they saw that strangers had come amongst them.

"They were with light skin, taller than the tallest man in the village – the people thought that they were gods. The strangers spoke in the language of the people and told them not to be afraid. The next day they were gone. From that day the village was known as Zigda, which means where the light came down. From that time until today, it is the most sacred place in Liberia.

"The man chosen as chief has a most important task – he must always protect the village from outsiders. It is the only place on Earth where *endosyms* cannot enter. I know we say that the Poro protects the village, and we say the Poro is very strong. But, in truth, there is something else that protects us. It is hidden in the Mountain of Darkness. During our civil wars, the ruthless armies destroyed many sacred sites. Until last night, no enemy had ever entered the village.

We believe the *endosyms* are growing in power. The time may come soon when Zigda itself will again be breached, and we will have no way to protect ourselves. That is why I must take you to the see the chamber and show you how the endosyms were defeated in the past. We go tomorrow."

Tim sat in silence, pondering Joe's story.

"I still don't understand all of this."

"Welcome to the club. Until three years ago, I did not know the true story of Zigda," said Joe.

"How was it that you learned the truth?"

"As you know, I left the village and joined the army as a young man. It was against my father's wishes. Yet, I must tell you, I have enjoyed every day of my life. I have traveled around the world. I am wealthy and can have any woman I desire. I never dreamed my life would unfold so differently.

"One day old Chea Geebe came to me in a dream and told me I would become the guardian of Zigda. I had never really believed the old superstitions, but when Chea Geebe told the tale, it became real to me. The council of *zos* who select the next chief visited me. They told me that when my father died, I would rule Zigda. But when that day came, I would have to denounce all my worldly possessions and return to Zigda. I would serve as chief until my death.

"You know that I laughed at them and said to them that one of my half brothers could be the chief. I told the men from the council to go away. But the dreams stayed with me. The more I resisted, the more often Chea Geebe's ghost came to me.

"One morning I awoke and realized that deep in my heart, I really wanted to be chief. I contacted the *zos*, and they began teaching me the secrets of Zigda. As part of my training, they took me to the chamber by the old ruins. When your dad and Charles Moray destroyed the compound, I assumed that the chamber had been closed off forever. But I was wrong. There was another entrance and the *zos* led me there. I was told that only the future chief would see the wonders. I am that man. That is where you and I will go tomorrow."

"Joe, I am honored that you chose to share this story with me," Tim said. "Probably more than anyone else, I understand the threat of the *endosyms*. For me it started in that valley twelve years ago. Then in Virginia six years ago I again battled the *endosym* George Sarday.

"Now it has happened again. This time they worked their evil ways in the dark tunnels under the United States Military Academy. That *endosym* escaped. But it showed up once more in New York when it tried to kill Sam and our baby. Fortunately, they survived. We've felt safe – at least until the other night when I killed that female *endosym*.

"I'm convinced," Tim continued, "that there is more than one *endosym* involved now. Somehow they are communicating with each other. I suspect they have some evil goal that involves the fate of the human race."

79

THE NEXT MORNING JOE LED TIM BACK TO THE VALLEY WHERE IT HAD ALL begun for Tim twelve years before.

Tim had mixed emotions about going back. He looked at his left hand, flexing his fingers and rubbing the stub of his little finger. Sarday had it cut off as a warning to his dad, Hank Martin. Tim wore the mutilation as a reminder of what the *endosym* had done to him.

After a ninety-minute drive from Gbarnga, they passed through the town of Gbalatoah, crossed the bridge and entered the village of Saint Paulsville. Joe turned onto a secondary road shifting the Land Rover into four-wheel drive. It was a winding trail just barely wide enough for the vehicle. The road was almost impassable. Joe shifted into low range. They crawled along, passing a number of rice and cassava farms. It was slow going, but easier than walking. After traveling about six miles, they ran out of road.

"From here, we walk," Joe said. Each of them carried a rucksack, a canteen and a machete. They both had semi-automatic pistols.

Initially, the trail was easy to negotiate, but it gradually worsened. They came to a raffia barrier, the classic Poro warning that the sacred bush lay ahead. The uninitiated could not enter. If they tried, the dark spirits would kill them. The barrier had partially collapsed. In some places a man could simply step over the decaying grass and sticks. The overgrown trail beyond it had almost vanished. Tim recalled traveling along this same path twelve years earlier. He and his friend Sabo had barely come out alive. Joe, Charles and Tim's dad had come to their rescue.

The two men stepped over a low point in the barrier and picked their way along the worn trail. In several areas they had to use the machetes to cut their way through the dense brush. Twice they came to forks in the trail. Tim marveled that Joe always seemed to know which fork to take. At mid-morning they reached a clearing at the top of a hill and could see down into the valley below. The forest had once been clear-cut, but now, small trees and underbrush had begun to reclaim the area.

From their viewpoint, they could make out the broken remains of a circular stockade about two hundred feet in diameter. Its walls, now mostly collapsed, had been constructed of six-inch diameter wooden poles, each twelve feet high. On one end, Tim could see a circular mud hut that had served as a jail for Tim and Sabo. Now, in its current state of collapse, it wouldn't serve to corral a goat.

Within the large circle, Tim could see that the ground had sunken inward and created a hole nearly forty feet deep in its center. Tim had been impressed by the power of the blast that had been set by his father and Charles Morray. After the explosion, they had left the area, leaving time and the jungle to erase its evil purpose.

"What now?" asked Tim, glancing at Joe.

"We head for that rock outcropping above the valley. From there, we can access the tunnels."

It took them another hour to descend into the valley and reach the tunnel entrance. There they opened their knapsacks and took out two high-intensity flashlights and extra batteries.

They passed through a cleft in the rocks with Joe leading the way. He seemed somewhat uncertain of which direction to take. Tim paused for a moment to inspect the opening in the rocks. It appeared that someone had enlarged the natural cleft in the hill. He could see lines in the rock indicating that a hand chisel had been used to widen the opening.

After going only another fifteen feet, they entered a natural limestone chamber. Tim's eyes had to readjust to the dim interior. He looked upward at the dark ceiling. It was covered with thousands of sleeping bats. He didn't know where to step, so thick was the accumulation of rotting guano. They stepped close to the wall to avoid wading through the deepest of the manure.

They tipped their lights upward and saw another opening to the right. It appeared to be man-made and very old.

"This way," Joe said without looking back to see if Tim was following.

They passed downward through the opening and went nearly three hundred and fifty feet until they came to an opening that led to another limestone cavern. They pointed their lights upward, but the beams couldn't reach the cavern's ceiling. They could see thousands of stalactites pointing downward like icicles. Dripping water echoed from deep inside the cave.

It was so similar to the cavern in Virginia that Tim now completely understood why Sarday had chosen that underground sanctuary as the ideal place to conduct his ghastly rituals.

As they moved along slowly, Tim realized how alike it was to other limestone caverns he knew about. He'd seen pictures of places like this before that had been taken in other parts of the world. In some places, the passageway became a tunnel so narrow that the two men had to crawl one after the other on their hands and knees.

Other passageways branched off to the right or to the left, but Joe stayed to the more worn path. They passed by several pools of crystal clear water. They heard no sounds other than the drip-drip of falling water.

When Tim stopped to touch a coral-red outcropping, the toe of his boot came in contact with a circular object, about eight inches across. He bent over and picked up a brass disc. It looked like an oversize doughnut, but had small, protruding bumps on its surface. When he picked it up, Tim was surprised at its weight. It felt heavy. Tim guessed it might weigh as much as five pounds.

"That's a tien or a water spirit," Joe said. "Formed from bronze, they are found throughout Sierra Leone and Liberia. Our people have forgotten how they were made. Many say they come from a lost wax-casting method, but I am uncertain how it was done.

"Occasionally, the change in current reveals them in the sand along the riverbanks. They are very old. There are thousands in this cavern.

They were used by the Egyptians to barter for slaves," said Joe. "The warriors who guard the Mountain of Darkness have the symbol of the tien carved on their chests."

They continued deeper downward into the cavern, stepping over more and more of the brass objects scattered along the trail. Tim was amazed at how many there were. He also was surprised at the variation in size, ranging from only a few ounces to nearly thirty pounds.

They came to another narrow spot. They crawled several hundred feet, sometimes holding in their breath or bumping their heads. Finally, the passageway opened up into a large, smooth-walled chamber.

"Wow!" said Tim, staring with wonder at the sights before him.

"This is the place," Joe said. "You aren't going to believe what all is in here."

Tim shined his light from side to side and top to bottom, gasping with surprise each time he came across something beyond belief. The cache of ancient artifacts included brass spears, large plates that appeared to be made of gold, and a wooden throne inlaid with precious gems. Two large carved wooden statues sat side-by-side at their left. The walls were decorated with hieroglyphics and multicolored drawings.

"This is unbelievable!" Tim whispered in awe.

Joe moved ahead to the far wall, flashing his light beam on primitive drawings on the stone. One scene depicted an open valley with groves of trees covering green rolling hills. A variety of crops and herds of fat livestock proved that this had indeed been a fertile valley. He rested his light beam on a large stone statue at the center of the scene.

"That's the Great Sphinx from Egypt," Joe said. "The drawing predates the pyramids. Look, you can see trees and grass, not desert."

To their right they examined a second drawing, this one featuring men bowing to two *endosyms*. One *endosym* was tall; the other short and dwarf-like, less than three feet tall.

The next drawing depicted the taller *endosym* leading a group of men toward the sphinx. In the next drawing, the smaller *endosym* seemed to be taking another group out of the valley.

"Wow, do you see that?" asked Tim, as he studied the next drawing. "It looks like they're cutting the heads off of some people."

"You're right, Tim. It's logical – there are lots of stories about *endosyms* and human sacrifice," Joe replied.

Another drawing appeared to be a map.

"That's the western coast of Africa thousands of years ago. Arrows indicated a route to West Africa by sea," Joe said while he pointed to a curving line. "See, that's the Saint Paul River."

Men dressed in Egyptian costumes seemed to be greeting naked black men. Other black men were tied and bound together. Piles of the bronze discs were stacked nearby.

"See, the tien are being used as money to barter for slaves," Joe explained.

Another drawing showed dark-skinned men building temples. In all the pictures, the dwarf-like *endosym* seemed to be directing the Egyptian priests.

A map showed a road leading from the city into a valley. One drawing illustrated the inside of a cavern. Another depicted the construction of more temples and an amphitheater.

They continued to follow the drawings. The next drawing showed demons stepping out of a round opening in the ground. The demon-like warriors appeared to be marching up to the Egyptians.

"An army of *endosym*s," said Joe. "Had the doorway remained open, they would have conquered the Earth."

The final group of drawings was more crudely done than the previous pictures. In these, black men attacked the Egyptians with spears. The city was in flames. Egyptians seemed to be placing stones across the entrance to the caverns.

The final drawing was a life-sized, full color rendition of a beautiful light-skinned woman with green eyes. She held a short sword over her head. The blade glowed green. Standing beside her was a huge leopard. Its fur was gray with black spots. "That's the same green glow as the leopard tooth," Tim said aloud.

The woman was naked except for a leopard hide loincloth tied around her waist. Her physical features were surprisingly realistic. She had small, well-formed breasts. The biceps in her arms and legs showed a high degree of fitness. She was thin — obviously well toned and strong. At her feet lay dozens of beheaded *endosyms*. Tim was startled to see how vigorous and alive she seemed.

"This is why I brought you here," said Joe. "Her name was Anaya. Ten thousand years ago, one of the visitors from The Night The Sun Came to Earth stepped out of the jungle. He was naked and sick. A young woman from our tribe nursed him back to health. She later gave birth to his child. This girl-child was only five years old, when the stranger died. She thrived as a member of our tribe. She grew tall, far taller than any of our men. People knew that the gods had given her to us.

"One day she went into the jungle. She returned several days later with a message from the gods. We were to form an army and defeat the *endosyms*. The warriors at first laughed at this young tall, light-skinned woman. But they quickly found that she possessed unbelievable strength and wisdom. Warriors gathered from all surrounding tribes and prepared for battle.

"Anaya led us to victory. After the *endosyms* were defeated, she returned to Zigda, married and had many children. The people of Zigda all claim to be descendents of Anaya," Joe concluded.

"She looks like Samantha, only her skin is lighter," said Tim staring at the woman's face.

But it wasn't Sam; it was Anaya, the female warrior who had defeated the *endosyms*. The woman could have been Sam's sister.

"My God, Joe, do you realize that Samantha's ancestors came from here?"

"Tim, now you know why the *endosyms* want to kill your son. He has to be one of Anaya's descendents."

"Does that mean my son will be able to defeat these *endosyms*?"

"I don't know," said Joe. "It is beyond my understanding. It is mystical. It's magic."

Neither man spoke. The two stood silently, gazing at the pictures that showed the past, yet foretold the future.

Finally, Joe lightly tapped Tim's shoulder.

"Come on, now you must see what can happen if the *endosyms* ever get a foothold on Earth."

The two of them went farther into the chamber. They passed a large pile of broken rocks. Joe must have noticed Tim's puzzled look.

"That happened when your dad blew up the tunnel leading into the valley," said Joe.

Even farther back they came to a doorway carved in the wall. Two wooden *endosym* statues, each almost ten feet tall, framed the doorway.

Joe didn't hesitate. He led Tim through the portal. Tim felt a sudden flow of cool air. They stepped forward and aimed their flashlights inside the tunnel. Far ahead, Tim saw a light. It became brighter and larger as they moved ahead.

They stepped into a grand chamber, more than a hundred feet in diameter. It had some of the features of a Roman amphitheater. Rows of benches were lined up parallel to what appeared to be a granite temple framed by tall marble columns.

Tim couldn't imagine the manpower and ingenuity – plus the time it took to construct such a grand stadium. The place was so large that it was difficult to see across to the opposite side. Just like the cavern in Virginia, it was illuminated by phosphorescent light. Sarday had conducted his ceremonies in a large cavern just like this one.

"It even has the same glowing algae," marveled Tim. "The *endosyms* must know how to locate these places throughout the world."

They moved deeper into the amphitheater. For the first time, Tim noticed thousands of round objects that had been placed side-by-side on the benches. Tim knew what they were – Sarday had started the same thing in Virginia. Even the cadets at West Point were collecting human skulls.

"Joe, this is what they plan to do," said Tim.

"Look at the scope of this," said Joe. "It's incredible."

They moved down a rocky pathway toward the center section. When they neared the first row, they paused to take in the enormity of the grisly scene. Some of the severed human heads still had pieces of dried flesh and strands of dark hair. The farther down they went, the more the heads resembled skulls.

"In the stories told by my people, they call this the temple of the skulls," Joe whispered. "All these people were sacrificed to *endosyms*. Imagine what would happen if hundreds of *endosyms* organized an army whose sole purpose was to destroy the human race."

"I've seen enough," Tim said firmly. "Let's get out of here."

They retraced their steps and entered the chamber of treasures. Joe stopped and pointed to a cache of bright stones.

"Tim, you need to fill your rucksack with those gems," he said.

"I can't do that, Joe. That treasure belongs to Liberia. Those gems are worth millions of dollars."

"No, Tim, it doesn't belong to Liberia. Only evil will befall us if we claim this treasure for ourselves," Joe said with conviction. "But your son may be the salvation of mankind. For you and Samantha to defeat the *endosyms*, you will need this wealth to hide the child from them until he comes of age. Those stones could well provide the means for him to save the world."

Joe scooped up two large handfuls of gems and poured them into Tim's knapsack.

"Leave the rest," said Joe. "Let this treasure remain here for eternity."

The two men made their way out of the cavern. Tim was relieved when they saw the Land Rover where they had left it under a tall, leafy tree. He sucked in deep breaths of fresh air and paused to reflect on what Joe had shown him.

"Joe?" Tim called to his friend.

"What is it?" Joe asked.

"Don't tell Sam what we saw. She doesn't need this burden now," Tim said. "I will tell her when the time is right."

80

Samantha drew an "x" on the date January 16 on her small calendar.

Each day since they had arrived in November, she had checked off the date as a new day began. The skin of her entire mid-section was now so tight that she thought she could bounce a quarter off of it. Shelly had guessed the birth date around January 21. Only one more week was left if her estimate was correct. Well, Sam concluded, anytime now is just fine. She had been ready for the last three weeks.

Tim and Sam had been in Zigda for only two months. Sometimes it seemed like they had been in the village for years, maybe even centuries, she concluded. At least, it felt like it.

With no radio, TV or news, time seemed to stand still. Surprisingly, some of the villagers had chosen to celebrate Christmas. She and Tim had joined a small group of Christian villagers who had learned to sing Christmas carols. The words were somewhat familiar, but the couple had to smile at the African rhythms they added.

They had no gifts to exchange, but Tim had kissed her and said that she was the only gift he would ever want. Then they had joked about their son being born on Christmas night. Then it would have truly been a holy night. But now it was January 16 and still nothing.

Sam needed to pee. That was becoming a continual problem as Trevor's growing size caused pressure on her bladder. Sam nodded at her female assistants and two of them joined her in the trek to the women's toilet. This morning she had experienced her weekly stomach cramps that had come regularly the day after she took her malaria pill.

"These stupid cramps," she mumbled as she clumsily made her way down the trail. One strong cramp nearly doubled her over.

Finally, they reached the trench. Sam pulled up her lappa and lowered herself to pee. It took both Mamamu and Lanai to keep her balanced. She started to urinate. Then, a gush of liquid poured from inside her.

And then she had a cramp from hell. She gasped. Mamamu begin jabbering in Kapel.

"Oh, my God," gasped Samantha. "We need to get back to the village. The baby is coming."

"Bath first," said Mamamu in broken Liberian English.

"No time," said Sam. "We need to get back right now."

Mamamu again said something in Kapel.

Lanai translated.

"Mamamu say you have lots of time. First baby takes much work. You must take a bath before we return to village. Mamamu say many hours before baby is ready."

"All right," said Sam. "But we must hurry."

She waddled down to the bathing pond and waded into the cool water. Once Mamamu was satisfied that Sam was clean enough, she dried in the sun then wrapped her lappa around her. During this entire process, her cramps had gone away. She thought she must have had a false alarm.

Then another one, far more severe, struck. It began with a pain in her lower back. Like a charlie horse, the cramp seemed to radiate from around her lower body until it faded at her navel. This cramp caused her to gasp. She sucked in her breath.

The trio started back up the trail to Zigda. As they stepped off the trail and into the village, they were greeted by a number of children and younger women. They jabbered in excitement. Sam wondered what she done to cause such a frenzy.

"They know it time for baby to come."

"How?" asked Sam.

"We always know," said Mamamu.

Sam was taken to her hut where she collapsed on a chair. She had caught the people's excitement, but she also felt a little fear. Finally, Trevor would make his appearance; soon she would be holding their son.

Her joy turned to anxiety when she realized she was about to give birth in an African village deep in the jungle. What if there were complications? No one here could perform an emergency Caesarian. She bowed her head and made a sincere prayer to God that she would experience a normal birth.

Another contraction struck, even stronger than the previous one. The women were at her side, watching and questioning.

"Do you want to lie down?" asked Ananau.

"Not yet," said Sam. "Where is Tim?"

"He is hunting with the men. They have sent him word," said Lanai. Just then Tim poked his head in the door.

"Are you OK?" he asked. Sam had never seen Tim as anxious.

She opened her lips and began to speak when suddenly another contraction almost bowled her over in pain.

Her screams upset Tim even more.

"What can I do, Sam?" he pleaded. "We've got to do something!"

Mamamu stood and pressed her palms against Tim's upper arms.

"Women's business. You, out!" she ordered. She planted both feet firmly on the floor and looked up at Tim like a pit bull ready to bite.

Tim searched Sam's face, looking for her answer.

"It's OK," said Sam, "I'll be fine. Women have done this since the beginning of time. Tim, babies are born every day."

"Not ours," said Tim.

"Just wait outside with the men, we'll handle things here," she said between pains.

"All right," said Tim. "But call me if you need me. I'll be right outside."

Sam watched Trevor's dad step out of the hut. She doubted that she would need Tim. Her women and her body seemed to know what to do.

81

THE SUN HAD SET MORE THAN SIX HOURS EARLIER. SHE WAS STRETCHED OUT on her side on her cot. She'd read lots of stories about childbirth and had watched re-runs of *Little House on the Prairie*. If the pioneer women could do it, she could. At least, between contractions, she thought she could. When the sharp pains struck, she wasn't so sure.

Now the contractions came every thirty minutes. Just before dark, a woman in her early twenties had come into the hut. Mamamu had squealed with excitement and hugged the woman. The newcomer was Mamamu's daughter by Togba. She was one of Joe's half sisters. Same father, different mother, as the Africans say about the children of the men who took multiple wives. She was Shana Weah, a nurse from Phoebe Hospital. Somehow, Joe had gotten word to her that Sam's baby was about to be born.

No, she wasn't Sam's doctor, Shelley, but it made Sam feel better to have someone with her who had modern medical experience. Shana had brought a small black bag that contained the medical instruments used to ease the baby from the womb. She also told Sam that she would sew up the tears to her tissues following the birth. She explained that her husband would definitely be happy with that procedure. Shana was very knowledgeable, and it helped having an educated nurse in the hut. Perhaps Shana's training would help in the birth, but the primitive medical equipment failed to calm Sam's concerns.

"Time to look again," announced Shana, patting Sam lightly on her bent knee. Sam dutifully spread her legs while Shana used the thin beam from a flashlight to peer into the dark space between her legs.

But Trevor chose to take his time. For Sam, the hours dragged by slowly. She had already been in labor for more than twelve hours. Sweaty and sore, Sam was near exhaustion. She'd fall into a brief slumber between contractions and then be jolted awake by the jarring pain.

"Sam, good news," Shana assured her. "Your cervix is ten centimeters. That's what we want. Now your contractions will truly begin."

Shana nodded at the other women, and they surrounded the cot.

"We're going to move you onto a mat on the ground. We're getting close," said Shana.

"Thank God," Sam said weakly. "Thank you, God."

She was helped from the cot and lowered to a straw mat on the dirt floor.

"Get ready, Sam," Shana said. "This is really going to hurt."

"Hurt?" gasped Sam. "Hurt? If this is going to hurt, what in the hell has been happening already for the past fourteen hours?"

"Nothing compared to what will happen now," Shana answered. "But hang in there. It will all be over soon."

Sam lay flat on her back. She was completely naked. The women spread Sam's legs so far apart that it hurt. Then Lanai and Ananau each clasped her ankles and held her feet up bending her knees. Mamamu wiped perspiration from Sam's forehead with a damp, cool cloth. Shanna knelt between Sam's legs and peered at her vagina. The contractions continued to increase in strength and frequency, coming one after another. Sam felt like a Sumo wrestler was jumping up and down on her belly.

"Push! Now you can push," Shana said. "Come on, push harder," she insisted.

"I am pushing!" screamed Sam.

"Harder," Shana said, "Push. Push."

"My God, it hurts so much!" moaned Sam.

Just then, Sam felt a searing pain. It was a tearing feeling like someone had just ripped her open with a butcher knife. She couldn't breathe; the pain was too severe. She was staring at the thatch ceiling above her. The room was dark, only illuminated by the dim light from two kerosene lanterns. She experienced a ringing in her ears. The ceiling began to fade from sight.

Then she saw the bright light. Hovering above her was what looked like a large bubble, many feet in diameter. A big soap bubble, she thought. In the center of the bubble was a pinpoint of light, but brighter than the sun. It was so bright that she had to close her eyes. Strange, she felt no pain.

Death she thought, I'm dying. The light. She opened her eyes. Looking down at her was the witchdoctor who had come to her in a dream. What was his name? Chea, that's it – Chea Geebe.

"Am I dead?" she asked.

"Oh, no," said the old man as he smiled at her. "You are very much alive, and today you have given the world a great gift. If you are careful, this child will save the world from the *endosyms*."

"I don't understand," said Sam, confused.

"Thousands of your earth years ago, Anaya drove away the demons."

"Anaya?"

"Yes, look carefully, and you will see."

Before her, Sam saw a scene from a recent battle. The dead were strewn on the ground. A young woman, perhaps in her late teens or early twenties, faced her. She wore a leopard loincloth like the one Chea wore. She was naked from the waist upward; she had small, firm breasts. Her skin was light, far lighter than Sam's. In her right hand she carried a bloody dagger that glowed with a green light. Next to her stood a huge gray cat bigger than a Bengal tiger, its muzzle dripping with fresh blood, its sharp fangs at least four inches long.

Sam stared at the young woman's face. Sam was confused. She thought momentarily that she was gazing into a mirror. The woman's features were similar to her own, except that this girl's features were finer. But it was her eyes that were striking. They were green.

Then Anaya disappeared; Chea Geebe had also vanished. She stared at the thatched ceiling above her. She felt no pain.

"Samantha? Samantha, can you hear me?" asked Shana.

"Yes. Yes, I can hear you," murmured Sam, still groggy from exhaustion. Then she heard the baby's cries.

"Trevor?" she called. "Trevor, is that you?"

Sam's arms reached around the bundle the woman had placed on her chest. This, thought Sam, is the most beautiful sight I've ever seen.

The child stared directly at her, as if he had heard her call.

"We'll get you cleaned up, and your husband can come in," said Shana. "By the way, we were fortunate. The placenta directly followed the baby. The women will take it to the sacred bush, so it cannot be used for evil intention."

But Sam ignored Shana's words. She cradled the baby in her arms. Finally, it was beginning to sink in – she was now a mother.

82

At the United States Military Academy in West Point, New York, it was 20:05 on 16 January.

Jim and Maggie Parkinson had both been reading in the den. Jim turned a page in his novel. Suddenly he began to perspire.

"Man, it's hot in here," he mumbled.

"It's just you," said Maggie. "I'm fine."

"I'm going to step outdoors for a few moments," said Jim.

"Put your coat on. It's freezing outside."

"But I'm hot," argued Jim.

"Right, then you'll get cold. Leave your coat unbuttoned, but put it on," ordered Maggie.

"Yes, dear," grumbled Jim. He might be the dean, but in this house his wife was the commanding general.

Jim went to the hall closet, pulled on his winter coat and stepped onto the front porch. The snow was piled along the sidewalks. It was a crisp, cold winter night with the temperature around twenty degrees.

Jim walked down the steps onto the shoveled sidewalk. The lights were on in the cadet barracks. Four thousand cadets were preparing for the next day's classes and activities.

Streetlights cast a yellow glow on the freshly fallen snow. He looked toward Washington Road. The gaping hole from the collapsed tunnels had been filled. New sidewalks and curbs were formed up, readied for the pouring of concrete. The road would be paved in the spring. The Corps of Engineers had restored power and heat to all buildings. Sadly, the bodies of the three cadets and their victims would remain buried beneath the plain forever.

Jim still was having trouble sleeping whenever he thought of that horrible night in the tunnels. In his dream the *endosym* was a member of the faculty. He had tried to find out which one of his fellow officers was not human but really an *endosym*. He would be about to open the door to his office where he knew the *endosym* would be hiding when he would wake up in terror.

It was a clear night, and when he looked upward he could see the brighter stars despite the glow from the streetlights. Then he felt dizzy. He closed his eyes, fearing he was about to be sick.

When he opened his eyes he was in a hut. It seemed like he was floating near a thatched ceiling. There was no sound, no smells, no feeling. Two Coleman lanterns lit up the interior. Lying on her back on a grass mat was a light-skinned black woman. She wore no clothes and her legs were spread apart. Two women held her feet up with her knees bent.

She was giving birth. He couldn't see her face. He watched as the child was expelled from her womb. The baby, a female, was washed off and wrapped in a worn blue towel. She was a light-skinned, white child, yet clearly this was an African hut. It reminded him of the huts that he had seen when they were stationed in Liberia twelve years earlier. The baby's eyes were a striking green color. He felt joy as he looked at her wrinkled features. She smiled.

Then the scene vanished, and he was in a modern hospital. A woman with her legs in stirrups was giving birth. He was unable to identify the woman. Surrounded by doctors and nurses, her face was hidden from view. Only an overhead observer, he floated above the scene.

In an instant, an infant was expelled from the woman's womb. A doctor in blue scrubs cut the umbilical cord and carried the infant to a hospital crib where he gently laid it down and took a step backward.

This, too, was a girl, but something was wrong. The skin was a gray color. The head was too large and two small bumps protruded from a high forehead. Then he saw a tail. The newborn had a long tail extending from the tailbone. Then he hovered closer. The small creature – that's what it was – couldn't be human. It opened its eyes and stared in his direction. The orbs appeared to be only black holes in the head. It opened its mouth and let out a pitiful cry, revealing two rows of razor-sharp teeth, like those in a shark's mouth. This creature was pure evil. He could feel it in his bones.

A cloud of darkness surrounded Jim Parkinson, and he felt a moment of sheer terror. Then he realized that his eyes had been closed and he had only imagined the two episodes. When he came back into full consciousness, he was standing on the sidewalk outside his quarters. Cool air streamed by his face. Now he felt chilled to the bone. Maggie had been right – he was cold, very cold. His fingers struggled to button his coat.

What time was it? He lifted his cuff and fumbled to find his watch. It was now ten minutes past eight o'clock. What had happened? He had never experienced hallucinations, yet he could still see the baby with the green eyes, the child in an African village, and he also saw the creature with the black eyes in a modern hospital. He felt unwell. Still somewhat dizzy, he felt a burning in his throat. Only heartburn, he reasoned.

He returned to the warm security of his home and the comfortable presence of his wife. Once inside, he opened the kitchen cupboard, found his pills and swallowed two Tums. After hanging up his coat in the hall closet, he returned to the den.

"Did the fresh air cool you off?" asked Maggie.

"Oh, yes," said Jim as he collapsed in his easy chair. He picked up his novel and thumbed through the pages, but he couldn't concentrate. All he could think about was the two births he had just witnessed.

Was it an omen? Was it a prophecy? Was he going crazy? God, this was weird.

83

A NURSE WHEELED THE PREMIE UNIT FROM THE DELIVERY ROOM STRAIGHT TO neo-natal care at Newburgh General Hospital.

Time was critical. At six months, the survivability of the small girl was good. She weighed in at three pounds twelve ounces. Smaller babies had survived. Her name, Sabrina NMI McDougal, was scrawled in felt marker and affixed to the end of the tiny bed. Time of birth 8:10 PM January 16.

Constance Marsh had come in by ambulance at eight o'clock in the morning. Marsh was in advanced labor, which seemed strange considering that she was only in the beginning of her sixth month of pregnancy. So far, she had experienced an unremarkable, normal pregnancy. The birth had been normal. The infant was Marsh's first child. Normally, a fetus born this early would have been stillborn without a Cesarean. But, despite the premature birth, the baby was breathing on her own.

Dr. Harold Goodfellow smiled confidently at the new mother.

"Don't worry," the genial man said. "We have the best neo-natal facility in the state."

"I know, doctor," replied Constance. "I know she will live. She will be the first of the new order."

Goodfellow smiled. New order? Obviously the woman was a little off. After all, she had a pentagram tattoo on her forehead.

"You just concentrate on getting your rest. Our staff will take good care of your child," he said as he turned to go out the door.

Constance lay back on the white pillow. She didn't know what had happened to bring on the early labor. She knew that Duncan would be pleased to learn of his daughter's birth. She believed that Sabrina would one day be a leader in the new world order promised by Duncan McDougal.

"Enough. That's enough for now," she said, her lips forming a satisfied smile. She closed her eyes and drifted into a dreamless sleep.

84

NOTHING IN TIM'S LIFE HAD BEEN AS DIFFICULT AS LISTENING TO SAM'S screams and not being able to do anything for her. Not the dangers he faced twelve years ago in Africa, not the escape from Sarday in Virginia, not the terror in the tunnels beneath West Point, nor his near-death encounter with the *endosym* in Zigda – the memory of Sam's screams as she gave birth to Trevor had shaken him to his very core.

Soon, Tim would hold his own child. He thought of the memories of his relationship with his own dad. He was an only child. The bond between his two parents and him was incredibly strong. Although he was often separated from his father due to his responsibilities as an army officer, his dad always gave him one hundred ten percent when he was at home. He was committed to having the same strong relationship with his son.

Forty-five minutes earlier, had Joe not stopped him, Tim would have rushed into the hut. Sam had been screaming as if she were dying. Then came an eerie silence. He hung his head and breathed deeply.

"Sam, Sam, please don't leave me," he pleaded.

Suddenly, he heard a baby cry – an angry, demanding wail that meant that his new son was ready to take on the world. Tim sighed with relief. He glanced at his watch. It was 1:10 in the morning on January 17.

The old woman came out of the hut. She looked right, then left, spotted Tim, and muttered a few words.

"They see you shortly," she said before abruptly turning on her heel and disappearing back inside the hut.

For thirty minutes, Tim had paced back and forth.

"She said it would be 'shortly'," Tim complained. "There's nothing short about this waiting!"

The villagers had ignited a huge bonfire in the clearing near their hut. Everyone was awake and up, even though it was two o'clock in the morning. Of course, Tim realized, how could anyone have slept what with Sam's screams?

"Your woman is ready to see you," said Mamamu, poking her head out quickly.

Tim had been immersed so deeply in his own thoughts that he jumped when he heard Mamamu speak.

Tim cautiously entered the hut, pushing the crude wooden door inward with his foot. He was astonished to see Sam sitting in one of the chairs. She wore a colorful lappa. Her hair had been combed. But he could tell that she was exhausted. She looked like she had just finished a marathon. Yet, there was a glow of excitement in her eyes. She held a small bundle in her arms.

"Trevor?" Tim said softly.

Sam looked directly at Tim.

"Tim, there is a little problem."

"A problem?" gasped Tim. "With the baby or with you?"

"It's the baby."

"Oh, my God, Sam. What's wrong? Is he deformed or blind – or does he have some kind of birth defect?"

"Not really a birth defect, but fifty percent of babies don't have one."

"One what?" asked Tim exasperated.

"A penis, Tim. I'm telling you that Trevor is a girl."

"A girl? You mean like a girl?"

Sam could see the disappointment in his eyes.

"I'm sorry, honey."

"You're sure it's a girl?"

"Either that or he has the shortest penis in the world. Tim, there is no question about it, we have a daughter."

"A girl?" asked Tim again.

"Do you want to hold your daughter?"

"I ... I can? I can do that so soon?"

"Of course, silly. She won't break."

She held their daughter out to her father's arms. Tim reached out and took the child from Sam. He cuddled the baby close to his chest.

Sam could only watch her husband's face as he embraced his daughter. He must be so disappointed, she thought. He so wanted a boy. Maybe they should have looked at the ultrasound. If they had known the baby's gender earlier, Tim might have had time to prepare himself emotionally. He wouldn't have had such high hopes for a son.

Would he reject the baby? She looked at his face, trying to assess his reaction. She saw tears running down his face.

"Tim, I'm so sorry that she wasn't a boy."

"What?" said Tim, "I didn't hear what you said."

"You're crying. I have never seen you cry."

"Oh, Sam. She's so beautiful; I have never seen a baby so beautiful. I know, every parent says that. But most babies are red, wrinkled little gnomes. Her eyes, they're green. Our daughter is beautiful."

Sam looked up at the picture of her husband and daughter meeting for the first time. She knew then that everything was going to be all right.

"We never discussed a girl's name. What are we going to name her?"

"Anaya," said Sam with a smile. "Her name will be Anaya."

85

SAM RESTED ON A WOODEN BENCH IN FRONT OF THE HUT.

The overhang of the thatched roof provided a block of shade away from the tropical sun. Anaya was happily tugging at her mother's right breast. As she greedily suckled, the baby's eyes were closed and her sweet face had an expression of absolute contentment. How bizarre, thought Sam. Here she sat – a college graduate, TV reporter and daughter of a billionaire, bare-naked to the waist, nursing her baby as people casually strolled by, often stopping to chat and peek at the new baby.

Sam's daddy would have suffered a coronary if he had seen her like this. She stifled a sob. She had cried a lot in the last three days. Tim should return by this afternoon. He had left to make arrangements for their departure from Zigda. It should be a joyous time; they would be returning to New York. She would show off her daughter to her friends. Both sets of parents would be ecstatic to meet their new granddaughter. But that wouldn't happen. That would never happen, and she cried each time she thought about it.

How could God be so cruel to do this to them? Of course, she chided herself for being such a fool; she should have realized that this change in plans was the only recourse. Anaya was five weeks old and ready to travel. Since Sam was overflowing with milk, transporting the baby would be easy.

After Anaya's birth, Tim had seemed so distant from Sam. He acted like he relished being with the baby, asking to hold her often. Sometimes, he looked deeply into his daughter's eyes, wondering what she was thinking, what she would become, and how she would change the world.

Too often, however, Tim seemed to fly off the handle, and hold back from his wife. Some women claim that their love life falters once a baby is born. Sam hoped that was not the case between her and Tim.

The books said that marital relations should be delayed for six weeks to allow the mother's body time to heal. For Sam, even thinking about having sex with her husband gave her a cringe of fear and a sense of anxiety.

Tim hadn't made it any easier. After Anaya's birth, Sam had asked Tim to text their parents with the news. He had reluctantly stomped into the bush, taking the satellite phone to a high point on a hill that promised better reception. He came back sooner than expected.

"Did you get through?" Sam asked, wanting to know how her parents had reacted to the news.

"Uh, no," Tim answered. "I couldn't get reception. Must be a solar storm or something."

Every day, Sam had insisted that he try again, but the results were the same each time.

If she couldn't talk to her parents from Zigda, then she was determined to return to America. She began to ask Tim when they were going home.

"Anaya is ready to travel. She has all the natural immunities to keep her safe from infection," Sam offered. "And I've been feeling just fine ever since the first week after her birth."

Sam knew she was pressing her luck. Then, just three days ago, Tim became angry over some stupid little thing she had said. That did it. Sam waded right into the argument and demanded that he tell her what was bugging him. She didn't pull any punches. Had he lost interest in her because her body had been stretched from having a baby? Was he so upset that Anaya was a girl that he had lost interest in both of them?

Sam never expected the answer Tim gave her. It had been worse than anything she had imagined.

"We can't go home," Tim said, plopping down on his cot and pressing the heels of his hands into his eyes.

"Why?" she demanded. "Just tell me why we can't go. Was it too difficult to arrange for the flight?"

"No, that's not exactly what the problem is," he said, concerned that Sam's anger had reached the boiling point. "The truth is that we can never go home. We can never contact anyone we know from home – including our parents."

"Have you lost your mind?" she screamed. The entire village must have heard her outburst.

"They are never going to give up," he said sadly. "They will never stop until Anaya is dead."

At first Sam didn't know what he was talking about. She didn't know what he meant by "they."

Finally, she heard him whisper the answer, *"endosyms."*

Well, none of that made sense to her. Tim had killed that one in the village. If more came, he could kill them, too.

"Listen, Sam," Tim said, reaching out to hold her hands as he spoke softly and looked directly in her eyes.

"Sam, I don't know why we have been selected to have this child. Long before I met you, my life had been under a cloud of something unreal.

"You know that when I was just fifteen and we first came here, evil entered my family's life. I saw an *endosym* when I was held captive here in Liberia. I lost the end of my finger because of their thirst for power. But I lost more than that. I lost my innocence,"

Tim bowed his head and stared at his folded hands. He continued speaking without waiting for Sam's reaction.

"Dad never talked about what happened to him when he defeated the *endosym* by killing Julius Carpai, the minister of defense. I don't hold that against him. Most soldiers don't talk about the men they kill in combat. The true heroes, like my dad, keep it to themselves.

"Until our paths crossed, I hadn't thought about the *endosyms*. I was just a normal human being, living my life day-by-day. Everything changed when George Sarday showed up in Johnsonville, Virginia. I knew that Sarday was the same *endosym* that took the end of my finger.

Then you and Eddie were kidnapped. My love for you led me to search for you in that cavern. I fought the *endosym* to save your life.

"I was beginning to feel invincible – I began to believe that that old witch doctor, Chea Geebe, had invested me with some special power to defeat the *endosyms*. You saw how the leopard tooth could glow when the *endosym* was here. The same thing happened in the tunnels at West Point. But something changed. I wasn't strong enough, and the *endosym* got away. I guess maybe I'm not really the super-hero I thought I was.

"Then when they found us in New York and you and our baby were almost killed, I believed that it was a mistake to have you be involved in my life. Your life was in jeopardy because of this thing with *endosyms*. I blamed myself. I even blamed my dad for even taking us to Africa. I blamed old Chea Geebe, and I even blamed God."

Tim lowered his eyes, still not daring to look up at Sam.

"Then we had that crazy dream that brought us here," he continued. "All the time I believed that I was the cause. Without me, you could have led a normal life. When the female *endosym* showed up in Zigda, where I had thought we would be safe, I realized that it had followed me here. Somehow, I must send out some signal. When I fought the damn thing and killed it, I was shocked when it said that they would never stop pursuing us until our child was dead. My God, that means they are working together. That's when I stopped making the cell phone calls to our folks."

"What?" she asked in disbelief.

She had held on to her hopes, confident that Tim had been sending weekly message to her parents by using the SAT phone.

Tim had continued his story, ignoring her rage.

"Don't you see? Those things are using the Internet and computers. Anyone with the know-how and the right equipment can pinpoint a satellite phone's location within a few feet. Our government has been doing it to intercept terrorists for years. Dumb me, I walked up the trail to the point where the phone worked and sent text messages to our folks and to your office. Each time I sent a message, the signal was traced. But how would they know where we were if the phone was turned off?"

"Tim, get serious. They can't be monitoring us twenty-four hours a day."

"That's the problem. They're monitoring our families."

"That's impossible," she argued.

"Sam, they found where we lived. I'll bet they know where we worked. Once they have that data, it doesn't take a rocket scientist to fill in the blanks."

Sam seethed with anger, arguing that his logic didn't hold up. Tim had killed the *endosym* in the cavern in Virginia, and then he won again in the fight in the village when he killed another *endosym*.

Unfortunately, that argument confirmed the fact that there was more than one of the horrible things. Was it possible that these creatures had organized and were bent on enslaving all mankind? She remembered the crazy vision she had the night of Anaya's birth.

Then Tim dropped the bombshell that would forever change their lives.

"Sam," he said, "Remember when Joe and I were gone for several days?"

"Yes," she said. "You said that you were coordinating our departure."

"Well, that was a half-truth," he admitted.

"What do you mean a half-truth?"

"Let me show you something."

Tim reached into his rucksack and grabbed two small leather bags. He reached into the first bag and pulled out a handful of rubies, emeralds and other stones. They were crudely cut, but sparkled in the narrow beam of daylight coming in from the door.

She looked at the gems.

"Are these real?" she asked.

"Yes, and they are very old. A jeweler in Monrovia said that they are worth tens of millions. But let me show you what's in the other bag. He reached in a pulled out a handful of what looked like pieces of quartz, some as big as walnuts.

"I suppose you're going to tell me that those are uncut diamonds?"

"Yes, you're exactly correct, and they are unusually pure. I sold two of them in Monrovia for nearly three quarters of a million dollars, and those were smaller than any of these. The money was deposited in a Swiss account. We will use that money to change our identities and disappear."

"Where did you get those?" she asked, astonished.

Tim told her of the hidden chamber and the ruins of the lost city. He explained that it was the same place where the *endosym's* worshipers had held him and Sabo. The gems were part of an ancient treasure that belonged to the *endosyms*.

He told her about the pictographic story of the *endosyms* coming to Africa and enslaving the people. Then he described the underground temple littered with thousands of human skulls, apparently sacrifices to the *endosyms*.

"Twelve years ago I was a normal teenager. I wanted to be a fireman or policeman or soldier when I grew up. I loved sports, and I loved my parents. When we were assigned to Liberia, my life changed completely. I met Chea Geebe. But I also encountered my first *endosym*.

"Even after facing the damn thing several times over the years, I still find it hard to believe such things really do exist. I still don't believe that I have the power to stop them.

"Despite what has happened, I'm not that religious. Yeah, Mom, Dad and I go to church once in a while, and I guess I believe in God and an after-life. But I'm not a miracle worker.

"But I know that something has happened to change me. I know that some of the things that people would never accept as fact are truly real. I was the source of this mystery, and I should never have gotten you involved. I love you so much, but I would walk away from you in a moment to save you.

"Then I saw her," Tim said.

"Her?"

"In the last pictograph I saw a woman who battled with the *endosym* ten thousand years ago. That woman looked just like you, and her name was Anaya according to the stories passed down through the ages.

"OK, I don't believe in fate or predestination or God's will. At least, I didn't until I saw that drawing on the wall," Tim concluded.

"Sam, this isn't just about me, it's us, all three of us together. Somehow we are here in this village with our daughter who is somehow destined to change the world.

"Whatever happens, these *endosym* things want to destroy our daughter. We are her guardians and protectors until the time comes when she will claim her own destiny."

Tim became quiet and finally raised his eyes to look in hers.

Sam was about ready to counter his arguments when she recalled the strange dream she had on the night their daughter was born. She had realized that the vision she had was that of the woman in the cave drawings. My God, she realized, Tim was right, their lives were part of some greater plan, something she would never grasp.

Sam bowed her head and whispered, "You're right, Tim. I know you're right."

She sobbed at the loss of everything she held dear. Tim embraced her and their baby. Sam finally controlled her tears. She looked directly into her husband's eyes and then down at their daughter, Anaya.

Then she realized it was she who had been wrong. Everything she loved the most was right here in the hut with her.

Nothing else mattered.

86

THE UNMARKED, BLACK HELICOPTER LIFTED OFF FROM ITS PAD ON THE REMOTE estate north of edinburgh.

The MD 902 had two direct-drive Pratt & Whitney Canada turbo shaft engines. Each engine had a single-channel control, rated at five hundred horsepower. The chopper was loaded with navigation and communication goodies. Its maximum speed exceeded one hundred and fifty miles per hour. The helicopter could operate for three and a half hours. Its range was four hundred and fifty miles.

The MD 902 had one of the industry's quietest rotors. It had a thirty-one gallon auxiliary fuel tank, exterior and interior night vision support, and room for eight, including pilot and co-pilot. The doors had been removed.

Black-clad figures sat ready in each doorway. The six men wore para-glide steerable chutes. Each man was armed with a sophisticated assault rifle. They all wore night-vision goggles.

The chopper climbed to fifteen thousand feet and headed south toward the Pentland Hills. Flight time was only forty minutes. The pilot checked the clock. It was 0200 – ten minutes to drop time.

The MD 902 silently circled high above Black Castle.

Two black-clad snipers lay flat on the ground on the hill above the guardhouse at the main gate. They drew beads on the foreheads of the two guards inside who were chatting as they sipped their coffee. Members of the assault team each had a radio with a throat mike and earpieces.

Simultaneously, they heard one word: "GO!"

The snipers squeezed the triggers and saw the guards' skulls explode. Fragments of bone and tissue spattered the walls around them.

Two bulletproof Hummers roared down the main road, crashing through the gate. The vehicles rushed up the winding pavement toward the castle.

At the same time, the six commandos exited the MD 902 and plummeted toward the castle's courtyard. Small arms fire burst out from positions along the top of the castle walls.

The two Hummers slammed to an abrupt stop. Twelve men exited the vehicles and directed their fire on the castle.

As the firefight raged, the jumpers quietly glided into the central courtyard. The six quickly took up positions, firing on the guards who were unaware that the enemy was not only outside – but also inside – the compound.

Soon it was all over. No member of the castle staff was spared. Each member of the domestic staff was shot in the head.

The assault team had been well briefed on the castle layout. They had entered through side doors and made certain that no guard or employee had survived. Now, all that remained was one man.

The team kicked in the door to the great room. Once inside, they spread out along the walls, each commando aiming his weapon at the man who sat calmly at a large oak table. A dozen red laser dots appeared on his forehead.

"Move a finger and you die!" said the one commando who apparently led the team.

Duncan didn't move. Within minutes, two men passed through the doorway and approached the table.

"Gentlemen, if you had called, I would have opened the gate. It is such a shame to lose such valuable employees," said Duncan, seemingly unfazed by the carnage.

"So, tell me what brings Krill Morozov and Roberto Mendoza back to my humble home?"

"You have gone too far," said Morozov.

"Yes," agreed Mendoza. "The *endosym* Florence is dead because of you. Now the *zoutari* will become aware of our activities. We told you that this was a mistake."

"So what are you going to do about it?" asked Duncan.

Morozov grinned.

"We are going to make you go away. I am afraid that we no longer need the likes of you."

"Kill him," said Morozov.

All of the commandos opened fire at once, emptying their weapons into Duncan McDougal. They knew to aim for the head. They knew that to kill an *endosym,* its brain must be destroyed. They all stood less than thirty feet from their target.

It was impossible to miss.

The barrage of bullets knocked Duncan backward. His crumpled body lay silently on the polished floor. The room filled with a smoky haze from the discharged weapons.

Mendoza and Morozov made their way slowly to the corpse, carefully choosing their steps. It was hard to see the body through the cloudy air. As they moved closer, Duncan's form became more distinct.

Duncan's eyes were wide open. His lips formed a satisfied smile. There wasn't a mark on him.

"Cut off his head! Now!" screamed Mendoza.

The men drew their knives and rushed toward Duncan. The commandos, given enhanced strength by the pair of *endosym*s, were invincible. Yet, because of the dense haze, it was difficult for Morozov and Mendoza to see what was really happening.

They could smell the blood, and they could hear the screams and grunts, but even with their enhanced vision, it was impossible to know who was winning.

The room filled with the electrical essence of one brain after another shutting down as the heads were severed from the bodies.

The fight didn't last long. Soon, there was silence.

One man rose from the bloody conflict. He was coated in blood from head to foot. He licked his lips and grinned. It was Duncan McDougal.

"Impossible!" roared Morozov.

Mendoza didn't hesitate. He turned and rushed toward the door. But he wasn't fast enough. Duncan got there first, slamming the door shut before the man could make his escape.

Duncan faced the two men. He could read their thoughts. They planned to charge.

"If you wish to continue to exist, I suggest you look around you. While you sat idle for centuries, I have learned the true power of the *endosym*. I can change my molecular structure, allowing bullets to pass through me. I have the power to rip your heads from your bodies. If you had listened to me, you could have joined me in this."

Duncan took a single step forward and ripped Mendoza's head from its body. A flash of lightning gave proof that the demon and the man had separated.

Morozov stood silently, anticipating his own demise.

"Would you prefer death or would you care to become my second in command?" asked Duncan.

"I will serve you," Morozov said without hesitation.

"Excellent. First, I want you to clean up this mess. Next, take over the financial holdings of Florence and Mendoza. Finally, report to me. Our next move will be to open the doorway to the demon world," Duncan said.

"Now, if you will excuse me," Duncan continued. "I need to get cleaned up."

Duncan left the room, leaving Krill Morozov standing there alone. Morozov pulled a radio out of his pocket.

"I need a clean-up crew," he demanded. "Also, I need damage control with the locals. Get on it now!"

87

A GROUP OF CHATTERING CHILDREN EMERGED FROM THE FOREST AND RAN directly to Sam's hut.

Sam could see as well as hear them coming.

"Missy, Missy Sam, Tim coming. He coming now," said a taller boy who had gotten there first.

Sam smiled broadly and thanked them for sounding the alarm. She pulled her nipple from Anaya's toothless gums, held the baby to her shoulder and patted her lightly on the back.

Tim and Joe Weah had left for Monrovia four days earlier to make the arrangements for the family's departure. The thought of leaving this peaceful village and its friendly villagers made Sam's heart ache with regret. They had been in Zigda for three months, yet in some ways, it seemed as if she had never known another life. Her past seemed distant and dreamlike. Right here, right now, was reality.

Had Tim been successful in arranging their way out of Liberia? Would they be able to hide from the *endosyms?* Could they ever lead a normal life, or would they be fugitives, always on the run?

Now the children buzzed like flies around the two men who stepped out of the forest. Sam beamed with pride when she saw Tim and Joe walking side-by-side, smiling and joking with the children around them. They walked with confidence – true leaders and good men.

God, did she ever love that man!

Sam remembered the first time she had ever seen Tim. That was seven years ago. She'd gone to his dorm to find her twin brother, Eddie, who was Tim's roommate. Never in her wildest dreams would she have thought they would get married and she would give birth to their precious daughter.

It seemed like only yesterday that Tim had stood in the doorway in his college dorm with only a towel around his waist. He had just gotten out of the shower. It was obvious that he hadn't expected company. She had fallen in love with him that very day, and their love had grown stronger every day since then.

Sam stood up to greet him, holding the baby on her hip.

"I see you, my husband," she said softly.

"I see you, my wife," he answered, pulling the two of them close to him. He kissed Sam on her lips.

"I love you," he whispered.

"And I love you, too," she answered.

He held his arms out for his child, gently lifting her high over his head. She beamed down at him, and he returned her look of love.

"I see you, my daughter," he said.

Sam was amazed. Anaya was only five weeks old, yet she seemed to giggle in response to her father every time she saw him.

"That's all I will ever need," whispered Sam.

"What? What did you say?" asked Tim.

"The two of you are all I will ever need," she said with a smile. "I will gladly give up my past life just to be with the two of you."

A tear ran down her cheek. She wiped it away. The men, women and children who had gathered around the little family smiled with approval and drifted away.

"We leave tomorrow morning," Tim told her. "A plane will pick us up in Sanniquellie tomorrow afternoon. Joe will have a vehicle waiting for us on the other side of the old bridge. He has Amos and Fuji to guard us, just in case. Joe and I will also be armed."

"Guard us?" Sam asked, her voice shaking.

"Don't worry," said Tim confidently. "Joe and I kept a low profile. There is no way the *endosyms* will know we're leaving tomorrow. "Come on," he said, tugging at her arm to pull her inside their hut. "We need to rest up for tonight."

"Tonight?" asked Sam.

"Yes, the entire village is planning a big farewell celebration."

For the rest of the day, villagers busied themselves getting ready for the evening's events. Haunches of venison and sides of goats roasted on spits over the open fires. The calm village had been transformed into a frenzy of activity.

"Let's put on our traditional tribal clothing," Sam suggested to her husband. "This is likely to be the last time we ever dress this way."

"Sure thing, Sam," replied Tim. "This is a special night for us."

To Sam's delight, she could now button up her jeans. Only five weeks after giving birth, Sam almost felt like her old self. The only thing that didn't fit was her bra. Nursing a baby gave her the large breasts that she'd always wanted. She wrapped the colorful lappa around her upper body to make the most of her full bust. Got to take advantage of it while I can, she sighed. Obviously once the milk dried up, she would be back to a B cup, possibly something smaller.

Just before dark, the beat of drums announced the arrival of lesser Poro spirits. Masked, costumed figures paraded into the village, trailed by clusters of small boys. These weren't the invisible spirits, but actual physical beings. People lined the wide pathways to watch their entrance. They laughed and poked at the spirits with blunt sticks.

This was only the first of many events. Elsewhere in the village, people came together to dance. Others formed impromptu bands, beating out the rhythms common to West Africa. At dusk, all the villagers gathered in the central square. People bumped purposefully into each other, laughed loudly, and collided with each other once again. By now, the brief twilight had been consumed by the dark of night. Small firepots had been arranged along the perimeter of the square, providing enough light for the celebration.

The Martin family had been led to seats of honor, right next to Joe. Sam looked away when she noticed that Joe had been checking her over as if he were examining a purebred filly. Joe was the same age as Tim's dad, but it seemed obvious that his glances were anything but fatherly. Sam wouldn't call his attention suggestive, but she knew he approved of her face and form. Likely, Joe was just showing his approval of Tim's selection of a mate, Sam thought, reassuring herself of Joe's intentions.

"We have festivals like this all the time," Joe explained. "They help pull the people together. If we can celebrate together, we can work together."

He told them that one of the biggest celebrations always came just before planting. The morning following the festivities, everyone would go out together to clear the land for new rice fields. In this part of the world, rice grew in open fields. Timed to coincide with the beginning of the rainy season, the young plants thrived in the soggy soil. No need for rice paddies here. The fertile new ground and heavy rains provided the ideal growing conditions.

The drums began to beat more loudly. People began to cheer.

"What's happening?" Samantha asked.

"In honor of you and your husband, the young warriors will compete in hand-to-hand combat," Joe answered.

"Combat?" asked Sam concerned.

"Well, I guess you could say it's more like wrestling," Joe said. "In bush school, the boys are taught ways to take down the enemy. Once the enemy is on the ground, it's easier to kill him with a spear or a knife.

"In this contest, two men stand on a ten-foot square mat. The first man to throw the other off the mat or on the ground is the winner. The top five winners earn the right to dance with the young virgins. Forty of the best warriors will compete to reach the top five," Joe told them.

Then he grinned mischievously.

"Sam, you know that twelve years ago, Tim participated in this event. He was one of the five winners."

"So, did you pick a wife?" asked Sam as she turned to look at Tim.

"No, I was just fifteen. Mom would have killed me," said Tim, blushing. "But I sure had an interesting night."

"I'll bet you did," Sam laughed.

The crowd parted and a line of young men emerged from the bush behind them. All were barefoot and wore only brief leather loincloths. Their well-oiled skin glistened in the firelight.

"No one gets hurt in these matches," Joe explained. "It's just a friendly competition."

Togba stood and made an announcement to the crowd. Joe quickly took to his feet and looked down at Tim.

"Come on, Tim," Joe said. "Father wants us to demonstrate our techniques for everyone."

"Sure," said Tim. "You don't need to worry, I'll be as gentle as I can be with an old man."

Joe reached out with his arm and pulled Tim to his feet. Together, the two bowed to the chief.

Both men wore the traditional fighting britches; both were barefoot. Joe, in his late forties, still had a magnificent build. His muscled arms were thick and powerful. Although Joe stood a half-foot shorter than Tim, he outweighed him by a good forty pounds.

But Sam had confidence in her man. She'd seen what Tim could do. He had earned a black belt in karate. Years ago when they visited Tim's parents in Hawaii, she had seen him nearly kill a young bully in a match. Then, too, Tim had added to his impressive skills in his training to become an FBI agent. He had extensive training in hand-to-hand combat. But then again, his opponent, Joe, had gone through Special Forces training at Fort Bragg. He wouldn't be a pushover for anyone.

"Men!" she said aloud, somewhat exasperated by their bravado. She hoped that they would remember that this was supposed to be a friendly contest. She didn't want either of them to get hurt.

The two men stepped onto the mat, bowed, then faced each other. The chief barked an order, and both men slowly moved forward.

Joe made the first move. He lunged forward, intent on knocking Tim off the mat. Tim saw him coming and stepped quickly to the right. Joe missed and barely recovered his balance. He let out a low animal growl and grabbed Tim's wrist. The move had always worked before, but Tim twisted his wrist inward, breaking the hold.

Now it was Tim's turn to move ahead in an attempt to throw Joe out of the circle. Because Tim had been focusing on his grip, he failed to heed Joe's footwork. Joe swept his right foot against Tim's left ankle. Tim struggled to keep his balance. He released his hold on Joe's wrist.

Without a pause, Tim resumed his stance and moved forward once again. Now, he held Joe's forearms. Joe countered by clasping Tim's upper arms. Locked together, they pushed each other around the mat, their muscles bulging.

Then Joe made a quick move that Tim should have blocked easily. Instead, Tim fell backward off the mat and landed on his rear. Joe stepped forward and offered his outstretched hand to Tim. He pulled Tim to his feet, and they both embraced. A cheer rose from the crowd. Both men turned to Togba and bowed.

They took their seats next to Sam and Anaya. The baby had missed all the action – she was sound asleep in her mother's arms. Sam looked down and spoke softly: "You missed seeing your daddy land on his bottom."

She leaned over and whispered in Tim's ear.

"You let him win."

"No, I was just out of shape," he replied, making sure no one else could hear his words.

"Sure," she said. "I don't believe a word you say!" She pressed her face against his cheek and kissed him gently.

Soon, the real competition began. Joe was right – this was like the judo matches she had seen on TV.

The chief called out the names of the combatants. Then the young men stepped forward. Their muscles glistened in the firelight. Together, they bowed to the chief.

As each match came to an end, the man who lost returned to his family. The winner stayed up front near the chief. The competition continued until only five warriors remained. Each beamed with pride and stole furtive glances at their loved ones.

"What happens now, Joe?" Sam asked.

"Just watch," he said.

The drumbeat intensified. The crowd parted and twenty young women surrounded the proud, but trembling, warriors. The girls' firm bodies moved to the rhythm of the drums. They wore short grass skirts tied around their waists. Pairs of dark breasts in a variety of shapes and sizes bobbed to the rhythm of the drumbeat. The women lifted their knees, some directly in front of the perspiring young men.

Samantha gasped when she realized that the women wore nothing under their skirts. Their bold leaps lifted their skirts, revealing the dark area between their thighs. Some reversed direction and leaned forward, offering their smooth dark buttocks to the gaze of the spellbound young men.

"You did that?" asked Sam, punching Tim playfully on his shoulder.

"Yes, Sam," he answered, leaning against Sam's shoulder. "Yes, I did that."

The dancers tightened their circle, moving to within an arm's length of the warriors. One warrior reached out, his fingertips only inches from a pointed nipple. Following his lead, other arms stretched out, some touching a female shoulder or leg. The girls pulled back, and then quickly moved in again.

Samantha shifted on the mat, and drew her hips nearer to her husband. Her thigh pressed against his upper leg. The drumbeat increased in volume and intensity.

Then Joe spoke loudly, interrupting her thoughts.

"The warriors see the most eligible young women in the village. Once the rice is harvested, they have first opportunity to offer a bride's price to the girl's father. That's why the men try so hard to win – not just for the honor, but also for the first choice of the women. I guess you could say the strongest males select the finest women."

The sound of drums began to fade. Sam watched as the young women vanished deep into the crowd; the warriors appeared tired and spent.

Two men came forward. One held a leather pouch filled with liquid. The other passed out five cups fashioned from black gourds.

"Now what's going on?" Samantha asked.

"The five get the first of the palm wine," Joe said.

"Palm wine?" she asked.

"It's a sort of homebrew. Let me get you some," Joe offered.

He got to his feet and quickly returned bringing with him three gourds filled with a milky white liquid. Sam took a sip. It had a sweet fermented taste. Tim and Joe downed theirs as if they were simply thirsty for a glass of water. Sam sipped once more then stopped.

"You don't like it?" asked Joe.

"No, it's OK, but I'm not sure Anaya will like it once it's processed into my milk."

Joe laughed, "I forgot, you're a nursing mother. I guess our women don't drink palm wine either."

By now the fires had died down. Only glowing coals remained where flames had once blazed so intensely. People began to leave, randomly returning to their huts. They nodded as they passed the honored guests.

88

SAM AND TIM KNEW IT WAS TIME FOR THEM TO RETURN TO THEIR HUT. THEY excused themselves and chose their steps carefully on their way back. Inside their hut, only the dim light of a lantern illuminated the interior. Tonight would be their last night to sleep in this home where they had experienced such love and acceptance. It was the birthplace of their daughter – a precious memory in the history of their family.

Anaya began to fuss. Sam pulled down her lappa. Her bulging breasts now released, she cupped her left side and offered a dark nipple to her baby. Anaya latched on, sucking greedily.

Women say that the act of nursing a baby can elicit erotic feelings for both men and women. For Sam, the pull on her nipple and the nearness of her husband stirred up an intense sexual desire. It had been a long time since she had felt a sexual need.

But it was more than that. She thought of the young virgins who danced so brazenly before the aroused young men. Tim had been there. He had watched the dark virgins dance in the firelight. Sam imagined that she herself was one of those virgins, and Tim her warrior. Sleep wouldn't come easily tonight.

After all the night's pandemonium, Sam should have been tired. The quiet should have calmed her emotions. Instead, she stood next to Tim's cot. She looked down at her mate. His eyes were closed, but she didn't hear him snoring. Perhaps he was still awake.

She laid Anaya on her bed. She untied her lappa and allowed it to fall carelessly on the ground. She stood in the lantern light and began to caress her own breasts, her firm belly and her inner thighs.

"Tim?" she whispered, reaching down and gently tapping his shoulder. "Tim, are you awake?"

Tim's eyes popped open.

"What? What is it, Sam?" he asked as if coming out of a dream.

"I want to do it," she said. "I want you inside me tonight."

He took in the vision of his wife standing naked beside him. He still had on the warrior britches, yet she could tell that he was immediately aroused.

"Are you sure?" he asked. "It's only been a month since Anaya was born."

"Actually, it's been five weeks, and, yes, I'm sure."

"I won't hurt you, will I?" he asked, his face showing his concern.

"Let's try not to get too rough," she whispered. "It's been almost three months since we've enjoyed good sex, and I'm telling you I want you now."

She bent over and kissed him hard on the lips.

He reached over and fondled one of her engorged breasts. Suddenly, he pulled his hand away.

"It's leaking!" he said in amazement.

"It's only milk. It won't hurt you," she laughed. She kissed him again. She reached down and began to pull down his britches.

"I want to do it on a mat on the floor," she said.

"OK," Tim whispered huskily.

Once pressed tightly to Sam's body, Tim couldn't stop thinking about the baby.

"What about Anaya?" Tim asked.

"Anaya?' asked Sam. "What do you mean?

"What if she sees us doing it?"

Sam almost laughed out loud.

"Oh, Tim, she's just five weeks old! Besides that, she doesn't care what Mommy and Daddy are doing. She's fed, and she's sleeping. That's all she needs now.

"But me, now that's a different story," Sam continued, her eyes sparkling. "Right now, I want to be one of those virgins who danced for you twelve years ago, and I want to be fucked."

All arguments over, they rolled on the floor together until Sam was on the bottom, and Tim arched above her. Fortunately, the exhausted villagers were deep in sleep. If they had been awake, they would have heard the sounds of pleasure coming from the hut.

Finally, Sam and Tim, too, fell into a satisfied slumber.

89

SAMANTHA WOKE AT FIRST LIGHT. THEY HAD SPENT THE NIGHT ON THE HARD clay floor – not exactly the most comfortable place to rest. She stood and moaned. She didn't feel like a young virgin now. She felt older than her twenty-eight years. She tied her lappa around her body and headed for the bathing pool. She carried her underwear, jeans, blouse and sneakers in her arms. Today, they would return to the civilized world.

Back at the hut, she woke Tim and nudged Anaya. She nursed the baby while Tim got dressed and packed their suitcase. The two took one last look around the hut. Now it was time to go.

Tim had purchased a modern day baby sling in Monrovia. It would allow her to carry the baby while leaving both hands free. She'd learned a great deal about babies from the village women. Once infants became accustomed to being carried in a sling, they could spend the day by their mothers' sides while the women worked. With the babies fed and sleeping, mother and the baby stayed close to each other. No day care necessary, Sam thought. This is the way life should be.

As they stepped out of the hut, the family was surrounded by villagers, each person anxious to say goodbye. Sam tearfully hugged the kind women who had helped her through her pregnancy, Anaya's birth and the care of her newborn.

The talking and hugging ceased and the crowd parted to allow the old chief, Togba, to come forward. His voice cracked as he spoke softly to Sam.

"Protect the child at all costs. Anaya is our only hope to save the world from the *endosyms*. We know this from the stories that have been passed down from generation to generation."

No one else heard what the chief had said to Sam.

Soon they began their trek up the hill toward the deep forest.

"What did Togba say to you?" whispered Tim as he fell in step with his wife.

"Nothing," Sam said. "He only wished us luck."

90

As they moved farther and farther away from Zigda, Sam realized what a special time this had been in their lives.

She was filled with contentment. The jungle seemed greener, and the sky looked bluer. Her vision had sharpened. She saw the shape of leaves and noted the quickness of insects. She breathed in deeply, taking in the scent of flowers and the rich odor of the jungle soil.

She wrapped her arm under her sleeping daughter and pulled her close to her breast. This was a new life, one that she and Tim had created.

Nothing could dampen her spirits.

They came to the stream and crossed the log bridge. A slight movement on the other side caught her attention. On a rotting log, she saw the same snake she had seen there more than three months earlier.

Impossible, simply impossible, she thought. She searched the surface of the log once again, but the snake had disappeared. She felt a chill, but shook it off. No snake would ruin the day.

Sam began to hum a familiar lullaby. She quickened her pace, vowing to ignore the creature behind her. She would only look ahead to their future together. She intensified her melody, adding lyrics to her song.

"Rock a bye baby, on the tree top. When the wind blows the cradle will rock. When the bough breaks ..."

Finally, they reached the waiting vehicle that would take them to Sanniquellie. It was only a one-hour drive, but Sam relished riding in a real automobile. After living the primitive life in Zigda, she found herself admiring the interior of the SUV. Such luxury, she thought. She would never take a gas-powered engine for granted ever again.

91

Sanniquellie, one of the larger towns in Nimba County also had a paved runway at its small airport. Several streets in the town were also paved. It even could boast of having a power generator.

Once again, the Martins had stayed in one of the presidential retreats. They were to spend several days in the small city to "re-adjust" to their new lives. To celebrate their last night in Liberia they dined in a local restaurant frequented by the city's wealthier residents.

"Wow, Tim!" Sam exclaimed. "Real American food and even a California wine!"

Although Sam didn't plan to drink alcohol while she was nursing, she couldn't resist a sip from Tim's glass. Joe and Tim told stories about the Martin family's stay in Liberia. It seemed like the stories all ended with a punch line that resulted in uncontrollable laughter.

The restaurant had been packed – there was hardly an empty table. Some guests had settled in to eat their meals at the bar. None of the members of the Martin party took notice of a single white man who sat alone at the bar, picking at his food. He frequently stared into the large mirror behind the bartender. If any of their group had been more attentive, they would have noticed him watching the party of six – Joe, Tim, Samantha, the sleeping Anaya and the two bodyguards.

After dinner, they had walked back to the retreat house. Tim and Sam had been thrilled at the prospect of sleeping on a real mattress with crisp cotton sheets and fluffy down pillows. Finally, they could enjoy showers in a large bathroom with double overhead sprinklers. They could use an actual porcelain toilet – no more of that standing with knees bent and peeing in a trench, thought Sam.

They planned to take off from Sanniquellie's airport and fly to Lagos, Nigeria. From there, they would take a commercial flight to Johannesburg, South Africa.

All their documents were in order.

"Tim, would you look at this?" Sam said. "See my passport photo. I'm Sally Ann Brown, and you're James Timothy Brown!"

Sally's passport had a tiny photo of her five-week old daughter – Amy Lynn Brown. The Martin family had already begun to disappear from the face of the Earth.

Their first night at the retreat had seemed like a dream come true. Tim couldn't resist bouncing on the mattress and stretching his legs from one side of the bed to the other. Tonight, he curled his body against his wife and nuzzled her neck.

"Uh, Sally," he whispered in her ear. "Sally, do you want to have sex with me tonight?"

"Sally? Did you call me Sally?" she asked, pretending to be shocked.

"Right," he grinned. "You, Sally. Me, James. Us, sex?"

"I guess I'll have to get used to my new name," she laughed. "But, James, you do realize that this is my first time with Mr. Brown."

Sam – or, Sally – didn't, or – couldn't say another word. Mr. Brown had rolled over to fondle her breasts. He'd already begun a slow rhythmic movement against her lower body.

Miss Brown – that's Miss Amy Brown, simply ignored her pre-occupied parents. Fed, pampered and safe, she continued to sleep soundly, a sweet smile forming on her delicate lips.

92

KRILL MOROZOV WATCHED FROM A BACK CORNER OF THE ROOM AS DUNCAN video-conferenced with a woman in new york.

Her name was Constance, an attractive American woman. Morozov shook his head in amazement – it seemed as if she were right there in the great room with them.

A member of Duncan's coven, the brilliant Constance was essential to their success. She had set up a website, *endosym.com*, that had gone world-wide, recruiting others to join their coven. Throughout the centuries, their kind had hidden from the humans. Now, via the Internet, they had gone public. It didn't seem to negatively impact their efforts. They could say whatever they wanted, and the world seemed like it could care less.

It wasn't long ago that Morozov had teamed up with Roberto Mendoza. Their men stormed the castle with orders to kill McDougal. But McDougal had bested them – Mendoza died a brutal death. Only Morozov survived, taking up Duncan's offer to serve as his second in command.

What choice did he have? If he didn't agree, Morozov would have suffered the same fate as Mendoza. Now, he could watch Duncan in action and learn from him. If his plan worked, he would work alongside Duncan and learn how he had obtained such formidable powers. Then he would kill Duncan McDougal.

However, to his surprise, Morozov began to understand that what Duncan was saying actually made sense.

Together, they had searched the web. The Russian mafia became a vital resource. They had located twelve *endosyms* who lived hidden lives among the humans. Duncan had used his impressive powers of persuasion and had recruited seven of them to work with him. He found the other five to be defective, and they were destroyed.

Morozov became convinced that Duncan would find a way to open the portal to the demon world. He was certain that eventually Duncan would create a master race of *endosyms*, capable of ruling the Earth and eventually the universe.

But Morozov couldn't be certain about Duncan. Sometimes he suspected that Duncan might have sunken into madness. A prime example of his lack of sanity could be seen in the relationship with this woman, Constance.

Morozov glanced at the large flat screen that had seemed to entrance Duncan. There she was again – that woman named Constance. She held up a small, wrinkled girl-child who appeared to be a resident of a hospital.

"Six weeks," said Constance. "She can come home in six weeks."

Morozov found Duncan's fascination with the infant to be disgusting. He giggled uncontrollably as he stared at the frail pink child. This girl, named Sabrina, had been born too early. Coincidentally, she was born on the same day at the same moment as the Martin woman's child. The premature birth threatened the child's very survival, yet she had thrived.

Morozov overheard Duncan praising this creature, apparently of his own flesh and blood.

"Both of you, Constance and Sabrina, will become *endosyms*," beamed Duncan.

But Morozov knew that the girl would have to wait until she reached adulthood before she could be transformed. Then she would become the first of a race of *endosyms* with the power to control the world.

The relentless vibration of his cell phone disrupted Morozov's thoughts. He pulled his phone from his front pocket.

"Demetir Gocheck here. Calling from Liberia," said the man on the phone.

"Yes," responded Morozov.

"They are here in Sanniquellie. They will fly out tomorrow morning."

"Wonderful. You will take care of it?"

"Yes, no problem. I have all the credentials of an aircraft mechanic. I will take care of everything."

"Excellent," Morozov said. He turned off the phone.

Duncan had been near enough to read Morozov's thoughts. He knew what had just transpired.

He closed his eyes for a moment and saw the future that was about to become a reality. The Martins were going to die.

Duncan would personally go to the memorial ceremony. He would easily meld into the crowd of mourners. He would sit three rows back from the woman's parents. Everyone would believe he was a close friend of the family.

Duncan chuckled. He was no stranger; he knew more about the Martins than anyone could ever suspect. After the ceremony, he would mingle with the crowd. His powers were so enhanced that he would be able to enter the minds of family members and read their thoughts. Then after the memorial, he would visit Constance and his daughter in New York, then fly to Edinburgh, and finally return to Black Castle.

"A good day," thought Duncan. "This has been a very good day. I hope the Martins have enjoyed it, too. It will be their last."

Duncan turned his attention back to the woman on the screen and to the tiny bundle she cuddled in her arms.

After completing the videoconference he walked over to the large oak table. The Codex Gigas, known as the Devil's Bible, sat on the table. Duncan caressed its leather cover. For centuries its origins had been shrouded in mystery.

Morozov's men had stolen it from Stockholm where it had been kept in a secure vault in Sweden's National Library. It had been insured for thirty million dollars – although, in truth, the book was priceless. The Swedish guards were no match for the ingenuity of an *endosym* and its minions.

This book, written in 1229, was now in his hands.

It was unfortunate that Duncan had to destroy Roberto Mendoza, author of the Codex Gigas. But an *endosym* of Mendoza's standing threatened Duncan's quest to rule the world. He kept Krill Morozov, another *endosym*, solely because the creature was resourceful and capable of enforcing Duncan's orders.

Roberto had been useless. He failed to understand the meaning of the book's hidden messages sent to him by unknown powers. Duncan would now devote himself to study and learning. He believed the volume would provide the guidance he sought. It would aid in the establishment of a new religion. The book would become his Bible, his Koran.

He opened the Codex to the passage that sharpened his focus. It was Mendoza's interpretation of Revelation, Chapter 14, Verse 14,

"The Harvest of the Earth." He read it aloud, the words slipping easily from his lips:

I looked and before me stood a black throne. Seated on the throne was an endosym. It held a sharp sword in its hand.

Then the Dark Master, Satan, the great destroyer of souls, came up to the throne and spoke in a loud voice to him on the throne: "Take your sword and kill. The time for the harvest of the human race is now."

The endosym will gather an army of endosyms, and mankind will be enslaved for all eternity.

Duncan McDougal closed the great book. He would study, he would learn, and he would reign supreme.

The battle for the conquest of Earth had begun.

93

Sally finished nursing Amy, burped her and placed her in the infant carrier.

Last night the true reality of what was happening hit them like a bolt of lighting. She had been changing Amy's diaper when Jim peeked over her shoulder.

"She's got dirt on her chest," said Jim. "Right there, that brown spot."

Sally glanced down at her daughter. She rubbed her finger on the spot. "That's not dirt," she said. "It's a birthmark."

"A birthmark?" asked Jim. "I don't recall seeing it before."

"I read somewhere that birthmarks may appear after several weeks. It's no big deal," said Sally.

Suddenly Jim turned pale. "Oh, my God," he said. "I've seen the mark before."

"Where?" asked Sally.

"On the drawing of the woman in the chamber. It was darker, but had the same shape and location. Remember, the FBI trained us to look for tattoos or birthmarks on people."

"It's just a coincidence," said Sally.

Suddenly, she remembered the vision the day the baby was born. She closed her eyes and tried to focus on what she had seen.

The woman stood in the midst of battle. She remembered the face, the eyes, and the color of her hair. She thought about her body. Yes, it was there on her chest – the birthmark. She let out a gasp. Opened her eyes. Tears began to flow down her cheeks.

"What's wrong?" asked Jim.

"Oh, my God," she sobbed. "The woman you saw in the drawing is our daughter."

"Whoa, wait a minute," said Jim. "You never saw the drawing, what are you talking about?"

"I saw her, right after Anaya was ... God, I've got to get used to our new names. I mean that I saw her right after Amy was born. The old man, Chea Geebe, was there. I had another one of those crazy out-of-body experiences," explained Sally.

"You didn't tell me," said Jim.

"Hey, I was a little tired after fourteen hours of labor. Besides, until today all you told me was that you saw a drawing that looked like me."

"OK, I'm sorry," said Jim. "Tell me what exactly did you see?" he asked his wife.

"Our daughter, she was maybe twenty or twenty-five years old. She had just killed some *endosyms*."

"What was she holding?" asked Jim.

She thought for a moment before she answered. "A crystal dagger," she said.

"Not a sword?" asked Jim.

"No, it was a crystal dagger. It seemed to glow green like the leopard tooth."

"Was there anything else you saw?" he asked.

"There was a terrible beast standing next to her," she answered.

"You mean a gray leopard?" asked Jim.

"No, no it wasn't a leopard. It was huge. If the Amy in my vision was as tall as I am, then this thing stood at least five feet tall. It must have weighed seven hundred pounds. It looked like a huge cat, but it had fangs four inches long. Its muzzle was covered with blood. But what were terrifying were the eyes. They weren't golden like a cat; they were red with black pupils. No way was it a leopard," explained Sally.

Jim stood there for a minute then said. "The drawing in the chamber showed the woman holding a sword, not a dagger, and the cat beside her was a gray leopard with black spots. But the drawing sure looked like a relative of yours."

"It was a drawing of your daughter," said Sally.

"I hope not," said Jim. "I wouldn't want guys looking at my daughter dressed like that."

"Oh God, Jim, I don't know if I can handle this," cried Sally.

"We have to," said Jim holding his wife.

When they went to bed, Sally brought Amy with her. She lay on her side with Amy's little body cuddled against her body. She tried to sleep, but all she could do was think. She relived her life from the time that she was a child.

She thought of the future, and it frightened her. Her hand caressed the soft skin of her sleeping daughter. She whispered to the child.

"I don't know what the future holds," Sally promised her daughter, "but you are going to be raised as a normal, healthy child that includes dolls and bikes and fun and love. Also, there will be no cats in the Brown household. Not even stuffed toy cats."

Sally closed he eyes as she drifted into a deep sleep. It seemed like only moments later that her alarm sounded.

Jim had just finished showering. He would be on baby duty while Sally took her turn in the bathroom. He wore tan slacks, a blue polo shirt and canvas loafers. His long brown hair, still not completely dry, had a center part. Once it dried, his hair would reach just to the top of his ears. He wore gold metal-rimmed glasses. He might have passed for an accountant, except for his remarkable physique. Jim stood six and a half feet tall. He had a narrow waist, broad shoulders and impressive biceps.

Jim tucked in his shirt and grinned at his wife.

"Your turn, sweetheart. I made sure to leave you lots of hot water."

Amy's daddy reached out for his darling daughter as Sally passed him the child. The baby's lips turned downward. She looked as if she was almost ready to cry.

"Hi, Amy," he said softly, "it's just Daddy."

He knew that the baby was too young to react to a stranger, but clearly his altered appearance had upset her. Only his familiar, soothing voice brought back her smile.

Poor child, thought Sally. Both Mommy and Daddy had changed, and she didn't know why. Jim hadn't had his black hair cut in weeks. It was trimmed neatly now. He had dyed it brown, and he'd put on glasses.

Of course, Mom's physical changes were even more startling. She no longer had long, straight light brown hair. Now it was short, curled and dyed black. She, too, had begun to wear glasses – thin rimmed and fashionable.

As a mixed race African-American, Sally had inherited light brown hair from her white grandmother. Her skin was mocha, not the ebony black like the Liberians. Her daughter would likely have lighter skin since her father was white. In Johannesburg, Sally Brown would fit right in. She looked like any other mixed-race colored.

A new identity, a new look and a new life awaited the Brown family in South Africa.

94

ON THE DAY OF THE FAMILY'S DEPARTURE, JOE WEAH SIPPED AT HIS THIRD cup of coffee while waiting for the Brown's in the retreat's dining room. When he saw them come in, he stood and reached out his hand to greet Jim and Sally. He patted Amy on the head and kissed Sally lightly on the cheek.

"Good morning, Jim ... Sally. We'll have a good breakfast then head for the airport. The plane should arrive in about two hours."

They talked very little; there wasn't much to say. Everything that needed to be done had been done. Each was aware that it would be a long time – perhaps never again – that they would sit together to enjoy a meal. Joe had been like a big brother to Jim. They would miss him.

After breakfast they loaded in the SUV and left for the airport.

It took fewer than five minutes to drive to the airport. The men unloaded their spotless suitcases, filled with new clothing and personal items – everything Brown. Nothing was left that had belonged to the Martin family.

Jim hesitated. "Well, almost nothing," he thought.

The Browns settled in on a bench in the air-conditioned terminal. Joe stood anxiously at the window, scanning the clear blue sky.

"Here comes your plane," he said turning to speak to them.

Jim joined Joe and the two others as they watched as the Beechcraft King Air 350i Turboprop circle and start its approach toward the runway.

The plane could carry as many as nine passengers. Its powerful twin Pratt and Whitney engines allowed it to cruise at more than thirty thousand feet at three hundred fifty miles per hour. Its range exceeded fifteen hundred miles.

Both men were concerned as they watched the plane approach. It seemed to drop too fast. As the plane hit the tarmac, it bounced once into the air, then settled down, finally coming to an abrupt halt using only half the length of the pavement.

"The pilot seems a little reckless on his landings," remarked Jim as the silver plane taxied to the terminal.

"The pilot has flown in Africa for years. He comes with the plane," said Joe. "The plane and the pilot are considered a CIA asset. I had to pull some strings to arrange for an unregistered flight out of here to Nigeria."

As the engines wound down, a grizzled man in a dirty white tee shirt, torn jeans and worn sneakers, walked down the stairway to the tarmac.

"Who's that?" asked Sally, somewhat astonished at the less-than-professional appearance of the man.

"That's your pilot," said Joe.

"My God, he looks like he's at least seventy years old," Sally said.

"He probably is. He flew in the special forces troops twelve years ago during the coup," said Joe.

"Shit," said Jim, "He's the guy that flew my dad into LAMCO's airport. I think his name was Ray or something?"

"Roy," answered Joe. "Just Roy, No-last-name, Roy. He's a little wild, but if he is still alive after all these years, I guess he is doing something right."

After the plane's tanks were topped off, Roy turned to make sure that Jim, Sally and Amy were strapped in.

Joe handed the pilot a thick envelope.

"This should cover your expenses."

Roy took it with a broad grin and fastened himself into the pilot's seat.

Joe bent down and kissed Sally for the last time.

"You take good care of that little girl."

He shook Jim's hand, placing his left hand on Jim's shoulder.

"Go in peace, my brother. We will all pray for you and your family."

Then Joe was gone. The plane was secure and ready for takeoff.

"Folks, as your pilot I need to explain emergency procedures. The windows over the wings can be popped open if necessary. To open the door, just rotate the handle on the right.

"Should we have a problem in flight, this aircraft can fly on one engine. If we crash, stay buckled up until the plane stops moving. I would encourage you to keep your seatbelts buckled at all times, except if you need the bathroom.

"That reminds me," Roy said with a smile. "There's a cooler in the back with cold beer and drinks. If you're hungry, there are several TV dinners in the freezer.

"One more thing, our flight time is three hours and twenty-eight minutes to Lagos, Nigeria, more or less. Enjoy your flight."

Sally reached to hold Jim's hand.

"God," she said, "I hope we live to make it back to Nigeria."

95

Joe walked back to stand in the shade of the terminal. He saw Fuji standing next to the Mercedes.

"Where is Amos?" asked Joe.

"He went over to take a leak behind that hangar. He should be back by now. He's been gone about ten minutes," said Fuji.

"Go get him. I want to leave as soon as the plane takes off," ordered Joe.

Fuji, following orders, jogged over to the hangar.

The Beechcraft's engines revved up, slowed down and revved up once again. With the engines idling, the door opened and the pilot stepped out and checked the left engine. He appeared satisfied and climbed back in the aircraft.

Joe looked around. Still, no men. Now both Fuji and Amos were missing.

"Damn," he said to himself. "They had better not be screwing some woman in the bush behind the hangar."

As the plane turned and taxied to the end of the runway, Joe began walking toward the hangar.

When he reached the hangar, he heard the plane's engines come up to their maximum RPM. He glanced back as the brakes were released, and the plane raced down the runway at increasingly faster speeds. When it had covered three thousand feet of runway, the wheels left the ground, and the aircraft was airborne.

Joe sighed. All morning he had felt tightness in his stomach. The Brown family was finally on its way. He'd done everything he could.

Their fate was now out of his hands. Now he was going to kick Fuji and Amos in their butts. He stepped around the corner of the hangar. Without thinking, his hand went for his shoulder holster. Lying on the ground was Amos. His throat had been slashed. Fuji was nowhere in sight.

He ran toward the far side of the hangar. Next to a pickup he saw the body of Fuji. What the hell was going on? The plane had already taken off.

He looked to the east and saw the plane bank to the right towards the Nimba Mountains. As he turned his head, he noticed a streak of smoke rising from behind the maintenance hangar. The line of smoke streaked across the sky toward the plane at the speed of sound. Joe froze in place.

He knew that a Russian surface-to-air missile, a SAM, had been fired. The old-style heat-seeking missile was designed to quickly lock onto a heat source. It had found one – the exhaust from the right engine.

He heard a loud explosion. Pieces of the engine dropped from the aircraft. The plane skewed to the left and began a rapid descent.

Amazingly, the plane dropped several thousand feet and then began to right itself.

"Impossible! Impossible!" screamed Joe. "Please, God, please!"

It began to bank to the left and head back to the airport. Then it changed course and resumed its flight toward the mountains, smoke trailing from its right wing.

Joe was puzzled. Why didn't it keep coming back to the airport?

Then Joe realized that the pilot must have assumed that whoever fired the SAM would launch a second missile once the plane was within range.

Joe ran towards the back of the maintenance hangar. He slowed as he approached the rear of the building. He kept his body tight to the wall and began working his way soundlessly along the south side. At the corner, he peeked his head around its edge.

He saw a white man. On the ground beside him lay an empty firing tube. The man held a loaded tube, aiming it in the general direction of the plane.

Joe didn't hesitate. He pulled his pistol, aimed, and emptied all fifteen rounds into the man. One round struck the SAM. A deafening explosion followed. Shreds of the man's flesh flew through the air and bloodied the ground around where he had been standing.

Joe turned and searched the sky for the plane. He saw it approach the mountains. He needed to get to the terminal and have them call back the plane.

He watched pieces of the right wing drop away. The plane banked to the right and disappeared into the thick blanket of green at the base of the mountains. He visualized the wings twisting and crumpling and falling hopelessly to the ground.

He listened. He heard nothing, no sound, no explosion – nothing. Then he saw a thin trail of white smoke rise from the base of the mountain just a short distance from where he'd last seen the plane. The smoke turned black as hundreds of gallons of jet fuel ignited.

It was over. Joe slowly began his trek through the dense forest to locate to the source of the fire. There would be no survivors, but at least he could recover their bodies.

SIX MONTHS LATER

"Prominent Washington Attorney Allen Dixon's daughter and son-in-law were eulogized yesterday in a private ceremony in Alexandria, Virginia.

The couple vanished when their plane crashed into dense jungle in a tragic accident in Liberia, West Africa six months ago. Their bodies were never found.

Witnesses said that the Beechcraft 350i had been engulfed in flames as it fell into the dense triple canopy jungle north of Sanniquellie, Liberia. After an exhaustive two-week search, government and private search teams were unable to locate the wreckage. Dixon delayed the funerals until the searchers were certain that the plane was unrecoverable.

Samantha Dixon-Martin was an anchor for WNY-TV. She was involved in investigative research for a documentary on Africa. Her husband, Tim Martin, worked at the Federal Bureau of Investigation. He had taken a three-month leave of absence to accompany his wife to Africa.

The endosyms are taking over the planet.
Book four coming in 2014

TRUST NO ONE

ENDOSYM
BOOK FOUR

RESURRECTION

SIXTEEN-YEAR-OLD AMY BROWN COMES HOME TO FIND BOTH OF HER PARENTS brutally murdered.

The Browns have no known relatives and Amy becomes a ward of the state and is placed in a foster home. The only information she has about her family is a key to a storage container. In the container she finds a strongbox holding millions of dollars in uncut diamonds, gold and two passports with pictures of her parents but with different names.

Homicide detective Mark Baker is convinced that the Brown murders are not just a home invasion gone wrong. When the mutilated bodies of three men are found in a storage container owned by the Browns and a bloody handprint on the door of the container is Amy Browns, he digs deeper.

What he and Amy Brown discover is a worldwide conspiracy. Who are the Browns? What is terrible secret that Amy and Mark will discover as they try to unravel the mystery of what she really is and can she stop the endosyms.

www.ingramcontent.com/pod-product-compliance
Lightning Source LLC
Chambersburg PA
CBHW070354260626
47161CB00001B/137